THIS SPELLS DISASTER

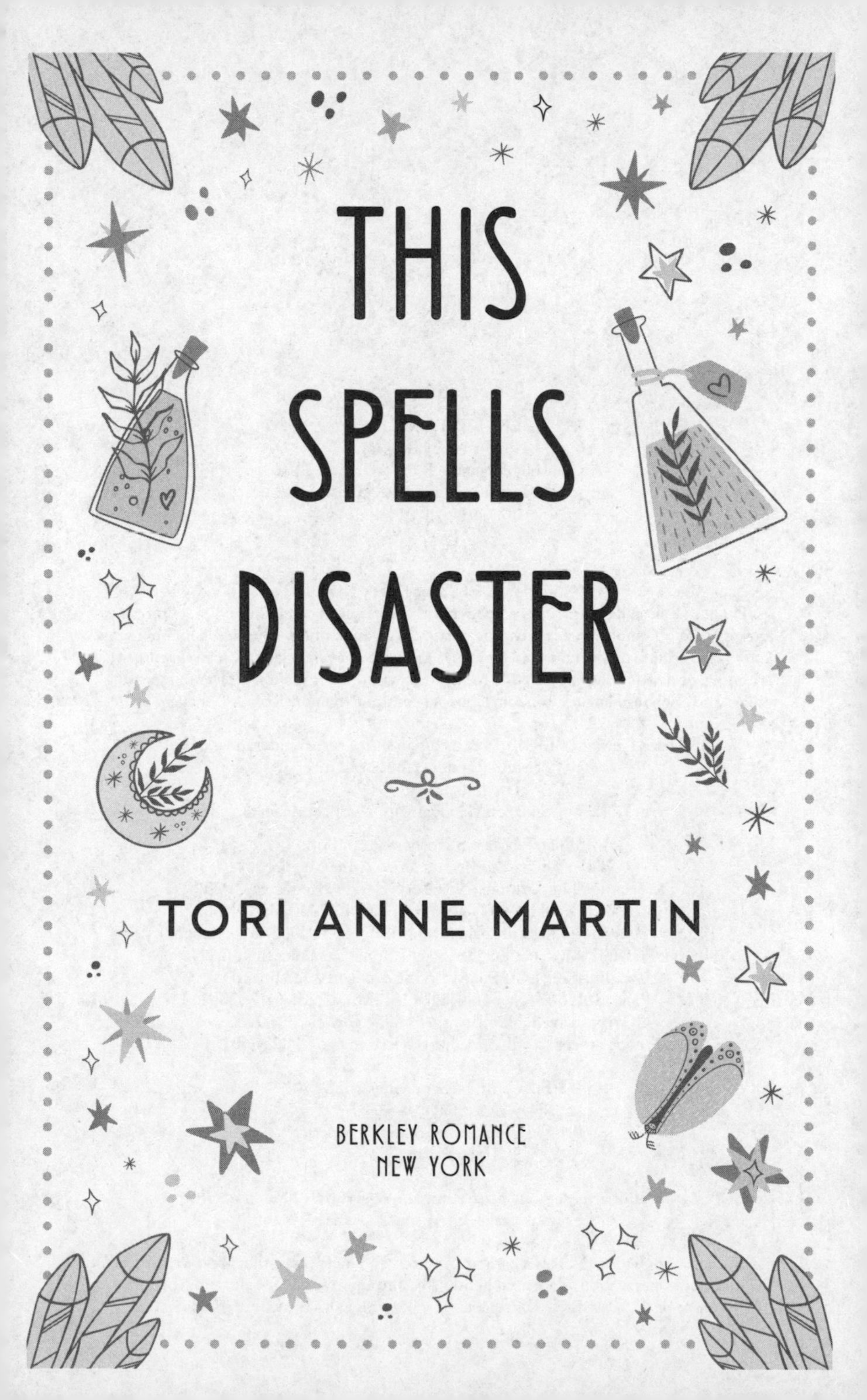

THIS SPELLS DISASTER

TORI ANNE MARTIN

BERKLEY ROMANCE
NEW YORK

BERKLEY ROMANCE
Published by Berkley
An imprint of Penguin Random House LLC
penguinrandomhouse.com

Library of Congress Cataloging-in-Publication Data

Names: Martin, Tori Anne, author.
Title: This spells disaster / Tori Anne Martin.
Description: First edition. | New York: Berkley Romance, 2023.
Identifiers: LCCN 2022060750 (print) | LCCN 2022060751 (ebook) |
ISBN 9780593548486 (trade paperback) | ISBN 9780593548493 (ebook)
Subjects: LCGFT: Witch fiction. | Lesbian fiction. | Romance fiction. | Novels.
Classification: LCC PS3613.A786246 T48 2023 (print) |
LCC PS3613.A786246 (ebook) | DDC 813/.6—dc23/eng/20230113
LC record available at https://lccn.loc.gov/2022060750
LC ebook record available at https://lccn.loc.gov/2022060751

First Edition: September 2023

Printed in the United States of America
1st Printing

Interior art: Magical background © SpicyTruffel / Shutterstock
Book design by Alison Cnockaert

To Tracey, who never questioned why so many
of her college friends were queer

AUTHOR'S NOTE

Thank you for picking up *This Spells Disaster.* Although this book is intended to be a light, romantic read, I can't ignore the fact that the plot revolves around a character being given a love potion. If love spells or potions existed, they would be a serious threat to bodily autonomy, yet many stories that include this type of magic disregard that potential or even treat such magic like a joke. Seeing as I spent years in school studying consent and sexual assault, this always left me uneasy, and when I got the idea for this book, I was determined to make sure that didn't happen. After all, at their very best, romance novels show what healthy consent can look like.

Before you begin, please be aware that the following issues are discussed: consent or the ability to consent to physical and sexual contact, magical drugging and loss of control, and anxiety and self-medication.

I hope you will love reading *This Spells Disaster* as much as I loved writing it, and that you find I treated the above topics with the seriousness they deserve. Finally, I want to assure you that while the possibility is addressed, there is no sexual assault in these pages.

THIS SPELLS DISASTER

WITCH COUNCIL DECREE #13

In order to ensure peace, to strengthen the bond between the magical and non-magical communities, and to promote the values of justice and tolerance, the Witch Council of the United States of America, on this day, October 22, 1944, hereby adopts the following laws by which all witches who reside in the United States are henceforth expected to abide.

1. The Law of Autonomy. No witch shall cast a spell nor give another a potion that violates one's free will.

2. The Law of Mind. No witch shall cast a spell nor give another a potion that interferes with one's mental state or memory unless they are explicitly given permission to do so.

3. The Law of Hexing. No witch shall hex a person or creature unable to magically defend themselves.

4. The Law of Discretion. No witch shall draw unnecessary attention to magic.

5. The Law of Community. All witches should strive to honor themselves, their magic, and their connection to all witches.

Failure to heed these laws, whether intentional or accidental, may lead to investigation by the Witch Council or a Council-designated Inquisitor. Punishment for harming witches or non-witches will be commensurate with the damage inflicted upon both individuals and the magical community.

1

IT WAS THE PERFECT NIGHT FOR A MESS, AND MORGAN GREENwood was precisely the sort of witch who couldn't resist a good mess.

Surrounded by her two closest friends, and with lively music filling her ears, Morgan had no worries. So even though some potions were powerful enough that they ought to be forbidden, she swallowed a mouthful of liquid and damned the consequences. To do otherwise would be a waste of a sultry Friday evening. Or at least a Friday evening that was as sultry as it ever got in Maine, which wasn't saying much.

Morgan knew her potions. A talented witch could create one that would make a person spill their darkest secrets or one that could erase their most traumatic memories. But no witch had yet found a way to combine those two effects. No, leave it to the mundanes to have discovered the power of the one she held in her hands.

Tequila.

If it were magical, surely the Witch Council would have banned it. Like a truth potion, tequila could make a person blab all of their secrets. Like a memory elixir, it could make someone forget their pain. And if you were really unlucky, tequila might convince you to dance naked around a bonfire beneath the full moon. Not that Morgan would know about that last one. She'd never done it herself.

Or had she, and tequila being what it was, she couldn't remember?

Best not to ask.

August evenings at the Empty Chalice were a blur of people and sound, even if one was abstaining from tequila. Summer meant the coastal town of Harborage was packed with tourists, and Fridays in the summer meant many of them joined the locals at what was generally known as the town's "witch bar," so called for the uncreative reason that it was owned by a couple of witches. There wasn't a whole lot else to do in the evenings in Harborage. If it wasn't the Empty Chalice, it would be another bar, and the Empty Chalice was the best of the bunch, even for the witches who didn't come to gawk at the overpriced magical cocktails on offer.

Along the far wall, the windows had been removed to let in the salty ocean breeze, and in the opposite corner from where Morgan sat, a fiddler played a jaunty tune. Morgan could hear but not see her through the mass of bodies circulating beneath the bar's open-beam ceiling and the enchanted lights that twinkled above like stars. Those lights moved nightly to reflect the changing constellations, creating the impression that what was indoors was actually out.

But in they were, and despite the Atlantic's cooling gusts, the bar was warm with people and the air thick with barely contained chaotic energy. It was on a summer evening like this that the first witch had probably been born. On a summer evening like this, it was easy to believe anything could happen.

Especially when tequila got involved.

Morgan's head swam, though this was her first drink, and she grabbed another lobster nacho from the plate she was sharing. The lobster nachos were the reason actual witches flocked to the Empty Chalice, and they were twice as addictive on her empty stomach. Still, it was easier to blame the tequila for her head feeling like it was stuffed with cotton rather than accept that forgetting to eat lunch hadn't done her any favors. Or the fact that she'd stayed up too late last night because she'd gotten sucked into watching cat videos. It was totally not her fault that cats were cute.

Come to think of it, why hadn't she adopted a new cat after her beloved Charlie had died? She should do that, then maybe she wouldn't waste time watching other people's cat videos.

Wait, what had she been thinking about a moment ago?

"Are the drinks extra strong tonight?" Morgan asked, desperately seeking validation of her blamelessness from Hazel and Andy. In a pinch, Andy's boyfriend, Trevor, who was also at their table, would do.

Hazel quirked a red eyebrow in her direction. "Mine seems normal, but maybe Rory was being nice to you."

Her tone was as sticky sweet as the strawberry syrup in Morgan's margarita, and Morgan poked her in the shoulder. She would not rise to the bait.

Would not.

Damn it. She glanced at the bar.

Rory Sandler was putting on a show as she made a drink for a couple of tourists. Amber liquid flowed from her shaker, spiraling and twisting in the air before landing gently in the martini glass. With another flick of her wrist and a light tap on the glass's side, the pair's faces alighted with delight. Morgan couldn't see what Rory had done yet, but she could guess. She'd frozen half the drink, and knowing Rory, she'd turned the ice into something more than boring cubes. Sure enough, a golden heart slowly rose above the rim, then settled into place, floating on top of the cocktail. Rory slid the glass over to her customer.

Elemental magic was simple magic, in theory. Any halfway competent witch could do it. Boiling or freezing water, lighting or extinguishing candles—they were the first sorts of spells a young witch learned. Making a complex liquid dance to her tune, like Rory had, or freezing only part of the drink and doing so in complicated shapes—that was another matter. Although for someone with Rory's skills, no doubt it was child's play. The sort of thing she could do in her sleep. One did not become the youngest national spellcasting champion ever by performing Magic 101.

Morgan had seen Rory compete several times before she'd ever met her, and the amount of power she hid behind her dark, often downcast, eyes was astonishing. How she'd ended up in Harborage a year ago and why she was slinging drinks at the Empty Chalice instead of competing for world dominance were both mysteries that no one in town had the answers to.

In fact, now that Morgan considered it, the possibility of being served a drink by *the* Rory Sandler was almost certainly another reason tourists beelined for the Empty Chalice. Rory had probably autographed hundreds of cocktail napkins over the past year. And while Harborage's witches might have gotten over their fangirling, speculation over Rory's sudden departure from the competitive spellcasting world remained rife in the witch media. Witches were a nosy bunch.

Rory's dark eyes finally glanced Morgan's way, and Morgan whipped around in her seat, her cheeks flaming.

Hazel sighed with something that sounded uncomfortably like sympathy, and the snake tattooed around her left arm circled her light skin in agitation. "You could just ask her out."

The mere thought of it made Morgan want to crawl under the table, and she sipped the dregs of her margarita to cool off. "Not happening."

"She's really nice."

"I know."

It was simply irrelevant. Rory had joined the local coven when she moved to town, so Morgan saw her plenty. Talking to her, on the other hand . . . Morgan's tongue had a tendency to tie itself in knots if Rory was within earshot, and looking at her caused Morgan's stomach to do the same.

Objectively, Morgan would have sworn Rory was not her type. She was too quiet. Her hair was too boyishly short, and the contrast between it and her pale skin was too stark. She dressed too plainly, her mostly black and gray wardrobe too dreary for Morgan, who loved bright colors. But there was something about the few freckles around Rory's nose that made Morgan long to kiss them, and she could waste hours daydreaming about running her fingers through the crop of dark hair on top of Rory's head. She wanted to know if Rory ever truly laughed as loudly as she did herself, and what it would take to make that happen.

She was a fool, and so was Hazel for suggesting she ask Rory out. A nobody like her did not ask out Rory fucking Sandler.

"I don't know if she'd be interested in that sort of thing," Morgan mumbled, the same lie she used to deflect whenever her friends teased her about her ridiculous crush.

It was a lie, because Morgan was nothing if not slightly obsessed, so she knew Rory had been in two semiserious relationships before moving to Harborage—one with a male witch and another with a female witch. Over the past three decades, the Witch Council had begun heavily marketing competitive spellcasting to mundane audiences—usually comparing it to figure skating—so even the non-magical press had paid attention to Rory during the U.S. national championships a few years ago, making that sort of research easy. And too hard to resist.

So yes, the possibility of dating Rory, in theory, was there. But a chasm the size of the Milky Way existed between theory and reality, even for people who performed magic on a daily basis. Morgan could no more conjure world peace than she could imagine Rory being interested in her.

"You never know unless you try," Hazel said, which was how these conversations always went. Hazel was the optimistic friend everybody needed in their life to goad them into making an ass out of themselves occasionally, but there were limits to Morgan's willingness to do so.

Let Hazel dare her to dress up as a sexy Glinda from *The Wizard of Oz* one year for mundane Halloween? Why not? Morgan had decided she was born to wear a sparkling pink bikini top and matching skirt. Go along with Hazel sweet-talking Morgan and Andy into a karaoke version of Olivia Newton-John's "Magic" during a coven fundraiser for the Harborage library? Who cared that Andy was the only one of the three of them who could belt out a tune when it was for a good cause? Morgan had been game.

But this was different. Her head might be fuzzy from the margarita, but all common sense hadn't fled her body yet.

"What's the worst she can say?" Andy added from across the table. "No?"

"Actually, yeah. 'No' sounds pretty terrible now that you mention it." Morgan snatched the last nacho in retaliation for the encouragement.

As different as they were, the three of them had grown up together—the inevitable result of their shared magical heritage and small-town existence. Hazel and Andy looked at Morgan and saw the same girl they'd known their whole lives. The first to volunteer for a wild scheme, the first to jump in someone's face when they threatened a friend, and the one who always got yelled at in class for never shutting up. Seven years post high school graduation, Morgan liked to believe she was still those things, or she tried to be.

Just not in this particular case. After her last disastrous relationship, Morgan had learned her limitations, and she had zero desire to subject herself to further romantic humiliation.

Trevor, the only non-witch at the table, glared at Morgan. "I had my sights set on that nacho, witch. That nacho was mine."

Morgan grinned at him. She liked Trevor, who was a physics doctoral student at the nearby university and who enjoyed deep, geeky conversations about the underlying so-called science of magic. Everything he said went way over her head, so Morgan had no idea if he was really smart or really full of shit, but he never got weirded out around her friends the way some mundanes did. And Andy really liked *him*, so that was something, too.

"Never get into a competition with me when it comes to food, especially when I'm hungry." Morgan popped the gooey nacho in her mouth. In spite of the congealing cheese and cold lobster, it tasted amazing.

"Fine. Another plate and another round." Trevor started to stand, then he turned Morgan's mischievous grin back on her. "Unless you'd like to go order so you can talk to Rory."

"Beat it before I turn you into a toad." She pointed a finger at him, and Trevor left, laughing. "And the two of you, stop staring at me with your pitying eyes. I mean it."

Hazel and Andy exchanged innocent expressions.

Oh, fine. If that's how they wanted to play it. This table needed a change of topic, fast. "Festival talk," Morgan said, slapping the wood and setting the candle in the center rattling inside its hurricane glass. "Am I the only one who has to work the whole time?"

She suspected she was. Her family's shop maintained a vendor booth at the New England Witches' Trust (aka NEWT, because weren't they clever?) biennial festival. Morgan wouldn't be working every shift, but she would need to be there every day. Something about responsibility and having bills to pay, blah blah blah. As far as jobs went, Morgan liked making potions, and having learned from two generations of witches, she was good at her work, but adulthood was overrated.

"I booked a few appointments Friday and Saturday," Hazel said. "I wasn't going to work, but . . ."

"But you're so in demand," Andy finished for her.

Hazel gave a modest shrug, which suggested Andy had been right.

People had probably begged Hazel for tattoos at the festival, and Hazel, being the sort of person who couldn't say no, had capitulated. Morgan got it. She'd been saying "no" for Hazel their whole lives. That's what best friends were for, when they weren't goading each other into acting like fools or practicing spells by magically curling or straightening each other's hair (and, on the unfortunate couple of occasions, removing each other's hair entirely).

"Well, I won't be working," Andy said. "I'm not arriving until Friday afternoon, because I've got bookings through Thursday. I promised my cousin's friend I'd do an assessment on this house she can't sell."

"It's early for haunting season to pick up, isn't it?" Hazel asked.

Andy shrugged and tucked her black braids behind her ears. "Yeah, but it's New England. There's no shortage of ghosts any time of the year. I just hope this is a we-can-negotiate kind of situation, and not an I-need-to-banish-this-thing one. If that's the case, I'll seriously be delayed."

"Eh, the festival doesn't get good until Friday," Morgan said, trying to console her, and it was true enough, depending on your reasons for attending.

Officially, the NEWT Festival was supposed to be an opportunity for the region's witches to strengthen inter-coven bonds and learn from one another. Unofficially, it was four days of partying and magical fun in Western Massachusetts. The festivities kicked off Wednesday afternoon, and there were networking events, workshops, concerts, and shopping available every day, but the crowds didn't really descend until Friday and Saturday. Naturally, the best of everything was saved for those days, whether it was the most famous musicians, the most sought-after instructors, or the most popular magical games. And it was all topped off by what was (in Morgan's opinion) the festival highlight—the spellcasting exhibition on Saturday. Which, coincidentally, was the first place she'd ever seen Rory perform in person. Back when Rory was just some witch from Boston, and not Rory fucking Sandler.

Trevor returned a moment later, and a server brought over a fresh round of margaritas and a new platter of nachos soon after. Morgan started on her second margarita while they discussed the festival schedule and any workshops they wanted to attend. If *fuzzy* had been the word of the evening so far, she was slowly creeping into *drunk* territory.

"You think Rory will perform at the exhibition?" she asked.

"Doubtful," Andy said. "I don't think she's performed since she dropped out of World's."

No, she hadn't, and Morgan knew it. The last time anyone had seen Rory perform was almost two years ago. Tequila and her wishful thinking were getting the best of her. "It's too bad."

"You are so hopeless, my dear." Andy placed her brown hand on Morgan's much paler arm and squeezed.

"It's a hopeless situation."

Hazel jerked up at that moment, a smile spreading over her face. "Rory!"

Beneath the table, Morgan kicked her. "Stop it."

Hazel kicked her back. "Hey!"

"Seriously?" Morgan flopped backward in her seat. "Don't call her over. Haven't you guys—"

Oh.

Hazel pulled on an empty chair, and from somewhere behind Morgan's back, Rory appeared. The room spun as the blood drained from Morgan's brain and flooded her face. Again.

Rory sat tentatively, smiled even more tentatively, and cast a glance at Morgan that suggested she'd overheard enough to assume Morgan didn't want her around.

Fuck.

"Hi." It was the most Morgan could squeak out before fumbling with her drink. Her options were now: 1) get completely blitzed so she couldn't remember this later, or 2) slide off her chair and hide under the table. Although she wasn't about to rule out attempting both. In the meantime, she pulled her blond braid around her face, trying to disappear behind it.

"Hi." Rory gave everyone a wave and bit her—very full, very tempting—lower lip.

Morgan took a large swallow of margarita.

"Taking a break?" Hazel asked.

"A brief one, yeah." Rory sipped from the water glass she'd carried over. Her face was a touch shiny from the heat, and the band T-shirt she wore clung to her curves. The Dragon Flies were a popular witch group, and Morgan was positive she'd seen their name on the festival lineup this year. She could mention that, but it would necessitate her brain engaging with her mouth in a way that made Morgan sound intelligent, and alcohol aside, that rarely happened in Rory's presence.

"We were talking about the festival," Hazel said. "You are going, right?"

Rory nodded with a grimace. "Yeah, I'm going."

"You sound absolutely delighted," Andy said. "What's wrong?"

A drop of condensation ran down Rory's glass, and she wiped it up with her finger before responding. "I'm not a big fan of crowds."

A laugh exploded from Morgan's lips, completely beyond her control. She wasn't even sure why. It wasn't like that was funny. Ironic maybe. Damn it. The tequila was doing her in. "Sorry. I just . . ." She waved a hand around them to indicate the packed bar. "Wrong profession."

Rory shrugged. "I'm tending bar; it's not the same thing as . . ."

Morgan could fill in the rest—as being approached by strangers wanting autographs and photos while she was trying to relax. Morgan had never seen Rory be anything but gracious to her fans, but it had to be exhausting.

"Anyway," Rory was saying, "I'm going because I want to see my brother and my nephew, but I just found out that my parents invited Archer Gregg to come with them."

"They asked another spellcasting competitor to join them?" Andy said.

"Yeah." Rory picked up her water, but her gaze hovered over the margarita glass in Hazel's hands, like she wouldn't mind a trade. "According to my brother, my parents have it in their heads that he can convince me to get back to competing."

"Oh, I've seen him perform. He is good *and* he's cute. What?" Andy stuck her tongue out at Trevor when he flashed her a look of annoyance. "I'm sorry, but it's true."

Morgan's stomach jerked violently, and she clasped her hands more tightly around her glass, hoping her internal struggle was hidden. She had no recollection of what Archer Gregg looked like, but she questioned the Sandlers' motives, or Rory's interpretation of them anyway.

No matter what centuries of patriarchal propaganda taught, there were no gender requirements for being born a witch, though male witches—be they cis or trans—were rare. It was also true, however, that magic tended to run through female bloodlines, so most witches had non-magical fathers. When a child was born from two magical parents, they were almost always extraordinarily powerful. Like Rory—her father was a witch.

Morgan figured she probably knew way too much about Rory, but the Sandlers were prominent in the community, even without Rory's fame. Rory's mother was on the Witch Council, and powerful people always tried to increase their already potent standing. Rory marrying a male witch would do the trick for her family, and Morgan read enough romance novels to recognize a setup when she heard one.

"You do not sound enthused by this idea," Hazel said, noting the obvious. She, too, had sensed where Rory's eyes had gone, and she held out her half-filled margarita glass.

Rory shook off the offer. "This is heavy-handed, even for them. I don't know what it's going to take for them to accept my decision to quit competing. I suppose I can just not go, but I can't decide if it's better to face this head-on or if I should wimp out. It's not like staying home will prevent the meddling for long, but postponing it would be nice."

"Face them," Morgan said. It was the advice she'd give anyone, and besides, she couldn't imagine a witch with Rory's power wimping out of anything.

Rory grimaced again. "You're right. Best to get it over with."

Her tone suggested she was walking into a trap and knew it but was determined to accept her fate and surrender to it quickly. Suddenly, Morgan had visions of Rory giving in. What if Rory went to the festival and agreed to spend time with Archer to make her family happy? What if he convinced her to compete again (yay!), but she fell for him in the process (boo!)? Then, she—Morgan—would have been partly responsible for this nightmare.

Get real. It's not like she would date you if she wasn't dating someone else, a voice in Morgan's head whispered. It sounded suspiciously like her ex-girlfriend, and Morgan drank another sip of her margarita, hoping to drown it.

No, Rory would never be interested in actually dating her, but that didn't matter. What if she could be a shield between Rory and her family's pressure? Not just to keep Rory from possibly dating someone else—although that was obviously part of the brilliance of this plan—but because it was the right thing to do. She didn't like to see Rory stressed, and Rory definitely looked stressed, from the little V between her eyebrows to the way she kept chewing on that lower lip, which was going to drive Morgan absolutely insane with lust. If she couldn't kiss away Rory's stress, she could do the next best thing.

You are a fool, and this is a fool's idea. Do not say this out loud. That was entirely her own voice in her head this time, a product of the few brain cells that hadn't succumbed to the power of tequila.

"What if you were dating someone here?" Morgan asked. Only the absurd idea popped out of her drunken lips so quickly it sounded like whatifyouweredatingsomeonehere? Those sober brain cells had done their best to stop this disaster, but their best was not good enough.

Shut up, shut up. SHUT UP!

Rory blinked. Hazel, Andy, and Trevor probably did, too, but Morgan's consciousness had shrunk to the size of the candle flame flickering on the table between her and Rory. It shuddered violently inside its glass cage, like the dying shreds of her dignity as they fought to control her tongue.

"What?" Rory asked eventually.

"I mean, like, not for real," Morgan said. Of course not. It could never be for real.

Her heart must have stopped momentarily, but she felt it now, kicking up a fuss inside her chest, her pulse racing as adrenaline flooded her body. It was too late to take back her drunken suggestion, so damn it, she would commit. Just like she always did when her propensity to speak first and think second got her into trouble.

"Pretend to date someone," Morgan said, concentrating on her words so she sounded more confident than she felt. "I could be your fake girlfriend, telling your parents how much you love your new life in Harborage. Your parents would see that you're happy and setting down roots here, and you could enjoy the festival without their interference."

Rory stared at her with an expression Morgan couldn't read—but she was thinking about it, Morgan was certain. A delightful giddiness swept over her. The magic in the air tonight was real. She could feel its tingle in her veins, an almost imperceptible hum that called to the blood like the moon beckoned the tides. *Witch up, and seize the moment. Unleash your power.*

She was brilliant.

She was bold.

She would be triumphant.

Then Rory laughed, a sharp, hollow sound that punctured Morgan's mood like a poisoned dart. "Good one. I've got to get back to work."

Who was she was kidding? She was a mess.

Murmurs of "later" and "good luck" rumbled around the table, but Morgan had a hard enough time faking a smile, never mind speaking. Her consciousness had expanded again, the tingle had vanished, and the room was a cacophony of noise and the reek of booze and fried food. She slumped in her chair, the bar spinning.

Fucking tequila. What had she just done?

2

THE VAGUE SENSE THAT SOMETHING WAS WRONG WOKE MORgan a minute before her alarm. Her brain felt like sludge, but her mouth tasted like stale toothpaste—a positive sign that suggested she'd been with it enough to brush her teeth before climbing into bed last night, though perhaps not with it enough to rinse them properly.

Yet something in the hazy depths of her mind bugged her, and it wasn't because she was up at eight on a Saturday morning. She normally worked Saturdays at the family shop.

The feeling stayed with her as she showered and brushed her teeth again, and it grew as her sluggish brain began to throb in tune with the jerk mowing his lawn outside, the incessant whine of the motor drowning out the morning's usual chirping birds. She knew who the culprit was—Mr. Abbott—and Morgan dearly wished to hex his lawn mower. His leaf blower, too, if she were being thorough. That would break Council Law #3 (aka the Law of Hexing, or—as Morgan thought of it—not being a magical asshole), although her neighbors would consider her a hero.

When Morgan finally opened her apartment blinds, the summer sunlight turned the throbbing in her head into an all-out attack on her senses.

"All right. Tequila, I get it. We are through, the two of us. No more meeting like that." She started the coffee, wondering if Rory actually had made her table's drinks extra strong last night, no matter what Hazel had claimed.

Rory.

Morgan frowned, her sense of unease latching onto the name for a reason she didn't understand. Sweet stars, she hoped she hadn't done anything humiliating last night while Rory had been working. Her memories of anything after that first margarita were hazy.

She stuck two thick slices of raisin bread into the toaster and poured her first cup of coffee—also seemingly magical, but not as dangerous as tequila. Once she'd added cream and sugar, Morgan retrieved the bottle of anti-hangover potion she kept in the kitchen cabinet. It would have been best to take some last night before bed, but only so much logic could be expected of a person who needed an anti-hangover potion in the first place.

Since that opportunity had passed, Morgan put a drop of the colorless, odorless potion in her coffee, wishing she'd been the one to make it. She could probably license the recipe from the witch who'd created it and make and sell it herself, but that wasn't the point. Credit went to the witch who was clever enough to create a brand-new spell or potion. That didn't merely bring in money; it brought renown. It brought respect. It brought accomplishment.

Basically, it brought everything Morgan longed for as much as she longed for Rory to notice her. More so, maybe, because she'd been chasing magical success for longer.

Chasing and subsequently failing to obtain it, so all of her desires had that in common.

Wow. Being hungover made her morose.

Morgan took a sip of coffee, and it burned her tongue. While she waited for the caffeine and the potion to kick in, she contemplated the bottle. The brown glass gave no indication as to what the thick solution contained, though Morgan could guess. Willow bark, blackberry seeds, perhaps some peppermint. If she were trying to create her own version, that's where she'd start, although those were easy guesses at the spell's basic building blocks. The recipe would get a lot more complicated from there. Likely, there were dozens of ingredients, and factors like the moon phase and how the ingredients were used and added, even harvested, would have a significant effect on the outcome.

Volumes upon volumes had been written about the generic magical properties of natural phenomena—the ingredients that went into potions or spells—and every witch's family had their own spell books, jealously guarded and passed down over generations. Morgan had gotten better at crafting the old family brews over the years while working at their shop, but potion-making was as much intuition as it was a recipe. Morgan could run her fingers over a new plant or catch a scent on the wind and get a feel for what effects she could glean from them.

Intuition would only get a witch so far, though. Like everything in life, to get ahead—to get *good* at magic—required practice. So every witch specialized, and then they shopped for anything they wanted that fell too far outside their areas of expertise, same as the non-magical community. The options were as countless as the stars in the sky. Morgan focused on potions for the family shop, Hazel bespelled inks to create her wondrous tattoos, and Andy possessed the rare ability of being able to talk to (and, when necessary, banish) ghosts. Other witches specialized in green craft (gardening or farming magic), kitchen witchery (cooking and baking magic-infused foods), healing, and even curse-breaking.

Of course, some things were best handled non-magically, period, including most things that involved the human body. Manipulating living systems got tricky. An anti-hangover potion sounded simple, but it was anything but. There was a reason witches saw mundane doctors for most ailments more serious than headaches or broken bones.

One-quarter of her coffee down, the throbbing in Morgan's head began to ease, and the cloud that covered her memories of last night began to dissipate. She'd almost finished the mug and was picking at her toast as she scrolled through social media when perfect clarity was restored.

She choked on a raisin as the clarity brought horror along with it.

Oh no. Oh shit. She should never have taken that anti-hangover potion.

No, she should never have drunk two large strawberry margaritas on a mostly empty stomach and a sleep-deprived brain. In her hand, the ceramic mug grew scalding hot and the coffee began to boil as stress roused the magic in Morgan's blood. Swearing, she set the mug on the table and breathed deeply, forcing her power back down. Strong emotions could have that effect, especially in adolescents who were still developing their power and control, but adults weren't immune. In retrospect, Morgan was lucky that embarrassment hadn't made her lose control like that last night, but she supposed tequila was to thank for it. Alcohol dulled the ability to perform magic, even unintentionally.

Failing to remember the time, or that Hazel would likely be asleep, Morgan almost knocked the remains of her coffee over as she grabbed her phone and sent a desperate text.

MORGAN: I did, didn't I?

She followed with a string of crying emojis.

Unable to stomach the rest of her breakfast, Morgan shoved her plate aside so she could stare blankly at her white cabinets and contemplate running away to join a circus. Certainly, she could never go back to the Empty Chalice. Or to a coven meeting. On that note, Harborage was a relatively small town. She should probably never leave her apartment again just in case she ran into Rory at the local Hannaford. From now on, it was food delivery all the time and a life of solitude. Her family would have to understand if she refused to ever cover another shift at their store.

From somewhere, a high-pitched alarm sounded, and it took Morgan a moment to realize she was whining out loud.

When her phone chimed with Hazel's return text, she grabbed it.

HAZEL: Are you referring to offering to fake date Rory? Yes, you did. Not as good as the real thing, but a first step. I was impressed.

Well, that was one of them.

MORGAN: She laughed at me!

The memory brought with it the distinct taste of vomit, so Morgan added an appropriate GIF.

There was a pause, followed by several ". . ." while Hazel must have been struggling for how to best comfort her.

HAZEL: I don't think she was laughing at you.

Morgan scowled. Hazel had chosen lies, but that could be forgiven. Comfort was impossible while acknowledging the truth.

MORGAN: I am such a dumbass. Why are you friends with me?

HAZEL: Because you are a lovable dumbass.

Yeah, right. Hazel might think so because they'd grown up together, but no one else did. Rory clearly didn't. She'd laughed like the idea of merely *fake* dating Morgan was ludicrous. Which, in fairness, it was. As if anyone—besides her wildly biased friends—could believe Rory would be interested in her. No wonder Rory had darted away like the table was on fire.

"No more tequila. Ever." For good measure, Morgan sent a text to that effect to Hazel as well. That ought to make it a vow.

The laughing emojis Hazel sent back disagreed.

How much would it cost to have someone remove this memory from her brain? As she got dressed, Morgan contemplated whether she knew anyone skilled enough for her to trust them with that sort of magic, but ultimately, she had to concede that this plan was no plan at all. For it to work, the memory would also have to be removed from Rory's brain, and Morgan was not so unethical as to violate Rory's mind that way, however tempting it was.

Back to her original plan it was, then. Hermit life, or as close to it as she could come.

Her travel cup of coffee in hand, Morgan slipped on her sunglasses and begrudgingly left for work. The town's historic district, where she lived, was only a few minutes' walk from downtown Harborage, making it a coveted location. Victorian monstrosities mingled with even larger colonial-style ones, their yards heavily gardened, lawns bursting with the color of mid-August blooms—white and blue hydrangeas, golden black-eyed Susans, cheerful-faced sunflowers in warm yellows and oranges, and dahlias in every shade of pink and red. Most of the houses had been converted into multifamily homes or apartments decades ago, and Morgan's was no exception. Her top-floor apartment resided in a pale pink Victorian with deeper pink trim that Morgan affectionately referred to as "the brothel" when describing it to visitors.

Two turns landed her on Main Street, where the ocean's scent clung to the air. Flags decorated with flowers flapped from the antique-style streetlamps. Neighbors walked their dogs, bikers weaved through the morning traffic, and tourists took their breakfasts to sit on the benches overlooking the rocky coastline and the fishing and sightseeing boats already out on the water.

Morgan normally enjoyed her morning commute, but today she was glad the bright sun provided an excuse to cover her face in sunglasses and the ocean's cool breeze was a reason to pull her sweatshirt hood down over her head. Rory would have been up late, closing the Empty Chalice, so the odds of seeing her at this time of day were slim, but why take chances?

Bed, Bath, and Broom had already opened, and the pungent scents of the products—many of which she'd made—hit Morgan's nose as she pulled on the polished wood door. The bells overhead jingled, temporarily drowning out the harp music that Tara, the morning clerk, had put on.

Her maternal grandmother had started the shop before Morgan was born, going from selling magically infused soaps and lotions out of her home work space to finding the perfect storefront in the quaintest, most tourist-friendly block of downtown. The many shelves were organized into categories—bath supplies, personal care, cosmetics, and more. Every glass jar, shiny tin, or lovingly paper-wrapped item promised self-care, and all their products were handmade by the family, as magic was not something that could be industrialized or scaled up easily. Besides, the potion recipes were the family's wealth of sorts. The more in-demand or popular a creation, the more a witch could charge for it.

But while there was nothing simple or boring about her ability to brew up a shampoo that could turn your hair any color you wanted, or a lip balm that adjusted to the most flattering shade for your face, or a moisturizer that could reduce wrinkles (or rather the appearance of wrinkles, which was far less complex than actually de-aging the skin), Morgan dreamed of more. She'd already improved upon some of her grandmom's signature potions, and no doubt the next generation would one day improve upon her improvements. But none of these things were meaningful.

Noteworthy. Important. *Significant.* The word came out tinged in her ex's voice.

Your family's shop is cute, but when are you going to show some ambition and do something significant *with your life? I thought you were more talented than that, but you're just a small thinker like the rest of them.*

And then, Nicole had dumped her.

Nicole had *significant* goals for her life. Getting elected to the Witch Council was first among them, which was not something she could do hanging around some tourist-trap Maine town, wasting her time with a witch who was content to infuse bubble bath with relaxation potions because she had no true talents of her own.

"You okay this morning?" Tara asked from where she was adjusting a display of energizing soaps.

Morgan caught her reflection in one of the many mirrors lining the shop and realized she was scowling. Luckily, the store was empty of customers at this time of day, so she wasn't scaring anyone off.

"Um, yeah." She glanced around the showroom's soothing pink and brown walls and up at the decorative bundles of dried lavender, rosemary, lemon balm, and more that were strung from the ceiling. Magic could be dangerous and it could get dark, but there was no evidence of that here, which was exactly how Morgan's grandmom wanted it.

Not to mention exactly how the Witch Council preferred magic be perceived by the general population. Helpful over harmful. Sweet instead of scary. If witches kept their heads down and blended in, everyone could live in harmony. That was the entire reason the Council had written its laws in the first place. Despite its history, New England was one of the safer places in the U.S. for witches to live openly these days, but the magical community was—and always would be—greatly outnumbered.

Shaking off these thoughts, Morgan propped the sunglasses on top of her head and glanced around. It only took a second to determine that Tara had everything well under control. "You all good out here?"

"All fine. I'll holler if I need help before Liv arrives."

Saturdays were always the busiest day. The day-trippers came up from Boston, joining the tourists who were staying for the whole Maine vacation experience, and people tended to do their online shopping, too, so the mail-order half of the business picked up. Morgan rarely worked the customer-facing side of Bed, Bath, and Broom these days. Once her skills had reached the point where she was allowed to make potions instead of selling them, that task had been left to the non-magical staff.

In the back room, Morgan took off her sweatshirt with a sigh. Her entire body, not just her face, still went hot when she thought about her outburst last night, but for a while, she could turn her focus onto something else.

The NEWT Festival was eleven days away, and there was a lot of prep work to be done for it. Festival shopping was a big draw for many people, and vendors came from all over the country. But despite the competition, Bed, Bath, and Broom had built a positive reputation over the years, and they always did good business.

Morgan's mother had put together a schedule that listed the tasks to be accomplished each day so they would have enough products to stock their booth and keep the store filled while they were gone. Then there was the packing of the products, the repacking of specific ingredients in case they needed to make additional items on-site for special orders or surprise bestsellers, and so much else.

Morgan regarded the day's tasks with distaste. What she really wanted to do was work on her personal project—one day, she was going to create a potion that made the magical community sit up and take notice. A potion that would show the world that she was a clever and talented witch. Worthy of respect, if not admiration. One day, she was going to prove Nicole wrong.

The problem was, Morgan didn't even have an idea for what that revolutionary potion might be, never mind the confidence that she was actually skilled enough to create an entirely new potion from scratch. Nicole had turned out to be a bitch, but she hadn't been wrong to call Morgan a small thinker. She was good at what she did, but what she did was tweak other people's spells. It made for a decent living, but it was far from significant.

"Focus," Morgan told herself, downing the rest of her coffee. If this bad mood of hers didn't pass by lunch, she'd have to stop by Sugar Spells and hope the magical bakery had something in stock that might snap her out of it. One of her own potions *could* do it, but why waste an opportunity to treat herself to cupcakes? It was just too bad that they wouldn't have anything to fix the cause of her mood, because that meant it would inevitably return.

In the meantime, there would be no thinking about Rory, and no thinking about her project. Everyone knew inspiration came only when your mind was busy elsewhere, so Morgan would work. She plugged in her phone, brought up her favorite playlist to put her in the right frame of mind, and got going. The faster she finished today's tasks, the faster she could get out of here, and . . . Oh, right, hide in her apartment.

Correction: the faster she finished, the faster she could get out of here and eat cupcakes and begin her search for a cat to adopt. That worked fine for motivation, and if she was going to be an apartment hermit, she'd need company. Goal set.

Soon, the music's beat chased away these worries, and Morgan activated the runes along the edge of her worktable with a dab of salt water, a touch of spit, and a whisper. The runes would concentrate her power, and had she been doing something risky, keep it contained. It wasn't as strong a barrier as a full protective spell circle would be, but it would do for her purposes. The benefit of making potions over casting spells was that Morgan didn't have to worry about magic slipping out of her control or releasing too quickly. Besides, nothing she did here was harmful.

While the same ingredients and tools could be used for hexing or creating illicit potions, magic was more than combining the right ingredients in the right ways. Intent and focus were the key to unlocking the power inside the objects used. Otherwise, they were just that—objects. Stagnant and inert. Magic came from within the witch as much as it did her tools.

In record time, Morgan finished prepping a new batch of the glamour potion that was the primary magical ingredient in the store's most popular lip balm, and her head swam as she screwed the lid on the glass jar. She grabbed the worktable to steady herself, the runes twinkling out.

Magic depletion felt an awful lot like being drunk, but minus all the fun aspects. Non-witches had this delusion that magic wasn't work, that all someone like her had to do was wiggle her nose *Bewitched*-style, and poof—she could restock the store. If only. Magic cost something internally, and it was only partly physical. Trevor had expounded on theories as to what and why that Morgan didn't understand, but she damned well knew what it felt like.

And it felt like snack time. Holding on to the table for balance, she glanced over at where she'd set her empty coffee cup and found nothing. In her miserable, distracted state this morning, she'd completely forgotten to bring her favorite snacks.

Perfect. Could she *not* screw something up for a change?

Grumbling to herself, Morgan threw open the supply closet and was rewarded with a giant container of her mother's preferred pick-me-up. Peanut butter–filled pretzels were not in Morgan's top ten, but the sweet and salty combination was no doubt better for replenishing her energy than what she normally carried, which were cheese crackers. Not high-quality cheese crackers, as her mother often lamented, but those bright orange squares that she could eat by the handful. Morgan could practically taste their overly salty, only vaguely cheese-like flavor if she closed her eyes. So when she shoved the first peanut butter–filled pretzel nugget in her mouth, the mismatch was jarring and oh so disappointing.

The pretzel did its job fine, though. As soon as the salt dissolved on her tongue, the room steadied and the headache she'd barely noticed before faded. Morgan crammed two more pretzels in her mouth and pulled out a fistful to munch on while she cleaned and packed up her supplies. The back room's door opened as she did so.

"Everything okay?" The syllables stuck together on her tongue, completely unintelligible thanks to the peanut butter, and Morgan spun around, expecting to find Tara or Liv. But it wasn't either of the clerks.

Rory stood in the doorway, one hand lingering on the wood frame. Her brow was as pinched as it had been last night. "Sorry to interrupt."

3

MORGAN SWORE, BUT THE PEANUT BUTTER SERVED HER WELL, muffling the f-bomb that Rory undoubtedly would have misconstrued into thinking Morgan didn't want to see her. Alas, peanut butter could do nothing to prevent the flush creeping up her neck, accentuating cheeks that were stuffed chipmunk-like with food.

Way to not further humiliate herself.

"I was told you were in the back, and . . ." Rory trailed off, leaving the room silent enough to make the sound of Morgan desperately chewing the sticky carbs as loud as thunder in her ears.

"Um, yes. I'm here." She hid her mouth behind her arm, licking the remains of peanut butter from her teeth, and grabbed her water bottle. Convinced she could be understood, Morgan cleared her throat and tried again. "Hi. Welcome to Bed, Bath, and Broom. How can I help you?"

Oh, and why are you in my back room? And which clerk do I need to hex for letting you in without warning me that Rory Sandler was in my shop?

Really, no one should have been allowed back here except for employees, but Tara and Liv, although mundanes, had hung around witches long enough to become enamored with competitive spellcasting and thus were starstruck by Rory, too.

Morgan dumped her handful of pretzels on the table and brushed crumbs off her shirt. There was nothing she could do about the rest of her appearance. Her hair was poorly clipped back, her leggings were faded, and her T-shirt was old and stained because potion work could get messy. She hadn't put on any makeup because she wasn't supposed to be seeing anyone.

Pop culture loved to depict potion-brewing witches wearing beautiful robes with long bell sleeves, their hair floating in a cauldron's steam. In truth, that was a quick path to a hefty cleaning bill and setting your head on fire. A witch only needed to singe a few inches before appreciating the magic of a simple hair tie, or Morgan's preferred accessory—a large clip.

Rory's gaze traveled from the pretzels to Morgan's face, and Morgan considered joining the crumbs on the floor. "Sorry. The woman out front told me you were packing back here, not working magic. I can . . . You know what? Never mind."

"No, it's fine." If it weren't for the worktable in her way, Morgan would have lunged for the door to prevent Rory from leaving. Any time in Rory's presence was better than no time, even if she was continuing to make a fool of herself. "I'm done. Just making a mess of my post-casting meal because I got dizzy. I'm sure it's nothing like post-competition exertion, but . . ."

She should stop babbling.

Rory shrugged, but her smile was sympathetic. "You can't possibly make a bigger mess than I have. I once poked myself in the eye with an energy bar. My arms were shaking so badly that I missed my mouth."

What had Hazel said last night? That Rory was really nice? Yeah, she was. Magic depletion only happened when something required effort, and the exhaustion and light-headedness were proportional to the amount of effort expended. Morgan could light candle flames all day and feel fine. The difference between what she'd been doing to make the glamour potion and what Rory would do during a competition was like the difference between a gentle summer drizzle and a hurricane.

"It's worse when you don't eat your breakfast," she mumbled, recalling her abandoned toast. Pretzels aside, if she kept being reminded of last night, she might never eat again.

Rory made a tsk noise. "Yeah, that'll do it."

Yes, it would, and she should have known better. She also shouldn't have tried excusing her poor manners since she'd only made herself sound like an incompetent witch in the process. Awesome. Next time, she'd let the peanut butter do its thing and keep her mouth glued shut.

Since she hadn't done that, though, Morgan drank more water, trying to assess Rory's purpose without looking like she was trying to assess her.

Rory was wearing a violet Empty Chalice T-shirt today over a pair of faded black jeans, and everything was rumpled like she'd recently rolled out of bed, including her hair. She'd taken the time to put on some eye makeup, though, and all seven silver rings she typically wore. (Morgan had counted them many times, noting which fingers went unadorned.) Yet all that effort couldn't hide the tiredness Rory seemed to be trying to conceal.

Of course, a somewhat slovenly Rory looked good, almost approachable for a change.

Morgan curled her fingers into her palms, possessed by the desire to comb Rory's hair and press her lips against the softness of those pale cheeks. She wanted to give Rory a shoulder to rest her head on, and to wrap her arms around Rory's slender body, lulling her to sleep. Morgan was softer than Rory was, curvier, and often thought she'd make a good pillow for the right person. It was pathetic how badly she wanted Rory to be that person.

"So, last night," Rory said, thankfully oblivious to Morgan's thoughts, "when I brought up what my family is doing—"

"Yeah, I'm sorry."

The V returned to Rory's forehead, forming a line that pointed down to those distracting freckles sprinkled across her nose. Morgan's pulse danced, and she averted her gaze.

"For what?" Rory asked.

Morgan rubbed her palms on her leggings. She was sweating more now than she had been making the glamour potion. "I was drunk last night. I forgot to eat lunch yesterday, so one margarita did me in, and I was saying nonsense."

"Huh." Rory crossed her arms. "I'm noticing a theme with you and missing meals."

"It's strange because I love to eat."

"Not sure I believe you."

Clearly, Rory had never noticed her stuffing her face during coven meetings. Morgan couldn't decide whether or not she was relieved by this.

"Is there any chance you remember what nonsense you were saying last night?" Rory asked the question warily, and Morgan couldn't blame her for doubting the answer.

Unfortunately, however, the anti-hangover potion had ensured she did. "Yup."

Which meant . . .

"I was thinking about it afterward," Rory said.

Here it came.

"Were you at all serious?"

Say no! No, say yes! Unable to choose, what came out sounded like, "Uh."

Just kill her now.

"Drunk or not, it didn't seem like a terrible idea," Rory said.

Had someone hexed Morgan as a baby? What had she done to deserve this?

Wait.

"What?" Morgan asked.

Rory shrugged again, sheepishly almost, like she was the one feeling awkward. It made no sense. "I thought it might be worth a shot. If you were at all serious, that is."

"I . . ." Morgan's brain screamed incoherently, a chorus alternating between *Is this really happening?* and *Holy shit!* and *Did I cast a spell on her in my sleep to make this real?*

"If not, don't worry about it," Rory said quickly. "I could ask Hazel."

"No! I mean, yes. I mean, I was serious. It could work, right? I'd be happy to be your fake girlfriend." Sweet stars, she had to get a grip. Morgan forced herself to eat another pretzel, fearing this was a post–magic drain hallucination.

Rory stared at her, and those dark eyes of hers felt like they were boring into Morgan's soul. Morgan wasn't sure what Rory saw there—the insecurities, the hopeless attraction, the freaking desperation—but she didn't run.

She nodded slowly. "If you're sure it wouldn't really be inconveniencing you."

"Positive. Couldn't be happier." Really, truly could not be, unless Rory was asking her to be her real girlfriend, but in that case, she'd have fainted.

"Okay." Rory's arms dropped to her sides, and she inspected the mess on the worktable.

Herbs, oils, and more were scattered everywhere—vervain and lavender and powdered ruby. An applewood wand rested in the cast-iron bowl Morgan used for mixing. Pink candles carved with runes and coated in rosemary oil, still with melted wax on top, contributed to the mix of scents in the air. Morgan barely noticed the smells anymore. The entire shop was perfumed from one item or another, but if she focused, she could identify exactly what potion she'd been working on from the aroma in the back room. To the visitor's eyes or nose, however, it must seem like chaos.

To be fair, it was chaos. But it was chaos Morgan knew like she knew her ABCs.

Rory dragged a finger along the table's edge, tracing some of the runes. Protection. Power. Healing. She tapped a finger against the last one and smiled ever so slightly. She didn't seem less tense, but she did somehow appear more alert. Morgan didn't know how to describe it, but she felt it, too. They'd known each other for a year, often hung out with the same people, and yet this was by far the longest they'd ever spoken directly to each other. The universe had shifted ever so slightly.

"Thank you," Rory said, staring at the table.

"It's nothing." It was everything, and not only because Rory had turned her entire day upside down with a single question. "You laughed at the idea last night, though. I'm surprised you changed your mind."

Rory acknowledged this with a tilt of her head. "I was surprised. I couldn't tell if you were serious, and it seemed . . ."

"Ridiculous?"

"Kind of. Faking a relationship sounds extreme. But the more I thought about it, or rather, the more I thought about the situation, the more willing I've become to try anything. My parents . . ." Rory pressed her lips thin, seeming to reconsider whatever she'd been about to say. "I hope that if I can convince them that I'm happy with my life, they'll stop pressuring me to get back to competing. Being in a relationship with someone from Harborage could help with that. You got it exactly right last night. It shows I've settled in here. That I have a new life and people in it that I like. That I'm not moping around because I miss competing. So, absurd as it might be, it's worth a shot."

Morgan's excitement deflated slightly. Rory still thought her plan was ridiculous.

But of course she did. It *was* absurd. But that didn't mean her willingness to try it was worth nothing. She would have to pay attention to

Morgan to pull it off, and that was far from nothing when Morgan had been wishing for Rory to pay attention to her for the past year.

"The situation is that bad?" Morgan asked, covering for the pinch of pain "absurd" had caused in her chest. She hadn't expected Rory's response, and she was dying to ask more, but she didn't know Rory well enough. What she did know was that Rory didn't talk about her former life, so pushing the topic might cause her to change her mind about this plan.

"It's complicated, but I'm trying to give my parents the benefit of the doubt and assume this is all because they want me to be happy. Archer is just their newest solution to a problem that doesn't exist. But he's a whole problem himself. I've met him a few times over the years when I was on the competition circuit. Let's just say, he prefers to be called a sorcerer." Rory's expression made her thoughts on that clear, and they seemed on par with Morgan's own.

The rarity of male witches meant the non-magical community (and often the magical one) granted them special treatment. Despite making up only about ten percent of the witch population, male witches were far more likely to achieve fame and success. They were coddled and placed on pedestals by people who ought to know better. If that wasn't enough, over the last decade, some of those men had taken to referring to themselves as sorcerers. As though "witch" were a gendered word. As though it were beneath them.

"One of *those*." Too flustered by Rory for a rant, Morgan let her tone speak for itself.

"Exactly," Rory said. "I thought he was arrogant before, but if he has my parents' favor, he's going to be intolerable. They're *all* going to be intolerable."

"Then I'm happy to be your shield." Did that sound cheesy? That sounded totally cheesy. "What I mean is—I'm tall. I'm good at standing between people, and I can block you from view."

Rory narrowed her eyes. "Are you making fun of my height?"

"I would never. I've seen you play with fire, and I would be too scared." She was joking, mostly, but Morgan frowned and pretended to give her next idea serious thought. "Come to think of it, you could just set Archer on fire if he gets obnoxious."

Rory snorted. "Don't think the idea hasn't crossed my mind, and I'm not ruling it out. But if I did, the Council would get involved, and I'm sure my mother would try to make an example out of me. And anyway, burning flesh smells awful." She held up her left hand, and for the first time, Morgan saw a large burn scar on her palm. "Theatrics aside, I'll do my best to keep us both far away from Archer and my family, unless you have any *sorcerer* repellent among your potions."

Morgan snapped her fingers. "No, but I'll get to work on creating one. I'd bet there's a market for that."

Rory grinned, and it was the most genuine smile Morgan had ever seen on her face. Her pulse didn't dance this time; it passed out, and she was light-headed again.

"I'll buy a case if you do," Rory said. "But in the meantime, we should get started."

"We should? What needs to happen?"

Rory looked at her in surprise. "If we're going to convince my family we're dating, we need to make it realistic—*everyone* needs to believe it. If the coven doesn't buy it, someone could slip up to my parents. You know how much Verbena likes to talk, and she knows my mom well since she's the Council liaison."

That made sense. That also meant spending more time with Rory, and that was not an opportunity Morgan was going to waste. "Right, I should have thought of that. I have to finish up here, but we can meet up anytime. Just let me know."

"I have to go to work in a couple of hours," Rory said, checking the time on her phone. "What about tomorrow evening?"

"Sundays are family dinners at my grandmom's." Morgan hesitated. "But you know what? I can skip this one." It wasn't like she was giving Rory more importance than her family, but Rory needed help and it was just one dinner. Her grandmom would understand.

"No, you don't need to do that."

Morgan started to protest that it wasn't a big deal, but Rory had already moved on.

"Let's just meet before the coven gathering on Monday evening. We've got to start the ruse somewhere. I feel bad deceiving everyone, but it's harmless, really, and I can't think of a better way." Rory held out her phone. "Put your number in, and I'll text you."

Morgan's fingers trembled as she entered her number into Rory's phone, and she didn't speak until she was finished, afraid she'd drop it. "You're right—Verbena and some of the others can't keep secrets to save their lives. It's risky enough with Hazel and Andy knowing."

"We could cast a spell that prevents them from telling the truth." Rory paused, then laughed at the dumbfounded expression Morgan felt on her face.

Morgan swallowed and reached for another pretzel. That would require an extremely complicated spell. "I'm sure they'd consent to it if you're really worried."

"I'm not. I was kidding. Anyway, messing with people's heads is outside my skill set. I'd probably end up convincing Hazel she was a tree or something."

Morgan doubted there was any form of magic that Rory couldn't manage if she put her mind to it. Making Hazel believe she was a tree was more like the sort of mistake *she'd* make.

Rory sent her a text with her contact information, and before she slipped out the back room door, they planned on meeting half an hour early on Monday. Morgan counted to ten—well, she made it to eight—after the door closed before spinning in a circle and stuffing her hand in her mouth to keep from screaming.

That had happened, and yet . . . She needed some proof that it had happened, so she brought up Rory's text and stared at it while she ate her final pretzel. It was a good thing she'd finished the magical work for the day, because there was no way she could possibly concentrate anymore. Stars above help her, she was going to be Rory's fake girlfriend, from now until the end of the NEWT Festival.

Rory's fake girlfriend. Two out of three of those words sent shivers of excitement down Morgan's spine.

Lowering her phone, Morgan glowered at the mess in front of her. She couldn't take a break and revel in this moment for long. She still had to clean and pack up the remaining ingredients into travel-ready containers that could be brought to the festival. Even without anything to distract her, that was the type of task Morgan loathed. The meticulous accounting of supplies, the organization, the labeling—to borrow Rory's phrase, those tasks were outside her skill set. The mental energy required of her was, in some ways, so much more intense than what went into actually performing magic.

Before getting to it, Morgan allowed herself one more indulgence. She texted Hazel and Andy on the group chat to let them know what happened and to ask for their assistance in pulling off the ruse—especially at Monday's gathering. Then, smiling, she got to work sorting herbs, measuring out and repacking oils, and labeling jars. Her phone exploded during the middle of this, and Morgan went back and forth between work and giddy typing.

MORGAN: I revoke my vow. Tequila and I are back on good terms.

ANDY: 🙄

MORGAN: Eleven days until the festival. Then four days there. Two whole weeks of fake dating.

HAZEL: See? I told you she wasn't laughing at you.

Maybe not, but Rory had laughed a real laugh in Morgan's shop. She'd smiled a real smile. As Morgan slapped a label on a jar of lavender buds, she wondered how many more times she'd be able to see those things before her two weeks were up. And if she could make that happen, was there the smallest chance she could turn this fake relationship into the real thing?

Her brain told her that hope was as ridiculous as this entire scheme, but surely there was nothing wrong with letting the heart dream.

4

MORGAN STARED AT HER BUREAU AND WONDERED HOW IT WAS possible that she had nothing suitable in it to wear. Literally nothing. Almost every scrap of clean clothing she owned, minus a few pairs of socks and some underwear that had seen better days, had been dumped on her bed and rejected.

This was a nightmare. Taking a deep breath, she shoved aside two shirts that had been perfectly acceptable only yesterday and found her phone amid the mess. Her fingers hovered over it until her better judgment kicked in. She should not be bothering Hazel or Andy with her fashion catastrophe. Her friends didn't need to know what a drama queen she was being.

"Shit." Morgan caught a glimpse of the time and dropped her phone, wishing that coven meetings had a dress code. If everyone gathered in matching black robes and pointed hats, or something equally cliché, she wouldn't have such a dilemma.

But since witches did not dress like they were in a Shakespearean play (unless they actually *were* in a Shakespearean play), she had to get practical and decide from her less-than-fabulous options. That meant it was time to trust the magic. Morgan pulled out her five best shirts, ones that didn't have slogans, graphics, or old stains on them. Then she grabbed a deck of tarot cards and removed an ace, two, three, four, and five, not caring about the suit.

Every witch studied some form of divination, usually starting with cards and progressing to more challenging but also more powerful methods. Some people liked crystals, others water or smoke. Morgan's preference was for people to do her readings for her. Divination required a patience and focus that she so often lacked.

This trick, however, came courtesy of one of her aunts, and it required little patience, even less magical ability, and absolutely no interpretive skills. So basically, it was perfect. She closed her eyes and shuffled the cards, clearing her mind just enough to feel the power beneath her skin rise to the surface. After a few seconds, one of the cards felt right, and she plucked it out of the set. The two of cups.

Morgan stared at the image—two lovers, their arms entwined, offering goblets to each other. In a reading, it would suggest love or a deep friendship, and Morgan's pulse skipped. She longed to believe that was significant, but she knew better. She wasn't doing a real reading, so all the card signified was the second shirt from the left—an emerald faux-wrap blouse that she rarely wore because it showed more cleavage than she was comfortable with. But maybe showing cleavage today wasn't a terrible idea? She wanted to look nice. She'd even put on some makeup.

"It's not a date," she reminded herself as she tossed on the shirt.

But it could be the first step toward one, something reminded her. Something being her heart or maybe her ovaries. Morgan bade them to shut up. There was no time for their bullshit if she was going to be punctual. Because she'd had to work today, she and Rory only had thirty minutes to meet before the full coven descended on their planning session.

No matter the season, the Harborage coven met at an apple orchard that was owned by one of their oldest members. The orchard provided them with privacy, atmosphere, a heated barn for the winter, and a seemingly endless supply of fruit. Rory was waiting for Morgan at a picnic table outside the charmingly rustic farm store, which was currently closed. A row of super tall sunflowers that had been planted against the building's red facade towered over her, their giant heads looking down as though unsure what to make of the woman in their midst. One who was ignoring their curiosity and all that soothing atmosphere as she kept her head down and wrote on what appeared to be an index card.

Since Morgan was tired after working all day and performing magic required energy, she normally fortified herself for coven meetings with coffee. But she couldn't bring a thermos for herself and not one for Rory, so she'd stopped by the Wicked Good Brew coffee shop on the way. As a result, she'd been five minutes late when she pulled into the orchard parking lot, but she considered that a justifiable delay.

Morgan slid the to-go cup toward Rory as Rory looked up from her writing. "I didn't know what you'd like, and I didn't remember that I could have texted you until after I placed my order."

As thrilled as she'd been to exchange numbers with Rory on Saturday, it had felt so momentous that Morgan's brain couldn't quite believe it had happened, or at least that was Morgan's theory for why she hadn't recalled this vital piece of information. Her brain was ridiculous—Hazel, Andy, and probably a dozen other coven members already had Rory's phone number—but Morgan had never pretended to *not* be ridiculous, especially where Rory was concerned.

Rory lifted the lid and sniffed. "Hazelnut?"

"Yeah, I got us both the same. I hope that's okay. Oh, and here." Morgan dumped a half dozen packets of sugar, fake sugar, and creamer on the table. "I wasn't sure how you took it."

"Black is perfect, actually. Thank you." She smiled so broadly that Morgan felt as though one of the sun's fading rays had singled her out, bathing her in a golden glow that warmed her like a hug. There was nothing fake or subdued about the smile that it elicited on Morgan's face in turn, as she tried and failed not to overdo her reaction.

Today was the first day of her plan to impress Rory, and this felt like an auspicious start.

"Wait." Rory held up her hand just as Morgan thought she might burst from smiling, and Morgan froze in alarm. "Yours is plain hazelnut, too? How is that possible? I took you more for a double hazelnut latte, half vanilla, half cinnamon, heavy foam, light ice, and ask-Hecate-for-a-blessing-on-it-before-you-pour kind of person."

Morgan's smile faded along with the worry that she'd done something wrong, and she chewed on air for a moment, unable to decide if she was offended by this assumption or thrilled that Rory had given her taste in coffee any thought at all. "Are you saying you think I'm high-maintenance?"

"Aren't all potion witches? Mixing stuff together is kind of your shtick."

"Yours, too, barkeep."

Rory laughed. "Yeah, exactly why I try not to inflict that shit on other people."

Hearing Rory laugh made Morgan practically bounce in her seat. "I'll have you know that's a totally unfair stereotype. And ask Hecate for a blessing—really? I'm insulted." She covered her heart in mock offense.

"It happened once, I swear. Given the way that witch tipped, she was lucky I didn't have a black candle on me."

A sign above the Empty Chalice's bar announced that *Poor tippers will be turned into iguanas*, but apparently not everyone could read. For a while, the original owners had kept an aquarium with two iguanas in it, as well, and they'd liked to tell mundane tourists it was proof of the policy. But the iguanas were taken when they sold the place a couple of years ago. No one was going to leave their pets behind. The sign, however, remained.

"Maybe the problem is that no one's ever been turned into an iguana, so the bar's sign is an empty threat," Morgan mused aloud.

Rory tapped her lips in what was likely supposed to be a thoughtful manner, but which had the rather ironic outcome of emptying Morgan's brain. "Maybe, but this was back in Boston when I was bartending at my aunt and uncle's restaurant. They were too *classy* for a sign like that." Her emphasis on *classy* suggested that what she meant was too boring.

"Is that how you got into bartending?" Morgan was surprised she hadn't learned about that in her—*cough*—research. "I wondered when you had the time to pick up more skills."

"I had to do something before I was earning enough in prize money and sponsorships to pay the bills." Rory shrugged. "I started off waiting tables until my aunt finally couldn't take my begging any longer and taught me how to make drinks. She's a bit of a potion witch. Everything I know about making magical cocktails is from her. So, what about you? Have you always worked at your family's shop?"

"Always, although I wasn't always allowed to make the products, obviously."

Rory nodded at this, and then a thought seemed to occur to her, and she jotted something down. She wasn't using index cards, Morgan realized, but some of the branded postcards that the Empty Chalice sold along with other souvenirs. Rory had a stack of ones that read *Witches brew good martinis*.

Morgan swallowed too much coffee, and the hot liquid burned the back of her throat. Should she have brought note-taking supplies, too?

Rory glanced up and must have seen the confusion on her face. "I started writing stuff down for us to discuss as I thought of it while I was working last night. I don't expect you to be as anal as I am."

"Oh, I'm not . . . You're not . . ."

"I'm a Virgo. It's okay. You can say it." Rory reached into her bag and pulled out two more pens, and she waved the three—black, red, and green—in Morgan's face. "It was too hard to type everything on my phone, so although postcards weren't ideal, this way I could color-code. See? I wrote out this whole list of questions we should review in different colors for different topics and levels of importance, and then there are the rules . . . Morgan?"

"What?" She'd spaced out in a color-coding panic. That there would be questions to answer and rules to be followed had never occurred to her. But of course there would be. Morgan probably knew more about Rory than she should, but only because Rory was famous. As for the things Rory likely knew about her—gets drunk on one margarita, is too disorganized to take notes, eats pretzels like a chipmunk . . .

Morgan suppressed a shudder.

"I'm scaring you, aren't I?" Rory asked, misinterpreting Morgan's silence. She started to stuff her notes away. "Sorry. Forget it."

"No!" Morgan made to grab Rory's arm and stop her, but it dawned on her that she'd never touched Rory before. They'd never even joined hands in a spell circle or casually bumped legs on Hazel's floor while watching TV. Touching Rory somehow felt forbidden, and Morgan wasn't sure it was a great idea to try it now. She might spontaneously combust if she did. "I'm in awe of your organizational skills. That's all."

Rory bit her lip, and Morgan wished that lip-biting habit didn't have such an effect on her body. It had to be unnatural for a behavior to be both so adorable and so hot at the same time. Like, there should be some kind of law against it. It was rude.

"You were saying something about rules?" Morgan asked, trying to distract herself.

Rory made an apologetic face. "Bad choice of words. More like, things I'm begging you to consider doing or not doing at the festival. If that's okay."

Whatever they were, they would all be totally okay. Morgan was not going to mess up what she'd begun referring to as Operation Impress Rory. She rested her chin on her hands and smiled deviously. "That might depend on what you're asking."

"Nothing tawdry, I promise. And in return, you're allowed to make requests of me."

"Do my requests have to be nothing tawdry?"

Wait. Had she just managed to untie her tongue long enough to flirt with Rory?

To her utter amazement, a little color crept up Rory's neck. "I suppose we can handle that on a case-by-case basis."

Was it getting warmer as the sun set? Was the orchard starting to spin? Morgan felt dizzy, and she took another sip of coffee. "Hit me with your asks."

Rory cleared her throat, looking uncertain about what had just transpired between them. "One—and I'm sorry about this—but I need to ask you to attend a couple of dinners with my family. They'll want to meet you, and they'll expect me to eat with them a few nights. This is going to be the key to convincing them that I'm happy."

Morgan shrugged, but her insides squirmed at the idea of eating with the Sandlers. Apparently, meeting the family was always intimidating, even when everything was fake. Operation Impress Rory was on, though, and this was a normal request to make. "Sure. I promise I can eat like a civilized person. I only stuff pretzels in my cheeks after working magic."

"I have complete confidence in you. Two—if my mother brings up having me attend a Council meeting with her, you'll be ready to back me up with an excuse about why I can't."

"Consider it done. I am there to be your shield." Morgan frowned. "I'm a terrible liar, though, so you'll need to have some reasons prepared."

"Got it." With an apologetic shrug, Rory retrieved a new postcard, which read *I drank a Truth Potion at the Empty Chalice*—Truth Potion being the name of the bar's most strongly alcoholic (and equally delicious) cocktail. "Making a note to myself to come up with excuses."

"And what color does that get? Red for importance? Green for go? What is your system?" She was only half teasing. Part of her was fascinated by this glimpse into Rory's mind.

Rory started to respond, but her words died away before they could fully form, and her eyes widened. It was only then that Morgan realized she'd heard tires crunching over the parking lot gravel, and the sound of car doors opening and shutting had grown more prominent over the past few minutes. The orchard was filling with people.

"Don't the two of you look sweet?" Verbena said from behind Morgan, and Morgan spun around. The coven elder motioned to Rory's postcard stack. "What are you working on?"

"Oh." Rory flipped the top postcard over with a guilty expression. "Morgan and I were just making plans for what to do together at the festival."

"I *see*," Verbena said, drawing out the word like a question.

Morgan normally loved Verbena. Like herself, Verbena had a reputation for being loud, and although they weren't blood related, she'd been like a great-aunt to Morgan for as long as Morgan could remember. With black-and-gray-streaked hair that cascaded down to her waist, a penchant for wearing flowing skirts, and more rings on her fingers than Rory, Verbena was also loved by mundanes because she matched their idea of what a witch would look like. For that reason alone, Verbena was often the spokeswoman for the coven, and she'd served many years as their liaison to the Witch Council.

But at the moment, Verbena was making Morgan strangely self-conscious. She and Rory were supposed to be convincing everyone of their relationship, but the way Verbena assessed them made it all feel too real yet simultaneously too fake. With one breath, Morgan worried Verbena wouldn't approve of Morgan and Rory dating. With the next, she worried Verbena was seeing right through them.

"I hope those plans include leading our coven to glory and a Golden Cauldron award," Verbena said after a heavy moment.

Amid all of the festivities, the NEWT Festival featured plenty of games and other competitions in which witches and covens could compete for prizes. Harborage's coven hadn't won the overall prize—the Golden Cauldron—since before Morgan was born, and older coven members, like Verbena, were always grumbling about it.

"The plans mostly involved dancing," Morgan said before Verbena could bring up Morgan entering the potion-making contest for the hundredth time.

"Really?" Verbena's younger sister, Ivy, appeared as though out of the sunset, struggling to carry four bottles of wine. Her head swiveled from Morgan to Rory and back again, and her gaze lingered for a second on Morgan's outfit, eliciting a slightly raised eyebrow.

"You know I love dancing." Morgan tugged on her shirt in a futile attempt to share less skin. What had she been thinking, dressing up for a coven meeting? Rory hadn't seemed to notice, but Ivy's reaction was proof that everyone else was going to. "And I get to dance with her, so . . ." She grinned at Rory, finally recalling that they were supposed to be selling a relationship.

This was all true enough in its own way that none of it could count as a lie. Not only were the nightly concerts and dancing Morgan's favorite parts of the festival (aside from the spellcasting exhibition), but she'd already been imagining that this year, she'd get to dance with Rory. It didn't matter that the circumstances would be fake. The thought of the cool night air on her skin, the scent of the crackling fires as their light flickered over the crowd, the live music blaring as she and Rory joined their friends, half-drunk on mead, taking Rory's hand in hers, skin to skin—Morgan could practically transport herself there already in her mind, and her stomach fluttered.

Which is probably why she failed to notice the look of panic Rory shot her until it was too late to retract her words.

"Aren't you the persuasive one, Morgan? Rory was just telling a bunch of us the other day that she doesn't dance." Ivy nodded meaningfully toward her sister, and Morgan yelped as Rory kicked her under the table.

Shit. How could Rory hate music and dancing? Oh, wait—Rory hated crowds.

New question: How could Morgan be screwing up their ruse so badly before it even got going? So much for her auspicious start.

"I mean, I'm working on persuading her," Morgan said, externally trying to course correct while internally sobbing at this development.

Rory wrapped her hands around her coffee cup, and Morgan could see the tension in the way she gripped it. She hoped no one else did. "We're negotiating. I told Morgan she could go without me."

That was a realistic possibility, Morgan supposed. She could meet up with the friends she only saw in person during festivals and dance with them, disappointing as it would be. But this was about her wanting to help Rory and doing her best damned job so that Rory would like her, even if it was only as a friend. Morgan would suck it up and avoid the music for one festival. Maybe it wouldn't be so bad if she could spend the time with Rory instead.

"I would never abandon you like that," Morgan said.

Rory reached across the table and squeezed Morgan's wrist, and her first touch sent Morgan's blood streaking through her veins. Yup, she'd been right. Spontaneous combustion was imminent. Rory's hand was not soft—unsurprising given the burn scar on it—but her fingers were lithe and her palm warm from holding her cup. Morgan hoped the way her breath hitched and the heat spread across her exposed skin wasn't obvious.

Or maybe she should hope it *was* obvious in order to sell their story. The trouble was, she didn't know what to think or do (and she barely remembered how to breathe) after Rory had touched her. Sure, it was only an act. Rory was only trying to fix Morgan's error. But skin was skin, and Rory's skin apparently had brain-melting effects.

Then Rory's hand was gone as quickly as it had arrived, and Morgan plastered a smile on her face that felt very fake as she mourned the loss of Rory's touch.

"I see," Verbena said again. And again, she and Ivy exchanged glances that suggested this ruse might be working in spite of Morgan's fuckup.

"Starting in five minutes!" someone yelled from the barn.

Verbena adjusted the bag of supplies she was carrying. "We'll talk more later."

Under the circumstances, Morgan had a hard time not taking that as a threat.

Suddenly, Morgan wished she'd forgotten all about her family dinner on Sunday when Rory had suggested they get together to flesh out a plan. Planning, after all, wasn't her thing; it was best left to the sort of witch who carried around pens in multiple colors. But Rory had been too polite to break up Morgan's dinner, and Morgan hadn't taken the planning seriously enough to insist, and now they were scrambling to pull this off at all.

As soon as Verbena, Ivy, and anyone else in the vicinity wandered away, Morgan lowered her head to the weathered table with a groan. "I almost blew everything."

"Nah. We recovered. Verbena just had spectacularly bad timing. No dancing was going to be Rule #3, and I am sorry about that. I didn't know you were looking forward to it."

Oh, wow. Rory felt strongly enough about dancing to make a whole rule? No wonder Ivy had appeared so shocked. "It's fine," Morgan lied, sitting back up. "You're not ruining anything."

"The way your face just fell suggests otherwise."

"I like dancing, but it's no big deal. It's all good."

"You're right. You are a terrible liar." Rory winced. "I'll make it up to you, promise. Any workshops you want me to attend with you—

name it. Need someone to help at your family's booth—I'll do my best. Got enemies you want me to light on fire—happy to burn them. Really—anything you want, it's yours."

That was unfair, because Morgan could still feel Rory's fingers on her wrist, and the only thing she could think about wanting at the moment was to kiss Rory, to taste the whisper of coffee left behind on those lusciously full lips and feel Rory's breath on her face, and her body ached so fiercely with that desire that she couldn't respond right away. Not that she could ask for that.

"I owe you," Rory added, and those three words were enough to break the spell. Morgan didn't want to be owed. This was her choice. She had seized the excuse to spend time with Rory, to make herself be noticed, but there was no way to convey that without admitting her crush and ruining everything.

Morgan faked another smile and got up from the table. Fakity-fake-fake. Ugh. And the evening had started off so promising, too. She headed down the dirt trail to the barn, wondering how she was going to get through two more hours when she'd almost flubbed everything within two minutes.

"You look nice, by the way," Rory said, catching up to her.

"I do?" Morgan nearly tripped over a pebble on the path. Those three words—*you look nice*—completely undid the damage to her mood that Rory's previous three had caused. "I mean, thanks."

"It's a good color on you. It really brings out the green in your eyes."

Morgan thought so, too, which was why she'd bought the shirt in spite of the cleavage issue, so thank the stars the tarot trick hadn't let her down. Or perhaps her cleavage hadn't.

Now if only she could get her brain and mouth with the program.

"You look nice, too," Morgan said, which was stupid because Rory was dressed in the same sort of thing she always wore. Tonight, that consisted of a light gray T-shirt and pair of dark jeans. Unlike Morgan, who was so obviously *trying*, Rory always looked naturally hot. Like she didn't give a shit what anyone thought.

Because of course she didn't. If she were Rory fucking Sandler, Morgan wouldn't give a shit, either.

Still, Rory grinned at the compliment, and Morgan's heart beat faster. Rory thought she looked nice, and there wasn't anyone around to overhear her say that, so those words weren't for an audience. Maybe not everything was fake after all.

5

NOT WANTING TO ACCIDENTALLY RUIN THE MOMENT, MORGAN didn't speak again until she and Rory arrived at the barn, and then there was enough commotion that trying would have been pointless. After a few minutes of greetings, announcements, and general confusion (in Morgan's opinion, gathering witches was an awful lot like herding cats, which was probably why they got along so well), everyone made their way outside to where a couple of coven members had lit a bonfire. The main business of every full moon coven meeting was coming together for community spell work. All witches performed magic on their own, of course, many of them for their jobs. But spells performed with other witches were more powerful, as everyone involved lent their magic to the combined task.

Morgan didn't have a defined role to play in the spell this month, but Rory was called upon, as she often was, to cast the protective circle. When she did it, the magic encasing the coven always felt thicker. Stronger. Morgan struggled more than usual to maintain her focus, conscious of dozens of pairs of eyes on her as Rory took her place next to Morgan in the circle after she finished, giving her a small smile. The subtle attention made Morgan nervous, but the not-so-subtle attention (mainly her grandmom winking at her from across the fire) made her want to run into the orchard and quietly die of embarrassment. Verbena and Ivy must have wasted no time in spreading around their earlier conversation.

Her grandmom's antics aside, Morgan felt bad about deceiving people, but it was for a good cause. Yet perhaps because of her conscience, or the feeling of being watched, or fear of what her grandmom might do next, the meeting's magical working seemed to take extra long. The coven was performing a healing spell for one of their members—Verbena's wife—who was recovering from a hip replacement. It would have taken a powerful witch who specialized in healing to fix Vanessa's hip without mundane intervention, but the coven's efforts could speed and ease her recovery.

By the time they'd finished, twilight was creeping over the orchard. The evening air had come alive with chirping insects, and the first hint of the approaching autumn crispness brushed Morgan's cheeks on the breeze. Hazel took her arm as they joined the group heading inside the barn where the potluck was waiting, saving her from more of the coven elders' sly smiles. Morgan had hoped for an excuse to hang out with Rory, but Rory had been detained by the casting fire, dragged into a heated debate on the relative merits of using red-skinned versus green-skinned apples in a prosperity spell.

That was the sort of minutiae that put an intuitive witch like Morgan to sleep. If she were as powerful as Rory, it wouldn't make a difference anyway. She would simply tell them that the best apples were whichever ones you had lying around and run off to hang out with her fake girlfriend. But Rory seemed to be enjoying the discussion, or if not, she preferred to be polite and fake it. No surprise since faking it was apparently the theme of the evening, and Rory was as polite as she was powerful.

"You barely spoke to each other," Hazel whispered, "and people are noticing anyway. Did you cast some sort of spell on yourselves to make it obvious?"

"Please," Andy said, coming up from behind and adding her contribution to the potluck table. "Did you see Morgan's face when Rory smiled at her after casting the circle? No magic needed. She's smitten and stopped hiding it."

"I did notice." Hazel sighed wistfully. "I miss having someone to look at that way."

"There is no real *that way* between us," Morgan reminded her. "Rory and I met up before the meeting, and Verbena and Ivy interrogated us. That's all."

"And what do you mean, you miss having someone?" Andy asked Hazel. "What happened to that guy you met at the tattoo convention last month?"

"That was just a weekend fling."

"What about the grad student Trevor introduced you to . . ."

Hazel shook her head, cutting Andy off. "We didn't really connect."

Andy started working backward through Hazel's list of would-be romantic partners, and Morgan wondered if she was going to run out of fingers before they got through last spring.

The three of them could not be more different this way. While Morgan had been silently crushing on Rory for a year, Andy had been with Trevor for even longer, and Hazel flitted from partner to partner like a honeybee in search of the perfect blossom. Hazel loved the idea of love, so she threw herself into any and every opportunity for it, but none lasted long. Morgan would need to be as organized as Rory to keep track of Hazel's romantic entanglements. It was no surprise, therefore, that Hazel was almost as committed to making Morgan and Rory happen for real as Morgan was.

Soon, the aromas of myriad dishes filled the air, replacing the smells of old wood and the hay that had long since been banished from the building. After filling their plates, everyone grabbed seats at one of the scattered tables, and Morgan's friends were forced to ease off on any teasing that might give away the ruse. Although Morgan was grateful for the reprieve, her frustration grew as the minutes passed and Rory didn't appear.

Honestly, could the apple debate have gotten that out of control? Were they doing experiments in the orchard? What was the point in fake dating her crush if she didn't have an excuse to spend more time with her?

Okay, that was selfish. The point was to help Rory, but still. Morgan had been looking forward to this gathering more than usual, and it wasn't only because Andy had contributed her cheesy mashed potatoes to the potluck.

When Rory hadn't appeared by the time she finished eating, and some of the food was starting to run low, Morgan got up to fix her a plate before they ran out of her favorites. Was it weird that she knew Rory loved Verbena's broccoli quiche? Probably. But unlike with Rory's coffee order, which Morgan had no reason to know, she'd been to enough coven dinners with Rory to observe her food choices. And if she was giving away her secret stalking habit, it was worth it when Rory finally arrived and gave Morgan a genuinely delighted smile upon being handed a warm plate and a glass of wine. Morgan's stomach congratulated her by doing a series of somersaults.

"Don't leave without picking up your coven T-shirts," Verbena called as dinner was cleared away and dessert brought out.

"And don't forget to give your affiliation when you arrive at the festival," said another one of the elders. "We haven't won that coven prize in two decades, and I'm getting too old to wait any longer. If we lose to my sister's coven in Portsmouth again, I'm never going to live it down."

A smattering of laughter rippled around the barn.

This was the second festival where Morgan had been asked why she wasn't entering anything into the potion contest, and the second time she'd had to demur. The witches who entered those competitions were excellent at their craft. What could she possibly create that wouldn't be a waste of everyone's time?

If the coven wanted a professional potion-maker to enter something, her mother or grandmom should be the one to do it, but no one ever bugged them. Morgan's mother, Lianne, was too busy with the practical side of work to get creative, especially now that she basically ran Bed, Bath, and Broom these days since Morgan's grandmom was mostly retired. But Morgan was young, and more importantly, she had a reputation as the loud, competitive one in the family. People expected her magic to be as noisy and explosive as she was. If not *significant*, then they at least expected her to do something attention-grabbing that could win a prize. Yet she couldn't even imagine something worthy of that.

Some of Morgan's good mood slipped away as she pondered the desserts.

"Why are you frowning?" Verbena asked, draping a heavy arm across Morgan's shoulders.

"I'm not frowning." She'd totally been frowning.

"You'd better not be." With a mischievous gleam, Verbena glanced in Rory's direction. "If you look at her, will you smile again?"

Morgan's cheeks burned and she stared resolutely at the dessert table, recalling the way Andy had teased her earlier. Verbena's knowing smile was all the more embarrassing since Morgan couldn't tell if she'd been successfully fooled by their act or if Morgan's true feelings were too obvious. "Hey, I don't need that from you, too."

"Need what?" Rory asked. She carried over a plate filled with cookies and held it out to Morgan. "Sugar? These are my contribution to the desserts—margarita-inspired rugelach. They were running out, so I snagged you some since I made them for you."

"You made them for me?" Since Rory was frequently asked to cast the protective circle, which was plenty draining, she rarely contributed to the potluck.

Morgan's fingers hesitated over the cookies while she pondered what Rory meant by "margarita-inspired." That sounded like lime was involved. Morgan wanted to gush over Rory's baking, but she was—as admitted—a terrible liar.

"It's my great-grandmother's rugelach recipe," Rory said. "But my spin on the filling since you like margaritas."

"They're delish," Verbena added. "Wicked tart, if you like that sort of thing."

Morgan, as it happened, did not like that sort of thing, and she was fairly certain that Verbena—who, like most of the older coven members, had known Morgan since she was born—was warning her. But damn it, Rory was offering her a homemade cookie. A cookie she'd made specifically for Morgan. She had to try it.

Once again, Morgan was regretting that she hadn't made more of an effort to meet with Rory before tonight. Odds were that Rory had a question about food preferences on one of her postcards.

Bracing herself, Morgan grabbed a cookie and bit down. Tart lime curd burst over her tongue, mixing with the much more palatable sweetness of the agave and walnut filling and the crust. She smiled, barely, and from the corner of her eye, caught Verbena failing to adequately suppress a laugh.

"Too tart for you." Rory nodded. "Got it."

"No, it's good. I mean, it's a bit tart, yeah." Morgan washed her bite down with some water. Rory was watching her with an unreadable expression, and Morgan couldn't help but think that she'd screwed up again. What kind of girlfriend—fake or otherwise—choked down a family cookie recipe? Answer: a terrible one.

Verbena had recovered from her not-laughing fit, and she waved a finger between them. "So when did you two become a thing?"

"A thing?" Rory asked. "Ouch."

"An item, then, if you prefer," Verbena said. "A couple. Whatever you youths call it these days. I've known Morgan since she was in diapers, and I've never seen her smile at anyone the way she smiles at you. I want answers." Verbena turned to Morgan. "Even your mother looked surprised. Tell me what happened and when."

What happened? Never mind that. What *was* happening was that, beneath her skin, Morgan was curling up into a ball of embarrassment. Verbena's comment was accurate, no doubt, and Rory was going to see right through her. If she figured out that Morgan's feelings weren't fake . . .

"What happened?" Rory asked, repeating Verbena's words a second time. She looked every bit as panicked and horrified as Morgan feared.

"Yes, what happened," Verbena said. "You're very good at not answering questions, Rory Sandler, but as the coven's nosiest member, I'm declaring that your attempts to deflect attention are not going to work this time. Humor me. I'm old and my wife is in the hospital."

"Kind of the usual *thing*, right?" Rory's gaze fixed on Morgan, and suddenly the panic on her face made sense. She wasn't horrified to figure out that Morgan's feelings were real. She was horrified to be caught off guard in the same way Morgan had been about the dancing.

Rory, with all her color-coded notes and lists of questions and requests, hadn't prepared for this. Either that, or she'd meant to bring this up earlier and they'd run out of time. But no matter what the cause, they had no story.

"It just happened, like she said." Morgan opened her mouth, trusting that something would spill out. Words always did with her, and it was about time her mouth followed her cleavage's example and started earning its keep. "I'd had a crush on Rory for a while, so I finally did something about it."

Oh. Well, those were words. Fuck.

If she got any warmer, she was going to explode. Luckily, that explanation seemed to satisfy Verbena. Morgan couldn't stand to look in Rory's direction, but Verbena was telling them how cute they were, and Morgan didn't think she breathed until Verbena walked away.

She gasped for air when Rory took her arm and practically dragged her back out into the night. Rory didn't stop walking until they were far enough from the barn that the other voices faded into the background.

"Sorry," Morgan blurted into the moonlit darkness, not even knowing what she was apologizing for. For making Rory uncomfortable by being so obvious about her true feelings? For not doing a better job of evading Verbena's questions in the first place? For not liking the cookies? The options were endless.

"No, that was okay." Rory dropped Morgan's arm, and Morgan's stomach seemed to drop with it. "It was better than I did, but it's not good enough. This meeting has made it perfectly clear that we have a lot of work to do. We need to improve at this for my family."

That was all? Morgan relaxed a touch. "You think they're going to ask a lot of questions?"

Rory stuffed her hands in her hoodie's pockets. "My mother will if she's unhappy, and questions are my brother's life. He's an Inquisitor. Everything is a chance for him to poke and prod for more information. I love him, but I don't know how my sister-in-law puts up with him."

An Inquisitor. She and Rory were supposed to fool an Inquisitor. Morgan tried to recall whether she'd known that about Rory's brother, but she was no longer relaxed, and panic interfered with rational thought. Was it actually possible to fool an Inquisitor?

They were so screwed.

Technically, Inquisitors were simply the investigative arm of the Witch Council, but that was like saying fire was hot. It didn't really convey the meaning.

Although magic could be powerful, witches were uncommon

enough that if they didn't do their best to blend in and appear non-threatening, history provided plenty of examples of what could happen to them. Enter Inquisitors. They were highly trained, carefully selected witches who were tasked to look into any matters where the Council's laws had been broken. In the course of their jobs, Inquisitors were allowed to perform all sorts of normally forbidden magic such as truth spells or memory reading. They could even remove a witch's magic temporarily.

Like most witches, Morgan believed self-policing was important for everyone's safety. Also like most witches, being around an Inquisitor made her nervous. Having to lie to one . . .

Her insides spun around like a tornado, and Morgan laughed shakily. "As long as he doesn't decide to slip us a truth potion, I'm sure we'll be fine."

Perhaps because it was her brother they were talking about, Rory didn't appear to share her freak-out. "I'd like to see him try. Just expect to be questioned. Even my mother jokes that Isaac's first word was 'why.' So we need a good origin story. I can't believe that didn't occur to me already, but I completely forgot about it." She swore and dug her boot into the soft dirt. "Tonight was my mistake. I'm sorry to have put you on the spot like that."

She sounded so put out that Morgan's anxiety receded in the face of her sympathy, and she had a hard time restraining herself from hugging Rory, which she wasn't sure would be welcome. Instead, Morgan shrugged, doing her best to hide her relief. Rory was upset with herself, not with Morgan. She'd be happier about that except she didn't like seeing Rory upset at all.

"I didn't think of it, either," Morgan pointed out.

"Yeah, but I'm the one asking you for help. It's not your responsibility to think of all the angles."

"Hey, I'm your fake girlfriend." Morgan held up a hand for a fist bump. "That makes us a team. Your fuckup is my fuckup, and my fuckup is your fuckup." She frowned. "You know what? Never mind. I'm sure I fuck up a lot more than you, so you'd be getting the raw end of that deal. Forget I said anything."

Rory laughed and fist-bumped her anyway. "Too late. Here's to team Fake Girlfriend."

Right then, in that moment, Morgan's knuckles became an erogenous zone. A zap of electricity shot up her arm and jolted her heart before sinking down to her nether regions. Along with it came the realization that Rory had just touched her again, voluntarily and with no audience this time.

Rationally, Morgan knew it was just a fist bump, but . . . Wait. Hadn't Rory taken her arm and walked her outside, too? Yes, she had, and while that had been in full view of the coven, Morgan couldn't shake the sense that things were shifting between them.

Casual touching of any sort was so not Rory. Even among friends, Rory kept her space. She wasn't a hugger. In fact, when Rory had brought up rules and requests earlier, Morgan had expected the very first one out of Rory's mouth would be about the number of times and the duration of any hand-holding in front of her family. Or possibly that there would be no kissing, not even on the cheek. Yet Rory had taken her requests in a totally different direction.

Morgan didn't know what to think about this, only that she wasn't going to be able to stop thinking about it.

The full moon's light shone down where they stood, and Morgan could feel the whisper of heat on her arms from the fire circle as the last logs burned down to ashes. Around the field, the sugar maples and oaks and birches that stood sentinel danced in silhouette against the indigo sky. It was almost a perfect scene, except Morgan couldn't pull Rory closer and kiss her.

"To team Fake Girlfriend." Morgan grinned. She was never going to get tired of seeing Rory smile like that. The tiny wrinkles in the corners of her eyes, the way her nose freckles squished together—Morgan's chest fluttered. "Are you off any nights this week? We could get together again and concoct a story."

"Only Wednesday," Rory said. "But I'm helping Verbena with the Welcome Home dinner she's hosting for Vanessa when she gets out of the hospital."

Morgan hadn't known Rory had offered to help with the dinner party, but she wasn't surprised. There was always a coven elder who mentored the younger members as they were coming into their powers—answering questions they might not feel comfortable asking their parents, teaching them spells at coven meetings, and performing their initiation into the coven—a "witch mother," so to speak. Verbena had played that role for Morgan, Andy, and Hazel. And when Rory had moved to Harborage, Verbena had adopted her, too. Rory hadn't needed the Intro to Magic stuff, but someone had to sponsor her into the coven since she hadn't been born into it.

Morgan and the others didn't owe Verbena anything for this, but it would never cross Morgan's mind not to help her with something important. Verbena was basically family, and Morgan was happy to see that Rory must feel the same way.

"Yeah, me, too," Morgan said. "Do you think we could get away with planning then? I promised I'd cook."

"I promised I'd make drinks." Rory ran her fingers through her hair. "We'll just have to take over the kitchen. Who else is helping with the prep work?"

"Hazel and Andy are on decorating duty," Morgan said. "I don't know who else will be there, but maybe they can run interference and keep people away."

Rory nodded with a grimace. "It'll have to do since we're running out of time." She gestured to the barn. Morgan wasn't ready to leave their private conversation behind, but they both had belongings to retrieve, so reluctantly, she followed Rory's lead. "Can I ask you a question?"

"Anything," Morgan said, hoping she wouldn't regret that answer.

"Do you not like lime, or do you not like sour foods?"

"Oh." Lying seemed pointless. "Actually, I don't like any citrus very much."

Rory paused, clearly not expecting that. "But when you guys go to the Chalice, you almost always order margaritas."

Was it a good thing that Rory knew her usual drink order, or was that a normal sort of thing for a bartender to notice? She refused to let herself get excited. "Only fruity ones—strawberry or blueberry or watermelon . . ." She trailed off.

"Ah, yeah. That's true." Rory tucked her hands back in her pockets and sighed. "We never got around to it, but I swear I had questions about what foods you liked, although I never thought to ask about dislikes. Or allergies. How did you know exactly what to get me for dinner?"

Because my heart leapt out of my chest the moment I saw you behind the bar at the Empty Chalice, and you've been carrying it around with you without knowing it ever since.

Thankfully, Morgan's proclivity for speaking first and thinking second let that one slide.

"Um, lucky guess?" she said. "Who doesn't love Verbena's quiche?"

Rory's brow pinched, and Morgan had the sense that this was the least convincing thing she'd said or done all evening.

6

VERBENA AND VANESSA LIVED IN MORGAN'S DREAM HOME, IF her dream home had more rooms than she cared to clean, which it definitely did not. The colonial-style farmhouse was huge, painted white with vivid lavender trim and boasting a large porch out front. Baskets hung at intervals, filled with a riotous blend of pansies, lobelia, and fuchsia, and the backyard was a year-round spectacle of color. Everything about the decor was the combined work of Verbena's talent for plant magic and Vanessa's love of magic-aided home renovation.

Only one thing truly set the house apart from its neighbors, and that was the pentacle charm dangling from the front window, but even that wasn't particularly noteworthy around here. Half of Harborage's tourism draw was due to its large—relatively speaking—witch population. Plenty of similar towns were scattered around the country, but not all small towns were as friendly, so not all covens could be as open as Harborage's. The Witch Council worked hard on public relations, using spellcasting competitions and promoting high-profile witches like Rory as a way to make mundanes comfortable with magic, but it was a job that never ended.

"So." Verbena stuck her hands on her ample hips. They were

standing in her enormous kitchen and listening to the sounds of furniture being shoved around in the living room, a subtle din punctuated by the occasional bang that would have worried Morgan but didn't seem to faze her host. "Do you have everything you need? You said vegetables, but you didn't say what kind of vegetables."

Morgan surveyed the selection of broccoli, onions, bell peppers, and summer squash arrayed before her on Verbena's counter. There was enough to feed an army, but there was already enough other food to feed an army, so it didn't make much difference. With the exception of Hazel and Andy, who were in charge of decorating, the other guests had all contributed food to the party. It was a little over-the-top, but Verbena never did anything that wasn't over-the-top when her wife was concerned. That drop-everything-and-party attitude, as well as her romantic devotion, were two of the things Morgan adored about her.

"I'll make do," she assured Verbena.

Verbena swept an arm along the kitchen island, which was covered with more ingredients and every kitchen implement Morgan could imagine. "Okay, everything else you said you needed is here, then. I need to go make sure Hazel and Andy aren't destroying my house before I leave, but thank you for making the stir-fry. Vanessa loved it so much that time you made it for the coven potluck. Honestly, I told Ivy she didn't need to make lasagna since you were doing this, but she never listens to me. Lasagna is *boring*."

She whispered the last part into Morgan's ear while wrapping her in a spine-crushing hug because Ivy was somewhere in the house, most likely helping Hazel and Andy destroy furniture.

The doorbell rang as Morgan was able to breathe again, and Ivy's voice rang out a moment later, "Rory's here!"

Verbena spun around and clasped her hands together. "I'm so happy you two will be sharing my kitchen. This is the best. Just remember—food safety and hygiene first. I don't require hairnets, but clothing must remain on at all times."

Rory appeared behind Verbena at that moment, and her eyes opened wide.

Morgan felt her cheeks burn. "Yeah, I don't think that will be a problem."

She turned to inspect the tofu that Verbena had started pressing in order to have an excuse to look away while Verbena gave Rory the grand tour of her bartending supplies.

"Is it just me," Rory asked after Verbena left, "or is Verbena being extra Verbena tonight?"

"Verbena is always extra, but yeah. She's in a good mood."

Rory picked through the pile of fruit Verbena had left her. "This is a cool house. I've never been here before. What's with the paintings?"

There was no question as to what she was referring to. With the exception of the kitchen, portrait paintings covered every inch of wall space in the Coleman-Chung abode.

Morgan grinned as she grabbed a knife and began chopping squash. "Vanessa's hobby. She buys them cheap at estate sales and antique shops. Then when strangers come over, she and Verbena make up stories about the people in them."

Rory paused in the middle of lining up the liquor bottles on the counter. "Seriously?"

"Until I was ten, I believed they were Vanessa's ancestors despite them all being white. In my defense, I was taught to trust my witch elders."

A slow smile spread over Rory's face. "Those two really are life goals, aren't they?"

"They are." Morgan sighed happily. It should be absolutely nothing to her that Rory shared the sentiment, but . . . Rory shared the sentiment. For a brief moment, Morgan imagined what it might be like if this was her kitchen. If she got to cook for Rory every night while Rory stared moodily at a bunch of fruit.

Then sounds of delighted squealing from the living room knocked some sense back into her. She was not dating Rory for real, and anyway, Rory worked at the Chalice so Rory wouldn't be home most nights for dinner. She had to get a grip. Stop wasting time with daydreams and focus. Morgan was not going to flub their story again.

To that end, she'd spent most of her free time since Monday night brainstorming, and she had a list of ideas ready to share. While she might not be a colored pens kind of witch, she had exactly the sort of talent necessary to concoct a good backstory—an overactive imagination. Operation Impress Rory was on, and Morgan was determined to nail it.

"What are you making?" Rory's gaze lingered over the spread of Morgan's ingredients. "I'm trying to figure out what kind of drinks will go with dinner."

"I'm making tofu stir-fry with peanut sauce. But Ivy made a lasagna, Olga brought blueberry bread, Eliza contributed salad, and Raina made naan and samosas." Merely mentioning Raina's samosas made Morgan's mouth water.

"Wow." Rory tossed a lime back and forth. "The only theme here is that there's no theme. Good thing there's an abundance of wine."

"Also champagne to go with the cake Verbena bought from Sugar Spells."

Rory set the lime down and grabbed one of the many bottles of red sitting out. "If I had a week to plan, I'd create a cocktail that adapts to whatever dish you're eating, but there's no time for that. Everyone's getting one pre-dinner drink and one after-dinner drink if they want it, and they can fend for themselves in between. Not that I'm complaining about the food. Two home-cooked meals in one week is way better than what I normally eat for dinner."

"What do you do when you work?" Morgan asked.

"Food from the bar kitchen, or I bring an energy bar with me. It's nice to have a fake girlfriend who's making me dinner instead." The cork popped from the bottle, punctuating Rory's words.

"Isn't it?" Wait, did that make sense? "I mean, it's not as good as the real thing, but it's good."

Shut up and cook, Morgan!

Rory looked amused as she slid a glass of wine over to her, and Morgan took a fortifying sip before she could blurt out anything else embarrassing.

Unfortunately for her, Verbena was there to take over where Morgan left off. "How are you lovebirds doing in here? Still dressed?"

"Really?" Morgan almost sliced off her finger as she glanced up in distress.

"I'm starting to wonder how you usually cook, Verbena," Rory said.

Verbena just winked. "I'm off to pick up my love. Thank you both again for all your help. Oh, and by the way . . ." She'd only made it two steps out the doorway before she stuck her head back in the kitchen. "I want all the details about you two later."

Rory joined Morgan in taking a large swallow of wine. "We should probably talk about that," she muttered when Verbena disappeared.

They totally should, especially while the voices of the other guests were far away, but the knife slipup had warned Morgan she could only pay attention to so much at once. "Give me a second to finish chopping."

A second was more like five minutes, and when she finished, Rory was concentrating on bespelling some liquors. Morgan watched her a moment—her eyes closed and dark lashes lying against her sharp cheekbones, her kissable lips moving silently. She'd seen Rory do elemental spell work dozens of times, but those were performances. And group spells with the coven were different, too, noisier and more participatory. This more typical solo spell work seemed strangely intimate as a result, although there was nothing necessarily private about it. It was just a side of Rory she'd never experienced before.

Not wanting to stare, Morgan returned to her sauce, so she didn't know Rory had finished her spell until she turned to reach for her wineglass.

Rory wore a slight smile, and apparently *she'd* been watching Morgan.

"What?" Morgan patted her back. "Is there something stuck to me?"

Rory laughed. "No, I'm enjoying watching you cook. Finally, I get to see the potion witch in action after you surprised me with your coffee."

Flustered, Morgan fumbled with the honey container. "It's just sauce. No magic involved."

Rory tapped her lips. Really, if Morgan didn't know that Rory couldn't possibly be interested in her, she'd start to suspect that Rory was drawing attention to them on purpose. "It's the principle of the thing," Rory said. "You're throwing everything into that bowl with abandon. No recipe, no measuring. It's magic to *me*."

"I've made this before. I know basically what needs to go in it. But I guess . . ."

Morgan frowned as she squeezed honey into the peanut sauce. She'd never thought about it before, but for her, cooking actually was a lot like making potions. There was a recipe and steps she had to follow, ingredients that were required and an order that had to be obeyed, but at some point, she trusted her instincts.

"Magic is about intuition, right?" Morgan said. "It's about learning how to make your own power interact with the power around you. Cooking's kind of the same. It's about knowing what to add together to get the right effect."

"Exactly. Which is why it doesn't surprise me that you'd be good at cooking. Whereas me?" Rory spun the cork around on the counter. "I can follow a recipe if it's simple, but anything that requires more creativity than boiling pasta and adding jarred sauce better be written down."

Rory wasn't making any sense. Morgan could understand if she wasn't much of a cook, but there was no way Rory was anything other than an immensely talented witch.

"Your metaphor is failing," Morgan said, raising her spoon from the bowl to better determine how thick the peanut sauce was. If she was only cooking for herself, she'd stick her finger in it and taste it. Intuition was great and all, but the tongue was the ultimate judge. "Magically speaking, you're like the equivalent of a Michelin-starred restaurant."

That earned her a choked laugh from Rory, and the cork went flying from her fingers. "No, I'm more like an expert water boiler. Literally—my specialty is elemental control. It's what every witch has to learn first. Controlling earth, water, fire, and air is just the basics of spell craft."

"What you do is anything but basic."

"In a way, sure." Rory waved a finger at her wineglass, and the pinot noir glided up the side in a graceful arc. With a few more hand motions, Rory had it dancing in the air and tying itself in an elaborate knot before returning it to the glass.

"Uh-huh," Morgan said, stirring the sauce aimlessly. "My point."

"That is simple."

"For you, maybe. For the rest of us, water is simple. But wine is water and alcohol and grape juice, and probably loads of other stuff that form a complex liquid. If I tried to do what you just did, the wine probably wouldn't budge. And if it did budge, it would go splashing all over the walls."

Rory took a sip of the wine and shook her head. "You're confusing simplicity with difficulty. Controlling elements is simple; it's what all other magic is based on. It can be easy, like boiling water, or it can be more challenging, like what I did with the wine, which takes more practice. Or it could even be something like summoning a tidal wave, which would be scary as hell, and we should all be thankful that no one is powerful enough to do it. But it's still magic at its most basic, so most witches stop practicing once they're good enough at it. At that point, they work on mastering more complex spells, and that's how they develop intuition. But I kept practicing elemental control. I never put the work into doing more complicated spells. So while I can cast easy ones, I have to follow the steps carefully. My results might be strong because I've spent years perfecting how to channel my power to do the elemental work, but they'll never have the nuance or refinement that someone like you could produce."

Morgan blinked, unable to entirely process what she was hearing. It made sense, and yet part of her had trouble getting over how Rory could possibly think someone like Morgan was in any way better at magic than she was. Rory was a living legend, and Morgan couldn't even create her own potions.

"I saw you in competition when you first did the fire trick," Morgan said, trying to collect herself. "You stood on a pyre that was covered in lighter fluid and had it set on fire. It went up in a flash, and you didn't even get singed. You made the flames do the most amazing things. I still think about it sometimes. It was incredible. You *are* incredible."

Witches loved playing with fire for spellcasting exhibitions and competitions. Obviously, it looked amazing, but there was also historic symbolism. While the Witch Council liked to remind everyone that "witches who play with fire get burned," meaning don't draw unnecessary, unsanctioned attention to magic (Law #4), competitive spellcasters liked to prove the opposite—real witches *couldn't* burn. Except, of course, they could, or those displays wouldn't be so astounding to watch.

Morgan had seen nationally ranked competitors part walls of fire or walk into bonfires, but those tricks were pale imitations of what Rory had done. They were slow and deliberate spells because those witches—the best at their craft—couldn't do them any other way. Until Rory had shown them all up.

Morgan had watched the video of Rory over and over once it had been posted online, and probably so had most of the world's witches. The trick had started a race for competitors to top it, and the results were not always pretty. At the time, there had been talk about banning it from competitions because it was too dangerous.

Rory had upped her game when she won the U.S. Nationals—a bigger fire to control, a more dramatic performance. But in retrospect, that original display of power was the moment when, in Morgan's head, she'd become Rory fucking Sandler. And judging by the world's reaction at the time, it hadn't only been her to think so.

Morgan assumed Rory would be used to hearing people gush over her, and maybe, if she'd thought otherwise, she would have felt weird about so openly fangirling her fake girlfriend. But to her surprise, Rory turned slightly pink and cast her gaze down. "Thanks. I think about it, too. Only I call it a nightmare."

"Really?"

"No, I'm kidding. Sort of." Rory took another sip of wine, and Morgan caught a glimpse of that burn scar on her left palm.

Sort of? A dozen questions bubbled up Morgan's throat, but she forced them back down. Rory did not talk about competing or why she quit competing. Ever. Morgan was treading on uncomfortable territory, and she didn't want Rory shutting down or thinking Morgan was just a fan prying for information.

Yet those questions were going to haunt her. She couldn't help but wonder if there were other scars on Rory's body in places that she couldn't see. Normally, thinking about Rory's body, especially the parts that were typically covered, had a rather pleasant effect on Morgan. But this time, she only felt pained.

“Anyway,” Rory continued, shaking off the moment, “my point was that you can throw food in a pot, and I’m sure it will turn out great. But if I don’t follow a recipe exactly, I’m dead. And now my metaphor has definitely failed.”

“Yeah, you make an excellent margarita, so I doubt your cooking is that bad.”

Rory laughed, and someone save her because Morgan could get used to that sound. “It’s true that I have never burned a pot of water.”

“Because you have excellent elemental control.”

“Exactly.” Rory snapped her fingers. “Anyway, how long is it going to take Verbena to get back? We haven’t started work on our story, and I expect we’re going to be grilled over dinner.”

Right. Crap. Morgan had been all prepared to lead this discussion, and it was Rory who’d brought it up twice now. Her fake girlfriend was totally going to believe Morgan was slacking.

The vegetables were chopped, the tofu and sauce were prepared, and the rice was cooking. Morgan wasn’t going to heat the wok until Verbena returned with Vanessa, so her time to shine had arrived. She reached into her purse and grabbed her phone.

“I’ve been making notes,” Morgan said. “They aren’t color-coded, but some words *are* in all caps.”

“All caps? I’m impressed.”

Morgan shimmied in place because punching the air in triumph would probably confuse Rory. “Thank you. I’ve been thinking about what you said at the coven meeting, and we don’t just need a believable story. We need a story that will charm your family enough so that they won’t want to ask questions. They’ll simply want to enjoy it. In other words, we need a meet-cute.”

Rory nodded but she didn’t look convinced. “Okay, but we’d already known each other for a while before we started fake dating.”

“Yes, but . . .” Morgan raised a finger. “There still has to be a *moment*, right? Like, something must have happened to make us look at each other differently one day. That's our story."

"Okay, that makes sense, too." Rory pulled the bowl with the peanut sauce closer and dipped a slice of pepper in it. "Oh, that's good. You don't even need to heat this. I could eat it cold." Morgan stuffed a piece of broccoli in her mouth to control her grin. Fuck yes! She was on a roll. First her notes, now her cooking. Stand her on a pyre and light it up because she was on fire.

"I've jotted down some ideas," Morgan said, pretending she was not picturing Rory's dreamy expression in her bedroom.

"Go for it."

Morgan started with her favorite. "A customer was harassing you at the bar, and I jumped in and flung my drink on them."

Rory clasped her hands together. "A touch overly dramatic, but very heroic of you."

"What happened?" Ivy's voice startled them both. Morgan had been paying so much attention to Rory that she'd completely forgotten there were people just a couple of rooms over who could overhear them. "Did Morgan just say she threw a drink at someone harassing you at the Chalice?"

"Um . . ." Morgan glanced at Rory for direction, but Rory was cringing into her wine.

Her lack of a quick response didn't make much difference. Ivy barely paused for breath as she pulled her lasagna out of the fridge. "That's awful, but I wish I'd been there to see that. Morgan, you always were the first to jump into a fight at school. Your poor mother. But you didn't tolerate bullies, and that's a good thing. Not that I'm positive Rory couldn't handle a nasty customer herself, but that's such a sweet story."

Andy appeared in the doorway while Ivy stuck the lasagna in the oven. She made an apologetic face and mouthed *sorry* in Morgan and

Rory's direction. "Ivy, hurry up. We need a tie-breaking vote on what spell to cast on the balloons."

"I'm coming, I'm coming. I needed to heat the food." Ivy flashed Morgan a winning smile as Andy ushered her out. "Good job."

"Um," Morgan said again.

Rory rubbed her temples. "It would be a sweet story, but I'm trying to convince my family that I didn't make a mistake by buying into ownership of the Chalice. Telling them I get harassed while working is not going to go over well."

"Oh, right. Scratch that." Morgan scrolled down her list of ideas and hoped Ivy wouldn't spread it around. "What about this? I was carrying a heavy box of potion supplies and tripped, and you caught the box before all the jars broke. That's when our hands touched for the first time, and we felt a spark."

She hadn't finished speaking before Hazel darted into the kitchen and dropped her voice to a whisper. "You have people incoming any second now; I'm sorry. But that story doesn't make sense anyway. What would Rory be doing near you while you were carrying potion supplies?"

Shit. Morgan had celebrated too soon. She was going down in flames after all.

"I don't know!" She raised her hands in despair. "Why are you and Andy so bad at keeping people out of the kitchen? We had a plan!"

Hazel crossed her arms. "Have you ever tried telling a bunch of middle-aged witches what to do? It's not my fault you haven't finished. Be thankful for what we've managed so far."

"Hazel's got a point," Rory said, setting out cocktail glasses.

"About the story or middle-aged witches?"

"Both."

"Ugh, fine, so moving on." Morgan deleted her next two ideas since the same criticism could apply. She was growing more frustrated, but she wasn't ready to give up. "A customer was flirting with you at the bar, and I realized it made me jealous."

That one was boring, but it had the stench of reality going for it. Rory always smiled politely at the customers who hit on her, but she never flirted back for bigger tips. Morgan lived in dread of the day that Rory did flirt back, since that would have to signal actual interest.

"Aw, that's so lovely." Raina came bustling into the kitchen, her statement earrings and bracelets jingling, and Hazel threw Morgan an exasperated look.

Damn it. Hazel *had* warned her, but she'd been too intent on getting this right. Rory lowered her head to the counter, shaking, and Morgan couldn't tell if it was with laughter or frustration.

Verbena and Vanessa's friend unwrapped her platters of naan and samosas, scowled at the temperature Ivy had set the oven to, then proceeded to stick the food in there to reheat it. "Is that the same person you threw a drink on?" she asked Morgan.

"No," Morgan said.

"Yes," Rory said.

"What?" Hazel asked.

So much for hoping Ivy wouldn't talk. That had taken under five minutes by Morgan's estimation. Meanwhile, Hazel and Raina were looking between her and Rory for an explanation.

"I've gotten jealous a lot." And because that was the truth, Morgan drained her wineglass and refused to glance in Rory's direction.

Olga stuck her blond head into the kitchen next. "Rory, could you be a dear and come into the living room when you can? Verbena texted that they're on their way home, and we're trying to drape some streamers and it's not going well. We were hoping you could do some fancy air magic kind of thing." She waved her hand around vaguely.

Rory cleared her throat. "Be there as soon as I finish making the garnish for the drinks."

Morgan groaned as the kitchen emptied for what she hoped was the last time. "Do you think they'll compare stories?"

"You're really asking that? Let's just hope the stories become so distorted as they're passed around that it doesn't matter. I bet there's some anti-gossip spell for that." Rory twisted a slice of lemon peel into a spiral. "You've put a lot of thought into this."

"I'm trying to help. And I read a lot of romance, so I did some research."

"Oh, using books for inspiration is smart. Wait." Rory ran to the doorway, presumably checking for lurkers and potential intruders. "Okay, how's this one? You were trying to convince a friend that you're not interested in the guy that she likes, and in desperation, you kissed me in front of her to make your point. Uncool not to ask first, by the way. But, on the upside, we both realized how much we liked it."

Morgan smacked her mouth with the wineglass she'd just refilled. "Is that from the book with the neuroscientists? You read it, too?"

"Hasn't everyone read that book?"

"You read romance?" Duh, of course Rory read romance, or she wouldn't have read that book, or known what a meet-cute was. Morgan could have smacked herself with more than her glass for asking silly questions, but she was too excited to discover something she and Rory actually had in common. "Who's your favorite author? How did you get into reading it? I used to sneak my grandmom's Nora Roberts and Danielle Steel books, or I thought I did."

Rory was biting her lip, apparently doing her best not to laugh at Morgan's latest outburst. "Thought you did?"

Morgan shrugged sheepishly. "I didn't like reading until I found those books, and then I didn't realize at first that my mom and grandmom were leaving their books around for me to find on purpose. I thought I was being sneaky, but it turned out they were."

"Aw, that's kind of charming."

Morgan felt her neck turning red. "What about you?"

Rory blew out a long breath. "My family reads nonfiction mostly. I think I started reading romance to annoy them, to be honest."

"That's . . ." Morgan cast about for the correct word.

"Not charming?" Rory suggested. "When your family is a bunch of overachievers, sometimes the only way to best them is to confound them with your choices. You'll understand soon enough."

They both drank long from their glasses while Morgan considered what to say to that. The more Rory talked about her family, the more Morgan wondered what she'd gotten herself into. But the more Morgan heard, the more annoyed she became with the Sandlers as well.

She was determined to protect Rory, as ridiculous as it would seem that someone like Rory fucking Sandler would need protection. But a witch's power was only one aspect of her, and magic couldn't replace every mundane thing. Like friendship. Or love. Or even a fake girlfriend having your back.

And that was one thing Morgan could do for her.

7

RORY: That wrap you dropped off for me was perfect! Thank you again!

Verbena had sent Morgan home with some of the extra peanut sauce the other night, so Morgan had marinated chicken in the leftovers. She'd eaten hers with rice, but since she didn't know if Rory would be able to heat up food while she worked, she'd put the rest into a wrap with veggies, and dropped it off at the Empty Chalice.

Although she'd worried that such a gesture might seem overly friendly and give her away, she'd figured she could explain it as part of their ruse. As it turned out, her worries had been for nothing. Rory had spontaneously hugged her, and Morgan had floated all the way home, reveling in that unexpected full-body contact.

MORGAN: I can't let my fake girlfriend starve.

RORY: You are the best fake girlfriend I've ever had.

MORGAN: Hold up. I'm not your first? I thought we had something special.

MORGAN: 😭

RORY: You are my one and only.

RORY: 😘

Morgan dropped her phone.

MORGAN: Have you read Flirting with a Vengeance?

RORY: No, but it's in my TBR pile with twenty other books.

MORGAN: Slacker. I have over forty in my pile.

RORY: Full-length novels or novellas, too? Novellas only count for half.

MORGAN: Says who?

RORY: The word counts.

MORGAN: Give up your word-count discrimination. Your creative math doesn't matter. I have more than twice as many. You can't win.

RORY: BRB, going to the bookstore.

MORGAN HOPED THE drink-tossing story wouldn't leave Verbena's house since Rory didn't like it, and considering how tipsy some of the guests had gotten, it wasn't impossible. Rory had made the drinks very, very strong in what had to have been a deliberate effort to ensure that outcome. As for the story they were going with, it was a variation on the one Rory had suggested.

MORGAN: I kissed you when we were at Andy's birthday brunch in July to convince Hazel that I didn't have any interest in that friend of Trevor's she thought was cute.

RORY: You'd had three of those blueberry mimosas I made, so it's not surprising you were acting impulsively.

The best lies were garnished by truth, so Rory claimed. And Morgan *had* drunk three of Rory's blueberry mimosas that day.

MORGAN: Kind of you to suggest I don't always act impulsively.

MORGAN: Those mimosas were amazing.

RORY: I am a professional.

MORGAN: You are a potion witch at heart.

RORY: 😊

RORY: Shit. A bachelorette party just walked in and wants three-layer bubble shots. I gotta get back to work. It's gonna be a long night.

Morgan snickered. Bubble shots were one of those gimmicky, overpriced magical drinks that mundanes loved. One layer allowed the drinker to blow a long-lasting, brightly colored bubble from their mouth in whatever simple form they wanted it to take. Adding multiple layers allowed for additional bubbles. Making a round of three-layer magical shots was probably a lot of work, and given it was for a bachelorette party, Morgan could guess what form the bubbles floating around the bar for the next twenty minutes would take.

RORY, THREE HOURS LATER: I totally forgot. You need to meet Lilith before the festival.

MORGAN: Your cat?

RORY: Yes. My girlfriend would totally have met my cat, and it will be obvious to my family if you haven't.

Morgan didn't quite follow how it would be obvious, but if Rory wanted her to come over, a hundred hexes couldn't get her to turn down that invitation. Especially since she hadn't been able to spend time with Rory since Verbena's party on Wednesday. Rory worked long hours on Fridays and Saturdays, so aside from their brief conversation when she'd dropped off dinner (and one hug that Morgan couldn't discount), their fake relationship had turned to texts for the past several days. Cell phones were more convenient than the old-fashioned scrying mirrors witches once used, but no substitute for being in the same room.

Not that Morgan needed to see Rory in person to imagine the thick eyelashes framing her eyes or her scattered freckles or that distracting pair of lips. The additional time she'd spent with Rory over the past week had cemented those images in her brain, and more than one night she'd fallen into bed, imagining kissing her way down Rory's face, then lower and lower down her body, until sleep had become damned near impossible. But the point remained—fantasizing was nice, but simply talking to the real Rory was better.

Rory had texted about her cat on Saturday while she was at work, and since Grandmom June had canceled the weekly family dinner because of festival prep exhaustion, on Sunday evening, Morgan was finally discovering where Rory lived.

It turned out to be in one of the newer condo developments that had gone up on the north side of Harborage over the past decade. The row of homes was built in a quintessential New England coastal style, and they each had a view out the back that overlooked the ocean. It would be a longer walk into downtown from here, but the view probably made the trek worthwhile—and probably made the condo far more expensive than Morgan's third-floor apartment.

Rory led Morgan past a narrow but sleek kitchen into the living room. The space was light and airy but decorated with substantial furniture. A cozy woodstove was set against one wall, facing a green sofa so dark it appeared black except for where the sunlight hit it. Two overstuffed chairs completed the seating area, and the table between them was covered in candles, as was the mantel above the woodstove. But it was the room's far wall that really drew the eye. It was almost entirely floor-to-ceiling glass. Morgan was temporarily distracted by the ocean view until a small black cat padded up to her.

"Lilith, this is Morgan. She's a friend." Rory knelt to pet her and glanced up at Morgan. "You should introduce yourself."

Morgan didn't question. She squatted and held out a hand. "It's nice to meet you, Lilith."

Lilith sniffed Morgan's hand a moment, then she gingerly placed her paw on it. Her bright green eyes appraised Morgan, and Morgan involuntarily tensed, hoping she passed whatever test she was being given. A heavy moment lingered until Lilith removed her paw, meowed, and rubbed against Morgan's ankle before wandering off to better things.

"She likes you," Rory said.

"You said I needed to meet your cat," Morgan said, standing up. "Not your familiar."

Because there was no way that Lilith was an ordinary cat. Morgan had never found a familiar of her own—or, rather, none had found her—but she knew the difference when she met one. And that explained why Rory had insisted they meet.

After the whole hug ordeal, Morgan had been hoping, so secretly that she could scarcely admit it to herself, that Rory had simply been looking for an excuse to see her again. So much for that.

"She's not much of a familiar." Rory stood, too, and glanced toward the stairs that led to the second-story loft. "Yeah, I'm talking about you!"

A clearly disgruntled meow came from above, and a moment later Lilith jumped onto the railing. Behind her were several bookshelves and what might have been a desk. Morgan longed to go exploring, especially to check out what Rory had on the shelves, but she turned away.

"Do you actually understand each other?" Witches who could communicate with animals were rare, but true familiars were different from ordinary pets. Besides, Morgan would put nothing past Rory's capabilities. Never mind whatever Rory claimed to the contrary.

Rory waved her hand in a so-so gesture. "She understands me way more than I understand her. So, uh, since you're here, do you want to get dinner? I can't cook like you, but I'm fantastic at ordering pizza."

Huh. Maybe Rory *did* want an excuse to see more of her? Morgan grabbed a nearby chair to keep from fainting. "That sounds great."

While they figured out their pizza order, Rory set a bowl of peaches on the counter, which was soon followed by various liquor bottles.

"What are you doing?" Morgan asked, scrolling through the menu on her phone. They'd already decided on the triple mushroom and gorgonzola, and she was internally debating a side of garlic bread.

Rory studied the bottles she'd set out—prosecco, elderflower liqueur, bourbon, and others that were less familiar to Morgan—moving them around as she contemplated. "Since I can't cook for you, I'm going to make you a drink after I put in the order."

"You can't order the pizza *and* make drinks."

"Of course I can." She frowned at Morgan with confusion.

"No, you can't. If you're making drinks, I'm ordering the pizza."

"Not happening, Put down your phone."

Oh no. It was on now. Morgan scrolled faster. "Forget it. You're too slow," she called out in singsong.

Taunting Rory and picking silly fights with her was too hard to resist. Over text, it was fun. In person, it wasn't merely fun, but hot. Rory was every bit as competitive as she was, and the gleam she got in her eyes when challenged made Morgan long to press her against the closest wall and do unspeakable things with her mouth. That might be completely out of the question, but the possibility hung in the air between them and stirred Morgan's blood.

Rory dropped the strainer in her hand and lunged for her phone. "Don't you dare!"

But Morgan was running to the corner of the living room, furiously entering their pizza order into the online form. Forget the garlic bread. There wasn't enough time, and no way was she going to give Rory the chance to beat her when Rory hadn't even had the website up.

"Done!" Morgan raised her phone in triumph. "I guess I'm more fantastic at ordering pizza than you."

Rory shook the strainer at her. "You'll pay for that."

This was how, an hour later, Morgan found herself on Rory's sofa, glad that she lived close enough to walk home because she was unsafe to drive. Her head was as fuzzy as a peach. That feeling likely had as much to do with the fact that she was hanging out with her fake girlfriend as it did with the drink, but there was no question that Rory had gotten her revenge.

"It doesn't taste like there's any alcohol in this," Morgan said. "But my head disagrees."

Rory had mixed juice from the peaches with Morgan-didn't-know-what, but the drinks were large enough that she'd served them in balloon goblets. Morgan was on her second.

"That's why I called it Evil Peach Punch," Rory said.

"So you're saying I shouldn't be sucking these down like water?"

Rory's eyes twinkled with such mischievous delight that Morgan felt her body flush. "Oh no, you absolutely should be."

Fuck. That was yet another comment she was going to analyze to death.

Still, Morgan slowed her drinking, knowing it was a bit late. She was rambling, which she was even more prone to do after drinking, but Rory was asking lots of questions about potion-making, which suggested Morgan hadn't bored her. Either that, or Rory was also too buzzed to care.

"I'm going to try to go to the workshop Elena Cortez is doing on strengthening the magic in essential oils," Morgan said in response to Rory's latest question. "She's a master potion-maker for a reason."

"Do you make all of your own oils?" Rory sat across from her on an overstuffed armchair, her bare feet dangling off the side. She'd ditched her usual jeans for a pair of capri leggings, and Morgan was having a hard time figuring out where to rest her eyes. Rory's freckles or her bare calves? Fortunately, Rory had the decency to wear a loose shirt so her chest wasn't an option or Morgan would have been in bigger trouble.

"When we can, yeah." Morgan tucked her legs under her butt, trying to sound more professional and less drunk. "We can control the potency that way. Makes for more consistent potions. What about you? I mean, are there any workshops you want to attend?"

"Not sure." Rory plucked at the upholstery. "My former coach contacted me. There's a witch who'll be participating in the spellcasting exhibition who's searching for someone to help them train. She asked me to take a look."

Morgan shifted, sitting up straighter. They were venturing close to shaky territory, and the realization helped uncloud her brain. She needed to be careful. "Like scout them out?"

"Kind of?" Rory's brow pinched. "I don't know if I'm going to go to the exhibition, though. It's weird."

"Going or not going?"

"Both. Either. My family wants me to go back to competing, but they won't be the only people expecting me to perform. Go or don't go—either way I'm going to have people watching me and asking questions." She spun a ring around her thumb with an unhappy expression.

Morgan picked at her chipped nail polish, remembering wishing out loud that Rory would perform in the exhibition not so long ago. She was glad she'd never brought it up around her.

Groaning, Rory removed her legs from the chair arm and cocked her head to the side. "Ugh, this took a serious turn. Quick, say something funny."

"What? Why me?"

"Because you're the funny one."

"You think I'm funny?" Intentionally? Did she want the answer to that?

Rory shut the mostly empty pizza box and set her glass down on top of it. "Everyone knows you're the funny one. Just like Hazel is the artsy one, and Andy is the smart one, and I'm . . . What am I?"

There were so many ways Morgan could answer that. The talented one. The hot one. The mysterious one. The one she wanted more every day. "The badass one."

Rory laughed and tripped over the table leg, falling onto the sofa next to Morgan. The cushions shifted under her weight, and Morgan's insides jostled for more reasons than one. "I thought you were going to say the quiet, boring one."

"Quiet, yeah. But I can't imagine anyone calling you boring."

"You are kind, but literally, my entire life has been boring. Until recently, the only things I ever did were eat, sleep, and practice, and then practice some more. I'm a snooze-fest."

"Nonsense. You are endlessly fascinating." Morgan buried the embarrassment of saying that out loud by drinking more, which was probably the worst way to handle it, but her mouth was already running away with her, so why not?

Rory sat up straighter, disbelief written over her face. "You never even wanted to be my friend."

"What?"

"I thought you didn't like me very much. You're so outgoing and cheerful with everyone else, but you always got quiet when I was around. I didn't know if I'd offended you or what."

The truth was very much the opposite, but even this tipsy, Morgan knew confessing the real reason why she used to clam up around Rory was a terrible idea. The question was: Could she prevent it from slipping out under the circumstances?

"You are quiet," she said, speaking slowly in hopes that it would provide better control of her tongue. "I thought, maybe, I annoyed you, so I tried to be less loud."

That was mostly true. She *hadn't* wanted to annoy Rory. But it was also true that Morgan assumed Rory never thought about her at all.

Rory stared at her a moment. "You don't annoy me. You're funny and fun."

Morgan's heart beat faster, chasing away some of her discomfort. "You're pretty fun and funny, too. I have never disliked you."

That seemed to placate Rory. She nodded but didn't say anything else, and Morgan wondered if she should fill the silence. It was what she'd typically do. Yet, for once, she wanted to simply sit with what had just transpired.

The sun had started to disappear, but rather than turn on the lights, Rory waved her hand, and the candle by the pizza box flickered to life. With a second gesture from Rory, its flame shot across the room, igniting each white pillar on the elaborate candelabra in front of the windows, then the candles atop the fireplace mantel.

"Show-off," Morgan muttered. She didn't know how fuzzy Rory's head was, but if Morgan had attempted that stone-cold sober, she'd have burned the building down. "I can see why you think you're boring. That's not cool at all."

"You should have heard me get in trouble for lighting our menorah when I was growing up. *You can't do it that way!*" She laughed and rested her head against the back of the sofa, closing her eyes.

Since Morgan didn't know how someone was supposed to light a menorah, she was tempted to ask. But in the flickering light, Rory looked so peaceful that Morgan had to conserve her energy lest she give in to the urge to scoot over and press her lips against Rory's mouth, to feel the way her chest rose and fell against her own. It physically hurt how much she wanted to run her hand down the smooth length of Rory's leg and feel the softness of her skin. Sitting here with the ocean melting to twilight black outside, with her head pleasantly fuzzy, everything about their fake relationship felt too real. Like if she actually leaned over and kissed Rory, she could make it so.

But there was magic, and then there was magical thinking. Wishes alone couldn't make desires come true.

Rory cracked an eyelid and turned in Morgan's direction. "What are you pondering?"

And because Morgan was in that half-dreaming state of drunkenness when it was hard to distinguish between feelings and reality, and because—damn it—she'd already used up the last bit of control she had over her mouth, she blurted out exactly what she'd been thinking. "We should kiss. Practice, I mean. In case we need to do it in front of your family."

Morgan's pulse skipped, the full force of what she was suggesting dawning on her. This could have been a cozy moment that, later, she could have pretended meant more than it did. Now, she'd ruined it, and Rory was probably about to toss her out the door. "It'll seem less awkward then if we get the awkwardness over now. But never mind. It's a terrible idea."

Rory stared at her, and a flush crept up Morgan's neck so scorching hot that she started to worry Rory was actually attempting to set her on fire.

But Rory sat up, and after a moment, she nodded. "No, that's a smart idea."

For the second time tonight, Morgan felt light-headed. "You think so?"

"We have to sell this relationship. It would be weird if we weren't physically comfortable around each other."

"Exactly." Morgan took a deep breath, though she was unconvinced that more oxygen would help. Certainly not when her heart was beating this quickly.

Maybe this *was* a terrible idea. She hadn't even kissed Rory yet.

Maybe she'd pass out for real when she did, and that would be humiliating.

"So, um." Rory slid closer until her knee touched Morgan's.

Shivers rippled through Morgan's body, which was absurd. It was just a knee.

Yeah, she really was not going to survive this kiss.

You could take the suggestion back, her weak sense of self-preservation whispered. Then it laughed, because fuck no. Morgan couldn't think of a better way to die than by kissing Rory.

"Right." Morgan leaned forward, and Rory's face was right there. Those heavy eyes, those precious freckles, those lips she'd spent way too much time dreaming about.

Morgan closed her eyes as their mouths brushed, and *sweet stars*. The tingles from touching knees had nothing on that. Rory had set her on fire for sure, her nerves erupting in a blaze of pleasurable heat that cascaded down her body. Rory's lips tasted vaguely of peach, and her hair smelled like lavender. Unable to stop herself, Morgan touched her hand to Rory's cheek, holding her lightly in place but otherwise not daring to move for what felt like an eternity.

In that eternity, Morgan struggled to commit every sensation to memory. To make this moment—fake though it might be—into one she could take with her.

Then Rory placed her hand over Morgan's and she lightly pulled on Morgan's upper lip, and Morgan couldn't memorize anything more because her brain ceased functioning. She was nothing but a series of exploding nerve endings and molten emotions that were pooling between her legs. Her mouth reacted on its own, taking control of Rory's lower lip like she'd so often fantasized about, until Rory sucked in a ragged breath, and Morgan realized she'd stopped breathing, too, and reality intruded.

Rory pulled away, wetting her lips, and Morgan inched back quickly. Her body burned, and the air between them felt extra cold because of the distance. Her head still swam, but it was clearly no longer just from the alcohol. The longing inside of her had gotten a taste of what it couldn't have, and it threatened to overpower her. Her emotions raged, and her power soared. Around the room, the candle flames flickered wildly in an invisible breeze.

Morgan willed her gaze to focus, even if her brain couldn't, and the candles returned to normal as she watched Rory. Did she look just as dazed? Was the flush on her cheeks from pleasure or embarrassment? Morgan had never expected Rory to agree to a kiss, and she would not be able to stop obsessing over whether Rory had felt what she felt.

Rory caught her looking finally, and she lobbed Morgan a lopsided smile before reaching for her glass and draining the melted ice. Was she trying to cool off, or wash away the taste of Morgan's lips? Had she noticed the candles?

"That was smart to get that out of the way," Rory said, although she seemed to be speaking more to her glass than to Morgan.

It didn't matter where her attention was directed. *Get that out of the way* said it all, didn't it? And yet Morgan would have sworn the way Rory breathed before the kiss broke up was not with repulsion but with the same need that had been coursing through her own veins.

Of course, Morgan could be very good at deluding herself, too. With trembling hands, she drained the dregs from her own glass. "Yeah, definitely."

Whatever Rory did or didn't feel, the kiss changed the atmosphere in the room. A tide of ice water had come in, bringing wave after wave of awkwardness. They talked for another half hour or so, and Rory began to yawn.

"Aren't you used to late nights?" Morgan asked. She needed to go home and sleep herself. With only one more full day until they hit the road, her to-do list was feeling insurmountable. That meant an early morning awaited her tomorrow.

"Late nights are fine. I just haven't been sleeping well lately," Rory said, clearing away their glasses. "I think the stress of what's coming is getting to me. I could use a good sleep potion, but I don't have one."

Morgan had a spell for one that her grandmom had developed, but she'd never made it, and experimenting on Rory didn't seem like a great idea. If it was too strong, Rory might collapse where she stood, or end up sleeping for twenty-four hours, or some other nightmare. Morgan did have experience with something almost as good, however.

"What about a relaxation potion?" she asked.

"I have some of your lotion," Rory said, shutting her dishwasher. "It helps, but honestly, I need something stronger."

Morgan shook her head. "The lotion is weak, diluted. I mean the real potion. Put a couple of drops on your tongue or in a mug of tea before bed, and it'll stop your brain from spinning out of control so you can sleep. Guaranteed. I'll make it for you tomorrow."

Yes, in all her free time tomorrow. But whatever. It was Rory. Morgan would get up an hour earlier and do it. Making a relaxation potion was as simple for her as the trick with the candles was for Rory.

"I didn't realize you sold pure potions."

"We don't sell them to the public, but we do make them custom order for other witches." Morgan brought over the pizza box. "Our more commercial products are way more profitable."

Rory smiled knowingly. "And more palatable for the mundanes. Makes sense. How much?"

"Don't worry about it. Consider it the fake-girlfriend discount."

Anyway, she already had all the supplies on hand, and it wouldn't take long. Although, technically, the supplies were the shop's, not hers, but she'd figure it out.

Rory looked like she wanted to object, but Morgan's glare cut her off. "Okay. Thank you. For everything."

Morgan swallowed. Her gaze fell to Rory's lips, and the mad urge to step closer and see what would happen if she tried to kiss her a second time took hold.

But the post-kiss awkwardness locked Morgan's feet in place, reminding her of how she used to be tongue-tied around Rory. Oddly, that seemed like ages ago, but no doubt it was for the best that she didn't forget again. She'd never have dreamed of that one kiss happening, and she'd be wise to take the memory of it with her and leave before she messed anything up.

"No problem," Morgan said, recalling she needed to say something, however inane. "I'll drop the potion off tomorrow."

And then she left. Every now and then, she could do the wise thing.

8

ALTHOUGH HER ALARM WOKE HER EXTRA EARLY ON MONDAY, Morgan was in no mood to complain. She'd fallen into bed replaying the kiss in her mind, feeling the sensation of Rory's lips so intensely that her dreams had taken over from there. It wasn't the first time her subconscious had gotten them naked, but it was definitely the most vivid. She still could hear Rory's sharp intake of breath before she'd pulled away, and that sound did things to her. Wonderful things.

But while Morgan's mood was as bright as the sun, part of her nevertheless fretted. Previously, she hadn't considered Rory a friend since that implied a level of closeness Morgan's crush had never allowed her to feel. They'd been more like acquaintances. But her crush on Rory, while stronger than ever, was changing along with their relationship. Now that Morgan felt comfortable categorizing Rory as "friend," her emotions and rampaging lust created confusion. Having sex dreams about a friend was . . . awkward, and a new-to-her dilemma.

Morgan had always thought most of her friends were objectively attractive people, but she'd never once ogled Trevor's calves or given any thought to Hazel's chest. Somehow, subconsciously, she'd maintained a line between friend and object of desire. Rory's chest, on the other hand, occupied Morgan's thoughts on a daily—perhaps hourly—basis, and getting closer to Rory had only intensified that fascination. Her line had been crossed for the first time. The distance between them, which had kept everything simple and neat, had vanished.

Morgan would be the first to describe herself as a messy witch, but she'd ventured into new and confusing territory. She would have to guard her heart, tie it up in tight little knots to hold it in place, because this was definitely the kind of mess that she could lose it in.

It was easy enough to push aside this dilemma by the time Morgan finished her coffee. Less easy was pushing aside the memory of the kiss. It invaded her walk to Bed, Bath, and Broom, and lingered in her brain as she tried to work. It was there in the smile she couldn't shake, and the way her feet didn't seem to touch the ground. Her mother was already at the shop, and though she raised an eyebrow at Morgan's cheerfulness, she assumed it was excitement about the festival, and Morgan was content to let her.

Unfortunately, since the shop's back room wasn't large, sharing it was a challenge. Morgan was basically a twenty-year-younger version of her mother, and they were both too tall and curvy for the space. At times, Morgan thought they were too loud as well.

Her mother typically used her own home workroom and left the shop's room to Morgan, who didn't have a workroom of her own. Today, though, no one was supposed to be doing any magic as all the pre-festival chores left were of the boring, mundane variety, and Morgan found it helpful to have the company in spite of the cramped quarters. She and her mother bumped elbows while packing boxes, and the only casualty of so much close contact was a jar of the ever-bubbling bubble bath that Lianne dropped when her arm and Morgan's collided. Mostly, her mother's not-distracted brain kept Morgan on target while Morgan did a lousy job of pretending her thoughts weren't a mile down the road on Rory's sofa.

After lunch, Lianne left to do her personal packing and deal with the final arrangements for tomorrow, giving Morgan the space she needed to make Rory's potion. Without her mother around to ensure she was triple-checking her work, Morgan fell back into her earlier daze, so it was a good thing that she was familiar enough with the relaxation potion that it didn't require much effort. Although, in her dreamy laziness, she simply grabbed some of the dried herbs and oils she'd already packed for the festival rather than measure out quantities from the shop's larger containers. It wouldn't be a huge deal if they were short one container of lavender oil and some chamomile, and she'd probably have made a mess if she tried to do it any other way.

Morgan poured the potion into one of her prettier glass vials and sealed the stopper in place with candle wax to keep it fresh until Rory used it. She'd made enough to last Rory one to two weeks, depending on how strong a dose she took. That complete, Morgan swiped her hand across the table's runes, and the glow dissipated with the candle flames.

With a happy sigh, she popped a few cheese crackers in her mouth and checked the time before texting Rory.

> MORGAN: I've got your potion. Where are you?
>
> RORY: On my way to work. Can you bring it there? We have to talk.

Cheese cracker turned to dust in Morgan's mouth. Was this about the practice kiss? It had to be, didn't it? And it didn't sound good. *We have to talk* was never good. If Rory was her real girlfriend, that would sound like a breakup was on the horizon.

Morgan forced herself to eat another handful of crackers, though her stomach rebelled. *Stop being ridiculous*, she told herself. *You can't break up with someone who you aren't actually dating.*

At least if Rory was fake dumping her, Morgan would be in a place that served alcohol.

Grabbing her keys and phone, Morgan swept her gaze over the workroom to make sure she hadn't forgotten anything important, like putting out a candle or the incense, or not clipping the cracker bag so that the contents went stale—which wouldn't be as tragic as burning down the shop but nonetheless a cause for sadness. But everything was in its place. The boxes were ready for loading into the van. It was all good. Except for her. She was not feeling good anymore.

She carefully tucked the potion vial in a pocket—did it seem pinker than usual?—and left the shop by the back door.

With anxiety driving her feet, Morgan made it to the Empty Chalice in record time. The bar was far emptier than it was on the nights Morgan and her friends hung out there, but the atmosphere was surprisingly lively given it wasn't much past four on a Monday. For people on vacation, every day was a Saturday, Morgan supposed.

Rory saw her as Morgan made her way to the dimly lit bar, and she nodded in acknowledgment. Taking a stool, Morgan pulled the potion from her pocket and examined it, but it looked utterly normal. Any discoloration she thought she'd seen earlier must have been a trick of the mind. She was stressed, after all.

Speaking of stressed, Rory's face conveyed the same feeling when she came over a minute later, although she smiled as she slid a drink across the bar to Morgan, and some of Morgan's unease dissolved just like that. Honestly. She needed to stop jumping to such negative conclusions all the time.

"Is this for me?" Morgan asked, eyeing the tall glass. The liquid inside appeared thicker than a normal drink, and a slice of apple was stuck to the rim as a garnish.

Rory pushed it closer to her. "I'm experimenting with fall drink recipes. The only overt magic in this one is that the apple slice isn't already browning, so I'll need to work on the presentation. But tell me what you think of the rest."

The drink smelled pleasantly of cider and bourbon, but Morgan regarded it suspiciously. "Your experimentation with peaches yesterday got me drunk."

"That was hardly my fault." Rory pressed her hand to her heart, seeming quite pleased with herself. "I promise you won't be so tempted to chug this one."

"We'll see about that."

Morgan took a sip and almost fell off the barstool as autumn exploded on her tongue. Apples and cinnamon, cardamom and woodsmoke—she was drinking a walk through an orchard, running her hand over the smooth sides of a pumpkin, catching the scent of a bonfire on a crisp wind. The sensations were so potent that for a second, she lost track of where she actually was. Then Morgan removed the straw from her lips, and the bar came back into focus. All that was left in her mouth was a delicious flavor reminiscent of cider but with undertones of bourbon and spice.

"Okay, *that* is a magical drink worth the money." Morgan pointed toward the glass. "Wow."

Rory grinned. "Excellent. I just need to make the presentation flashier, then."

"I don't suppose that's why you wanted to talk?"

Morgan regretted the question immediately, because Rory's grin vanished. She gestured to the potion. "Is that mine?"

"One custom relaxation potion. I'd start with a single drop and go from there. I do not recommend taking more than three at a time, or I can't guarantee that your bowels won't relax so much that, well, you know."

"Got it. I don't need to give Lilith a reason to laugh at me. Thank you." Rory leaned forward, and for a moment, Morgan thought she might kiss her. Then Rory stopped abruptly and stuck the potion in her jeans pocket.

"So, what's wrong, then?" Morgan asked, trying to not feel disappointed that Rory hadn't kissed her since the very idea of it was absurd.

Clearly, more than yesterday's alcohol had gone to her head, and Morgan took another sip of the magical drink. The effect wasn't as strong this time, but it still tasted good.

Rory pulled out a stack of menus with each night's magical drink specials listed on them and tapped the top one with a pen. Tap—Wednesday's special was now the same as Friday's. Tap—Thursday's was now also Saturday's. Tap, tap—Friday and Saturday each went from two drinks on offer to one. Rory set the menu aside and began repeating the process with the rest of the stack.

"We're going to be magically short-staffed during the festival, so I need to pare this down," she explained in answer to Morgan's questioning expression.

Like Bed, Bath, and Broom, the Empty Chalice hired mundane help along with the witches who worked there, but obviously the mundanes couldn't make magical drinks. All that work would fall on the witches who weren't attending the festival.

"What's wrong is nothing specific," Rory continued. "I keep thinking of stuff we should have discussed but never did. Where are you staying during the festival?"

"I'm sharing a tent site with my mom and my grandmom."

"Would it be possible . . ." Rory winced. "Would you be interested in staying with me instead? I found out this morning that Archer is staying with my family. I should have anticipated that when I heard he was their guest, but I never put it together. My parents were not happy when I told them I have a girlfriend and I'd be busy. I got the 'but we asked Archer to stay with us so you could spend time together' speech."

She tapped a menu especially hard and Thursday's drink special disappeared entirely.

"Oh." Morgan's head spun as she attempted to take this all in. "And you're staying with your family?"

Rory shot a glance down the bar as a couple of new patrons took stools, but the other bartender wandered over to them. "It's a big cabin, more like a house, because my mother's on the Council. It'll be me, my parents, my brother and his family, and apparently Archer."

Oh, sweet stars. Staying with Rory was a giant fuck yes. Staying with Rory's family was a whole other matter. "Will there be space for me?"

"I'll have my own room. We'll make it work if you're okay with it."

Rory was biting her lip, and how was Morgan supposed to say no when she did that? Didn't Rory know what effect that had on her?

Actually, hopefully not.

"Okay, sure." Morgan took a deep breath. "Even sleeping on your floor will be better than a tent."

"You won't have to sleep on the floor. I promise."

No, she would just have to sleep in the same room as Rory. She might be able to hear Rory breathing. See her curled up in bed. Wearing her pajamas. In the morning with sleep-tousled hair.

Oh shit, oh shit, oh shit. She was going to make a complete fool out of herself at some point. Morgan knew it in her bones.

"Thank you," Rory said, snapping Morgan out of her panic. "I'm sorry I keep throwing these new problems at you. I will make it up to you somehow."

"It's fine. Like I said, sounds better than a tent."

"You say that now. Remember, these people are why I haven't slept in a week."

Before she knew what she was doing, Morgan reached over and squeezed Rory's hand. Surprise flashed over Rory's face, but it passed, and she squeezed Morgan back in turn. That pressure, light as it was, felt like Rory was gripping her actual heart.

Screw her concerns. Never mind her panic about sharing a room with Rory or worrying about not meeting her family's standards. These people were ruining Rory's sleep and promising to make her miserable during what should be a fun time, and there was no way Morgan was going to let that happen.

Rory was a friend—okay, she was way more important than that in Morgan's head, but moving on—Rory was a friend. And when you messed with Morgan's friends, especially this one, you messed with her. Morgan was going to do her damned best to make sure Rory got to enjoy herself at the festival, and if that meant standing up to a member of the Witch Council or a spellcasting champion or a freaking Inquisitor, then hex it. Challenge accepted.

9

TUESDAY MORNING PASSED IN A FAMILIAR BLUR. WHILE HE WASN'T a witch and wouldn't be attending the NEWT Festival, Morgan's grandfather took off from work in the morning to help load the van and bid three generations of his family goodbye. He always seemed cheerful enough, looking forward to a weekend fishing with friends, but Morgan often wondered if he'd ever been resentful about not going to the festival with the rest of his family. He'd never acted that way, and witches marrying non-witches was extremely common, but still. It was hard when two people were so different.

This specific difference had been what drove her parents apart. Her mother had wanted to stay in magic-friendly Harborage, work at Bed, Bath, and Broom, and raise Morgan among the family's witches. Her father was too ambitious and focused on his career for that. He'd left when Morgan was only five years old and was now a professor at some college in Oregon. For a while, Morgan used to fly out once a year to visit him, and he would always make time to see her when his work took him to the East Coast, but their relationship had gotten more distant after she'd told him she didn't want to go to Oregon for college. Or go to college at all.

When she thought about it, the situation with her father reminded her of her doomed relationship with Nicole. Though their expectations were wildly different, both Nicole and her father believed that Morgan was failing to live up to her potential.

Her mother drove the van from Harborage to Western Massachusetts where the festival's permanent grounds were located, and Morgan followed in her mother's car, which was loaded with the family's luggage. It was raining in Harborage when they left, but the forecast promised sunny skies with only possible afternoon thunderstorms for the rest of the week where they were going. Weather magic was something that required permission to perform since it could have far-reaching impacts (and a tendency to frighten mundanes), but who was to say permission hadn't been granted?

The drive took over four hours, and Morgan spent the next several after their arrival helping unload the van and set up the campsite, even though she wouldn't be staying there.

RORY: It took you four and a half hours? My nana drives faster than that!

MORGAN: Hey! I was following the van with our supplies in it.

MORGAN: That my mom was driving.

RORY: You come by your slowness naturally is what you're saying.

MORGAN: I thought you weren't in a hurry to see your family anyway.

RORY: I'm not. That's why I want you to be faster. So we can get together sooner.

With her brain fixated on the various interpretations of that last message, Morgan walked into the side of the vendor booth and banged her hip hard enough to leave a bruise.

Since then, afternoon had passed into early evening, and the grounds had grown increasingly noisy as more and more people arrived. Officially, the festival didn't begin until tomorrow at noon, but lots of people came the day before, including all the vendors, the New England–based members of the Witch Council, and the many NEWT volunteers who were helping check people in. Even at its busiest, though, the festival grounds were enormous, and it was easy to wander the tree-lined paths that connected various sites and forget where you were.

Morgan loved it, and she loved the unapologetic displays of magic. Witches—well, most of them—tried so hard to blend in, to keep the non-magical world from considering them a threat. But here, in their own makeshift hamlet for a few days, there was no need to hide. That didn't change much, but small things stood out, like the way people didn't feel the need to discuss magic with hushed voices in public, and the way they dressed, whether it was in T-shirts with cheesy sayings (*resting witch face*) or young girls wearing butterfly barrettes with wings that flapped in their hair. Decorations hung everywhere, too. There were garlands of flowers that didn't wilt strung between tents, enchanted metal bees that flew around the largest mead-seller's booth, and a lack of electricity in favor of conjured lights that hovered in the breeze (even places like the Empty Chalice used a combination of the two).

But it was more than the sights and sounds that ensnared Morgan's attention. The concentrated magic from so many people, cast over so many decades, had seeped into the woods and the fields. It was evident in the trees that sported the occasional magenta or turquoise leaves, the grass that glowed a touch too green, and the wildflowers that bloomed near continuously. Morgan would swear she could taste it in the air. Smell it. It was woodsier than the pine, hotter than the bonfire smoke, a sweet nothing like crystal clear water. If she had no words for it, that was precisely because pure magic was always out of reach. The best a witch could ever do was harness it through her own body.

Sometimes Morgan felt bad that non-witches couldn't attend the festival when many of them loved to watch elemental spellcasting shows, too, or would enjoy the concerts. But it was for all these reasons that she understood why NEWT restricted the festival to witches. This way, everyone here could relax a little easier. Could feel a little more normal. Besides, concerts and spellcasting shows—whether just-for-fun exhibitions or serious competitions that factored into a witch's national ranking—existed outside of the festival. The general public had plenty of other opportunities to experience her world, and the Witch Council encouraged it.

"Are you sure you want to stay with the Sandlers?" Morgan's mother asked, not for the first time since Morgan had told her of the change of plans.

"Of course she's sure," her grandmom replied since Morgan's mouth was stuffed with a cheeseburger hot off the grill. "Haven't you seen the way she's always made moon eyes at Rory? She's had it bad for a long time."

"What?" Morgan cried out. Or rather, she tried to, but the burger made it difficult.

Her grandmom snorted. "Just because Lianne wasn't paying attention doesn't mean the rest of us weren't."

Morgan's mother shot a disapproving look at *her* mother as she popped the cap off her beer bottle. "It's not her feelings for Rory that I was questioning. It just seems so sudden. I miss my girl telling me about all her crushes."

"Oh, you mean the way you used to tell me everything at her age?" Grandmom June replied with a nearly lethal dose of sarcasm.

"I was married at her age, Mom. I didn't think you'd want the details of my love life."

Morgan forced herself to swallow her food before she choked on it. "No one wants those details. And Mom, I haven't told you about my crushes since middle school."

"I know, but do you remember that heart-shaped pink candle you would light?" Her mother sighed wistfully, and Morgan cringed. There was nothing about it that deserved to be remembered wistfully.

"Do I remember being a cliché? Yes, very much so."

Grandmom June cackled. "Every teenage witch tries to do a love spell. Lucky for the world, there aren't many who could pull one off at that age."

Morgan would bet that Rory could have, if she'd tried. She, on the other hand, had certainly not had the focus nor the power then, and she was old enough now to know better—not to mention to be fully subject to the Council Laws if she attempted it.

"Anyway," Morgan said, preferring not to dwell on her adolescent self's experiments in angst, "for the record, I have not been making moon eyes at Rory."

She totally had; she just hadn't realized she'd been noticed.

Her grandmom rolled her eyes. She'd shown up this morning with bright pink hair, courtesy of the shop's choose-your-own-color shampoo, and her attitude seemed to be regressing with her appearance. "All you had to do to figure out where Rory was during a coven meeting was see where Morgan was staring." She batted her eyelashes, making a face that was probably supposed to imitate Morgan's pining, and almost fell off her chair with her theatrics.

Morgan stuck her hands on her hips, torn between indignation and laughter as the camp chair eventually collapsed on her grandmom. "Did something go wrong with that batch of shampoo? It's affecting her brain."

Lianne chuckled while her mother fought the furniture. "She's on her second beer. Your grandmom can't hold her alcohol."

"Lies," Grandmom June said, glowering at her chair. "I know I'm right. You never acted this way about what's-her-face. The one that walked around like she had a broomstick up her butt."

Morgan smacked her beer bottle into a tooth, and now it was her grandmom's turn to laugh at her. Which was fine. She'd earned the right; broomstick up her butt was an apt description of Nicole. But Morgan wasn't about to remind anyone of her ex's name. The sooner she was forgotten, the better.

"Oh no, I never liked her," Morgan's mom said. "Rory is a much better choice. She's very nice."

"Cute, too." Grandmom June nodded.

"Casts a strong circle."

"Knows how to make a decent old-fashioned."

"Hasn't let fame go to her head."

"I bet *she'd* never laugh if a chair tried to murder her grandmother."

"Then you've never heard her talk about her family," Morgan said, putting an end to the teasing. Neither her mom nor grandmom had mentioned Rory's freckles, so they clearly understood nothing about Morgan's infatuation.

Lianne got up and kissed her on the head. "We're just happy for you, sweetie."

"Yeah, yeah." She knew they meant well, but those words only made it harder to take the teasing. They had no idea there was truly no reason to be happy for her.

"Speaking of," Grandmom June said, "don't have so much fun tonight that you're late to help set up tomorrow morning."

"I won't." Morgan held up her phone, doubting there would be much fun in meeting Rory's family. "Alarm already set."

"There are spells for that, too."

"Yeah, but the phone's easier." Honestly, half the time her grandmom's generation of witches seemed at war with mundane technology. The rest of the time, her grandmom did things like charm her gas tank to improve her mileage. Morgan didn't get it.

The phone vibrated in her hand, and a text from Rory flashed on the screen.

> **RORY:** We're done with dinner. You still busy?
>
> **MORGAN:** Will be there soon. Start any fires?
>
> **RORY:** Nope, but considering a hex on Archer's tongue so he can't talk. Got a black candle on you?

Morgan crammed the last of her burger in her mouth.

> **MORGAN:** No, but I do have some blackberry thorns in the booth. Should I get them?
>
> **RORY:** Not if it's going to delay you getting here.

"I've got to go," Morgan said. "Rory's about to hex someone, and I need to watch."

A few minutes later, she grabbed her pack and headed down the main dirt road in the direction of the festival gate.

The cabins were all clustered together in their own neighborhood, not far from the entrance. There was no illusion of privacy surrounding them like there was with the tent-camping sites, but the amenities made up for it. They ranged in size from squat, single-story log buildings to multistory stucco houses. Each was named after a type of crystal used in spell work, with a plaque noting the name by the front door. Most were reserved for high-ranking Council members who would need private meeting spaces during the festival, but others were shared by older members of the community or those with physical limitations that made tent or RV camping a challenge.

Morgan double-checked the name of the Sandlers' cabin (Celestite) to make sure she found the correct building. As Rory had said, it looked more like a house than a cabin—three stories tall and with a deck partially encircling it. Rustic for sure, but a far cry from anything like camping. Solar panels on the roof would even provide electricity. Fancy.

Two adults, one carrying a baby in a sling, were climbing down from the deck as Morgan approached. The one on Morgan's right raised his sunglasses at the sight of her, leaving no question as to his identity. His hair was several shades lighter than Rory's, and his style, from the khaki shorts to the plaid button-down shirt, was her very opposite, but the resemblance was too strong for him to be anyone but her brother. The woman with him was on the shorter side, with long brown hair and such perfect eyebrows that Morgan wondered if she'd achieved them via magic.

"You must be Isaac," Morgan said as the group approached.

"And you must be Morgan." He dropped the sunglasses back in place and shook her hand before making the rest of the introductions. "I'm glad you're staying here."

"You are?" Morgan silently cursed the genuine shock in her voice. From the sound of it, her presence had not been welcomed by the family, so this was a surprise if true.

Isaac didn't seem to take offense, and his wife—Erika of the perfect eyebrows—laughed. "Rory needs someone to keep her calm," he said, "or there'll be blood in that house by midnight."

Morgan adjusted her pack and peered around him. "Be honest, is someone other than Rory going to hex me if I walk in there?"

"Nah, but it's a bit tense." Isaac shook his head, and the baby began fussing. "I tried to get Rory to go walking with us, but she said you were on the way, so good timing. Although I'm sure she'll try to get away as soon as you drop off your pack."

"Here." Erika pulled a snowflake obsidian bead from a pocket and handed it to Morgan. It matched a bead on one of the many bracelets she wore. "No idea where this came from, but it's one of mine. Should help ward off negativity."

Well, that was a great sign. Morgan hadn't considered whether she should carry a spell bag with her for that purpose, and maybe that was an oversight. Tomorrow, she could buy one or find the ingredients to make one herself if she had time. "Thanks."

"It'll be fine," Isaac said. "Our parents, our mother especially, do not like having their plans thwarted is all."

"And I am the thwart." It was what she'd volunteered for, so it was a bit late to worry about it.

"Yeah, but they just want Rory to be happy. Once they see that she is, they'll come around."

Did that mean Isaac believed the concocted story Rory had told him? That was promising, since Morgan had assumed an Inquisitor would be able to see straight through their ruse.

He certainly couldn't be convinced because their feelings were mutually real—right?

"We'll catch you later," Erika said, taking the baby from her husband. "This one did not nap in the car, so he needs to be walked until he sleeps."

"He needs a damned sleep potion," Isaac muttered as they set off. "He's being a twerp."

"Don't you dare. He is way too young for that."

"Then I need another mead."

Morgan chuckled to herself as they continued to playfully argue. So far Isaac didn't seem nearly as scary as she'd expected, but it was hard to judge after such a short conversation. Yet it gave her some hope for the rest of the Sandlers.

Rory must have seen her coming. The cabin door swung open before Morgan could knock. "Oh, thank the goddesses," she whispered, ushering Morgan inside. "You can drop your pack here and we can—"

"Rory, is that your friend?" a woman's voice called out. "Bring her in here so we can meet her."

Morgan showed Rory the bead. "It's okay. Erika gave me this."

Rory smirked. "I knew I liked her. Erika custom bespells jewelry, but I don't think one bead is going to be enough protection. We could sneak out and ignore them?"

It was tempting. But so was Rory's face, which was mere inches from hers as they huddled in the cabin's doorway, and Morgan promised herself she was going to protect the happiness on that face. Leaving would only delay the inevitable and make it worse when it occurred. Besides, Morgan Greenwood did not run from confrontation.

Embarrassment, yes. Fights, no.

"Better to get it over with," she said, although part of her wished to be contradicted.

Rory sighed. "You're always right when you say that."

Morgan followed her through the spacious, if somewhat dated, living space and dining area, and into a large kitchen. It, too, looked like it hadn't been updated since the eighties, but simply the fact that there was a kitchen rated this cabin a five-star hotel compared to most of the festival accommodations.

Three people stood around a central island, an assortment of wineglasses and a mostly finished pie of some kind in the center. Two were obviously Rory's parents, though she and her brother were a mix of their features. The third had to be Archer. Morgan had seen him compete before, but up close, he was shorter than she had expected, with reddish-brown hair and a baby face he was trying unsuccessfully to hide beneath a layer of scruff. Not really her type, but she could see why Andy had thought he was cute. Three sets of eyes—two brown and Archer's bright blue—wasted no time giving her the same once-over that Morgan was giving them.

"Mom, Dad, Archer—this is Morgan." Rory grabbed her free hand, seeming to remember something like that might be a good idea.

Her touch ignited the same flurry of sparks beneath Morgan's skin as it always did, but she was better able to ignore them, too conscious of the scrutiny she was receiving.

"Nice to meet you," Morgan said, adopting her customer-facing retail perkiness. She set the bottle of locally made hard cider she'd brought from home onto the island, and the clunking sound rattled her already on-edge nerves. She suspected Rory's parents were more into wine, but it *was* good cider, and it wasn't like she'd had a lot of time to come up with something better since Rory had only asked her yesterday to stay with them. The bottle had been sitting in Morgan's kitchen. "Thank you for letting me crash here."

"A pleasure," Wanda Sandler replied. Rory clearly took after her both in build and in her penchant for dressing in dark colors, though Wanda's clothes appeared far more expensive to Morgan's untrained eye. She didn't offer her hand, and neither did anyone else, but Rory's mother acknowledged the bottle with a polite nod. "That's very kind of you. Unfortunately, I've heard surprisingly little about you until recently."

"Rory doesn't share much with us about anything," said Brett Sandler, Rory's father, before Morgan could decide whether she'd just been expertly insulted or if Rory's mother was casually voicing her suspicions about their convenient timing.

Morgan swung their arms, pulling Rory closer. "I always thought she was very quiet, too, until I got to know her better."

Rory dug her nails into Morgan's palm, so maybe returning the subtle dig was the wrong approach. That was fine with her. Rory's mother was a politician, and Morgan was out of her depth. Still, Morgan wasn't going to take any implied insults about Rory quietly. She had never agreed to that.

“We’re going for a walk,” Rory said. “I’ll stick Morgan’s belongings in my room when we get back.”

“Oh, don’t rush off so soon.” Wanda slid the open wine bottle down the island toward Morgan and Rory. “Morgan, I’m sorry you missed dessert, but would you like a drink? Archer brought us some lovely mead.”

The absolute last thing Morgan needed was alcohol loosening her tongue when she was trying to be on her best behavior. “I’m good. Thank you.”

“Well, tell us about yourself, then,” Wanda said. “Rory said you work in a shop in that touristy town?”

“Harborage,” Rory muttered. “You know its name.”

This time, Morgan squeezed *her* hand. “Bed, Bath, and Broom is the shop my grandmom started. We make magical products for the home and self-care.”

Since Morgan had refused a drink, Wanda poured herself more. “How cute.”

Morgan tensed, the words reverberating in her ears.

Your family’s shop is cute, but when are you going to show some ambition and do something significant with your life? Nicole’s derisive tone had nothing on Wanda Sandler’s polite condescension. Morgan briefly wondered if they knew each other. Rory’s mother had Nicole’s dream job.

Do not react. Remember why you’re here.

But that was easier said than done. Morgan could defend Rory all day, but she had nothing to say for herself. Her brain was stuck on “cute,” and she was trying so hard to not react to that word that she’d lost the ability to do anything other than gape.

“It is cute,” Rory said, breaking the awkward silence. “Their products are fantastic—it’s one of my favorite shops. Morgan’s an extremely talented potion-maker. They can barely keep up with demand.”

That last part wasn't technically wrong, but the rest . . . Morgan told herself Rory was only jumping to her defense, like any real girlfriend would. Nonetheless, hearing Rory call her "an extremely talented potion-maker" was going to be another one of those moments that she would look back on and mourn, knowing it was fake. Even her work being called cute didn't sound insulting coming from Rory's lips. She made it sound like a compliment.

"You know what? I'll buy you a bottle of their calming hand lotion tomorrow," Rory continued. "It might improve the atmosphere around here if everyone used some."

It was a damned good thing she'd been frozen, otherwise Morgan was certain she'd have burst out laughing. Rory's comment did spur the rest of the room into agitated movement. Rory's father winced, and Archer poured himself more mead. He'd seemed pretty relaxed around Rory's family until a moment ago, but he clearly didn't enjoy the sudden increase in tension, either. This had to be awkward for him, as well, especially if Morgan's suspicions about a romantic setup were correct.

Wanda forced a smile. "It sounds delightful."

"We'll certainly stop by your family's booth during the festival," Brett said. "I just don't understand why my daughter can't also be using her talents for a living."

And there they went again. As soon as Rory was back in the family crosshairs, Morgan forgot about any past or present slights against herself. Her muscles relaxed even as her blood heated.

Bring it, bitches.

"Rory does use her talents," Morgan said, "and people love it."

"She works at a bar," Archer said, speaking up for the first time.

"And she performs every time she makes a drink. Like I said, people love to watch her. The nights she works are always packed." Rory always worked Fridays and Saturdays, so naturally, but her family didn't need the details.

Rory shrugged. "See? It's fun."

Archer snorted. "It's a waste of your talents."

Morgan retracted her previous assumption. Archer clearly enjoyed certain kinds of tension.

"My talents are mine to waste." A harsher edge crept into Rory's voice, and she turned to her mother. "I've offered to reimburse you for the cost of my coaching over the years if that's what this is about."

A collective groan emanated from her parents. "We don't care about the money," Wanda said. "We care about you. You quit bartending once you made enough money from competing, so I can't understand why you'd go back to it now."

"Look, everyone has setbacks," Archer started, and Rory cut him off with an expression that would have had Morgan praying for a quick death if it had been aimed at her.

"I never had a setback." Despite the look, Rory's voice was dangerously sweet and utterly dismissive. "You don't know what you're talking about."

"Rory—" her father began.

"No." She crossed her arms.

"We can do a pairs performance in the exhibition," Archer said. Morgan could feel her magic awakening beneath her skin as her temper flared, but Rory appeared as calm as ever. Not a hair on her head had lifted, nor had a glass rattled. "We'll ease back into something. It'll be fun."

"Well, I think that's a wonderful idea." Wanda raised her glass. "I think you two would enjoy working together if you could stop picking fights, Aurora."

Oh, now they'd done it. Although Morgan had promised herself she'd only defend Rory calmly and politely, she couldn't hold her frustration in any longer. She was supposed to be protecting Rory. To be a shield. To make it clear that Rory was happy.

"She doesn't want to!" Morgan startled the room into silence.

There went any chance she had of Rory's parents not hating her, but screw it. She wasn't here to be liked.

Archer glared at her, and Morgan glared right back.

Wanda set her glass down with a sigh. "I appreciate that you care about my daughter, but you haven't known her very long, and you didn't meet her until . . ." She waved a hand around. "All this."

"You mean until after I moved to Harborage and found a life that makes me happy?" Rory asked. "That's what I'm trying to tell you. I'm happy *now*. Morgan's part of the reason I'm happy. Let's go."

She spun around and dragged Morgan out of the room. Kicking herself over her outburst, Morgan followed without a sound. Usually, she knew exactly how and when she'd messed up, but this time, she honestly had no clue whether she actually had. The entire situation was messed up enough on its own.

10

"AURORA ROSE!" RORY'S MOTHER'S VOICE WAS CUT OFF BY Rory slamming the cabin door shut behind her.

"Aurora Rose—wow." Morgan giggled and half stumbled down the stairs to the grass. It must have been from the relief of escaping that tension. "You have the witchiest name ever."

Whatever post-argument giddiness had infected her had apparently infected Rory, as well. She giggled alongside her. "Please, *Morgan Greenwood.*"

"First of all, Greenwood is my dad's last name, and he's a math professor, not a witch."

"Your father's a math professor?"

Given that she'd once attempted to hex an algebra textbook after a particularly abysmal exam grade, Morgan didn't feel insulted by how incredulous Rory sounded. "I know—it makes no sense. The only thing I inherited from him is my last name. Which brings us back to the names, and my middle name is Elizabeth, which is about as boring and mundane a middle name as there is. It might only be topped by Anne."

"I was named after a couple of great-aunts."

Despite her laughter, Rory made Morgan keep up a quick pace. "I was named after no one," Morgan said. "I think my parents opened a baby name book to a random page and claimed Hecate guided their hands."

Rory snorted. "Sounds legit."

Once they reached the end of the dirt path leading to the cabin, putting some distance between themselves and her family, Rory's giddiness dissolved into a groan. "I'm sorry. I can't decide if that went better or worse than expected."

"No one tried to set anyone else on fire, so let's go with better."

"No one's tried yet. Don't count me out so soon."

"I would never." Morgan looped her arm around Rory's and only belatedly realized what she'd done. Rory didn't pull away or tense up, so Morgan tried to pass it off like it was a normal, natural thing to do and not the sort of casual touching that caused her to have heart palpitations. Had it really only been eight days since she'd freaked out over Rory fist-bumping her?

For a couple of minutes, they wandered aimlessly through the cluster of cabins, and Morgan glanced toward the sky. The sun was sinking beneath the trees, casting their crowns in silhouette and turning the wooded path an early dark. In the distance, smoke curled above the leaves.

"Where are we going?" Morgan asked.

"Anywhere but here." Rory nudged Morgan toward the main footpath. "Think any food vendors will be open? I could use a drink."

"Vendors aren't allowed to open until tomorrow, but we've got beer at my family's campsite."

Rory wrinkled her nose. "I already had that mead at dinner. I should refrain anyway."

"Was it actually good?"

"Unfortunately. Archer has done no wrong so far." She slipped her arm from Morgan's grip and rubbed her temples. "I know you don't want me apologizing for my family, so I'll just promise to do my best to keep you as far from them as possible for the rest of the festival. And thank you for so valiantly defending me."

"I'm here to be your shield, remember."

"My shield is one thing. My sword is another. I don't want you to feel like you need to come out swinging that way, although . . ." Rory smiled slightly. "I did appreciate seeing their reactions. You made an impression, which is more than I can do. They don't listen to a word I say anymore, as you might have noticed."

According to Rory's father, Rory didn't tell them anything. Clearly, they weren't listening to what Rory *was* saying to them, but Morgan wondered what else she was missing. Isaac had said they just wanted Rory to be happy, and while he might be a biased source, Morgan was having a hard time entirely discounting his opinion. The Sandlers were pushy, yes, but when Rory's mother had said she was concerned about Rory's happiness, she'd seemed sincere enough. But then, maybe Morgan wasn't a clearheaded observer, either. She'd always gotten along great with her mother, and when she disappointed people—Nicole, her father—they'd simply abandoned her, instead of pushing her harder. Surely Rory knew her own family and their intentions better than she did.

"Archer . . ." Morgan cut herself off, unsure of what she was asking. Whether Archer knew something she didn't? Jealousy kicked her in the gut, which was absurd. The only time Archer had gotten animated earlier was when competing came up. Any romantic intentions he or the Sandlers had for him and Rory were likely all in Morgan's head. Yet the idea that Archer might know more about Rory than she did irritated her.

Rory rolled her eyes. "His arrogance slays me. Don't get me wrong—you have to be an overconfident bitch to do things like have people light you on fire and trust you can prevent yourself from burning alive—but there's arrogance when it comes to magic and then there's being a general schmuck."

"Did you just call yourself an overconfident bitch? Because honestly, I don't see it."

"Oh, I totally am. But that's the difference between me and Archer. I know when to be overconfident, and when to admit I'm the same as everyone else."

Morgan shook her head. "I would never say you were wrong, but . . ."

"Because you're too kind. But the point is—Archer really believes he can convince me to return to competing, because my parents have convinced *him* that I've lost confidence and need to get it back. I haven't, in case you're wondering. They're all arrogant for assuming they know my reasons."

That was more than Morgan had ever previously heard Rory talk about why she quit competing, and a hundred questions danced on her tongue. They all made her afraid, though. Afraid of Rory shutting down. Afraid of ruining the better mood she was in. Afraid of assuming they'd grown closer than they actually had.

Morgan kicked a pebble down the path and made herself wait for it to roll to a stop before choosing her words. "Okay, how's this, then? I'll tell you that you're wrong right now. Maybe you do need an absurd amount of confidence to do what you do, but you're definitely not a bitch, and I will fight you on that."

"That's not fair because I don't want to fight you."

"Says the woman who fought me to order a pizza a few days ago, who spent twenty minutes arguing with me about whether pineapple counts as citrus—"

"I was right then, too," Rory said.

"Who gets competitive about how many books are in her to-be-read pile—"

"You started that."

"Who challenged me to a rugelach eating contest last night, then cheated by leaving all the lemon curd ones for last—"

"Hey." Rory put her hands on her hips. "That wasn't cheating. Those were my favorites. I was saving them."

"Conveniently."

"And you want to argue that I'm not a bitch?" Rory asked with a grin.

No, you are so perfect that sometimes I can barely breathe when I look at you.

Afraid she might say it out loud, Morgan bent down and plucked a couple of dandelions from the side of the path to give herself something to do until her mouth and her brain linked up. "Yes. Admit I'm right."

Rory narrowed her eyes.

"Any day now," Morgan said, weaving the dandelion stems together with the aid of just a touch of earth magic. It was the sort of elemental control her potion-making skills had made her best at. "Admit it, and I'll make you a beautiful loser's crown."

"I'll think on it."

She tucked the dandelions behind Rory's ear, hoping the pounding in her chest wasn't obvious. Then she backed up quickly in case it had been. "That is not an answer."

Rory didn't remove the dandelions, but she raised her hands, and the next thing Morgan knew, a pile of fallen leaves flew straight at her. Morgan shrieked as they whipped harmlessly by, circling her once before falling back to the ground. Loose strands of Morgan's hair that had picked up in Rory's highly focused gust resettled against her face and neck.

Sweet stars. Although they'd been talking about competing, somehow Morgan had forgotten that she was walking with Rory fucking Sandler. Come to think of it, she hadn't truly thought of Rory that way in a while. But whether Morgan remembered it or not, Rory was still her badass self.

Of all the types of elemental magic, air was considered the most difficult to master. By its very nature, it was hard to visualize and hard to focus on. Even Rory had needed to pause to lift those leaves, but she'd done it so precisely that it took Morgan's breath away.

"That's not an answer, either," Morgan said, collecting herself. "Although if you were trying to remind me that I'd lose to you in a real fight, you were successful."

"Not a chance. I'm secretly a wimp. I could never actually hurt anyone in a real fight. I'm all about flashy, showy stuff. My whole life has been about training for competitions. Nothing useful. Not like you."

"Your whole life?" She wasn't supposed to ask about this topic, but that surprised her too much.

Rory shrugged. "Since I came into my powers. My dad competed a bit before I was born, and he was the first person to train both me and my brother. My brother is powerful—I mean, it's wicked hard to pass the tests to become an Inquisitor—but he's good at by-the-book magic. Mastering normal spells. They gave up on him and focused everything on me. I wasn't really exaggerating about my life being one continuous cycle of eat, sleep, and practice."

"It paid off."

"But for what purpose? Did you know all these elemental spell-casting competitions came about because of combat? It's all rooted in the idea that witches should learn how to fight with magic. Not the hex-your-enemies kind of magic, which takes planning and supplies, but to fight like soldiers. Something immediately tangible that requires only the materials around you."

"They did?" That was news to Morgan, and it added a certain irony to the fact that the Council marketed competitive spellcasting to mundanes as a way to bridge the two communities. Although if its origins were martial in nature, there was also something nice about it now being used to promote intergroup relations. Everyone and everything could evolve for the better.

"They did," Rory reiterated. "Of course, the Council would absolutely deny that history because it would scare people, so . . ." She trailed her fingers along some low-hanging leaves. "It's about entertainment now. But you know, so's working at the Chalice. What's really the difference?"

"Drunk people hitting on you?"

"Nope. Got plenty of that both ways."

The path opened into the center of the festival grounds, acres of fields dotted with colorful tents and rows and rows of semipermanent wooden structures in a variety of shapes and sizes. One of those wood booths would be where Morgan spent many hours tomorrow and on subsequent days, but not one Morgan could see from here. The closest buildings would be for the food vendors.

A crew of volunteers was finishing up decorating the nearest tent. Based on the table configuration beneath it, Morgan guessed this would be the judges' tent for some of the smaller competitions held throughout the festival. They watched as a couple of witches were hanging a banner that announced tomorrow's kitchen witch baking competition, confirming her suspicion.

"You know, speaking of competing," Rory said, watching the witches struggle. They were using air magic to straighten the sign, but with far less precise control than Rory had demonstrated. "Why didn't you enter anything in the potion competition?"

Because your mother is right, and all I do is make stuff that's cute and pointless? Morgan swallowed down the thought.

"The competition is fierce. You have to come up with something either super powerful or innovative," she said. "When I make something that has any chance of winning, I'll enter. Let me show you our booth so you can find me tomorrow."

Rory looked like she might ask more, so Morgan took off at a jog, forcing her to catch up.

They spent the next couple of hours wandering the grounds, running into people they knew but hadn't seen in a while. Most of Morgan's friends required no introduction to Rory. Rory's friends, on the other hand, needed to be introduced to Morgan, and Rory decided on her own that they were the ideal candidates to test out their meet-cute on. After the initial shock of hearing Rory call Morgan "her girlfriend" during the first run-through, Morgan recovered and realized she'd better pay close attention, because Rory liked to embellish the story with each telling.

"When did we decide that you kissed me at the shop?" Morgan demanded quietly between conversations.

"Just now?" Rory cocked her head to the side and smiled sheepishly. "We had the basics down, but we needed flourish. A good story is like a spellcasting routine—once you have the trick mastered, you have to add some flair if you want to score well."

"But now I have more to remember."

Rory patted her cheek in a sarcastic manner. "I am positive you can do it."

Morgan was less certain, but by the third telling, she was adding her own details, and by the time they stopped at her family's campsite, she could envision the entire scenario in her head. Thinking about kissing Rory wasn't difficult, after all. She likely had entire lobes of her brain dedicated to it.

All this practice turned out to be fortuitous. Morgan hadn't expected her grandmom to be their toughest interrogator, but life was full of surprises. Grandmom June had refrained from questions all week, but as soon as they'd nestled around the campfire with a bag of marshmallows, she had Morgan and Rory cornered.

"Let me get this straight," her grandmom said. "You kissed Rory for Hazel's benefit, and Rory retaliated by kissing you back when you weren't expecting it? This all sounds needlessly complicated when you could have simply asked each other out on a date."

Morgan shrugged, wondering how Grandmom June could think such things when Morgan knew for a fact that the more bonkers a romance novel was, the more she loved it.

"When did this revenge kiss occur?" her grandmom asked.

"Saturday before the last coven meeting." The day Rory had agreed to this harebrained scheme seemed logical to Morgan. Pleased with her ability to ad-lib as well as Rory, even if lying to her grandmom felt wrong, she gave in to her impatience and shoved a marshmallow into the fire rather than wait for it to gently brown.

Grandmom June leaned forward in her chair, studying them long enough to make Morgan worry they'd given conflicting details and forget about her marshmallow. "That's a long time to wait for revenge," her grandmom said at last to Rory, her voice tinged with suspicion.

"It was all the more unexpected that way." Rory elbowed Morgan, but it was too late. Morgan's marshmallow had erupted in flames.

While Morgan desperately tried to salvage her dessert, her grandmom let out a sharp laugh. "I like that deviousness. Maybe some of your patience will wear off on Morgan."

"Hey!" It was hard to be indignant, though, with proof of her grandmom's point burning at the end of a roasting stick.

"So my daughter didn't fling her drink on someone?" Lianne asked, joining them at the campfire. Her mom offered Morgan a fresh marshmallow, and Morgan silently vowed not to waste another.

Rory buried her head in her knees, but Morgan made an innocent face as she scraped the blackened coal of the old marshmallow into the flames. "Would I do that? Who's making stuff up about me?"

Her mother didn't look entirely convinced—she knew Morgan well enough to know that scenario was entirely plausible—but she accepted the real fake version of their story easily enough.

Over the next hour, the sun dipped beneath the trees and disappeared, and the sky turned a velvety blue—not quite full black, but darker than it ever got in Harborage. The insects sang a noisy and repetitive lullaby that was occasionally interrupted by shouts of happy laughter or joyful yelling. They left when Morgan's grandmom, who had (thankfully) sobered up, reminded Morgan about how early she needed to get up the next day.

Morgan conjured her own magical light to guide them back to the cabin. Although it wasn't truly needed, she so rarely had an excuse to perform this kind of fun spell. Her grandmom's grandmother had probably grumbled about the younger generations turning to electricity when there was such a simple magical alternative.

Light shone from the cabin windows when they arrived, and Rory placed a hand on Morgan's arm. "I should have brought some supplies with me. I could have cast a silence spell around us so we could sneak in."

Morgan felt around in her pockets, but all she had was the bead from Erika, her phone, and an old movie ticket stub that looked like it had gone through the laundry a few times. While her shirt was cotton, from which she could purloin a thread, without a random button and a scrap of blank paper on her, tearing apart her clothes was pointless. "Can't help."

"Guess we're doing this the mundane way. I haven't tried sneaking around without magic since Isaac taught me how to create a silence bubble when I was fifteen."

When she was *fifteen*? Morgan had totally been right earlier. If teenage Rory had ever attempted to cast a love spell, she could absolutely have succeeded.

"He sounds like a good brother. I assumed he would side with your parents, but it seems like he supports your career move?" Morgan was still parsing out Isaac's take on everything.

"Yeah, he's on my side, mostly. He thinks I've lost my mind to have given up competing to work at the Chalice, but he'll respect my decision." Rory crept lightly up to the door and made a sheepish face. "I feel ridiculous, but I don't want to deal with them anymore tonight."

It turned out they didn't need to worry. Morgan could hear voices coming from somewhere in the enormous cabin, but the creaky staircase was only steps away from the entrance, and they didn't run into anyone as Rory quietly shut the door and led her to the third floor. There were two small rooms up here and a closet-sized bathroom, connected by a landing from the stairwell. Morgan hadn't noticed earlier, but the cabin smelled musty and faintly of vervain and vanilla. It was an odd and not exactly pleasant combination.

"Oh, right. I forgot to warn you about this." Rory opened the door to the room farthest from the stairs.

"About what?" Morgan placed her bag on the floor of the room and looked around as Rory flicked her wrist and flames ignited on a couple of candles. "Oh."

The room was barely big enough for a narrow desk against the open window and a bunk bed. Except it wasn't really a bunk bed, more like a loft bed. A sofa sat tucked away in the space below it.

Oh. The bed looked like a double, big enough for two people, but . . . Morgan's stomach spun in circles that left her nauseated. What was Rory expecting her to say? To do?

Before Morgan could decide, Lilith, who until that moment had apparently been snoozing on the bed, jumped up. Rory's familiar blinked disdainfully at them, then hopped down on the desk, deftly avoiding the candles, and streaked out the door.

"Rude. You didn't say hello to Morgan," Rory called after Lilith as the cat vanished down the stairwell. Turning back to Morgan, she continued. "I should've warned you about the space when you arrived. That's a sofa bed." Rory used her foot to gesture to the tiny couch. "In case you were worried. We don't have to share."

Right. That would have been truly horrible. She'd probably have rolled into Rory during the night. Tossed an arm over her. Grabbed a boob. Yup. Disaster averted. Morgan was glad for the dimness so Rory couldn't see the way she'd flushed.

"Ah." She lacked the wits to say anything else, visions of spooning a sleeping Rory with their bare legs entwined and the scent of Rory's shampoo taunting her mind's eye.

"I'll take it," Rory added quickly. "You're my guest, so you get the bed as long as you don't mind climbing up there."

"I don't mind." Morgan also spoke quickly, afraid anything else would give away her disappointment. "But I have to get up early, so I might as well take the sofa bed. Less likely I'll wake you in the morning."

Rory nudged her suitcase closer to the desk. "You'll wake me no matter what. I'm a light sleeper. So, you get the bed."

"Rock, paper, scissors?" Morgan suggested.

"No." Rory removed the dandelions that had miraculously not fallen off, and she tucked them into Morgan's hair. "The loser's crown is yours now, along with the bed."

Morgan didn't breathe until Rory stepped away, but she could smell her and felt slightly faint. "Why don't we agree to take turns?"

There, she was being eminently reasonable. There was nothing awkward going on here at all.

Rory pursed her lips, staring at her long enough for Morgan to fear she'd spoken some of these thoughts out loud. "Fine. We'll trade off. But you start with the bed. You deserve it after what you had to deal with today. You can say what you like, but I know you didn't sign up for so much shit when you offered to do me this favor."

"Fine," Morgan said. It was easier than arguing, and Rory's words had zapped her will to fight about it any further. As of this moment, she wanted nothing more than to crawl into the bed and not sleep.

Regardless of what her imagination had tricked her into believing, or how real things might have started feeling on her end, Rory had reminded her of the reality between them. Morgan was doing her a favor. Nothing more.

It was a lot easier to keep it in mind when Rory said it than when Morgan told it to herself. Probably because when Rory said it, it felt like a punch in the gut.

11

AFTER A FITFUL NIGHT'S SLEEP, FOR WHICH SHE HAD NO ONE to blame but herself, Morgan managed to sneak out of the Sandler family's cabin with only minimal human interaction. Rory groggily offered to have breakfast with her, but Morgan—still feeling stupidly morose—said she was planning on eating at the booth. Which meant she would spend the morning stupidly morose *and* stupidly hungry.

The morning air was shockingly hot, even for August, and Morgan was sweating far earlier in the day than she would have thought likely—partially because her mother had bought her a hot coffee instead of an iced, and partially because there were a lot of boxes to unpack and not a lot of space to do it in. In her grumpy mood, Morgan preferred to blame the coffee.

Unsurprisingly, it did not get any cooler as the sun climbed higher and the crowds descended on the festival grounds in earnest. The Bed, Bath, and Broom booth officially opened at noon, along with the festival itself, and although Morgan longed to go exploring, it wasn't an option. Hazel and other coven members stopped by to share gossip and make plans, but Rory wasn't among them. A few times, Morgan thought about texting her, but to what purpose? She was supposed to be there for Rory when Rory needed her. Presumably, when that happened, Rory would make it known. That was the favor Morgan was offering her.

Favor, favor, favor. The word had taken on the same unpleasant vibe as "cute," but this was no one's fault but her own. How many times had she told herself that she was only Rory's *fake* girlfriend? Even last night, while embellishing their meet-cute story, she hadn't truly accepted that it was all fake. A few moments here and there when they acted friendly had twisted her all up inside and made her believe there was a chance she could be more.

"And that's it," Morgan's mother announced. "We're all out of the sunblock. I didn't foresee that happening."

Grandmom June snorted. "What did I tell you? You should have done some scrying to know what to prepare."

"*You* could have done some scrying," Lianne retorted.

Morgan kept her mouth shut so no one would suggest that *she* should have done it. Instead, she shoved aside the pink curtain they'd hung and went into the back of the booth to sort through their inventory and make sure she hadn't forgotten to pack anything. Miraculously, she hadn't. They hadn't prepared a lot of the cooling sunblock, because historically it wasn't a big seller. Today's weather had simply affected purchases—even the weather forecasters hadn't divined the temperature would climb into the upper 90s.

Morgan discreetly tucked her own sunblock tube deeper into her purse, along with the one she'd set aside for Rory. It and her water bottle, which was charmed to chill its contents, were all that were keeping her from wilting.

"Do we have enough ingredients to make more?" Lianne asked. "It's supposed to cool off tomorrow, but it would be good to have some on hand. If people like it, they might want to stock up before leaving."

"We have most of what we need." Morgan scrolled through the inventory list on the shop's tablet. "No lemon balm, though."

Lianne popped the last bite of her lunch in her mouth. It was well after noon, but her mother hadn't slowed down to eat. "I'm sure someone's selling high-quality lemon balm. Grab me enough for a small batch, and I'll start it tonight."

"Morgan, your girlfriend's here!" her grandmom yelled from the front of the booth.

Fake girlfriend, her brain automatically corrected.

"I can do it," Morgan said, ignoring her grandmom. The sunblock was one of her mother's specialties, but spending more time with Rory was asking for trouble until she got her emotions firmly in check. Rory couldn't be annoyed with her if Morgan had to work, so it was a perfect excuse for avoiding the Sandlers.

"Don't be silly." Morgan's mother patted her arm. "Drop off the lemon balm before dinner. Things are starting to slow down."

Morgan grimaced into the tablet. She couldn't ignore Rory forever. And honestly, she didn't want to. She merely had to get her head on straight. There ought to be a spell for that, damn it. Morgan took a second to fix her hair, then recalled there was no point trying to look good for Rory. Grabbing her purse, she exited out the back of the booth. "Hi."

Rory spun around, looking significantly more cheerful and significantly less overheated than Morgan had expected. "Busy day?"

"At times, yeah. I didn't expect it to be this hot, either."

"No one did. Well, except this divination specialist in a workshop Hazel dragged me to this morning. Supposedly, she did." Morgan couldn't see Rory's eyes through her sunglasses, but she could hear the eye roll in her tone.

"Hazel's still determined, is she?" Hazel's mother and sister were both well regarded for their scrying talents, a gift Hazel did not seem to have inherited.

"We all have our magical hang-ups." Rory took a sip from her water bottle. "Did you eat lunch? Do you need anything? I stopped by earlier, but your mother said you were taking a break. It's been so busy, I didn't bother texting you since I doubted you could respond."

Rory had tried to see her? A drop of sweat ran down Morgan's cheek, and she brushed it away, feeling a touch lighter and less gloomy. "My mom didn't tell me that."

"She probably forgot."

Like Lianne kept forgetting to eat her lunch. That was certainly plausible. Morgan came by her tendency to be scatterbrained naturally.

"I have to buy some lemon balm, but otherwise I'm free the rest of the day." Morgan scanned the crowds and the lines of booths that spanned all directions.

Anything and everything magical or magic-related was for sale— from simple ingredients to prepared spells-in-a-bag. There were rare book sellers, jewelry-makers like Erika, and potion-makers like Morgan herself. Artisans sold beautiful scrying instruments and candleholders and censers. Talented green witches and herbalists sold custom incense blends, bags of dried leaves and seeds, or live plants. There were vendors selling ingredients for darker magics, too. Bones and dried blood for curses, live and dead insects, and more items that you had to know to ask for. If it was possible to put a spell on something or use it to that end, someone was probably selling it.

Since she hadn't left Bed, Bath, and Broom all day, Morgan wasn't sure where to go. For the moment, though, she simply wanted to get out of the teeming crowd and sit for a couple of minutes. Her feet were aching. "What have you been up to besides the workshop with Hazel?"

"Hiding from my family," Rory said. "I ran into some friends I used to know from back when but left when they started asking questions. So then I cheered myself up by going shopping. Which reminds me, I bought you a couple things."

"You didn't need to do that."

"Shush. I wanted to, okay?" Rory was wearing a tiny backpack, and she pulled it around to the side so she could reach into it.

They'd stopped under a tent that had been set up with picnic tables, although at this time in the afternoon, they had it largely to themselves. Morgan took a seat and drank more water, watching Rory.

Rory's sole concession to the heat was wearing a tank top, and Morgan realized she was searching Rory's arms for additional scars to match the one on her hand. She didn't see any, and while that was a good thing, it meant she was no closer to understanding why Rory had quit competing. Not that it was any of her business.

"Oh, here." Morgan handed her the tube of the cooling sunblock, thankful she could make a trade for the surprise gifts. "I saved you some when we started running low, in case you didn't have any."

Rory oohed as she examined the tube. "Thank you. I've never tried this before."

"It's good," Morgan said. "If I can say so myself. I mean, I didn't make it. My mom did. But it feels really nice when it's hot out."

"Of course you can say so yourself. And now for you—this is one of Erika's." Rory unwrapped a bracelet made of a string of snowflake obsidian beads and handed it to Morgan. It was beautiful, and Morgan could feel the power in the beads as soon as she touched it. "That should provide more protection from negativity than a single bead."

"It's gorgeous." It also had to be worth way more than the tube of sunblock. Morgan couldn't get away from the nagging voice in her head telling her that this was Rory paying her back for her help.

Ugh. If only the beads could ward off her internal negative energy as well as the external.

"That gift had a purpose," Rory said, pulling a small box out next. "This one is for fun." Smiling slyly, she opened the box, revealing what appeared to be four chocolate truffles. "They're called chocolate orgasms. I didn't know what flavors you'd like, besides no citrus, so there are double chocolate, hazelnut, cherry, and mocha."

Okay, aside from the heat rising up her neck when Rory said "orgasm" (and the momentary lapse in breathing as her imagination went places), this was a gift Morgan didn't feel weird about accepting. The truffles couldn't have cost nearly as much as the bracelet, and they looked amazing They were definitely magical, too, because they hadn't melted into a pile of chocolate sauce. "Ooh."

She reached for the box, and Rory snapped the lid shut on her fingers. "Don't eat them until later."

"I have terrible impulse control. You can't give me chocolate and tell me not to eat any."

"Morgan." Rory grabbed her wrist. "They are chocolate *orgasms*. I really don't think you want to eat one in public."

"Oh. Wait, what?" *Shit.* Had Rory seriously given her literal orgasmic chocolate?

Rory released her arm. "And now if my brother puts you under a truth potion, you can honestly say I've given you an orgasm. Four, actually."

That was funny and clever, but Morgan had to force herself to laugh through the shock. Was that flirting? It felt like flirting. If Hazel had given her these . . .

Scratch that. Hazel would not have given her these. Hazel might have bought some for herself, and shared them with a laugh, but she would not have bought a box solely and specifically for Morgan. And she certainly would not be smiling so mischievously at her if she did.

So no, there was no other way to interpret this except as flirting, right? Hands trembling, Morgan tucked the chocolates in her purse, hoping Rory wouldn't notice how badly she'd been knocked senseless. She made a second attempt at a laugh, and it was as unsteady as her fingers. "This is a first, then. I've never had anyone give me orgasms in public before. Well done."

"I can truly say it was my pleasure."

"But you can't say under truth potion that I've returned the favor. I should definitely rectify that." She barely resisted clamping a hand across her lips when she registered her own words. What if she'd been wrong and Rory hadn't been flirting? Why couldn't she keep her mouth shut?

Rory's wicked smile broadened. "Possibly you should. But for what it's worth, I prefer mine in private."

Fuck. Morgan suddenly felt like she was about to pass out. How could she be sitting in the middle of a field on a hot, sunny summer day and not be getting enough oxygen?

The bracelet Rory had given her twitched on her wrist as her magic flared, but luckily it was too heavy to move easily. Still, not great. Morgan inhaled, slowly, deeply, focusing on her breaths like she would for working a spell, and her pulse subsided.

She wished she could see Rory's eyes beneath her sunglasses, to have a better idea what she was thinking. As it was, all Morgan could see were nose freckles, and those lips, and the way Rory's tank top was clinging to her breasts, the skin of her collarbone shiny with perspiration. She yearned to kiss that divot at Rory's throat, then work her way up to Rory's face. Or down. Down was extremely promising, too. Rory was rubbing the sunblock on her arms, and what Morgan wouldn't give to be the one doing all of that touching.

She had to get up and move before she became incapable of it.

Wherever Rory's thoughts were, or perhaps whatever she saw on Morgan's face, her timing was perfect. She closed the tube and stuck it in her bag. "You said you needed lemon balm, right? Dried or fresh? There's a big tent where most of the herb vendors have set up shop."

"Um, yeah." Morgan pressed the water bottle against her forehead, wishing the bottle itself were as cold as magic was keeping its contents. "Fresh is ideal, but I'll probably have better luck getting what I need dried."

Rory tossed her backpack on. "This way."

They crossed through the milling crowds, past tents and booths selling everything from completely mundane food and drink to spellcasting supplies so odd or rare that Morgan didn't know their uses. She scarcely glanced at any one place for too long, her attention fully focused on the woman in front of her. Occasionally, she noticed someone nudge the person next to them, and a head swiveled in Rory's direction, but Rory moved with purpose, unaware of the attention or unwilling to become so.

At last they reached the enormous tent with tables spread out in a mazelike pattern. Jars and bundles of herbs and potted plants were displayed everywhere Morgan looked—from spell basics, like lavender and mint, to harder-to-obtain herbs, like mullein or betony. It was darker and cooler in this tent, charmed in an effort to keep the place chilled so the plants wouldn't wilt.

Rory perched her sunglasses on her head while Morgan figured out where to go. She picked a promising direction, leading the way around a merchant with several small lemon trees for sale.

On the other side of a sheet that had been hung to separate tables, she stopped abruptly at the sound of a woman's familiar voice. The water she'd been drinking curdled in Morgan's stomach as she turned.

Some twenty feet away, Nicole was talking to a group of unfamiliar people. Her ex looked the same as Morgan remembered her, only more Nicole-ish, if that were possible. Like the past two years had distilled her core personality traits into more potent versions of themselves.

Definitely a bad sign when Morgan had discovered those core traits were ambition, arrogance, and bitchiness.

Morgan took a step backward before she was spotted. Some confrontations were not worth it. They could not be won, and the last thing Morgan needed on top of her Rory-induced confusion was an encore of *cute* ripping open the scars she'd been doing her best to heal.

"What's wrong?" Rory placed a steadying hand on her back.

Morgan turned away, but Nicole remained a fuzzy presence in her peripheral vision. The mistake that had been haunting her for two years had become corporeal. "It's my ex. I'd rather avoid her."

"Bad breakup?"

"You could say that. I should have seen it coming, but I didn't, and she dumped me, and . . ." *Told me I'd amount to nothing and that she deserved better.*

Rory bit her lip. "Do you still have feelings for her?"

Morgan blinked, not expecting that question. "If by feelings you mean nausea, yes. I can't believe I ever cared for someone that shallow, and the memory makes me want to vomit. If you mean romantically, I'd rather kiss a swamp hag. In fact, I'm pretty sure that's exactly what I did, although she's disguised herself well."

"Hey, some of my favorite relatives are swamp hags." The tension drained from Rory's face, and she punched Morgan lightly on the arm. Morgan smiled in spite of herself.

"Shit. I think she spotted me." Although her perception of Nicole was skewed from this angle, Morgan would swear she could feel Nicole's eyes on her like the malicious poltergeist she was. If only Andy were here, maybe she could have banished her.

"Quick, look busy," Rory said.

"Doing—"

Rory kissed her.

This was not the practice kiss. Rory's hands were on her arms, and she was pressing her chest into Morgan's. Her lips were every bit as soft and sweet as Morgan remembered—and had replayed many times in her head—but they weren't as hesitant or enticingly awkward as they'd been before.

Rory was playing a role, Morgan reminded herself. And she was good at it, like she'd kissed Morgan a dozen times before. Like she'd never needed to practice it in the first place, because they were meant to kiss, their lips made for each other.

It was easier for Rory to pretend, maybe. Was Rory's blood on fire from this kiss? Was her body reacting like a million fireworks were exploding along her skin, mouth tingling, nipples tightening, heat spreading between her legs?

Fake! Morgan screamed at her body. *Knock it off!*

But her ovaries didn't know the difference, and honestly, wasn't that what the rest of her had been struggling with all day? That inability to tell? The kiss felt real—it all felt real—and she needed to act like it was, or this was going to look supremely weird.

Morgan raised her hand and brushed Rory's cheek. Somehow that intensified the sensation of Rory's mouth, her tongue caressing Morgan's lips, her breath mingling with Morgan's own. Then Rory pulled away, and it was over just as it was beginning. It wasn't a long, publicly inappropriate kiss at all, at least as long as no one knew how Morgan's body had reacted to it.

Rory inhaled sharply and her lips quirked into a half smile, but her eyes. Fuck, her eyes didn't drop Morgan's gaze. They were dark and heavy with longing, and even Morgan's battered self-confidence couldn't pretend she was the only one affected by that kiss. Something within Morgan's chest seemed to burst open, spreading warmth throughout her body, as though her heart had been waiting for a sign to let loose.

Of course, why simply have a crush on a woman who was so hopelessly out of her league when she could let herself go truly wild and free-fall toward . . .

Morgan slammed the door shut on that thought. Being turned on by a kiss was not the same thing as having real emotions.

"Is she gone?" Rory asked. Her voice was hoarse, and damn if that wasn't also a turn-on.

Swallowing, Morgan glanced sideways. "Think so."

"Good. Let's get you some lemon balm and get out of here."

Morgan approached the table with Rory at her side, and a witch with spiky hair that was alternating between shades of purple and blue every few seconds walked over to them. "Can I . . . ?" She gasped. "Are you Rory Sandler?"

Rory turned somewhat pink, and Morgan suppressed a chuckle. Kissing Morgan in public, gifting her chocolate orgasms? None of that could make her blush. But being recognized by a stranger? That, apparently, was a line too far. It was completely adorable.

Rory's discomfort lasted only a second, then she smiled the charming sort of smile that only a couple of weeks ago would have made Morgan weak in the knees. Before Morgan had discovered Rory's best smiles were the ones she kept hidden from strangers.

"I am."

"Would you mind . . . Could I get your autograph?" the spiky-haired woman asked.

"Can I help you?" An older woman approached, and Morgan dragged her attention away from Rory.

Morgan shook herself back to the task at hand. "Yes. Do you have lemon balm, and can you tell me how it was harvested?"

Morgan followed the woman down the length of the table while she answered her questions. Satisfied that it would work, Morgan requested two ounces. It was more than they needed, but it wouldn't hurt to have some extra in case the potion went weird.

Emboldened by the spiky-haired witch, several other people had approached Rory as well, and Morgan watched her sign autographs and chat. She didn't seem particularly at ease, but she did seem well practiced at it.

"Rory Sandler, huh, Morgan? Got to admit, I didn't think you had it in you."

That voice, so close to Morgan's ear, stiffened her shoulders. This time, Nicole wasn't speaking in her head. Morgan forced a smile as she thanked the herb vendor for the lemon balm, and turned to face Nicole. So much for hoping she'd dodged that hex.

"Perhaps you're not as unambitious as I thought," Nicole said. Up close, there was nothing ghostly about her. She was so solid and physically perfect that she might have been made of plastic. Her hair was pulled back into a low bun with not a strand out of place, and her floral-print sundress didn't show a wrinkle despite the heat. The silver studs in her ears gave off the faint glow of some kind of magic—subtle yet obvious at the same time. The witchy equivalent of a simple strand of pearls.

Morgan had once thought that such cool perfection made Nicole her ideal partner. After all, the way Nicole was always so put together was everything Morgan wasn't, so they must complement each other. But clearly she'd been wrong. Such cool perfection was nothing compared to Rory's casual hotness.

"Do you want me to hex you into next week?" Morgan asked.

"Like you could." Nicole pursed her coral lips. "I passed by your family's booth earlier. You're still working there? I truly believed you could do better. I hope you know that."

Morgan's grip tightened on the herb bag, and she shoved it in her purse. "I did do better," she said, nodding toward Rory. It was petty nonsense, and a lie, obviously, but Nicole hardly brought out her more mature side.

Nicole laughed. "Ouch. I'd ask what she sees in you, but you are pretty. That's enough for some people, and anyway, no one can figure out what's up with Rory these days. It's sad that she threw away her life like that."

"You know what else is sad? That you think I'd want to listen to anything you have to say."

Nicole tucked a strand of hair behind Morgan's ear. A chastisement. "I just came by to congratulate you on—"

"Morgan, you ready to go?" Rory interrupted, appearing at her side.

"Definitely."

Nicole held out her hand. "Nicole Miller. I'm an old friend of Morgan's."

Rory glanced down at Nicole's hand but didn't take it. Instead, she held hers out to Morgan. "Lovely to meet you."

Only after Morgan had pushed by Nicole while squeezing the life out of Rory's hand did she realize Rory had never given Nicole the courtesy of reciprocating the introduction. Clearly, Rory had learned a subtle insult or two from her political family, and Morgan giggled as they strolled away.

Once she started, she couldn't stop. Her emotional turmoil from the inescapable roller coaster she'd been on all day poured out of her in a fit of wild laughter. And the more she laughed, the more everything hurt, until she tasted salt on her lips and realized she was crying, and there were violets blooming at her feet. They glimmered as iridescent as amethysts for a second before turning solid. She'd lost control of herself *and* her magic, and that was not good. So not good.

Rory noticed, too, and she wrapped an arm around her, leading her out of the crowd. Half-blind in her hysteria, Morgan trudged along.

"Come on," Rory said, "we need to talk."

12

THEY WALKED IN SILENCE FOR A WHILE, MORGAN TRYING TO get herself under control, and Rory with a grim but determined expression. She led Morgan away from the vendor field, down well-trod trails and overgrown paths, winding them past campsites until Morgan—in her bleary confusion—wasn't sure where they were. Vaguely, she was aware that the temperature was cooling, and the sky was graying, but it took too much out of her to focus on that, and she risked another bout of tears if she did. Not to mention sprouting more magical plants.

Eventually, Rory stopped them in the middle of a path in front of an enormous boulder. Moss covered it in lazy trails that almost resembled a door, too green to be real but as soft and lush as a carpet. Somewhere nearby, the river that paraded through the center of the festival grounds sang out, but Morgan had no idea where she'd ended up.

With a quick glance around, Rory took her hand again. "Come on."

"Where?" But Rory was already pulling her forward, and half of Morgan's arm disappeared into the rock along with Rory. Surprise snapped Morgan out of her funk, and she followed. They were on another path, this one leading down to the river.

"A cousin showed me this secret trail years ago," Rory said. "Someone showed her, and so on. It's been this way since before we were born. No idea who did it originally, or who's been maintaining the illusion, but someone must have really wanted their own private path. I used to come down here sometimes and practice my water magic where there wouldn't be an audience."

The tightness around Morgan's lungs had lifted, but her mental state remained questionable. She was okay for now, but who knew how long that would last? Strangely, she wasn't embarrassed. She'd lost her shit in front of Rory—behavior that once would have made her want to lie down and let the earth reclaim her body—and it didn't bother her. Or, well, it bothered her to have lost it so thoroughly, but Rory's presence was a comfort and not an escalating factor, and that was really something she ought to give more thought to when she was feeling stable.

It was a short walk from the hidden door to a bank about three feet above the river. The current was slow here, the water clear enough to see the colorful stones below. Dragonflies shimmered in shades of red and blue as they flitted through the reeds, their lacy wings sprinkling trails of silver dust that evaporated into the air. More than just the plant life around the festival grounds had absorbed magic.

Rory sat on a rock that looked as though it had been carved to make a bench. "Tell me, do I need to set your ex on fire," she asked, "or is that too easy? We could turn her hair into snakes, or what about a spell so all of her words come out backward?"

"That one. That would be fitting." Morgan sat next to her, all of her willpower keeping her upright when she'd rather rest her head on Rory's shoulder.

Rory must have sensed that. She cautiously stroked Morgan's arm like Morgan was a feral animal who might strike at her throat at any moment. "I know I said we should talk, but do you actually want to talk? We could craft our hex instead, or just enjoy the view."

Morgan lowered her head, rubbing her thumbs together. "I don't even know why I flipped out exactly. I mean, it's stress. That's all."

"So she didn't say something particularly rude?"

Oh, Nicole had, but since one of the things was about Rory, Morgan would keep that to herself. "Same old shit. Nicole wants to get elected to the Witch Council someday. I have no idea what she's doing to that end, but when I met her, she was in Harborage for a summer, supposedly working on a book about New England's magical history."

"A very original topic." Rory was only trying to cheer her up, but her sarcasm wasn't misplaced.

"Harborage has one of the longest active covens in the country, so she was interviewing lots of people, doing research." Apparently, her mouth had decided to talk, regardless of what her brain preferred. Typical. "I think, in retrospect, she was looking for an excuse to introduce herself to anyone she thought was important. When she figured out that most of our coven doesn't have a lot of political connections—and doesn't care about them—she got angry about wasting her time and left."

"And took it out on you?"

Just like it should have been embarrassing to have become hysterical in front of Rory, it should have been humiliating to talk about Nicole. But the more the words dribbled out, the more anger warmed Morgan's blood. And the anger felt better than the pain. In anger, she could reclaim some dignity. "At first, she tried to convince me to leave with her. I thought that was a sign that she really loved me, you know? But when I had no interest in leaving—when I tried to convince her to stay—she lost it. She told me I had no ambition. That what I did was cute but meaningless, and I was wasting my talents. That she deserved someone who was better than that."

"Oh, I'm definitely hexing her, but I was being too nice. Boils, it is. Or spiders." Rory snapped her fingers. "No—spider-filled boils."

Morgan couldn't believe that got a laugh out of her, but it was hardly the first time today that Rory had made her emotions swing erratically. "That's disgusting."

"That's the goal. To make the hex fitting."

"She wasn't totally wrong, though." Morgan sighed. "What I do is cute but meaningless."

"Bullshit. What you do is create things that make people happy. That's not meaningless."

"But it's not important."

Rory frowned at her. "You're going to tell me, right now, when you're clearly unhappy, that happiness isn't important? Making someone happy is one of the greatest gifts you can give them."

Morgan rubbed her eyes. "I'm not explaining myself well. I mean, yes, happiness is good. But what I do and the potions I make aren't significant. It's not anything that makes a real impact. It's not even anything I could enter into the potion contest if I hope to place in it. I want to prove I can do more than tweak my grandmom's spells."

"To other people, or yourself?"

"Both?"

A shadow passed over Rory's face, and she shook her head. "You don't need to prove anything to anyone. If you want to dream big and create something because it's your goal to win a contest or find professional success or save the world, then okay. But if you're doing it because some spiteful witch made you feel like you're not worthy of being loved or valued unless you make a name for yourself, then fuck that. Fuck *her*. You are enough as you are."

Oh, sweet stars, she was going to cry again. Morgan forced down the prickling sensation behind her eyes. It was easy for Rory to say these things. Rory had done something significant. People might not understand why she quit competing, but there was no question that Rory's talents in elemental spellcasting placed her in a category all her own. Even if Rory spent the rest of her life working at the Empty Chalice, Rory would go down in history.

Still, she was trying to make Morgan feel better, and that wasn't meaningless. There might be nothing special about her, but Rory taking the time to talk to her, to listen, made Morgan feel special anyway. The knots holding Morgan's heart in check slipped a little more.

She was so screwed.

She stared at her knees, listening to the stream gurgle past and feeling the breeze pick up. After a few steadying breaths, she raised her head.

"Thank you. But I'm going to keep working on that potion for world peace, because someone's got to create it." Morgan hoped the obvious humor in that would offset the real desperation behind it.

"It is a worthy goal."

"I honestly don't have any ideas." *Because you're a small thinker,* Nicole said in her mind, and Morgan grimaced.

Rory poked her in the arm. "Come on. I just gave you a great one. A spell that causes spider-filled boils."

It worked as well to cheer her up the second time as the first, and Morgan laughed and pretended to shudder. "Gross. What's with you and spiders?"

"Spiders are poorly understood creatures. They eat other, actually gross insects. But fine. I'll help you brainstorm something without spiders, but I'm disappointed in your anti-arachnid stance."

"Hey, don't make me out to be the bad witch here. The spiders started it by having all those legs."

"Oh, it's the legs that bother you?" Rory grabbed her arm and walked her fingers up it in imitation of a spider, and Morgan screeched in surprise.

She barely had time to process how close Rory was, how much they were casually touching, before something *else* touched her forehead. "What the . . . ?"

A drop of water. The sky rumbled, and too late, Morgan realized how dark the clouds had gotten over the last few minutes.

"Oh no. My lemon balm is going to get wet." Morgan clutched her purse. It was made of mundane cloth with no magic to protect the contents.

Rory jumped up. "Your lemon balm, my phone, your chocolates. We should walk quickly."

Oh yeah. Morgan had her phone in her purse, too. Shit.

The need to move and move fast didn't allow her to wallow any longer. They jogged back onto the not-so-hidden path as the water droplets came down faster and fatter. Morgan let Rory lead the way again since she was unsure of the most direct route to shelter. Thunder cracked the sky, and in the distance, Morgan could hear other people yelling. Raindrops became rain by the time they hit the main road, and wind whipped hair about her mouth and leaves around her ankles.

Rory grabbed her arm. "Hold still."

Rain was already plastering Morgan's clothes to her body, although she futilely clutched her purse against her chest. Her head down—she was cradling her purse like a baby—she watched through her eyelashes as Rory whispered an incantation. Her face was strained until prickles of magic swept over Morgan's skin.

The rain around them stopped.

Morgan gaped.

Rory's posture relaxed, but her eyes remained dark with concentration, and she pushed wet hair off her forehead. "Walk slowly."

Morgan was amazed they could walk at all, but she did, following the pace Rory set. Rory couldn't keep the spell perfectly in unison with their motion for the entire distance, but by the time they came upon the Sandlers' cabin, Morgan was only slightly wetter than she'd been when Rory had told her to stop moving. As far as flashiness and showmanship went, this sort of thing was unlikely to win any trophies, but Morgan was suitably impressed.

The cabin appeared to be deserted, but just in case, they headed straight upstairs. Rory had folded the sofa bed back into a sofa after Morgan left this morning, and after she took off her backpack, she tossed herself on it. Rain swept into the room through the open window, covering the desk in mist, and Morgan shut it all but an inch.

"That was exciting." Rory's wet hair stood straight up, and Morgan turned away so she wouldn't be tempted to run her fingers through it.

"Do you need something for the magic depletion?" she asked, removing the lemon balm from her purse. Her fingers bumped the box with the chocolate orgasms, and a shiver rippled through her. Doing her best to ignore the box and the sensation, she placed the bag with the herbs on top of her pack. It was completely dry, so that was a relief.

"I'll be fine, but I might sit here for a moment and stare into space."

Morgan wouldn't have minded peeling off her damp clothes and putting on some dry ones, but with Rory resting on the sofa, even with her eyes closed . . . She was sure Rory wouldn't mind if she changed, or she could do it in the bathroom, but either way, the concept of removing clothing and Rory were now linked in Morgan's head, and the best way to handle that was to put both ideas out of her mind. Much easier said than done, especially with everything that had happened today.

Catching her reflection in the tiny mirror above the desk, Morgan scowled. Thank the stars Rory had shut her eyes. Her braid, which she'd been fairly certain was falling apart before the rain, was an utter loss. A couple of tiny leaves were stuck to her, too. She looked fantastic.

Morgan pulled the wet tie from her hair, and it splattered water across the desk.

"Can I fix it?" Rory asked.

Startled, Morgan spun around. Rory had opened her eyes and was watching her with an eager expression. Morgan combed through her wet strands with her fingers, trying to act as though she didn't want to fling herself at Rory's feet. "I'm not sure you're exactly qualified, are you? How much braiding experience do you have with that inch of hair on your head?"

Rory ran her hand through her hair. "Oh, come on. It's got to be closer to two inches in some places. And for the record, I'm perfectly capable of braiding hair. Just not my own, which is why I chopped it all off. That, and I was tired of it catching on fire."

Ignoring the voice of caution, Morgan sat next to Rory and hoped it wasn't obvious how quickly her heart was beating. It had to be her imagination, but she thought she could feel the heat rising off Rory's body as she shifted beside her. When Rory's fingers began detangling her hair, Morgan dug her nails into her palms.

Rory's fingers were far more gentle on her hair than Morgan ever was, yet every time one made contact with her scalp, Morgan was afraid she was noticeably twitching.

Still, her eyes were closing. Even as her body was wide-awake with barely suppressed need, her brain was shutting down. Lulling her into a contented—albeit also painfully turned-on—state. It was an odd combination, and a blissful one.

Then Rory snagged a knot with her finger. She swore and let the braid fall apart. "Sorry. I guess I am out of practice."

Morgan winced, but it wasn't especially painful, and anyway, the pain jolted her back to reality. So that was good.

"It's fine." Morgan reached behind to finish undoing the braid, and her hand collided with Rory's. This time, there was no hiding the way her breath hitched when their skin touched. No pretending a streak of pure fire hadn't shot straight down into her core.

Flailing internally, Morgan didn't dare move as she tried to figure out what to do next. She expected Rory to yank her hand away, but she, too, seemed frozen in place, letting her skin linger against Morgan's. Was that such a surprise? It couldn't have been more than an hour ago that she'd started to truly question Rory's behavior. Had been convinced Rory was flirting with her.

Morgan wet her lips. "When you kissed me earlier . . ."

Oh, sweet stars. Oh, fuck. Was she actually doing this?

Ridiculous questions. Was it a terrible idea? Then, yes, of course she was doing this. Although even her tendency to blurt out everything going through her head was having trouble with these particular words.

Morgan tried again. "Was it just because of my ex?"

She couldn't have brought herself to ask the question if she'd been facing Rory, but this way, she could stare at her own leg and focus on the bit of mud that had spattered around her ankles. She could pretend she was as fearless as she acted, when in reality, her heart was stuck somewhere in her throat, and if her pulse beat any faster, she might faint.

"Yes?" Rory sounded uncertain, and Morgan's insides shriveled. Only the weight of her disappointment held her down on the sofa. It was suffocating. "It wasn't one of my better decisions, and I'm sorry. Our fake meet-cute story aside, I should have asked before I did it."

"It's okay." Nothing was okay, and any moment, Morgan would appreciate regaining control of her limbs so she could bolt out of the cabin. She'd have to find some way to uphold her promise to Rory, to continue being her fake—very, very fake—girlfriend, but first she'd need to go back to the river and drown herself in it. Stand in one of the fields and ask the lightning flashing outside to strike her down. If she stayed here a second longer, the embarrassment was going to kill her, and that would be a humiliation all of its own.

Thunder rumbled, and it was like the blood pumping through Morgan's ears. The storm was gaining in intensity, and it made her want to scream.

Rory dropped her hand at last. "It's not, though. You mentioned your ex, and I got jealous."

"Oh." Hold on. That actually didn't sound awful.

"So, I mean, that's why I did it." Rory's voice had grown so quiet that she was hard to hear over the rain lashing at the cabin windows. "I should have asked first, but it seemed like a good excuse to kiss you again."

13

MORGAN HAD THE BRIEF THOUGHT THAT SHE WAS GLAD SHE WASN'T tent-camping, as if her mind couldn't handle what it had heard and needed something simple and boring to focus on. Something that made sense.

Then again, fuck sense.

She spun around on the sofa so quickly she was sure she'd be left with fabric burns on the undersides of her legs. "You did want to kiss me?"

Rory's expression was adorably confused. Like she was also trying to piece together what was happening. The look in her eyes made Morgan's insides melt.

The room had gotten dark, and Morgan longed to turn on the light so she could see Rory better, but now she *didn't* want to move. Her knee was touching Rory's, and when in the world had her knee become an erogenous zone? Rory's face was inches away, her lips slightly parted. She was so close. Too close.

It felt like gravity was pulling Morgan into her. Rory was the sun—the object around which Morgan's world had circled for the past year, the source of so much light and warmth—and with Rory's words, Morgan's orbit had broken and she was descending into her at last.

"Yeah?" Rory quirked a small smile when she seemed to pick up on Morgan's thoughts. "And here I was thinking I was being way obvious this past week."

"I'm a little slow some—" She never finished the thought because her face finally crashed into Rory's in an explosion of stars that should have rocked the galaxy.

Morgan closed her eyes, at an utter loss as to what to do. This wasn't the practice kiss or the kiss for show in the herb sellers' tent. While the first two had been amazing in their own way, her heart recognized the difference. This was a real kiss. She was hesitant all over again, overwhelmed by emotions that were riding as high and as wild as the storm outside. But also confident, for the first time, knowing this kiss meant something. Was truly wanted. That *she* was wanted.

And she wanted Rory. Sweet stars, she'd wanted this so much for so long, was it any wonder she was having a complete meltdown now that she had it? She'd dreamed about kissing Rory, fantasized about a whole lot more. But the reality found her unprepared because she'd never expected it to happen.

How is this happening? Why? That deep pool of self-doubt Nicole had first dug two years ago, and then stirred up again today, wouldn't entirely be silenced, but Morgan could ignore it when Rory's hands cupped her cheeks, pulling her in closer.

Morgan caressed her arms. She could smell the rain on Rory's skin, taste it on her lips. Her tongue was liquid fire, and so was the ache building in her body. Morgan moaned, and they both startled as the wind changed direction and slapped the window glass.

Rory pulled back, her fingers trailing down Morgan's chin. Her cheeks were flushed, her lips bright red. She rested her head against the sofa and gazed at Morgan in a way that made Morgan feel like she was far more than mere Morgan Greenwood. Like she was one of the many goddesses around the world to whom witches owed their creation.

And, honestly, more practically, in a way that made her want to tear her clothes off.

"Can we safely say we crossed the boundary from fake dating to real?" Rory asked.

"Can I admit that the only reason I offered to be your fake girlfriend was because I wanted to be your real one?"

Surprise knocked away Rory's smile, and she sat up straighter. "Seriously?"

"I mean, I wanted to help you, don't get me wrong. But that was basically what drove my whole drunken offer."

Rory laughed, an incredulous sound. "I wondered why you did, since I really was convinced you didn't like me."

"Oh, well, now you know the truth. I liked you too much to be my loud and obnoxious self around you."

"Let's go with your vibrant self."

Vibrant? Morgan liked that way better than loud and obnoxious. No wonder she had such a crush on Rory.

Such a *crush*? Those knots holding her heart in place had come completely undone right along with Morgan's braid. So okay, maybe this was more than a crush. Or it had become so over the last couple of weeks.

Blood rushed to Morgan's face. "Every time I tried talking to you, my tongue would get tied in knots. I was so intimidated."

"I am *not* intimidating."

It was Morgan's turn to look incredulous. "You are Rory fucking Sandler. You are talented and smart and beautiful, and you have the most adorable freckles around your nose. You are the dictionary definition of intimidating."

Rory lightly shoved Morgan's legs. "No. First of all, I'm pretty sure you're the only person to ever call me beautiful. I'm happy when I get called cute, and since I cut my hair off, I'm just happy when people don't mistake me for a boy. Although that doesn't bother me so much as it confuses me, since my body isn't particularly boy-shaped."

Morgan was very aware of that fact at the moment as Rory shifted position, and her gaze flickered from Rory's face to the way her chest strained against her tank top. Rory seemed to notice, and she smirked.

"Secondly," she continued, making a point to lift Morgan's chin and redirect her attention, "I like to pretend I don't have freckles. Never mention them again. Thirdly . . . Okay, fine. I do like to think I'm smart and talented. I'm an overconfident bitch, remember? But I am not intimidating. Please tell me I'm not intimidating you."

Morgan tossed her hair back and pretended she had some dignity left. All it took was one for-real kiss with Rory and she was confessing all of her foolishness. Rory's lips were more powerful than a truth potion.

"Not right now. You became a lot less intimidating once I got to know you." Morgan paused. "You're still a little, though."

Rory shook her head. Then she leaned forward, grabbed Morgan's face, and kissed her again. Pure, ecstatic happiness toppled Morgan over, and Rory landed partially on top of her. Her head hit the sofa arm harder than she would have preferred, but it didn't make a difference. Her body was entangled with Rory's, their legs entwined, arms wrapped around each other for support. Morgan couldn't feel any pain. Only damp skin, soft curves, and need burning inside of her.

"You are a completely charming, gorgeous dork," Rory said, pushing Morgan's hair back, and that was perfect, too. Morgan would take vibrant, take dork—damn it, she'd accept dumbass, even—if Rory called her that while kissing her.

"Can I kiss your freckles?"

"What?"

Morgan reached up and brushed Rory's nose with her finger. "They're adorable."

"I just got through telling you how much I hate them. I've tried a dozen spells to remove them, and nothing has worked for long. The last time they came back, I think I made them worse."

"You tried to get rid of them?" Morgan practically shrieked. "Never do that. I love them."

"You are so weird."

"So was that a yes?"

Rory leaned over until their mouths barely touched, and she kissed Morgan's lower lip. Her mouth was as light and soft as a feather, but Morgan's blood was turning to lava, and she sucked in a breath. "You can kiss me anywhere you want," Rory said.

Oh no. She should not have said that, not even if she meant it, and the gleam in Rory's eyes suggested she did.

"That's . . ." Morgan lost her thought as Rory kissed her chin and began slowly nibbling her way down Morgan's throat. Each kiss was like that first—featherlight—and each one burned Morgan from the inside out. "I'll take you up on that."

Rory tugged aside the loose collar of Morgan's shirt, exposing more skin. She was going to lose her mind. Had she ever been this turned on before in her life? Every piece of fabric touching her chafed. She wanted to pull everything off, to hurry Rory's descent down her body. But she wanted to hold on to every moment, too. To make this exquisite agony last forever.

Rory's fingers skimmed along the edge of Morgan's waistband, and Morgan squirmed beneath her. "I don't think you're capable of taking me up on anything at the moment," she whispered.

"Fair." She wasn't sure how she was managing to speak. "But I'll turn the tables." She gasped. "Eventually."

She tried to add more—to tell Rory exactly all the places where she wanted to kiss her—but Rory had pressed her lips to Morgan's stomach, and the only sound emanating from Morgan's mouth was a moan that she hoped there was no one else in the cabin to hear. She'd occasionally wished she was less soft around the middle, but the way Rory nipped at her, that slight pressure of teeth was enough to change her mind. Rory licking and sucking on her delicate skin had played a significant role in Morgan's fantasies, but clearly she'd done herself a disservice by leaving her least favorite body parts out of them. That would be no more.

She whimpered, and Morgan stuffed one hand in her mouth. With the other, she grasped for Rory, needing to touch her, but she couldn't reach more than her head. That would have to do, and she curled her fingers around a fistful of Rory's hair.

Then Rory changed direction, shoving aside the damp fabric of Morgan's shirt. That was almost more bearable, though her nipples were screaming out in anticipation of their turn and her mouth hungered to kiss Rory's again. She was an absolute mess of need and sensation and longing. Part of her wished for nothing more than to touch Rory's face, to stare into her eyes, to feel her silently breathe against Morgan's body. And that felt dangerously more intimate than any kisses, and frankly, it kind of scared the shit out of her.

From two stories below, a door slammed and the voices of Rory's brother and Erika drifted up the stairs. The baby fussed, and Isaac called up, "Anyone here?"

Morgan groaned.

Shifting her weight, Rory swore. "There's no way we aren't about to be interrupted."

As disappointed as she was, Morgan was also the tiniest bit relieved. The intensity of kissing Rory was almost too much. She was normally the dive-headfirst-into-the-pool kind of girl, but in this case, she feared she'd drown. It wouldn't hurt to take this slowly, to enjoy and savor it.

Maybe Rory was thinking the same things, because the kiss she planted on Morgan's cheek was deliciously sweet, as was her smile. "I'm glad we had this conversation."

Morgan laughed, stealing one last caress of Rory's face. Then she reached up and kissed Rory's nose. "Yes, finally."

Rory smacked her with a pillow. "Ugh. You were referring to my freckles, weren't you?"

"Totally." The bewildered expression Rory shot her made Morgan grin harder. In fact, she might just end up grinning for the rest of her life.

14

THE REST OF THE DAY AND EVENING PASSED MORGAN BY IN A blur. Even having dinner with Rory's family and Archer, and enduring the strained conversation that came with it, couldn't lower her mood. If anything, each time she caught Archer glowering at her, Morgan floated a bit higher.

She stayed up late with Rory, Isaac, and Erika, drinking mead and playing card games, and she barely had a moment to spare for being sad about missing the first night's concert. When she went to bed at last, her head full of thoughts of kissing Rory, she was so tired and drunk on her own happiness that she fell asleep before it could happen. She even forgot to argue with Rory about switching beds.

That was okay. Rory got up with her in the morning, had breakfast with her, and kissed her goodbye before Morgan made her way to the Bed, Bath, and Broom booth. Thanks to the rain, the air smelled extra fragrant. Water droplets hung thick and heavy on the trees, and branches and leaves sparkled like diamonds in the morning sun, blinding in their beauty. The world was vibrant, and Morgan smiled.

Although yesterday's storm had passed quickly and the skies had cleared overnight, puddles remained on the paths. Morgan had to resist the urge to jump in them like she was five years old again. Instead, she put on one of her favorite playlists and danced about the booth while she worked. She had zero cares in the world until her mother arrived around noon and reminded Morgan that she hadn't dropped off the lemon balm last night.

Morgan swore, cringed about swearing in front of her mother, and pulled the bag out of her purse. "I lost track of time yesterday."

That was a regular enough occurrence that Lianne didn't question why, which was a relief. Morgan was bursting with the need to scream that she'd kissed Rory, but that wasn't supposed to be news, since they'd already been allegedly dating. Frustrating.

"It's not a problem," her mother said, taking the lemon balm. "The rain would have made it impossible to start, but can you update the inventory this morning while I work on it? I pulled the rest of the ingredients yesterday, and we got a special order for a handfasting blessing potion. See if we have what's needed here?"

The blessing potion was essentially a happiness potion, one that tied the two would-be spouses (or really, anyone who drank it) emotionally together for a brief period. It was one of those items that wasn't generally available for sale, but witches in the know might ask for it. Given her state of mind, thinking about it made Morgan herself happy, though it was a challenging potion to create.

Shaking her hips to the music, Morgan pulled a jar of dried chamomile from the inventory. And frowned. That didn't look quite right. Her handwriting on the label declared it to be chamomile, but when she unscrewed the lid and sniffed it, her nose confirmed what her eyes had already insisted upon. It wasn't chamomile in the jar, but yarrow. Morgan's good mood evaporated like last night's storm remnants, and she switched off the music as she assessed the extent of her mistake.

Conclusion: big.

She'd mislabeled more than one jar, and one of those jars was partially depleted. Morgan searched her brain for where the chamomile-that-was-not-chamomile had gone, and realized she was the one who'd used it—in Rory's relaxation potion.

She'd been horribly distracted that day when she made the potion, too busy remembering her practice kiss with Rory the night before. She *knew* she hadn't double-checked the ingredients and had just trusted the labels. She'd made the relaxation potion so often that there was no point in thinking about it.

She very clearly should have thought about it.

Because—oh shit.

Heart hammering, Morgan sank back on her heels, walking herself through the rest of the potion-making process. Hadn't she thought the potion looked off-color at one point? She'd dismissed that concern, but what if it had been a mistake to do so? Rory had said nothing about the potion not working, but Rory was kind and Morgan had gifted her the potion, so there was a good chance she'd have shrugged it off and kept quiet.

The chamomile in the potion was there to induce relaxation and sleep. Yarrow would induce . . . Morgan ran through a mental list of its properties and clasped a hand over her mouth.

Oh shit turned to *oh fuck*.

Yarrow was used in potions to promote love or success. Or maybe success *in* love—it was an old witches' tale that giving the object of your affection a bouquet of yarrow during a full moon was tantamount to casting a love spell. It wasn't true, but it was the sort of scandalous story that very young witches whispered to one another.

The point was, combine the yarrow with where her distracted thoughts had been that day, the way she'd been daydreaming about kissing Rory, about wanting that kiss to be for real, and . . . No, no, no. Fuck, no. A scream clawed its way up Morgan's throat, and she bit her hand to hold it in.

Her vision temporarily blackened. The air in her lungs turned to stone.

The store's spell book was locked up in a chest in one of the boxes; Grandmom June always insisted they bring it in case they got a request for one of their less popular potions and needed to consult it. As soon as she recovered, Morgan flipped through the pages, her hands trembling. She'd seen a spell for a love potion in there once, written in her grandmom's old-fashioned handwriting. Practically every witch had one—a love potion or a love spell that they'd formulated or found in their younger years. They were against the laws, of course, but so were lots of spells, and only giving one to someone counted. Designing one was fine.

By the time she found her grandmom's version, tucked in the back, her lips had gone dry. It wasn't precisely what she'd made, but it might be close enough. So much of magic was about intention and will, more so than ingredients. And there was no question where Morgan's intentions had been that day.

She was going to be sick. Morgan closed her eyes, dizziness washing over her.

How is this happening? Why? The questions that had intruded on Morgan's thoughts yesterday when Rory kissed her returned with a vengeance. Now she thought she had the answer. It was the only logical explanation.

Why would Rory fucking Sandler kiss her? Tell her she was a gorgeous, vibrant dork?

Because Morgan had accidentally given her a love potion.

Fuck. Fuck. FUCK.

She couldn't breathe. Every hair on her arms and the back of her neck rose to attention with her power, which was threatening to spiral out of control. Half-blind with her increasing panic, Morgan texted Hazel. She hadn't even told Hazel what happened between her and Rory yesterday. She'd wanted to do it in person. Needless to say, this was not how she'd envisioned that conversation.

MORGAN: Where are you? I need you. Now.

Morgan tugged aside the curtain separating the front of the booth from the storage and work area. Her mother and Grandmom June were busy chatting with old friends, oblivious to her meltdown. Good. She couldn't handle questions or concerns. She couldn't handle *anything*, as this disaster was proving. She discreetly pulled the curtain closed.

Morgan shoved the spell book back in the chest and tossed the mislabeled herbs all over the ground outside before Hazel responded.

HAZEL: On my way. BB&B?

MORGAN: NO. I'll meet you.

Where did she meet Hazel in private? Think, she had to think, but she was incapable of thinking as panic clouded her brain.

MORGAN: By the fire circle.

It wasn't a particularly secluded area, but at this time of the day, no one had any reason to be there. It would do.

HAZEL: Ok. You all right?

No, absolutely not.

Naturally, her mother chose that moment to enter the back of the booth. "Morgan? Are you sick?"

She nodded, afraid if she opened her mouth too much, she'd vomit. All she managed to mumble was, "Sorry," before dashing out.

Morgan ran, darting and weaving her way through the shoppers and gawkers meandering around the vendor area. The midday sun had burned off the puddles or she'd have trounced through them without noticing. Her sandals dug into her feet, and she ignored them, too. She ignored everything—the air scraping at her lungs, the burn in her calves, the sweat forming on her forehead. The exercise didn't clear her head, but it made the panic temporarily subside and winded her too much for her magic to let loose.

As long as she moved, she could run from the mess she'd created.

And as long as she ran, she might avoid seeing Rory, or Rory's brother, or someone else connected to Rory. Someone she couldn't look in the eye. She was barely holding it together as it was.

She had to stop eventually, though, and Morgan skidded to a halt as she crossed an empty field, approaching the fire circle. The moment she did, panic overtook her once more.

Hazel must have been close by, because she'd beaten Morgan there. She was sitting on one of the logs around the perimeter, her hair braided in two Princess Leia–style buns. Morgan always teased Hazel when she did that, but she didn't have it in her to do so today. She barely made it to the log before she burst into tears.

"Oh no." Hazel rested a hand on her back. "Your hair is flying around your head. It's scary. You need to calm down. Is this about Rory?"

Morgan nodded through her sniffling, willing herself to get her magic and voice under control so she could speak, but the weather seemed to be mocking her.

Where was the storm now? Where was the oppressive heat? It was a fine, sunny day. Hot but not too hot. Humid but not unbearable. The grass was cool on her feet, the breeze was alive in the trees, and the air drifting her way from last night's fires smelled faintly sweet with herbs and magic.

It was perfect, and it was a lie. It had to be. Everything perfect was a lie. That's why she should have known yesterday was, too.

"Talk to me," Hazel said.

Morgan drew a deep, shuddering breath. "I really, really, *really* fucked up this time."

Hazel gave her a moment to collect herself and offer more information, but even those few words had been hard enough to get out. Her mouth rebelled against them, as though saying more would make everything real. Magic worked like that sometimes, although in this case, the damage was already done.

"Specifics would help," Hazel said eventually.

"I gave Rory a love potion," she whispered into her hands.

A pause followed, and Morgan couldn't blame Hazel for needing to process that. It was a lot.

"No. How? When?"

Goose bumps broke out on Morgan's arms despite the temperature. "I made her a relaxation potion earlier this week. Before we left for the festival. At least, I thought that's what I was making, but I mislabeled the ingredient jars and used yarrow instead of chamomile, and I *knew* it looked off, but I gave it to her anyway because I thought it was a trick of the light. I mean, I make the potion so often I figured I could do it basically unconscious. But I gave it to her, and now she thinks she likes me, and it's all wrong. It's all a lie."

Hazel had been patting Morgan's back, and though shock had stilled her hand, she didn't remove it. "One ingredient being off might have made the potion ineffective, but it shouldn't have turned a relaxation potion into a love potion. Should it?"

"Maybe, maybe not. There's a lot of similarities in ingredients, and my intentions when I made it . . ." Morgan wiped away fresh tears. "I was thinking about kissing her, so that definitely would have messed things up. That plus the yarrow, and her behavior—it all makes sense."

Hazel sighed. "Because you think she can't possibly like you without a magical cause? Wait—she likes you? For real? Why didn't you say anything?"

"I would have! It all happened yesterday, but that's not the point. The point is that she doesn't truly like me. She's under the influence of a love potion."

"Maybe."

"Definitely, and I *kissed* her." Morgan groaned through her fingers, fresh horror coursing through her body. The grass beneath her feet browned and wilted with it, and Morgan scooted away from Hazel lest her raging magic be contagious. "I kissed her because I thought it was real, and she kissed me, and it wasn't real. It wasn't real. I am a monster."

Nausea bubbled up her throat again, and Morgan had to shut her lips. If Rory was being affected by a love potion, then Rory actually couldn't have consented to kissing her. She'd not only violated Rory's will, but her body.

There was a reason love potions and love spells were number one on the Council's banned magic list, but Morgan was less concerned about violating Council Law than she was about hurting Rory. Although, possibly, she should be concerned about both. Rory's brother was an Inquisitor. The punishment for something like this would be nothing less than having her magic stripped from her, and Morgan couldn't argue with that.

"Breathe," Hazel said.

Morgan tried. The earth beneath her swam, but no more grass died.

"First, you don't know—"

"I do."

"Fine." Morgan couldn't raise her head, but she heard Hazel's resignation, so she didn't need to see the disagreement on her face. "Second, it was an accident. You are not a monster. You did not purposely try to hurt Rory or take advantage of her. Anyone who knows you, including Rory, would know that."

Her nose was running, and Morgan wiped it with the back of her hand. She was a monster, and she was gross and awful, so it was fitting. "If you run over someone in your car without meaning to and they die, you're still a killer."

"No one is dead."

"I want to be. She'll want to be if she finds out."

"I rather doubt that about both of you." Hazel resumed stroking her hair, which, given how Morgan's magic was sputtering about, made her rather brave. "You need to calm down. I'd say take a relaxation potion, but maybe that's not the best idea."

Morgan snorted. She might never make a relaxation potion—any potion—again.

And yet. Yet she had to. Morgan wet her lips, clarity piercing its way through her panic like a sunbeam through the clouds.

"I need to fix this," Morgan said. Her head pounded with the tears she was holding back and the pressure of what she had to do. But it was the only way.

"Yes, agreed." Hazel dropped her arm. "When did Rory last take the potion?"

Morgan rubbed her eyes. "I don't know. I don't think she took any last night or the night before, but I might not have seen her."

She'd fallen asleep so fast last night—and in retrospect, thank the stars for that or she might be feeling sicker had she done more than kiss Rory yesterday. But as for the first night in the cabin, Morgan couldn't say. She'd been lost in her own miserable thoughts and hadn't paid attention to Rory getting ready for bed. That would put Rory's last for-certain dose on the Monday when Morgan had given her the potion.

"Spells like that don't last forever," Hazel reminded her. "It will wear off as long as she doesn't take it again."

Theoretically, yes. Potions were notoriously short-lived magic. Trevor had theories about why that was—something about human metabolisms—but whatever the reason, the timing wasn't adding up.

"It could take days," Morgan said. "Weeks. Who can tell? The relaxation potion is only supposed to last a few hours. Most ingested potions only last a couple of days at most, and I don't see why love potions would be different. If Rory's still being influenced by whatever I gave her, who knows how strong it must be? I can't wait it out."

"No, I wasn't suggesting that."

Morgan nodded to herself. They were in agreement, then. Her headache worsened at the thought of the impossible task ahead of her, but having something she could do besides be sick to her stomach was calming her down. She'd wanted a big project, the chance to create something monumental and prove her worth. Now she had one. It just wasn't exactly how she'd wanted it to happen. "I need to make a love potion antidote."

Hazel cut off whatever she was about to say and re-formed her words. So, apparently, they hadn't been in agreement. "Fine. Sure. But since you don't know how, first you need to tell Rory what's going on."

Morgan shook her head so fast that her stomach recoiled from the motion. "I can't."

"Morgan."

"No. I *made out with her* yesterday, Hazel. I can't tell her!" The sheer horror of the idea launched Morgan to her feet. She didn't even glance around to make sure they were alone until after the words had spilled out. "It will be humiliating. She's going to be horrified. I've already caused her way too much trauma, and the only thing protecting her is that she doesn't know about it."

Hazel rubbed her wrist where her snake tattoo was spinning in circles like Morgan's insides. "Is this about her feelings or yours?"

"Can't it be about both?"

"Is it about her mother being on the Council? Her brother being an Inquisitor?"

No and no, although that didn't help the situation. Morgan was certain Rory's mother already hated her. And while Isaac seemed like a decent guy—and wasn't half as nosy as Rory had claimed he was or half as scary as Morgan had expected—she didn't want to see him go full-on Inquisitor around her, either.

But their wrath, which would be justified, wasn't the reason. Morgan wouldn't lie to herself—the idea of standing trial and having her powers removed, even temporarily, was terrifying—but it wasn't like she wouldn't deserve her fate. If that happened, though, she couldn't fix the situation, and she owed it to Rory to fix this as expediently and painlessly as possible. To do that, she needed to be left alone with her magic.

"Rory isn't vindictive," Hazel said, getting up. "She's not going to be happy, obviously, but she'll understand if it was an accident. She's not going to hex you or turn you in to the Council over an honest mistake. And if there's any doubt about whether it was one, a truth potion would answer that question."

"I can't do it. Not yet. If it doesn't wear off first, I'll tell her when I know how to fix it. In the meantime, I'll just have to keep my distance. Try to make her realize what happened between us was a mistake. Simple incompatibility has got to be the least traumatic solution. It'll feel natural."

Hazel pressed her lips thin in disapproval. "I don't agree with this plan."

"I know, but just give me a couple of days."

"The potion might wear off in a couple of days."

"And if it does, good!" She grabbed Hazel's arms. "Look, I promise I'll tell her then. It will be better if her emotions are back under her control, and she'll probably be so relieved that she didn't do something stupid, like actually fall for me, that it won't be as embarrassing."

And Morgan could go on being miserable because any hope she'd had of honestly making Rory like her would be dead.

Morgan squeezed her eyes shut as a new round of tears threatened.

There was no time for that nonsense. No time for self-pity. She had to focus.

Step 1: Figure out how to create an antidote.

Step 2, in case Step 1 failed or took too long: Avoid Rory as much as possible. Make Rory fall out of love with her. Convince her they'd made a huge mistake yesterday.

Given what a colossal fuckup she was, Step 2 ought to be a snap.

15

ALMOST TWO WEEKS AFTER HER DRUNKEN OFFER TO FAKE date Rory *hadn't* resulted in Morgan becoming an apartment hermit, she found herself becoming a booth hermit instead. It was the decidedly worse option of the two, what with the entire booth being about the size of her living room and not having a bathroom to speak of, but what she'd done to bring about this fate was also a whole lot worse. So that was fitting.

She ignored Rory's texts for the rest of the day, and when Rory stopped by to ask when she was leaving, Morgan snuck out the back and hid in the crowds until Rory gave up waiting. Morgan felt awful, especially since Rory stared at her phone (and presumably the ignored texts) with a hurt expression before she left. Not running after her was surprisingly the hardest thing Morgan had endured all day. Previously, it had been not vomiting.

While hiding from Rory, Morgan purchased another book on magical phenomena. She didn't need one, but she did need inspiration for where to start with her anti-love potion, and the act of doing something useful made her feel less awful. When she wasn't forced to do work for the shop, she flipped through its pages, reteaching herself things she'd known for years.

The book contained plenty of descriptions for how to use negative energies in hexes, but making someone fall out of love wasn't the same as causing them harm. As for simply undoing a spell, that was a magic all its own, and a difficult type to master. Inquisitors had to learn it, and had special tools for doing it, but Morgan didn't know how to use them, and she didn't think asking Rory's brother for assistance would go well. For all she knew, that sort of magic wouldn't even work in this situation.

Meanwhile, her phone chimed steadily throughout the afternoon.

RORY: You okay? Your mom said you weren't feeling well. Can I bring you anything?

HAZEL: Rory is looking for you. Answer her texts.

RORY: Can you let me know if you're going to make dinner with my family tonight?

HAZEL: Would you please text Rory already? She's worried she did something to upset you.

RORY: I guess you're not making dinner.

Sweet stars, she was such an asshole.

To be fair, she was doing her best to be one, but ugh. Why did it have to be so hard?

Around dinnertime, Bed, Bath, and Broom closed for the day. Morgan had bought herself some food about forty-five minutes ago, but she hadn't been able to stomach more than a few bites. That was fine. Her stomach hadn't unknotted itself enough for her to feel especially hungry anyway.

She flipped to a new page in her notebook as someone knocked on the booth's rear door.

"Hold on!" The words came out automatically, and Morgan silently swore. She should have been pretending to not be in here in case it was Rory. But what were the odds?

Apparently, the odds were excellent. Morgan cracked open the door and found Rory glaring at her. The sun was starting to creep below the tree line, and her face was half-illuminated in golden light and half-covered in shadow. She looked powerful and pissed off.

"Why are you ignoring me?" Rory asked. She didn't wait for Morgan's answer and pushed her way inside the booth.

On the upside, it wasn't clear what Morgan had been researching.

On the downside, that was because she hadn't made much progress.

"Um . . ." She wracked her brain for an excuse that wasn't a complete lie. "I've been working on something and got lost in it. If it makes you feel better, I've also been ignoring Hazel."

"Hazel saw you this morning."

"I saw you this morning, too."

Rory's expression suggested she was unimpressed by that technicality. "My parents were not happy that you weren't there for dinner when you told us last night that you were coming. And I could have used you being my shield maiden again. It was not a pleasant meal."

Morgan sank to the floor, feeling even more like shit. One job. She'd had one job she'd promised to do, and she was letting Rory down on top of everything else. "What happened?"

"Archer signed me up to perform in Saturday's exhibition. Word that I'm on the roster is already spreading, which is how I found out." The space in the back of the booth wasn't large, especially with the boxes of supplies strewn about, but Rory found a way to pace through the clutter. The tension—the rage—emanating from her was electric. Morgan wouldn't have been surprised to see lightning sparking at her fingertips, but Rory was ever in control of her magic. "Naturally, my parents think it's a great idea, and I shouldn't refuse because that would disappoint my fans. I didn't set anyone on fire, but a few glasses of wine can make quite a mess when they go flying."

"I'm sorry." The words seemed inadequate when she should have been there, but that was good. Right? She was supposed to be inadequate.

"I'm sorry, too," Rory grumbled. Her shoulders sagged, frustration dissipating into dejection. She flipped a page in Morgan's new book, looking utterly huggable.

Morgan stopped herself just in time before she moved to give her one. She wouldn't dare touch Rory now.

"What have you been working on that's kept you so busy?" Rory asked. "Wait—did you get that inspiration you were looking for? Is that why you have this book? I could use that spidery hex I suggested yesterday."

Morgan's laugh was strained, but Rory had formed her excuse for her. She wanted to be grateful. "Kind of, yeah."

"That's amazing!" Rory got down on the floor with her and kissed her cheek. Against her will, warmth bloomed in Morgan's chest, and she winced. Then she hoped Rory didn't see it. "So something good came out of running into your evil ex. Can you tell me what, or would talking about it ruin it?"

Oh, damn it. Why was Rory happy for her? She'd blown her off all day. Rory should be furious, not excited.

Morgan dragged a finger along the booth's rough wood floor, half wishing she'd get a much-deserved splinter. "Um, that. I'd rather not say yet."

"Okay, that's fair. I hate talking about my ideas until they're fully formed. They're always so much better in my head. Trying to convey them makes me decide they're actually terrible."

If only that was her problem.

If only the way Rory was looking at her, as though she was feeling all the joy Morgan should have been feeling, didn't hurt so much. Morgan would give anything for Rory's smile to mean something. But just because Rory didn't know what she felt was a lie, didn't make her caring for Morgan any less of one. If anything, the lie was crueler this way. It made it clear just how perfect Rory was, and therefore harder for Morgan to follow through with what she knew she needed to do.

Be strong, she told herself. *Be an asshole.*

She slammed her notebook shut. "I need to get out of here," Morgan said, which was true enough. The booth had never felt so claustrophobic as it did now with her emotions smothering her. It wasn't meant to be occupied this late, either, and the magical light hovering over her head did a poor job of illuminating the wooden walls, which were as dark and oppressive as her mood.

"Good idea." Rory climbed to her feet and held out a hand. "Go for a walk? I can't go back to the cabin for a while."

Oh, sweet stars. It was like Rory was orchestrating her excuses and lies for her. Still, she was going to hate what Morgan had in mind, and Morgan's heart stuttered, perhaps angry at her for what she was about to do.

"The concert should be starting," Morgan said, checking the time on her phone. "Let's walk there."

As anticipated, Rory's face lost some of its luster. She leaned against the far wall and twirled one of her many rings. "You really love dancing, don't you?"

"I do. But you know what? Forget it. I know you don't want to go."

What the fuck? That was not what she was supposed to say.

Be. An. Asshole.

Rory sucked on her lower lip, and Morgan had to turn away. That gesture never failed to heat her blood, and it was way worse now that she knew what it was like to kiss Rory and feel those lips on her body.

Never again.

You asshole.

"No, let's go," Rory said, standing straighter with her resolve.

"What?"

"I can guarantee my parents won't be there, and that's more than enough reason. Besides, if you had some brilliant idea today, you deserve to celebrate."

Morgan sank her nails into her palms. She'd won, but this didn't feel like a victory.

After sending a quick text to Hazel to let her know they could meet her, they left for the bonfires. It was a peaceful evening, and the contrast between the weather and Morgan's mood set her teeth on edge, just as it had during the day. The air was filled with insect song, and Morgan could have sworn she picked up on the scents of burning sweetgrass and incense before she could see the tendrils of smoke rising above the trees. As they got closer, the sounds of voices and laughter drowned out those of the woods, and the magical, multicolored lights lining the paths gave way to open sky. There was no need for additional light when five large bonfires sent their glows stretching to the stars.

Morgan had kept Rory talking about her day during their walk so she wouldn't have to answer questions about her own, but their conversation faded as they crossed the field. It was the same field she'd sat in with Hazel earlier, where she'd confessed what a monster she was, and it stirred up her emotions. Morgan pushed them down into the deepest pit of her stomach and felt sick all over again.

On the opposite side of the fires, the band finished their warm-up, and a hush swept through the crowd as several hundred people looked on in anticipation. The first notes sent cheers rippling across the grass. Morgan recognized the song and the performers immediately, as did Rory. She'd been wearing one of the band's T-shirts on the night Morgan had set this whole disaster in motion.

"One of your favorites?" she asked, seeing Rory grin. Morgan was unsure whether to be happy about this development or disappointed. With the Dragon Flies playing, Rory was less likely to hate Morgan for dragging her here.

"The bassist is a friend of mine."

"Should we dance, then?" She didn't give Rory the chance to refuse.

Morgan pulled her through the swarm of people hovering around the edge of the fires, and right into the chaos of those letting loose near the stage. Rory didn't protest verbally, but she didn't exactly come willingly, either.

Morgan spun her around, locked arms with her, and forced her to join in the group revelry for a couple of songs. Under the circumstances, it was more touching than she ought to allow, but it was innocent enough and in view of hundreds of people. She told herself it was okay. This was friend-level touching, no matter what the sensation of Rory's skin against hers did to her pulse.

Hazel found them soon after, as did more of their friends. Rory bought them each a cup of mead, and with every sip, she seemed to relax more. Morgan wanted to be happy about that. She wanted to share with Rory the joy that dancing usually made her feel. But she couldn't be happy trying to make Rory miserable, even if Rory didn't look as miserable as she expected.

To keep her mind off her own frustrations, Morgan focused on Hazel. The bonfires were as good a place to meet new people as any, but for whatever reason (and Morgan suspected it was partially her fault, given the unhappy glances Hazel occasionally shot her), Hazel wasn't her usual perky self. There, Morgan could help. Her own life was a trash fire that she questioned her ability to fix, but Hazel was the human embodiment of sunshine, and Morgan would walk through fire to cheer her up.

Fortunately, nothing so dramatic was required. A few whispered words to Rory, and Rory sought out her friends that Morgan had briefly met the other night, one of whom was an artist. And single. And just happened to be as *Star Wars*–obsessed as Hazel was, and couldn't fail to comment on Hazel's hair.

"Did you know about the fandom thing?" Morgan whispered to Rory, as Hazel's face lit up while talking to Rory's friend.

Rory shook her head. "Must be festival magic."

Morgan smiled weakly, but that quip cut too close for comfort. Love and magic were the last concepts she wanted to meddle with. Yet Hazel's demeanor had brightened considerably, and Morgan temporarily felt less like a shitty person.

When the band went on break, Morgan hoped to sit for a few minutes and give her tired feet a rest, but Rory snagged her arm. "You drag me, I drag you now," she said, literally pulling Morgan away from Hazel and the others.

Half the band had disappeared somewhere, but several members were hanging around behind the temporary stage. Rory made quick work of this second round of introductions, but Morgan's initial excitement to meet the band faded to awkwardness as their attention was all directed Rory's way. All except for Rory's friend Bea, who'd known Rory since kindergarten and therefore didn't find her as interesting as the rest, and who kept giving Morgan looks like she was considering whether her very muscular arms could pick Morgan up and toss her away.

Morgan got it. Everyone here was cool and famous except for her, but it was too crowded behind the stage to slip into the shadows. She sipped her mead, her miserable mood returning as she wondered how her plan to annoy Rory was crashing and burning already, if Hazel was still talking to her Boston counterpart, and whether it would be rude to plop to the ground and give herself a foot massage. And then whether anyone would notice if she did.

Then Bea slapped part of the stage's rigging, jolting Morgan out of her head. "That's why I recognize you." She pointed at Morgan, who'd been slowly lowering herself to the grass, and Morgan froze with her knees awkwardly bent. "You work at the shop that makes the massage potion. I saw you there yesterday."

Morgan tried to straighten her legs in a natural way, one that did not suggest she'd been about to do something rude, but it was no use. Her legs were tired, her feet more so, and her head was stuffed with mead and regrets. Pausing for that split second had been a mistake. She wobbled, grabbed Rory's arm for balance, and hit the grass anyway.

"Morgan!" Rory squeezed her hand but managed not to fall on top of her.

"I'm fine. Totally fine. I needed to sit for a minute." Only now that she was down, down wasn't so great. Her knees hurt right along with her feet, but Morgan wasn't about to let that stop her from pretending she'd fallen over on purpose. "You mean the muscle balm in a bottle lotion?" she asked Bea.

Rory's face lit up. "I told you about that. You tried it?"

"That stuff is the shit," Bea said, looking down on Morgan unfazed, like people dropped to their knees in front of her all the time. Given that she resembled one of Wonder Woman's Amazonian sisters (leather bustier included), maybe they did. "I'm going back tomorrow and buying more."

Morgan took a hasty swallow of her drink, or what was left after half of it had sloshed out the sides of her cup. "It's just a variation on a relaxation potion. I tweaked it to work more on the body than the mind."

Rory gazed at her with such an adoring expression that it would have made Morgan weak in the knees (too late) if she couldn't explain it away as the result of a love potion. Not to mention some strong mead. Either one alone could have been enough. "Morgan is very modest about her talents."

Morgan wanted to deny it, but there was no point. Especially once

Bea started hyping up her potion to the other band members, and they began looking at Morgan with more interest.

Maybe she *was* being too modest. Morgan had never seen anyone else create a similar product. It wasn't innovative enough to win her any contests, but she'd put her own spin on a tried-and-true recipe with success, and that took creativity. Plus, hearing Bea tell her bandmates that they had to use it on their sore bodies after performing felt kind of nice. Morgan didn't know the last time she'd used it herself. She made so many products for the shop, but aside from the calming hand lotion, she rarely used any of them. Could it be that she needed a reminder of what she did?

At the moment, both her feet and her knees were screaming yes.

When her head was swimmy wasn't the ideal state of mind for pondering, though, and Morgan didn't have much time anyway. Soon enough, the band was preparing to get back to playing, which meant it was their cue to leave. Unless . . .

Thanks to the strong mead and the buzz from Bea's compliments, Morgan had almost forgotten why she'd dragged Rory to the concert in the first place. But while her initial attempt to convince Rory they were incompatible had failed thanks to some bad musical luck, Morgan had a second chance. Coincidentally, a chance that involved her getting to do something she'd always wanted to do.

16

"HEY." MORGAN CAUGHT BEA'S ATTENTION AS THE BASSIST FINished off the drink she'd been chugging. "Any chance we could get up there?" She motioned toward an empty corner of the stage. Before the break, a group of people had been dancing on the stage, but they were gone now, and Morgan was back on her feet, ready to be devious. Rory hated being the center of attention, so it would be a shame to haul her adorably tipsy fake girlfriend into the spotlight.

"Oh, hell yeah." Bea punched her arm. "You belong in the VIP section."

"We do what?" Rory asked, because she hadn't seen what Morgan was referring to.

"You're a VIP," Morgan said, grabbing her arm before Rory could run away.

Morgan hadn't been expecting it, but Bea turned out to be an ally. She grabbed Rory's other arm. "Come on."

"Morgan!" Rory stumbled up the metal stairs, but she was no match for either Morgan with her additional inches or Bea with her additional mass.

Morgan pushed the remains of her mead at Rory. "Drink this. You said you hate crowds. I'm totally doing you a favor."

Rory gaped at her, then muttering a curse, she downed the rest of the mead.

"That's the spirit." Bea slapped her on the back, possibly a touch too hard.

Rory lurched forward and a spray of honey wine flew from her mouth and landed all over Morgan's shirt. Rory snorted at the mess she'd made. "That's what you deserve."

With a low whine, Morgan glanced down. She'd already spilled mead on herself when she'd fallen over, and now she was well and truly sticky. At least her shirt wasn't white.

"Whatever," she said, shaking off this minor setback. "It's not like I need a clean shirt."

"Take it off." Rory raised a suggestive eyebrow and burst into giggles.

In retaliation, Morgan yanked on her, drawing her deeper into the stage area over Rory's protests.

More people joined them as the band began playing again, and in the thick of the excitement, Morgan soon forgot all about her shirt. She was up here with the band and their select guests, and Rory had gotten another cup of something and appeared to be trying very hard not to sway to the music. Her stubbornness was adorable. Even her glaring was adorable. Morgan would be in such deep shit if she hadn't already wandered into that lagoon and drowned in it.

"Come on!" She took Rory's hands and tried twirling her around. But Rory resisted, her feet locked in place, which is how Morgan's feet got tangled up in hers, their arms twisted too tightly around each other for Morgan's comfort.

"I hate you!" Rory leaned into her, yelling over the music.

"You can't say that while you're smiling."

"I . . . Fuck!" Rory tried without a smile and failed. "I hate . . ."

"Nope."

"I—"

"You're not even trying."

"Damn it!"

Seizing her momentary distraction, Morgan grabbed Rory's hands again. Instead of trying to twirl her, she spun them in circles, and oh, that might have been a mistake, because they'd both drunk a bit too much. People-colored blurs streaked by before Morgan collided with the safety railing, and she swore.

Rory doubled over, shaking. "I'm going to hex you for this."

"Liar."

"I swear I—" Rory shrieked as the night suddenly burst with color.

She wasn't the only one. Sparkles rained down on the area around the stage, temporarily blinding Morgan as they flashed gold and silver and purple in the firelight. She held out her hand, and tiny iridescent stars landed on her palm. "Why is the sky vomiting on us?"

Rory stood with her face glancing upward, every inch of her shimmering. "I am covered in glitter. Morgan, this is all your fault."

"You look like a fairy," Morgan said.

"You look like a craft store exploded on you."

"A drunk and pissed-off fairy."

Rory screamed and shook her head futilely, trying to cast off the glitter as though color and sparkles offended her black and gray outfit. But more was falling, swirling around in the breeze. Delighted, along with most of the crowd, Morgan twirled in place with the music, watching her skin catch fire in the light, watching the people below do the same.

From somewhere to the right came a pop, and Morgan recognized the sound that had preceded the last glitter bomb. Sure enough, a new cloud streaked upward before gently floating down on the happily yelling crowd.

"Not this time, bitches." With a maniacal grin that spoiled her attempt to look annoyed, Rory shoved by Morgan and raised her arms. The wind picked up as she redirected the air currents, and the mass of glitter changed course, drifting farther into the dancers below.

Someone screamed out Rory's name, just audible over the music, but the stage lights and the fires made it impossible to see who. Then the cloud switched direction again, flying back at the stage.

Morgan managed to duck out of the way as Rory lifted her arms a second time and flung the glitter back toward the crowd with more force. The delighted voices increased in number and volume. Through the flickering shadows, Morgan could see people gathering, arms raising. A group formed near their corner of the stage, and the breeze rocked wildly. Glitter swirled in all directions, and so did Morgan's hair.

Morgan staggered back. Thanks to the erratic wind, glitter crawled its way up her nose, into her ears, and who knew what other orifices. She shuddered to think. Yup, Rory was going to hex her for sure.

Just when she thought it was ending at last, the air whipped around her head anew. Glitter that had already fallen to the ground shot upward, and Morgan squinted into the twinkling wind. To her amazement, Rory's grin hadn't faded. And not only that, she was moving to the beat as she manipulated the air to toss the glitter at the crowd.

The crowd loved it. Faceless figures in the dark called out Rory's name, begging her to fling the glitter at them. Rory did, laughing and taunting them as they attempted to overpower her and send it back.

Where was the witch who'd seemed embarrassed by the autograph seekers yesterday? Where was the woman who hated crowds? Who was this drunken pixie pretending to be her fake girlfriend?

Morgan's hair was going to be a giant knot, and glitter was probably embedding itself in her skin. And Rory was having fun.

Fun!

How dare she? Despite the dancing. Despite the glitter. Despite Morgan's best attempt to make her realize they were incompatible.

What the ever-loving glittery fuck?

Morgan couldn't do anything amid the frantic beat of the music but find an empty patch of the stage, and she wheezed with laughter as the glitter resettled over her, hoping she wasn't swallowing too much of it. That had not gone as planned, but it was hard to be upset when Rory seemed to be having a blast.

Morgan's own good mood held until the band wrapped up, which coincidentally was probably when the mead's effects started wearing off and the glitter started itching. Exhaustion set in as she climbed down from the stage. Her emotional swings were catching up to her, leaving Morgan utterly spent. Climbing into bed, where she'd likely cry herself to sleep, didn't hold much appeal, but she'd collapse at some point if she didn't.

Rory collided with her, her body pressing close—soft, tempting, and sparkling like unicorn vomit. Morgan took a quick step backward.

"Time to leave?" Rory asked.

"Yeah, I need to get up early again."

"Then let's go." She slipped her arm around Morgan's, and Morgan didn't dare pull away. She wasn't sure she could. "I know I was grumpy about coming here, but it was a good idea. I had fun."

"I noticed." She was glad, too. She'd simply have to try harder tomorrow to prove that they were incompatible.

For now, she had to survive the rest of the night. Alone. With Rory. Remembering the way she'd danced and gleefully played off the crowd. When Morgan wanted nothing more than to kiss her and would likely have every opportunity.

She was so screwed.

On the positive side, the glitter turned out to have been nothing more than a spell. By the time they made it to the Sandlers' cabin, it had vanished.

Like the first day, they crept up to their third-floor room, although this time it was more of a challenge. They were aided by Isaac and Erika, who were sitting out on the deck, and who warned them where

Rory's parents were. Archer had left, so there was one fewer person to avoid.

Rory peeked her head in the other third-floor room and frowned. "Archer's crap is in there. I was hoping by 'left' that Isaac meant he'd been forced to pack up and stay somewhere else after our fight. I should have known better."

"I'm really sorry he did that to you. I can punch him if you want." Morgan hadn't tried to throw a punch since elementary school, but she also hadn't spoken more than two words directly to Archer since they'd met ("thank you" after he handed her the butter at dinner last night, because she wasn't rude). It was two more words than he'd spoken to her. Since he seemed content to let his body language do the talking, she would as well.

Rory shook her head. "He's not worth the damage to your hand. If people are disappointed Saturday, it's on him. I'm not doing it."

"Is this the wrong time to point out that you had fun putting on a show tonight?"

"That's different. I chose that. Even if I'd been considering performing in the exhibition, I'd be extra not doing it now. It's the principle of the thing. I don't like people trying to manipulate me."

Hysterical laughter bubbled up Morgan's throat. She managed to hold it in, but she didn't know how long she'd be able to live like this. That potion needed to wear off immediately, but it seemed to be proving far more stubborn than the glitter.

Rory tossed the hoodie she'd tied around her waist onto her luggage, and Morgan's eyes fixed on her bag. The love potion. If Rory had it on her, she had to get rid of it before she could take another dose.

"I'll be right there," Morgan said as Rory headed to the bathroom to brush her teeth.

Her pulse quickened as she knelt on the floor. Given the space she had available in the cabin, Rory hadn't felt the need to pack light. She was, predictably, perfectly organized, though. Her clothes were neatly folded into packing cubes (even her underwear), her shoes were wrapped to keep the rest from getting dirty, and her makeup and toiletries were in their own case in labeled travel-size bottles. If Morgan didn't like her so damned much, she'd be terrified by this blatant display of Virgo organization.

Morgan tried to be as methodical as Rory (something that would have been challenging enough if she hadn't been drinking earlier), opening each packing cube and case, and putting everything back the way she'd found it. Especially Rory's underwear, which was difficult because Morgan had dropped that cube like it burned her when she discovered the contents. But there was no potion in sight. Not tucked away in Rory's underwear (why was she so fixated on this one cube?) or in any of the dozen highly organized pockets in her suitcase.

Unless the potion was in the bathroom—and Morgan hadn't seen it there yesterday—Rory hadn't brought it. That was a relief in a way. Rory couldn't take more while she was here. In another way, however, it did indeed suggest the effects of the potion were long-lasting, and that was not so great. Although in any other situation, Morgan would have been rather proud of her power.

She carefully placed Rory's belongings back as best she could, and was in the process of rearranging her hoodie into the same rumpled heap, when Rory returned. Morgan startled, positive guilt was written all over her face.

"Sorry. I kicked your hoodie onto the floor," she said.

Rory gave her a weird look, as though she didn't quite buy that but couldn't figure out why else Morgan would be on her knees next to her suitcase. "Sure you weren't searching for my underwear?"

"What? No." Oh crap, please let her have replaced that cube perfectly.

"Okay. Just asking, because if you want to see it, all you have to do is ask."

Heat crept up Morgan's neck. "I'll keep that in mind."

"I hope you do."

This night was going to be absolute torture, and she would deserve it.

"I should go brush my teeth before Archer returns," Morgan said, and she darted out of the room.

Rory had pulled out the sofa bed and changed into her pajamas while Morgan was gone, and Morgan averted her eyes as much as possible while she got out her own nightclothes. Rory's consisted of nothing more than a loose T-shirt that barely covered her ass and that wasn't thick enough to conceal that she was chilly. It was just lucky that her propensity for wearing dark colors meant that her shirt wasn't more revealing. But at some point, Morgan digging her nails into her palms wasn't going to cut it. Especially when she could feel Rory watching her as she changed herself.

More especially when Rory climbed over the sofa bed and wrapped her arms around Morgan's neck.

Shove her away! Morgan's conscience screamed at her, even as her body softened against Rory's. If she hadn't made her horrible discovery this morning, she'd press her hands around Rory's hips, lift her shirt until she found bare skin . . .

Breathing shakily, Morgan pulled back as Rory tried to kiss her. She would do no more damage here.

"What's wrong?" Rory asked, her brow pinching with concern.

In that moment, it dawned on Morgan that there was no such thing as doing no more damage. Everything she did, no matter which choices she made, was going to hurt Rory. The confusion in Rory's eyes cut Morgan to her core. The truth would alleviate that, but the truth would bring its own pain. Humiliation on top of it. Both options were shitty, but one would double the dose.

Surely that meant her current course of action remained the best.

Morgan touched Rory's cheek before dropping her hand. That

was the most she could do. She didn't want Rory to think she was upset with her, but she couldn't encourage her, either.

"Nothing. It's just . . ." Just what? Why did she have to be so bad at this? "We both drank a bit at the concert."

Rory raised her eyebrows, but she removed her hands from Morgan's neck. "That was over an hour ago, and we didn't drink much."

"Excuse me. We drank enough for you to dance onstage while covered in glitter."

Rory chewed her lip, considering this. "True, but I feel fine now. Are you feeling drunk?"

"A touch? I got so caught up in my work that I didn't eat much today." Part of that was true. Maybe it would be enough to sell the rest.

"Ah yes. If I recall, you have a habit of skipping meals when you work. You know, if you'll answer my texts tomorrow, I'll be sure to bring you sustenance."

Morgan smiled but she doubted it looked like a happy one. "Why do you have to be so good? I was rude to you today."

Rory kissed her cheek. "Don't worry about it. You're sweet, and I'm happy for you."

"Thanks." She didn't bother to attempt a smile this time, but Rory had already turned away and didn't notice.

"Did you see Lilith when I was in the bathroom, by the way?" Rory asked, shutting the door. "I feel like she's been avoiding me since we got here."

"Maybe it's me she's avoiding, and you're guilty by association." Could Lilith know what she'd done? Morgan had no idea how perceptive a familiar could be, but it was the first thought that popped to mind. It *was* odd that she hadn't seen more of Lilith the last couple of days. Given the way Rory had insisted that Morgan meet her, Morgan had expected it.

"No, she liked you. She's probably finding lots of mice around here and is having fun without me." Rory climbed onto the sofa bed. "I told you—she's a terrible familiar. No loyalty."

"You took the sofa bed the last two nights," Morgan said, because that was something she could do. "It's mine tonight. Get out."

"It's fine."

"Out." Morgan crossed her arms.

Rory tossed off the blanket and swung her bare legs over the side. "Fine, but you'll regret that."

She extinguished the candles before climbing into the bunk bed with her pillow. A moment later, she tossed Morgan's down to her.

With a huff, Morgan got into the sofa bed, hoping the sheets hadn't picked up too much of the scent of Rory's soap over the last couple of nights. That would be all she needed to be extra tormented. But when she lay down, she bolted upright a second later. "What the . . . ?"

"Told you," said Rory into the darkness.

"Is there any spring in this thing that's not broken?"

It sounded like Rory snorted into her pillow. "If you curl up in a ball all the way on the left, it's almost comfortable."

Morgan did as suggested and found that position didn't work so well, either. The additional inches she had on Rory likely weren't helping. On the other hand, she deserved to be tortured, right? Not getting any sleep, or waking up in pain—that was a just punishment.

Justified or not, though, Morgan twisted and turned, searching for a position where she didn't feel a metal spring poking her.

"You can come up here and share with me," Rory said after a minute, during which the sound of Morgan's agonized movement filled the room.

"I'll be okay."

"Not if you keep me up with your fussing all night, you won't."

Morgan shifted again, trying to recapture the one spot that had sucked less than the others. "Sorry."

"Morgan, it's a double bed. There's plenty of room for two people up here. I promise not to compromise your virtue while you're drunk."

Morgan groaned from the physical and emotional toll this night was taking on her. "I'll sleep on the floor."

"With the mice and the spiders Lilith hasn't caught?" Rory's tone had gone from flirty to amused to exasperated in short order.

That made Morgan freeze. She *had* seen a lot of spiders around the cabin.

"I toss and turn a lot in my sleep," Morgan said. She needed to convince Rory this was a bad idea, because she was starting to become convinced otherwise herself.

"So do I."

"What if I roll on top of you during the night? Or grab one of your boobs?"

Rory was definitely laughing into her pillow this time. "I do not believe for a moment that you're going to suffocate me. And if you grope a boob, all you'll do is make the other one jealous."

Morgan buried her head in her knees to stop herself from screaming.

"Morgan?"

"Okay." Okay, because she needed to sleep. Being exhausted tomorrow would not help her create an anti-love potion. And okay, because surely it was possible to share a bed platonically. As Rory had said, it was a double. They could each stick to their own sides.

Morgan tossed her pillow up to Rory and climbed into the bed. Although she did her best not to touch Rory, the sheets were already warm with her body, and this close, Morgan could breathe in the scent of her shampoo. Her heart fluttered, her nerves sang, and Morgan closed her eyes, bidding them all to shut up.

It felt like she lay there awake half the night, listening to Rory's even breaths. She tensed her muscles every time Rory shifted, afraid of letting the slightest bit of skin brush. But mostly, her mind raced with questions. Was she handling this the best way possible? What should she be researching to create her potion? How could she ever make this up to the one person who'd come to mean so much more to her than a simple crush?

At some point, she fell asleep with tears stinging her eyes and the joyful sound of Rory's laughter ringing in her ears.

17

IT WASN'T MORGAN'S ALARM THAT WOKE HER THE NEXT MORNing. It was voices drifting up the stairwell and through the floorboards. Agitated voices.

Blearily, she opened her eyes, consciousness returning like a slow, drawn-out punch to the face. One that made sure every muscle, every nerve, every fiber of her being knew that a new day had dawned and it was going to hurt.

To be fair, she was surprised she'd fallen asleep at all. For a while last night, she'd believed that no matter what object she lay on, she was doomed to spend the hours stewing in her despair, tormented by half-lucid what-if scenarios until the sun pierced the cabin's blinds and stabbed her with the sharp, hot pain of reality. A reality that screamed—*you really fucked everything up, didn't you? Good morning to the queen of disasters, the witch out of everyone's nightmares, you absolute suckiest of human beings.*

Morgan closed her eyes again. The sun *was* coming in golden and furious through breaks in the window covering, but the room remained dim and dreary in the half-light. Or it did thanks to her mood. Either way, she was lying on her back, and the room's ceiling was too close for comfort. Next to her, Rory stirred.

Rory was too close for comfort as well.

Panic snapped Morgan's eyes back open, and she turned her head. Rory was curled up next to her, their arms just touching, her knees resting against Morgan's leg. Right. She'd climbed in bed with Rory last night, which hadn't been a terrible idea at all.

Morgan rolled onto her side, careful not to disturb Rory, and her chest ached with a sweet desperation. The feeling had gradually replaced her tongue-tied butterflies over the past couple of weeks, but it was no less intense.

Did everyone look so beautiful when they slept? Rory could say whatever she wanted about no one using that word for her before, but Morgan stood by it. Maybe Rory didn't resemble some Hollywood starlet, but honestly, that was a bland kind of beauty anyway. What made someone special was their particular features—freckles, full lips, eyelashes that left Morgan envious—and how they accentuated a smile or lit up with a laugh. It was the way Rory referred to herself as overconfident, yet her eyes were often vulnerable when she thought no one was paying attention.

Morgan paid attention. She'd always paid attention, but finally, she wasn't so distracted by her wild emotions to miss these precious details.

She longed to reach out and trace Rory's lips, to see if she could coax a smile out of her in her sleep. And more—to lean over and kiss each freckle, one by one, until Rory woke up and laughed at her and called her weird. In another life, one where she hadn't screwed up so spectacularly, it might have been possible to one day wake up next to Rory and do all those things. To fall asleep holding her and with the taste of Rory's lips on her mouth.

But she had screwed up, so any chance of Operation Impress Rory succeeding had failed in a far worse manner than Morgan would have believed she was capable of. Part of her was sardonically impressed with her own creativity. Never in a million years would Morgan have dreamed she'd give Rory a love potion.

Proof that you are, indeed, a small thinker, her heart whispered.

Rory shifted again, her face strained as she struggled to hold on to sleep. Morgan caught herself reaching for her, as though to stroke her cheek and lull her back to slumber.

Shit. She couldn't do that.

Guilt washed over Morgan in suffocating waves. She didn't want to ruin Rory's peace, but how could she continue to lie? Rory deserved better than what Morgan had done, but lying about it, even if it was to protect her, was only compounding the problem.

"Morgan?" Rory's eyes fluttered open.

"Good morning."

Rory's sleepy smile made Morgan's breath catch. "What's that noise?"

"Some commotion downstairs." Which was odd. The last couple of days, Morgan had been out of the cabin before Rory's family or Archer had stirred from bed. "There's something I need to tell you."

As usual, her mouth was getting ahead of her brain. Morgan's pulse sped up. Did she really want to do this? Once she confessed, she could stop lying, but would she be upsetting Rory more than necessary? Or was waiting for these magic-given feelings to end the coward's way out? Every time Morgan thought she'd landed on her answer, she had second thoughts.

"Yeah?" Rory raised her head slightly. Her hair stuck out in all directions, and it was adorable, especially combined with the sleep lines on her face.

Morgan wet her dry lips. If she was doing this, she had to get out of this bed first. They should be dressed, too. Half-naked and lying a hair's breadth apart was absolutely the wrong way to go about telling the woman you cared about that you'd accidentally given her a love potion.

"We should get up first. My alarm's going to go off."

Rory rested her head back on her pillow. "Okay. I'm going to see what's going on downstairs."

Perfect. That would give Morgan plenty of time to practice how she was going to do this, because it wasn't like she could just straight-out say, *By the way, I accidentally gave you a love potion*, while they were having breakfast, as if they were discussing the weather. Rory was likely to choke on her bagel or spill hot coffee everywhere, and burns plus a lack of oxygen were not going to improve an already awful situation.

So no. Morgan needed a lead-in, an opening so Rory could brace herself for what was coming, if such a thing was possible.

Morgan cleared her throat under the shower spray and addressed her shampoo bottle. "You remember that relaxation potion I gave you? Boy, are you going to need one in a minute."

Just kidding.

She pushed down the pessimistic sarcasm and tried for real. "I'm really, really sorry, but there's something awful I need to tell you, and I think you should sit down first."

That was better, although Rory might think someone had died. Maybe the third time would be the charm.

"Rory, I gave you a . . ." Morgan floundered on the word, and then gagged on the shower spray as she stood there mouthing silence.

Great. Morgan spit out hot water. If she couldn't make the words form while talking to a shampoo bottle, how was she going to do this with the actual person?

As if it couldn't take any more of her dithering, said bottle slipped through Morgan's fingers and hit the tile, spilling part of its contents. Morgan glowered at it before remembering that this was the froufrou organic shampoo Hazel had convinced her to buy, and that stream of pink liquid running down the drain could be measured in dollars.

"Shit! You are no help," she snapped, slamming the bottle back on the rack. "And for the record, my hair was just as shiny with the cheap stuff."

By the time she'd emerged from her quick shower and had thrown on her clothes for the day, Rory had disappeared from the bedroom. Warily, Morgan tiptoed down the stairs, still searching for the perfect phrasing. A way to say, *I totally fucked up and you should hate me*, without the other person actually agreeing.

In other words, something not even potent magic could conjure.

Rory poked her head into the living room, temporarily ending Morgan's internal struggle. She was braless in her sleep shirt, but she'd thrown on a pair of shorts that covered a bit more of her legs. Thank the stars for small favors. "I made you breakfast."

Since it had just been her and Rory yesterday morning, they'd eaten while standing around the kitchen island. Now that multiple people were awake, Rory had set out plates for both of them with toasted bagels on the dining room table. Like every other room in the cabin, the decor was outdated but clean, and Morgan's chair squeaked as she sat.

Isaac sat across from Rory, drinking coffee and frowning at his phone. "Morning."

"Morning." Morgan took the mug Rory offered her and sipped it. Rory had added exactly the right amount of sugar. "You're up early."

So was Rory's mother. The back door was propped open a few inches, a light breeze blowing in through the screen, and Morgan could hear her on the deck. It sounded like she was on the phone.

"Drama," Rory said. "So much drama that we were oblivious to last night."

Isaac shot his sister an expression that suggested he thought she was way too cheerful for the hour and current situation. "Someone was slipped a charming potion last night at the bonfires."

Morgan paused spreading cream cheese on her bagel. "Get out. Really?"

Charming potions and spells, like love potions and spells, were strictly forbidden by Council Laws, and for the same reason—they overpowered another person's will. Morgan knew even less about charming potions than she did love potions, but her understanding was that they were a lot harder to make and the results were a lot more powerful.

Someone who was charmed, by whatever the means, was susceptible to being controlled by the person who made the potion or performed the spell. With a potent version of such magic, a person could—in theory—be made to do anything. Most witches probably weren't skilled enough or powerful enough to completely override a person's mind, but that hardly changed the morality of it.

Morgan couldn't believe someone would have the audacity to attempt such a thing at the NEWT Festival. But then, no witch would ever attempt it if they expected to be caught, and if people didn't think they could get away with that kind of magic, Isaac wouldn't have a job. *That* was true overconfidence.

"Did you get any sleep at all?" Rory asked, breaking off part of her bagel.

"Not much." Isaac poured himself more coffee. "I'm the only Inquisitor on-site, and since I'm here, the Council doesn't feel the need to bring in anyone else. So I was up preparing spells. Some vacation this has turned into."

Morgan forced herself to swallow her food. "Truth potion?"

"That's one of them. But first we have to narrow down the suspects." He yawned, and Morgan noted the dark circles under his eyes for the first time. "If it's not a baby keeping me up, it's some shithead."

Rory reached over and ruffled his hair. "The baby was your own doing. There are magical and mundane ways to prevent them from happening."

"I wanted the baby."

"Well, then. That's totally your fault, so no complaining." She shrugged and her brother raised his middle finger along with his coffee mug.

Morgan tried to smile at the sibling camaraderie, but she kept thinking about the resolution she'd reached in bed this morning. Granted, what she'd done had been an accident, but Isaac's comment about preparing spells had nonetheless opened a pit in her stomach. Apparently, she was more afraid of Rory's brother than she'd been willing to admit to herself yesterday. Seeing them banter didn't help. Rory might believe that Morgan's intentions had been good, but would Isaac? A truth potion would reveal that giving the potion to Rory was an accident, but it was still against the rules, accident or not. Irresponsible, accidental magic could be every bit as dangerous as intentional magic.

The back door opened, and Rory's mother set her phone down and grabbed a mug. She noticed Morgan and Rory through the kitchen doorway only after she filled her cup with coffee, and she entered the dining room. "Good morning."

Rory waved, and Morgan returned the greeting.

Whatever fight had occurred in this cabin yesterday evening, it seemed all but forgotten today, or perhaps Rory and her mother were too tired or un-caffeinated to resume it. Wanda didn't look as disheveled as her son or daughter—in fact, she looked like the sort of woman who was always put together—but she did look tired. Older. Morgan assumed she'd been up late last night dealing with the fallout of the charming potion, as well.

"I just got off the phone with Tabitha," Wanda said to Isaac. "She'll meet you in an hour to get started."

Isaac acknowledged the information with a nod into his mug.

"This is going to be a hell of a day." Rory's mother leaned against the wall. "Morgan, how are you feeling? Rory said you were unwell yesterday."

The question startled Morgan. After her recent behavior, she hadn't expected politeness. Although, given that there was a known criminal wandering the festival, perhaps Morgan wasn't looking so bad anymore in comparison.

Given what Morgan had done to Rory, that thought was almost but not quite funny.

"I'm feeling better, yeah," Morgan lied. "I'm sorry for flaking out on dinner."

Wanda waved off the apology. "Don't worry about it. I'm glad you're doing better. There's nothing worse than being sick while traveling."

Morgan wanted to turn to Rory and ask what had just happened, but this was clearly not the time.

Wanda's phone rang, and Rory's mother took it and her coffee back outside to answer it. A few minutes later, Isaac finished his cup and lumbered upstairs to get ready for his meeting. He continued to strike Morgan more as a tired dad than a badass witch, but there was a grim hardness in his face that she hadn't seen before. Morgan suspected that once the caffeine finally did its job, Isaac would look pretty damned scary after all. It was not exactly a pleasant thought.

Left alone in the room, Morgan feared Rory would ask what she'd wanted to talk about, and she'd need another excuse to delay it. Obviously, she couldn't discuss it in this house, or under these circumstances.

Obviously, she was getting cold feet.

"You all right?" Rory asked. She pushed a stray strand of Morgan's hair out of her face.

Morgan jumped at her touch, hating that she had to fight the craving to lean into it. "Yeah, why?"

"You've been quiet."

"Haven't finished my coffee. I thought your mother would be angry at me."

To Morgan's relief, Rory dropped her hand and picked up her

mug. "My mother doesn't get angry. It's far worse—she gets disappointed. But you're not family, so she's not disappointed in you. No need to worry. Actually, last night, she was concerned for you. The words 'chicken soup' left her mouth, but lucky for you, that wasn't an option at the festival."

Morgan swallowed another bite of her bagel. Unable to parse out the Sandler family dynamics, she went for the obvious question. "You don't like your mother's chicken soup?"

"I think my mother's chicken soup is the reason why I don't like any chicken soup." Rory pretended to shudder. "It's safest when my dad does the cooking. He understands the importance of salt. But really, they don't dislike you."

"Even after my outburst?"

Rory snickered into her coffee. "That little thing? Morgan, I might be quiet and boring in public, but we are not a quiet *family* in case you haven't noticed. That barely counted as an outburst around here, but it did show that you care about me—thank you—and that's not going to make them dislike you."

Rory placed a hand over Morgan's, and a lump swelled up in Morgan's throat. "Oh." She needed to change the topic. "What happens next? I mean, what did happen? With the charming potion."

If Rory was confused by the abrupt shift, she didn't show it. She pulled her feet up on the chair. "I'm sure we'll hear whatever Isaac can share later, and whatever he can't share will be spread around the festival by tonight. Although half of that will be bullshit."

At least half of it, Morgan was certain. Another quarter would be partial truths and misinterpreted visions, as the nosiest among their kind would scry for information.

"I hope the person who was charmed is okay," Morgan said.

"She is. I asked Isaac that before you came down. Physically she's okay, anyway. I'm sure mentally, knowing what happened, is another thing." Rory grimaced and slid her plate down the table. "I'm glad someone figured it out quickly. From the sound of it, things could have been a lot worse. Having your mind overtaken like that—I can't imagine how violating that must feel."

Morgan shivered and tried to hide her emotions behind her coffee mug. She was in one hundred percent agreement with Rory, and yet . . .

Rory's words cemented her decision. She could not tell her about the love potion. She simply had to end its effects, one way or another. Lying to her, ignoring her, annoying her—Rory would be upset, but it was a normal kind of upset. People dealt with failed relationships all the time, and theirs hadn't gone on for long. She'd be fine soon enough. Rory having to live with knowing her mind had been violated was something else. That sort of trauma had much longer-lasting effects.

Morgan's phone vibrated in her pocket, and she checked her message.

> HAZEL: Did you hear what happened last night?

Hazel wasn't normally one to gossip, so Morgan did not like that she'd immediately heard the news and felt the need to contact her. She already knew Hazel didn't support her decision to keep Rory in the dark.

"So what did you want to tell me?" Rory asked, and Morgan flipped her phone over guiltily.

"Oh, um, just I think I'm going to be busy again today." In her imagination, her shampoo bottle stared accusingly at her from the shower floor. It had spilled its overpriced guts far more easily than she could.

"With your brilliant idea?"

Morgan nodded. The bagel had turned into a hard, unhappy lump in her stomach.

Rory sipped her coffee, looking as suspicious as she had last night when she'd almost caught Morgan snooping through her suitcase. "Are you sure everything is okay? I didn't punch you in your sleep, did I?"

"No, definitely not. I'm just distracted. You know me, totally distractable." Morgan feigned a laugh and waved her phone around. "That was my mom. I need to get to the booth."

"Okay. I'll stop by later. How about I bring you lunch so you don't forget to eat again?"

How about no? Better yet—how about Morgan inconveniently disappear around lunch so when Rory showed up, she got annoyed with her?

She hated herself for thinking of these things, but it was always possible she'd have an epiphany by lunch. A potion in the works by the evening?

Yeah, right.

Morgan got up, forcing down a wave of nausea. "Sure. Yeah, see you then."

Only if she couldn't avoid it.

18

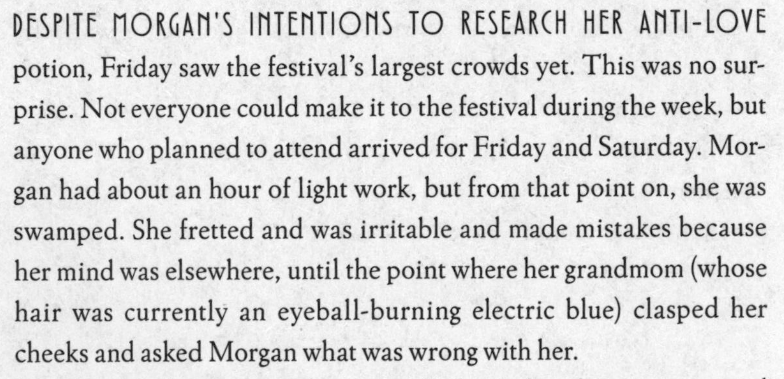

DESPITE MORGAN'S INTENTIONS TO RESEARCH HER ANTI-LOVE potion, Friday saw the festival's largest crowds yet. This was no surprise. Not everyone could make it to the festival during the week, but anyone who planned to attend arrived for Friday and Saturday. Morgan had about an hour of light work, but from that point on, she was swamped. She fretted and was irritable and made mistakes because her mind was elsewhere, until the point where her grandmom (whose hair was currently an eyeball-burning electric blue) clasped her cheeks and asked Morgan what was wrong with her.

Morgan's face crumpled. It was only due to them being interrupted by another customer that she didn't break down, confess everything, and beg for help. While she took a few minutes in the back of the booth to collect herself, she jotted down more ideas in her phone. This wasn't a generic anti-love potion she was trying to create. It was one tailored to Rory. It seemed to Morgan, therefore, that the potion ought to include stuff that Rory hated. The trouble was, Morgan only had a few ideas as to what those things were, and last night had shown her that even things Rory claimed to hate, like crowds and dancing, were negotiable.

MORGAN: What does Rory hate?

HAZEL: Why don't you ask Rory?

MORGAN: Because I don't want Rory asking questions about why I'm asking questions. Obviously.

HAZEL: 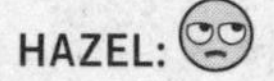

MORGAN: Pleeeeeeaaaaaaase. Help a witch out.

HAZEL: Ugh, fine. I once heard her say high heels are an abomination.

MORGAN: Yeah, but who doesn't think that?

HAZEL: I'd guess lots of people considering how many people wear them.

MORGAN: Fair.

HAZEL: I also think she has that aversion to patterns with holes. Trypophobia? She got squeamish when I showed her those honeycomb candles I bought. Does that count?

If she got desperate, Morgan supposed it would do.

MORGAN: TBF, I got squeamish looking at those candles, too. Is that it?

HAZEL: We've never sat around and discussed our mutual hates. If I had to guess, I'd say she hates something about competing, but she doesn't talk about that.

Hazel raised a good point, and Morgan tapped her thumb along the edge of her phone, trying to banish images of honeycomb from her mind. Although she'd opened up a little recently, Rory clearly avoided discussing her previous life. That was pretty powerful stuff if Morgan could figure out a way to use it in a spell.

"Morgan!" her grandmom called. "Could use your help if you're okay back there."

Damn it. When was everyone going to stop asking if she was okay?

Hazel hadn't replied, probably too busy kissing Rory's friend, so Morgan put her phone away. "Coming!"

The next few hours passed in a whirlwind. Morgan lost track of time, and hence her plan to disappear before Rory arrived with lunch failed thanks to her pathetic attention span. She saw Rory approach through the throng of people loitering around the booth, and would have dived into the back, but Rory saw her first. Morgan considered it anyway, but it wasn't like no one else would have seen her do it and dragged her out.

"Busy?" Rory asked. She stood off to the side, allowing a couple of women the space to debate the merits of the perfect-shade lip balm versus the antiaging balm and wonder why they couldn't be combined. (Because infusing the lip balm with two potions risked causing a magical interaction. Duh.)

"Yeah, I probably can't do lunch," Morgan said. Rory didn't appear to be carrying any food, so Morgan wouldn't be truly inconveniencing her. That wasn't supposed to be good, but it was a relief. Being an asshole to someone you cared about was fucking hard.

"Nonsense." Grandmom June shooed her away. "Raina is due to arrive soon, and she's working all afternoon."

Morgan had almost forgotten that Raina would be helping at the booth today and tomorrow. Back in Harborage, Raina only covered shifts around the holidays when the shop got extra busy, but the rest of the store's retail help were all mundanes, and the festival was for witches only.

"Go have fun," her grandmom continued. "You've been living here the past two days."

"It's my job."

"It's also your vacation. You've been here more than any of us."

Rory leaned over the counter and sniffed the contents of a jar of energizing bodywash. She frowned lightly, though she tried to hide it, and Morgan made a mental note. The key aroma in it was peppermint. Maybe Rory didn't like mint.

"Morgan's been working on some secret project," Rory said, screwing the bodywash's cap back on. "She's going to dazzle us all with her brilliance."

Morgan suppressed a groan. She should have asked Rory not to tell anyone about that. This was her own fault for lying, and one more reason—besides sucking at it—why she tried to avoid doing it. Lies spread faster than gossip and were harder to contain.

Her grandmom gave her a curious look. "I didn't know you were working on something special."

Sweat beaded on the back of Morgan's neck. "That's what 'secret' means."

"Hmm. I suppose." Her grandmom pursed her lips. "It's about time, anyway."

Morgan let out a slow breath. Did that mean her grandmother would side with her now if she used the project as an excuse to avoid Rory? "About time?"

"About time you tried working on your own thing." Grandmom June checked her practically neon hair in the booth's mirror as though admiring her own handiwork. "You've done a good job tweaking the family potions, but you should be out there creating your own, too. At your age, you're supposed to think you can do anything."

"Sounds like a good way to set yourself up for failure," Morgan muttered.

"Well of course. You'll be wrong, but the trying is where you discover what you actually can do. A wise woman once said to shoot for the stars. Even if you miss, you might reach the moon."

"That wise woman's ass never smacked the hard earth on the way down."

Grandmom June swatted Morgan's ponytail. "Everyone falls on their butt occasionally. You get back up. I'm sure Rory can tell you stories. But you've got my genes, so I know you're talented. Don't let it go to waste."

That sounded so much like what Rory's family was telling Rory that Morgan shot her a concerned glance, but Rory was looking right back at Morgan with a smug expression.

Brat. It made Morgan want to kiss her.

Instead, she crossed her arms. "That's why I need to get to work on my project."

"Nonsense. You'll have plenty of time to work on it when we're back in Harborage," her grandmom said. "Go on and enjoy yourself while you can."

Rory's smile somehow turned even more smug. After all her talk about not liking other people trying to manipulate her, Morgan wondered if she was the one who'd just been manipulated by Rory. If so, it was well done.

"I wasn't sure what you'd want for lunch," Rory said once Morgan exited the booth, "so I figured I'd see if I could tear you away for a bit."

The temperature was cooler than it had been over the last couple of days, and Rory had given up shorts for a pair of tight black pants. In fact, her entire outfit was black. Her black scoop-neck shirt hung partially off one shoulder, revealing a black bra strap. Her feet were tucked into black sandals, and she'd painted her toenails black as well. Rory normally stuck to drab colors, but she had outdone herself today, and Morgan couldn't help but suspect this was in response to the fight she'd had with her family during dinner yesterday. The charming-potion drama might have distracted everyone this morning, but Morgan wouldn't be surprised if arguing had started anew after she'd left.

Rory's parents and Archer had better beware. If Morgan had never met her and someone had just pointed out to her that the woman in black over there was Rory Sandler, she definitely would have been intimidated.

That word brought up memories, though. Memories of Rory lying on the sofa, her eyes filled with desire and finding Morgan's confession hilarious. What had she called her—a charming, gorgeous dork? She'd kissed Rory and been kissed, and for such a brief, amazing moment, she'd thought she could never be happier.

"You okay?" Rory grabbed her wrist.

That question again. "Yeah, light-headed. I guess I need to eat."

"Then let's get you some food."

Unable to think of a sufficient excuse not to do that, Morgan clomped along with her as they perused their options. There were as many stalls selling mundane food as there were vendors selling magical treats, and most did a mix of both. Aromas of fried potatoes and dough, peanuts and garlic, coffee and sugar mingled in the air, the fragrances rising and falling in dominance with every few steps in any direction. Morgan's stomach grumbled, and she grudgingly allowed that it had every right to. The bagel she'd forced down at breakfast had been the most she'd eaten in a day. Whether her guilt would actually allow her to eat lunch was another story.

In the end, she followed Rory's lead, and they settled down at one of the empty tables beneath the largest tent with slices of pizza—veggie lovers for Rory and plain for Morgan, who questioned her ability to stomach anything more—plus bowls filled with ice cream that had been enchanted so it wouldn't melt for dessert. Rory had declared that festival sugar wasn't unhealthy, and Morgan thought about arguing simply as an excuse to be annoying. Once her nose caught a whiff of the food, however, she decided she'd prefer to eat.

It was almost noon, and the tent was starting to fill. The buzz of voices grew louder every minute. Rory wisely found them a corner as far from the food stalls as possible, so it would take longer to be crowded out, but that was no safe haven, either. A noisy group of teen girls gathered at a nearby table, their hands laden with a variety of snacks that suggested they agreed with Rory's opinion about festival sugar.

That had been her and Hazel and Andy once, along with other friends Morgan no longer saw as often. At that age, Morgan had yearned for more magical responsibilities, dreamed of honing her craft well enough to work at Bed, Bath, and Broom and be considered a fully capable witch, one ready to be welcomed into the Harborage coven. She suddenly felt way older than her twenty-five years, and a lot more depressed about what all that yearning and dreaming had gotten her.

"So how's it going with your project this morning?" Rory asked.

"It's not going," Morgan said. "We've been too busy for me to work on it. I've always believed inspiration comes when you're not trying to find it"—and hadn't that been the truth—"but I'm feeling stuck in that area, too." Morgan wondered if there was a way to work in a question about Rory's dislikes based on that bit of information, but she couldn't think of one. She settled for the next best thing. "I'll probably stay late at the booth again today."

Rory cast her eyes down and broke her last bit of crust into pieces. She knew she was being pushed aside but seemed reluctant to bring it up, perhaps remembering how she'd told Morgan that she'd once put her practicing above all else. After a moment, she tossed aside part of the crust to feed some squirrels who were braving the humans in search of food. "Just take it easy on yourself, okay? Inspiration is great, but creating new spells is hard. Like your grandmom said, you can't expect to be successful overnight, and you might fail a lot before you succeed. It doesn't make you any less of an amazing person."

Morgan swallowed, a lump growing in her throat.

Rory doesn't mean it, truly. She's only saying these things because you bespelled her. Why the hell had her conscience taken on Nicole's voice?

"You're thinking about her, aren't you?" Rory said.

"What?"

"Your ex."

Morgan reached for her water and nearly knocked the bottle over. "Why do you think that?"

"Gee, I don't know. That deeply unhappy expression on your face?" Rory raised an eyebrow. "Look, don't think I haven't noticed the timing here. On Wednesday, you had a bad run-in with the ex who told you that you weren't good enough for her, and yesterday you became obsessed with this idea you have for creating a new potion. Tell me that's a coincidence."

"It's a coincidence." Bizarrely enough, it was. Although the irony was like a dagger through Morgan's heart. "She has nothing to do with it, I swear. To be honest, you were the inspiration."

Rory stared at her, clearly unsure whether to believe this, which was almost funny. But although it was the truth, Morgan had to drop her gaze to her empty plate. All the parts she was leaving out—the entire, bigger truth—were killing her.

"Okay, then. I hope so." Rory smiled tentatively at her. "That is, I hope it's not your ex inside your head driving this, and I look forward to someday seeing what you're working on. Especially if it involves spiders. But in the meantime, please don't get so caught up in your quest for greatness that you ignore the people who love you for who you are, and not for what you can do."

Oh fuck. Was Rory intent on completely breaking her? Morgan's lip trembled, and she quickly grabbed her ice cream. "Thank you."

Rory's sincerity, real or false, had Morgan close to tears. Everything Rory said, everything she did, made her fall harder. Her brain might know it all meant nothing, but her heart didn't care. It had chosen Rory, and there was no tying up her emotions anymore. No constraining them.

She loved Rory, and that was that.

And she'd never wanted to kiss her more than she did now when she absolutely couldn't.

She needed to get out of here. She remained determined to help Rory with her family—she owed her that much and was doing a terrible job of it—but being in her company unnecessarily was too difficult.

If hiding in the booth was out, Morgan would just have to find somewhere else to go. Since it was Friday, there would be no shortage of workshops or lectures she could pick from. Odds were good that she could find one that might teach her something relevant to her dilemma. Morgan brought up the festival itinerary on her phone and read through the workshops on offer this afternoon while she ate her ice cream.

When she'd scraped the bottom of the dish without settling on one, she turned her head in the direction where Rory was looking. In spite of her gloom, she had to smile at the girl who was walking their way. She couldn't have been more than six, her curly black hair pulled into two fluffy pigtails atop her head. Each pigtail was wrapped with several yellow ribbons, and at the end of each ribbon was a tiny, magical butterfly that flew around her hair. The effect was utterly charming, but the girl didn't seem to notice. She was too enraptured by her ice cream cone, which had been enchanted to turn into a rainbow of glittering colors. With each lick, the ice cream morphed from blue to purple to pink and back again. Who knew if it tasted any good, but that was exactly the sort of treat Morgan would have begged for at that age.

Enthralled as she was, the girl took another careless step forward and stumbled over an uneven patch of ground. Morgan caught her breath as the whole scene seemed to unfold in slow motion. The child didn't fall, but the cone lurched forward as she tried to maintain her balance, and ice cream flew into the air. Morgan was already cringing in sympathy when the ice cream froze in place and poured itself back into the cone.

From the corner of her eye, she caught Rory lowering her hand, and Morgan blinked. It should have been impossible for Rory—for anyone—to cast that quickly, but when she recalled Rory's trick with the lighter fluid and the pyre, Morgan reminded herself that *should have* didn't apply to her fake girlfriend.

The girl gasped, and so did several of the onlookers. Soon enough, their surprised and curious faces latched onto Rory. Her role in averting that tragedy must have been clear from either the way Morgan had turned to her, or because one or more people recognized her. A few of them clapped.

"Thank you so much." The girl's mother led the child over to Rory so her daughter could thank her as well.

Rory shook off the thanks. "Glad I got a sense that was coming, so I was ready."

"We would have heard the cries all the way across the festival site," the girl's mother said. A few more thanks and pleasantries later, she and her daughter moved on, and Morgan heard her urging the girl to eat the ice cream before she spilled it again.

"Heroine." Morgan nudged Rory in the ribs before she could think better of it. "Reflexes like that must come in handy at the Chalice."

"I wish, but trust me—I've spilled many glasses and bottles in my time." Rory winced as though recalling a specific incident. "I really did just get lucky and anticipate that."

"It was impressive," called a man from down their table, a compliment that struck Morgan as a rather vast understatement. The newcomer looked to be around the same age as the girl's mother, with crystal beads woven into his sandy blond beard. "With some practice, your control could be quite good. Your hand movements need sharpening, though. They're weak, but that's fixable."

Was this guy for real? He might not recognize Rory, but he had to know how few witches could ever hope to demonstrate that level of elemental control. The complexity of the ice cream, the speed at which Rory had overpowered it—that was intense magic, regardless of whether Rory had anticipated anything.

Morgan glared at the stranger, but Rory merely looked amused. Her expression suggested she didn't know him, so this wasn't some former rival or rival's coach trying to get under her skin. He was just another mediocre white man, one who probably called himself a sorcerer, inserting his bad opinion where it was neither needed nor wanted.

Rory simply acknowledged the guy had spoken with a half-hearted nod, and she put her sunglasses on, giving Morgan the sense that she'd like to disappear into the crowd.

But of course. Rory was not comfortable in the spotlight. Last night and the effect of a couple of glasses of mead excepted, that had been perfectly obvious over the entire year Morgan had known her. Rory was gracious when approached, but she kept her head down. She would be fine letting some stranger, who had no idea what he was talking about or who he was talking to, criticize her technique. No doubt she found it amusing. Morgan supposed that if she were the sort of witch who could laugh in the face of fire, she'd find this jackass's arrogance funny, too.

A good girlfriend would respect Rory's preference for keeping a low profile, which meant that finally—*finally*—this was an opportunity that Morgan couldn't screw up. She could be honestly and truly annoying because doing so would be giving in to exactly what her instincts were screaming at her to do.

For the first time in twenty-four hours, Morgan's blood pumped with something akin to glee. No one put down her friends when she was within earshot.

She stepped between Rory and the crystal hipster. "I'm sorry, are you seriously criticizing her technique? Do you know who she is?"

"Morgan." Rory grabbed at her arm.

Morgan ignored her and pointed with her free hand. "That is Rory fucking Sandler. You know, the youngest national spellcasting champion ever. The woman who pioneered a trick so dangerous it almost got banned from competition. Do you really expect me to believe you could have reacted quickly enough, with enough control, to stop that spill because you flick your wrist more sharply?"

Her voice carried throughout the immediate vicinity, her mouth running free of any restraint. Rory was probably a breath away from lighting her on fire, and Morgan didn't care. Later, she would regret embarrassing Rory, but at the moment, her tirade felt unapologetically right. The guy was glaring at her like she had nerve for lecturing him, and now she couldn't have stopped herself from going full-on bitch if she'd wanted to.

"Do you also give Simone Biles advice on how to do a cartwheel?" Morgan asked. "Do you tell Taylor Swift how to write a song?"

"Okay, seriously, that's enough, Morgan." Rory's grip on her arm tightened painfully, her voice louder than before.

Morgan took a deep breath. Rory's cheeks and neck gave the impression that she was suffering from a massive sunburn, and her lips were pressed as thin as Morgan had ever seen them in disapproval. The urge to apologize rose up Morgan's throat, but no more than a second of silence passed between the end of Morgan's tirade and new voices rising to defend Rory.

"Yeah, get real!" The group of teen girls sitting nearby had jumped up and were loudly expressing their outrage. "Like you could do better?"

Unable to handle the negative attention, the guy stormed off, shaking his head. But the girls didn't stop voicing their disapproval until he disappeared from sight, and one of them approached Rory shyly.

"I can't believe he said that to you." The girl's olive-toned cheeks turned almost as bright red as Rory's.

"It's . . ." Rory flailed about, clearly at a loss for how to expand. "It's okay. Thank you."

"No way. I bet he wouldn't have said that if you were a guy."

Rory bit her lip, and her cheeks started returning more to their normal shade. "No, probably not."

"Definitely not," Morgan said loudly. She took a long sip of water and pretended she didn't see the less-than-pleased expression Rory shot her.

The girl who'd approached Rory clearly wanted to say something else, and she kicked at the grass until one of her friends ran up to her and shoved her. She cleared her throat anxiously. "Okay, so I didn't want to bother you while you were eating, but I'm going to perform in the junior spellcasting exhibition today, and I wanted you to know that it's because of you. You're my inspiration, and I've been practicing elemental magic since I came into my powers because of you. You're amazing."

The words poured out of her in such a rapid torrent that it took Morgan a moment to decipher them. The girl's cheeks, already red, flushed so deeply that Morgan feared her face might explode. She'd have handed her water bottle to the girl if she hadn't already been holding her own.

The girl turned around and buried her face in her friend's shoulder while Rory stood there, her jaw hanging partially open. Morgan wondered if she needed help translating that rapid-fire speech, but then she realized Rory had simply been struck into silence.

Morgan pressed her fingertips against Rory's back, and Rory snapped out of her daze.

"That's really nice." She sounded confused at first, but her tone grew more confident as she spoke. "Thank you for telling me that. I'm glad you did. Is this the first time you're going to perform for an audience?"

Slowly, the girl turned around and nodded. "I was too young to do it at the last festival."

"Okay, just remember, it can be kind of scary at first when you see strangers watching you, but you can use that nervous energy to feed your power. Just don't feed it more than you can control, or you might cause explosions when you don't mean to." Rory smiled.

The girl nodded again, earnestly. "I'm in our school band. It's probably a lot like playing in front of people, right?"

"I'll bet, and I'm sure you'll do great. What's your name?"

Rory might be furious with her, but Morgan couldn't suppress her grin as she watched Rory sign autographs for the girls and offer more encouragement. The whole group had come forward, and they'd gathered in a semicircle around her, hanging on her every word.

Face it, said the hateful voice in Morgan's head, the Nicole-like one. *Even if you hadn't fucked everything up, how long do you think your fling with Rory would have lasted anyway? She's way too good for you. Too kind. Too powerful. Too special. Even if she never performs again, she was somebody, and you are nobody.*

Morgan pushed the cruel thoughts aside. She had half a mind to sneak out of the tent while Rory was distracted, but she feared Rory would chase after her as soon as she noticed Morgan was gone. She'd rather Rory give the girls her full attention.

When Rory turned toward her a few minutes later, the anger that had been simmering in her eyes had vanished, and Morgan didn't know how to feel about that. She only became more confused when they stepped back into the sunshine and Rory kissed her on the cheek.

"Thank you," she said.

"I thought you'd be furious at me."

How could Rory not be furious? She'd definitely sounded furious a few minutes ago.

"I was. Never do that again, or I will be forced to hex your tongue into knots." Rory poked Morgan in the arm, then smiled sheepishly. "But I do appreciate your willingness to always speak up, and how fearless you are when you're defending people you care about."

Oh. Wait. That wasn't how this was supposed to work.

"I don't think those girls would have talked to me if you hadn't made them brave," Rory continued. "It was good for them to see that. I've always hated drawing attention to myself, but I forget that sometimes being seen is helpful."

WHAT. THE. HELL?

The universe had to be messing with her. How did she keep failing at being obnoxious? First dancing and now this—she was such a spectacular screwup that she was fucking up the things that should have been un-fuck-up-able. It was wholly absurd.

Morgan couldn't hold in a wild laugh. "I told you that you were intimidating."

"I definitely wasn't intimidating to that guy."

"Yeah, well, luckily, the world doesn't entirely consist of mediocre white men." Morgan pretended to shudder. "But you did intimidate those girls."

"I don't want to be intimidating."

"Maybe stop dressing all in black?"

"I like black. It hides the bloodstains of my enemies."

Morgan snorted. "Why do you have to be so adorable?"

"See? Adorable. That's the antithesis of intimidating. You, however, jumping into strangers' faces when you're trying to protect people—most intimidating. And, I have to add, even though it pissed me off, supremely hot."

Oh, fuck her. This was so not fair.

"Seriously, it's a very admirable quality," Rory said, driving the knife in further, "and part of what makes you special. Not your ability to create a kick-ass potion."

"I'll keep that in mind."

Translation: she would replay this conversation in her head a thousand times, each one cutting deeper into her psyche until she was catatonic in her misery.

Or she would have, but Morgan's thoughts were interrupted by a familiar voice calling out her name and Rory's.

They both turned as Verbena plowed through the throngs of people, her black and gray hair streaming behind her. "Oh, thank the stars. There you are! We have an emergency!"

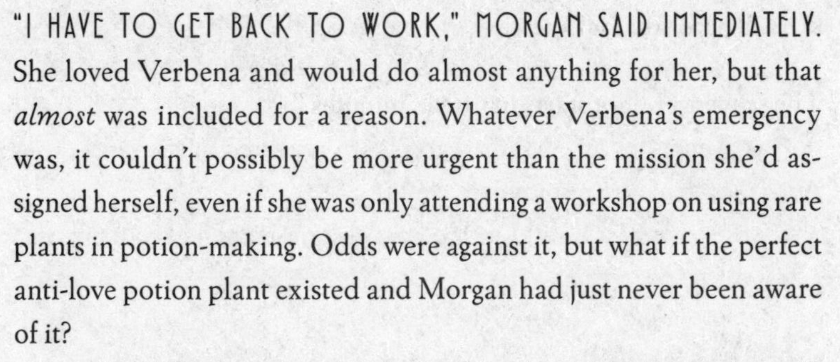

19

"I HAVE TO GET BACK TO WORK," MORGAN SAID IMMEDIATELY. She loved Verbena and would do almost anything for her, but that *almost* was included for a reason. Whatever Verbena's emergency was, it couldn't possibly be more urgent than the mission she'd assigned herself, even if she was only attending a workshop on using rare plants in potion-making. Odds were against it, but what if the perfect anti-love potion plant existed and Morgan had just never been aware of it?

Verbena's bracelets jingled as she stuck her hands on her hips. "I was just at your family's booth, and your mother and grandmother both volunteered your services. I believe Lianne's words were, 'It'll be good for her.'"

Morgan bit down a curse. The last time her mother had said something to that effect had been when Morgan was fourteen. She'd shot up in height over the summer, making her one of the tallest girls in her class, and she'd been recruited to play for the junior varsity basketball team. Morgan hadn't figured she'd be any good, but her mother and grandmom had encouraged her to try. She'd lasted two games, until her competitive streak and her still-developing magical talents had somehow resulted in an exploding ball, a 911 call, and a girl on the opposing team needing to be detangled from a suspiciously large hoop.

Morgan had assumed the ruckus caused by a half dozen firefighters and a news crew recording the incident for posterity would have made a stronger impression. But it appeared that over the past decade, her mother had forgotten the lessons they'd all learned that day—never tell Morgan that something would be good for her, and never permit her to participate in contact sports.

Verbena turned a challenging eye on Rory. "What's your excuse?"

Rory cocked her head to the side thoughtfully. "Depends on the emergency."

With a "humph," Verbena linked arms with them and began maneuvering them through the crowd as only someone of her age and imposing aura could. "You'll have to think of it while we walk, then. The scavenger hunt starts in fifteen minutes."

"Scavenger hunt?" Morgan and Rory repeated at the same time, giving Verbena their opinion in stereo.

"Yes, scavenger hunt. Our coven's second team had to drop out. They all tried some new recipe for galvanizing gooseberry scones that Moira made this morning, and this is why mixing magic with your meals is a risky proposition without lots of prior testing."

"Are they okay?" Morgan asked.

Verbena snorted. "They're fine if you can catch them. The magic will have to wear off eventually, but they can't focus on anything long enough to say a word with as many syllables as scavenger. There's no way they can participate, which is a shame. They'd be so fast."

Morgan glanced around Verbena at Rory, who looked like she was trying not to break into a fit of laughter. This was not good. It wasn't even that she thought she'd make headway on her potion this afternoon, but she'd just vowed at lunch to spend less time with Rory for both their sakes.

Unless . . . maybe there was a way to work this to her advantage?

Rory was competitive. If she agreed to this, Rory would be in it to win, and if Morgan sabotaged their chances, Rory would be irritated by her incompetence. It would be a mark against Morgan as good girlfriend material.

Of course, there were two major problems with this plan. One, Morgan wouldn't just be ruining things for Rory, but for the whole coven. And two, Morgan hated losing as much as her fake girlfriend did. Hence, the basketball incident.

"Every coven is allowed two teams," Verbena was saying. "We can't cut our chances of winning in half."

"But why us?" Morgan asked. The entire coven wasn't at the festival, but there had to be others free to put together a second team without them.

Verbena sighed at her like she was an unruly child. Which was only fair since Verbena had helped change her diapers once. "Because you're available, and because every team needs people with a variety of skills. And, if we're being frank here, the two of you aren't doing anything else to bring us festival glory. Nothing entered in the potion competition"—she looked at Morgan like the disappointed "witch mother" that she was—"and you're not . . ." Verbena cut herself off, although they all knew what she was going to say to Rory.

Rory grimaced. "I'm glad you're sensible enough not to believe the rumor going around about the exhibition. Fine. I'm in."

"Who else is on our team?" Morgan asked, resigned to her fate. She merely hoped the answer was someone, anyone, so it wouldn't be more time for her and Rory alone together.

Teams could consist of up to four people, and as Verbena had pointed out, the best strategy was to mix up a variety of skills and specialties. Morgan would be bringing potion knowledge. Rory was the elemental witch. That meant they needed someone who excelled at general spellcasting.

Verbena had whipped out her phone and was furiously texting as they started toward the crowd that had gathered around one of the many open-sided workshop buildings that dotted the grounds, so she didn't respond immediately. Probably close to a hundred people milled about, many in matching shirts. Since Morgan hadn't anticipated competing, she wasn't wearing her Harborage coven T-shirt, and neither was Rory, but Verbena had hers on.

Those shirts made it easy to spot the other Harborage team members as they headed over, along with Hazel, who was also not wearing a coven shirt. Perhaps that answered Morgan's question about the rest of her team.

"They roped you in, too?" she asked.

"Hazel volunteered," Verbena corrected her.

The dubious expression on Hazel's face suggested that she and their coven elder had different definitions of that word.

"You couldn't say no, could you?" Morgan whispered as they crossed the grass, slowly dividing into their two teams.

Hazel whimpered. "You didn't, either."

"We were ambushed and dragged here," Rory said. Although she joked, she didn't seem too displeased about the predicament. Already she was flexing her hands at her sides and scoping out the competition.

Her eagerness heated Morgan's blood. Damn it, she wanted to win, too, or at least not embarrass herself.

Glancing down the field, she noted Archer hanging out with Isaac and Erika. They weren't wearing matching shirts, either, but Morgan had learned that they all belonged to the same coven in Massachusetts, so they were likely working as a team. Isaac was yawning into a travel mug, and she wondered if his presence here meant the charming-potion investigation was already completed.

As she pondered, Isaac turned her way and smiled. It was a friendly—if somewhat tired—smile, but he stared in her direction a little too long for comfort, and Morgan glanced away after returning the gesture, her nerves prickling.

There was no way Isaac could have stumbled onto any clues to make him suspect she'd accidentally love-potioned his sister, right? None of the spells he'd performed for the charming-potion investigation should have revealed it. To do so, they would have needed to be focused on her. So yeah, everything was fine, Morgan reassured herself. Isaac was probably just exhausted and staring into space, and not at her at all.

Still, craving confirmation that Isaac was acting normally, Morgan nudged Rory and motioned to her brother, hoping she'd comment if anything seemed amiss. But Rory merely narrowed her eyes at Isaac in joyful anticipation. Since Morgan wasn't about to bring up her worries, because that would definitely be weird, Rory's lack of concern about his behavior would have to suffice.

Morgan had never participated in the scavenger hunt before, so she listened closely as the NEWT volunteers running the event went over the rules. Each team had been given a bag of supplies that should contain all they needed to complete each of the thirteen magical challenges. Every team's clues would be presented in a random order, so it would be hard to know who was ahead or behind you in the race, which would last three hours. At the end of that time, the first team back with the most ribbons won. The challenges—and ribbons to collect—were spread throughout the grounds; theoretically, it was possible to get them all if you worked quickly.

As soon as "Go!" left the witch's mouth, the teams scattered to open their bags and complete the first challenge that would tell them where to head next. Since the challenges were presented in a different order for each team, they got lucky at first. Morgan, Rory, and Hazel blew through the first few fast enough to give Morgan hope that they could do well.

They encountered a bit of frustration on the fifth challenge. They found their ribbon tied around a candle easily, but the paper containing the next clue was blank. Once they figured out it was invisible ink,

Hazel snapped her fingers to light the candle and . . . nothing. Perplexed, she tried again, and when she failed again, Rory did it. Or she tried to, and she also failed.

Given that Morgan had once seen Rory conjure a flame out of wet wood, the answer seemed pretty obvious to her. "It's a trick candle. My cousin gave me one once. The wick's been bespelled."

Rory glared at it like she was personally offended by such a thing. "I can overpower it."

"I'm sure," Hazel said, pulling one of the candles from their supply bag, "but since it's meant to be a time-wasting distraction, and we don't need you draining yourself so quickly, let's use this one."

Rory grumbled, but they got the clue and were off. "I hope you got back at your cousin for that candle," she said to Morgan as they raced toward the next challenge.

"Oh, I did. I modified the glamour potion in our lip balm, so five minutes after she put it on, it turned her lips black. She had no idea, and it lasted for almost a day."

Rory cracked up as Hazel pointed to an elaborate setup in a clearing ahead. "I didn't realize you had such a devious side. I like it. Also, remind me not to give you gag gifts."

Morgan grinned, then swore to herself. She was not supposed to be making Rory like her.

"I think you're up for this one," Hazel said, turning to her. "It looks like we need to make a potion."

Morgan's annoyance with herself faded under the pressure. Sure enough, three stations had been prepared with various supplies, all of which looked like they'd already been used by other teams—mortars and pestles, jars of unidentified herbs, bowls, eyedroppers, and more.

"Are we positive it's a potion and not a spell?" Morgan asked.

"Yup." Hazel handed her the sheet of paper on the nearest station that explained the challenge.

The ribbons had been bespelled to be hidden, which was as close as anyone had ever gotten to a true invisibility spell. Basically, the spell made it hard for human eyes to focus on them, so the brain interpreted that space as being empty. Only a person who took a revelation potion would be able to see them.

Morgan clenched her jaw. Taking a revelation potion was like putting on a pair of magical contact lenses, in the form of eye drops. It was hard enough to be challenging, but simple enough that it was often one of the first real potions a witch might learn, and with a practical reason. At one time, it was the sort of magic witches might use to pass messages they didn't want other people to see. Texting and email, however, had rendered that trick as useless as scrying mirrors. Morgan hadn't made a potion like this since around the last time her mother had threatened her with doing something that was good for her.

Her stomach twisted at the idea of failing at something that ought to be basic. "If I'd known I was going to get sucked into competing in this, I might have studied first."

She picked up the various packets of herbs on the table, but of course they weren't labeled. The potion-maker would be expected to identify the correct ingredients and know how to use them. She'd known the last few challenges had been too easy. Maybe she wouldn't have to worry about sabotaging their chances after all.

Fuck. If they were going to lose, she wanted it to be intentional, not because she sucked.

Fifteen minutes later, and aided by the standard supplies in their kit, Morgan frowned at the tiny amount of clear potion in her cup. There was just enough there for one person, so that suggested she'd done something right. But otherwise . . .

She'd used the marigold flowers, the oak bowl, a touch of rosemary oil, the mirror, and some silver filings, but she had zero clue as to what half the other ingredients on the table were meant for. If they were meant to be used at all and hadn't been placed there as distractions, that was.

"The quantity seems right," she said, taking a bite of the chocolate energy bar Rory handed her for the magic depletion. She was still stuffed from lunch, but it did stop the trees from swaying.

"If you're not sure," Rory said, placing a hand on her arm, "don't risk it."

"It's just . . ." Morgan took another bite and stuffed the remaining bar away. "I thought the cinnamon was supposed to be burned, but there's no censer, and we're not supposed to need anything they don't give us."

"It looks right," Hazel said, but she sounded worried. "Doesn't it?"

"Kind of." The truth was, Morgan didn't remember well enough to be certain.

The sound of voices startled her, and Morgan spun around as another team emerged into the clearing. They nodded in acknowledgment and took one of the other two tables.

"Maybe we should skip this one?" Rory asked. "Or we could scry to see if you did it right, if nothing else."

Scrying would be the safe option, but neither she nor Hazel were great at it, and Rory claimed she didn't have much talent for it, either. Getting a good, accurate answer here would take time, and the other team was already starting.

Morgan appreciated Rory's caution, and she knew it was the smart decision, but they didn't have time for that if they wanted to win. Besides, *she* was not cautious. What better way was there to show Rory how incompatible they were than by doing the opposite of what she was suggesting?

"Fuck it," Morgan said. She suctioned the potion into the eyedropper.

Rory had been in the process of removing the scrying crystal from their bag, and she dropped it in alarm. "Morgan, maybe that's not such a great idea!"

Hazel squeaked as Morgan let the first drop fall. It landed at the corner of her left eye. She rolled her head around to get it in, then repeated with her right. The potion stung for a second and the world turned blurry.

Heart racing, because she knew this was not one of her wisest moments, Morgan blinked a few times while Rory cursed next to her. The final time she opened her eyes, the world shimmered, a hazy magic overlaying everything. Then that, too, dissipated, and all returned to normal.

Disappointment, and no small amount of relief, washed over her. She could see, so that was a positive. Just no better than normal, which was definitely not.

"Are you okay?" Rory asked.

"Can you see?" Hazel asked.

"Everything looks . . ." The words "the same" were about to slide off her tongue, but when she looked into the trees, she discovered she was wrong. Colorful ribbons hung like streamers from the branches. Morgan let out a whoop. "Found them!"

Unfortunately, the other team would know where she was going, but they couldn't simply fumble around and take any old ribbon. They had to take the one meant for their team, which meant they needed to complete the potion. It took Morgan another couple of minutes to find theirs, and Rory was still scowling at her by the time she produced it.

As they hurried away, Rory squeezed Morgan's wrist. "That was incredibly reckless. You could have gotten seriously hurt."

Morgan's triumph deflated slightly. Rory didn't seem angry with her, just concerned. "I was mostly certain it was right. Ninety-five percent. Well, eighty-five percent. No less than seventy-five."

"Seriously?"

"Oh, come on. Don't talk to me about being reckless when you've asked people to set you on fire!"

Rory made a noise like a growl, so lost in her frustration she almost tripped over a pebble in the path. "A stunt that I'd practiced for months. That I worked up to."

"Yes, and I always rely on my instincts—that's what I've worked on. And my instincts weren't screaming danger. Relax. You want to win, right?"

The glare she received in response answered Morgan's question. Rory let out an "ugh," and caught up to Hazel. Morgan wasn't sure if that meant Rory was annoyed with her or annoyed with herself for agreeing with Morgan's strategy.

They ran into more and more people over the next few clues, including Verbena's team. With time running short (in part thanks to the need for an emergency bathroom break), and three clues left, they headed down a path toward the river.

Morgan's stomach sank, and not only because she could tell this next challenge was going to be hard. Archer, Isaac, and Erika were already there. From the looks of it, Isaac was preparing a spell with Erika's assistance.

Probably a third of the team ribbons remained, telling Morgan they were faring better than most of the competition. But that was where the good news ended. The ribbons were tied to a rope that crossed the river, high above the water and unreachable.

Isaac glanced over, sparing just enough time to smile wickedly at his sister, then he returned to work. Archer crossed his arms, assessing Morgan's team.

"A floating spell," Rory said, keeping her voice low. "But it will have to be a strong one, and we'll have to work fast."

Hazel groaned, and Morgan didn't blame her. Contrary to popular belief, there was no such thing as flying brooms. There were spells to make people or objects float, but floating was a poor substitute for flying. Whoever performed this spell would raise themselves off the ground, then have to pull themselves along the rope over the river while they searched for the correct ribbon. Then, if they were lucky, make it back to land before their spell ran out of power.

"I know how to do it," Hazel said. "I use a variation on it in my inks to get lifting effects, but I don't know about putting enough power into it. I'm beat from the last challenge."

Rory clapped her arm. "I'll help with the power."

Of the three of them, she was the only one who wasn't suffering from any magic-induced exhaustion yet. Not a surprise.

While Hazel and Rory went down to the riverbank to get to work, Morgan scoped out a good rock to sit and rest on. This patch of land reminded her a bit of the spot Rory had taken her to two days ago, and sadness crept into Morgan's heart. Wearily, she pushed it away. This wasn't the time to indulge, especially not while Rory's family and Archer were around.

Speaking of them, Morgan glanced up as a shadow darkened her view of where the two teams were working on their spells. After doing nothing but glare at her the past couple of days, Archer had apparently decided to break his silence. Morgan braced for the worst.

"You know you're never going to win over Rory's parents while you're enabling her," he said, taking the next rock over. Morgan hadn't noticed it before, but sitting down, they were the same height.

She could have laughed. The only person she'd wanted to win over had been Rory. "Are we really going to have this conversation?"

"We have to. If you actually care about her, stop. You're not doing her any favors. She needs people to push her back into competing, not help her be a quitter."

"I'm not enabling her; I'm supporting her. What she chooses to do is her choice. If you actually aren't a douchebag, you'll let her be happy."

Archer rubbed his scruff. "You think she's happy? She won the national title when she was twenty-four. She probably would have placed at the world championships—maybe won the whole thing. You don't work that hard and accomplish that much if you're not ambitious. And if you're that ambitious, you don't give everything up on a whim and ride off into the sunset, content to pour people drinks for a living."

Morgan frowned. She still didn't know why Rory had done what she'd done, and though she hated to admit it, Archer's words were clawing their way under her skin. She couldn't exactly argue the point.

Worse, Archer was unknowingly veering close to her own sore subject. While Morgan didn't know what Rory needed to be happy, she did know what *she* wanted and that she hadn't found a way to accomplish it yet. And when she thought about their situations that way, some part of her did have a hard time believing Rory was truly happy with where she was in life. But who was she to ask Rory about her goals? She was just a fake girlfriend and a terrible friend.

"What do you get out of all this?" Morgan snapped, because these thoughts annoyed her.

Archer's baby face turned almost dreamy for a second with whatever he was thinking. Then his cool blue eyes hardened like steel. "I want one of the most powerful witches in the world as my training partner. But she's got to get back to competing first. You see my dilemma?"

She'd expected Archer to feed her more crap about Rory's happiness, but his response sounded self-serving enough to be honesty. Since she hadn't been expecting it, Morgan blustered to cover up her surprise. "Oh, that's all?"

"Were you afraid I wanted to steal your girlfriend?"

Morgan shrugged. At one point, yes, but that had passed. Now she was simply curious about Archer's motives. Perhaps she should have been able to guess the truth. "Like you could steal her."

Like you could, because I gave her a love potion.

Oh fuck, that wasn't funny at all, and yet Morgan felt like laughing. The stress must be getting to her.

"Rory!" Hazel's scream snapped Morgan out of her stupor, and she and Archer darted for the riverbank in time to see Rory take a running leap toward the water.

"What the hell is she doing?" Archer yelled.

Sadly, Morgan had to admit it was a good question.

She froze in shock a moment later as Rory flew—fucking flew—over the water and up to the ribbons. If everyone else hadn't been gaping the same way, Morgan would have thought the revealing potion was messing with her eyesight. But no, Rory was in the air, and obviously not from a floating spell. That would have been a calm, gentle motion. Rory, on the other hand, moved awkwardly and unsteadily, as though the ground below her kept shifting. Only it wasn't ground beneath her, but air—wind, specifically. Her hair and clothes whipped about her body, as did the ribbons as she searched for the right one.

"She's manipulating the air," Archer said a moment later. Morgan couldn't drag her eyes away from Rory to see his expression, but she heard the awe in his voice without issue and she imagined he had that dreamy look about him again. No wonder he wanted to train with her.

"Got it!" The river made it hard to hear Rory's cry of triumph, but she held the ribbon high in her hand and pumped her fist.

Morgan hollered with delight, unable to believe what she was seeing.

Grinning wildly, Rory floated back toward the riverbank. "This is amazing! Can you believe—"

Then she plummeted into the water.

Hazel and Erika screamed, and Morgan swore, dashing down to the bank. But Rory was already climbing up the dirt path by the time she got there. Laughing and trembling with what had to be magic depletion (at last), Rory thrust the wet ribbon at Hazel to add to their collection. She was completely drenched but appeared positively delighted with herself.

"Did you see that?" she yelled, as if anyone could have watched anything else. "That was awesome!"

The only person who didn't seem fazed was Isaac, who was probably used to his sister's antics, and who'd finished his spell and was beginning to float himself in a much more controlled and undoubtedly safer manner. Archer was shaking his head—amazement and jealousy, Morgan decided—and she and Hazel practically carried a dripping Rory away, as fast as they could.

"What did you just do?" Morgan asked, handing Rory one of the last energy bars.

"The spell was taking too long," Rory said, huffing up the hill back to the path. "Not Hazel's fault, but I thought why not try something faster."

"You flew," Hazel said, stating the obvious.

"You fell," Morgan added, "into the river. You could have gotten seriously hurt."

Oh, fuck her. She was saying the same words to Rory that Rory had said to her only minutes ago.

Rory shook her wet head, flinging water droplets all over Morgan. "It was a controlled fall. I got too tired. Not how I'd wanted to end that experiment, granted, but I didn't think I'd get hurt. Eighty-five, seventy-five percent chance anyway." She stuck her tongue out at Morgan.

"Are you really throwing my words back at me?" Morgan wanted to slap her.

No, she wanted to slap herself.

Rory, she wanted to tackle and pin to the ground where she'd be safe while Morgan kissed her and told her over and over again what an unbelievable badass she was.

Rory looped her arm around Morgan's. "What can I say? You're a bad influence, but you were right. If we want to win this thing, we need to be less cautious and just go for it. We're so close."

"That was not—"

Thankfully, Rory was already consulting Hazel about their next stop, and she didn't hear Morgan almost blurt out that this wasn't the lesson she was supposed to have taken away from Morgan's recklessness.

Unlike the other times her plans had failed, though, Morgan couldn't even spare a couple of minutes to berate herself into misery. Rory's happiness was infectious. However tired she must have been, she propelled them through the last two challenges. Morgan and Hazel had a hard time keeping up.

"You okay?" Hazel asked Morgan as Rory worked to get their last ribbon. "You seem suspiciously cheerful for someone who's been miserable for the last twenty-four hours."

The reminder that she should be miserable extinguished some of Morgan's mood. "It'll pass. It's just—holy shit. She's amazing, right?"

"I assume we're talking about Rory. Yes, that's well established. As is the fact that you have a huge crush on her."

Morgan closed her eyes. "I think I love her."

Saying it out loud made it real in a way it hadn't been before. Like magic being released, the words were out there now. The meaning behind them impossible to restrain or undo, and impossible for her to pretend otherwise. She'd unleashed her power into the wind and given up control over her heart.

"Do you really?" Hazel asked.

"Getting to spend all this time with her . . ." She took a deep breath. "Before, I was attracted to her, but I think it was the idea of her that I was crushing on. I mean, she's hot and super talented, and she has that whole mysterious past thing going for her—totally crushable. Right? But she's so much more interesting than that. She's funny and smart and sweet."

And adorably competitive about the stupidest shit. Always kind to strangers who approached her. Quick to offer encouragement to girls who wanted to follow in her footsteps, even if she hated her former life so much that she wouldn't talk about it. Allegedly overconfident yet clearly soft and vulnerable. Rory always knew what words to say, like she could see right down into Morgan's soul and blast away the insecurities lurking there with her power.

Reminding herself of all these things made Morgan's heart feel like it would burst. Then it deflated in her chest with defeat.

How did she stop hurting the woman she loved when her every attempt was a disaster?

20

TO MORGAN'S ABSOLUTE DELIGHT, RORY'S GRUMBLING DISAPpointment, and Hazel's utter shock, they took second place in the scavenger hunt. Barely. Archer, Isaac, and Erika were a close third, and the only thing that placated Rory was that she could rub it into her brother's face that she'd beaten him. Since the top three teams were all awarded points, Morgan would accept no more guilt about not contributing to their coven's festival glory. Particularly since Verbena's team finished eleventh.

Hazel had plans to meet up with Rory's friend again, and she rubbed her eyes. "I need a nap after this. Do you think I should cancel?"

"I think you should track down those scones Verbena was telling us about," Morgan said. "Put a new meaning to speed dating."

"Speed kissing?" Rory suggested.

"Speed fu—Ow!" Morgan's usually nonviolent friend had punched her in the shoulder.

Hazel massaged her hand. "I think I'll get an iced chai. That'll help."

"A dirty chai?" Morgan asked, and she hid behind Rory before Hazel could punch her again.

"Speaking of dirty." Rory sniffed herself as Hazel strode away after giving them both looks that could also be described as dirty. "I smell like the river."

Morgan resisted the intense urge to press her face against Rory's hair and confirm. "I wonder why."

Rory ignored that. "I have enough time to take a quick shower before heading over to the junior exhibition and offering moral support. Want to come?"

"To the shower or the exhibition?" Damn it. Why did she have to say that out loud?

Rory smirked. "Both are options, although the first will slow us down."

There was an opportunity to make another speed joke there, but Morgan dug her nails into her palms and held it in. "I want to do some shopping, actually. I'll meet you at the exhibition?"

She hadn't realized Rory had committed to going to the junior exhibition, but aside from the fact that she wasn't supposed to be spending more time with Rory, Morgan had no reason not to go and a good reason to do so. Rory might be attending to offer moral support, but Morgan suspected she might need some support of her own. Her presence was going to cause a stir.

Morgan took her time wandering the vendor booths, her first stop at the handful of wineries, meaderies, and orchards. The magical offerings were vast—cider that attracted true love, wines that allowed you to reexperience your happiest memories, mead that tasted like summer (which made Morgan think of the cocktail Rory had been creating for the Empty Chalice), and even drinks that promised to promote clarity of mind, which seemed to Morgan to be rather counterproductive to the reason for drinking alcohol in the first place. She settled on a strawberry wine that boasted no magic except for the ability to chill itself when uncorked, and she stuffed the bottle awkwardly in her bag before resuming her shopping.

It was after five o'clock by the time Morgan made it to the exhibition, and her purchases weighed her down as she neared the field closest to the festival entryway. Although the NEWT Festival itself was only held every other year, the stadium on the grounds saw far more action. Between amateur local leagues, and regional and national events, spellcasting exhibitions and competitions were nearly year-round activities, and the stadium reflected that. It was enormous, a giant wood and stone bowl decorated in colorful banners that celebrated various NEWT milestones of decades past.

Morgan had come here to watch competitions on a couple of occasions, but unlike those events, which might draw a crowd of a thousand or so, the dirt parking lot was mostly empty today, and the stadium would be as well. No tickets were required for admission, so she passed through the gates and scanned the area.

On the field, one of the performers must have recently finished their act. Clapping died away as the young witch paused by the festival volunteers, and the four witches maintaining the magic circle released it. The candles positioned at each cardinal point snuffed out, and the air shimmered as the invisible force field vanished. It was probably unnecessary to maintain a protective circle during the junior exhibition since the witches were too young to be especially powerful, but good practice was good practice. One of the events Morgan had once attended in this very stadium had made her grateful for that magical shield when the performer had lost control of the tornado she'd conjured.

Maybe a hundred people sat in the bleachers today, watching the action on the field. Another dozen or so witches stood off to the side of the circle casting area, observing from ground level.

Although she'd changed clothes and her back was toward Morgan, Morgan's gaze homed in on Rory, as usual feeling the pull of her gravity. Rory was some distance away from the others on the field, between the eastern and southern candles, and standing next to Archer. No one stopped her, so Morgan went down a flight of stairs, climbed over a railing, and passed a couple who were more intent on staring at Rory than the teenage witch who had taken to the field in the intervening minutes. The girl was demonstrating her prowess with water control by creating an ice sculpture via magic and a bucket filled with water.

"Hi," she whispered close to Rory's ear.

"Glad you made it." She gave Morgan's fingers a light squeeze and jerked her head in Archer's direction, rolling her eyes in an exaggerated fashion. Morgan had acknowledged his presence with a polite smile, but Archer hadn't bothered to glance her way, and he wasn't looking at Rory, either.

"She has more talent as an artist than an elementalist," Archer said, not taking his eyes off the girl. She had to be at the upper age range of the performers, but it was hard to tell with her elaborate stage makeup. Anyone eighteen or older was no longer classified as a junior, though, regardless of their skill.

Rory shrugged. "She's fun to watch."

"It's as interesting as watching any other artist work." Archer's tone made it clear that he thought that was not interesting at all.

Elementalist? Morgan mouthed to Rory. That was as pretentious as describing oneself as a sorcerer. She hadn't heard Archer do that (to be fair, the situation had never arisen), but Rory claimed he did, and Morgan believed her. She hadn't been disposed to like Archer anyway, for reasons that were arguably *not* fair, but her conversation with him during the scavenger hunt had justified her opinion. Archer didn't care about Rory's happiness, only his own ambition. He was just another Nicole.

The young witch bowed next to her finished creation—an ice-sculpted dragon—and Morgan applauded with the rest of the audience. She couldn't see the detail on the dragon from where she stood, but she could make out that it was, in fact, a dragon, so the girl had more artistic skills than she did.

Rory tapped her lips. "If she could learn to move the ice so it looked like it was flying, that would serve her well. Judges always like seeing multiple types of control."

Archer grunted.

"Although she could try to actually make it fly," Rory amended. "That would be a lot harder, though."

Archer didn't even respond to that.

"Did the girl we met earlier perform already?" Morgan asked.

"Phaedra? Yeah, she was one of the first. She was good."

"For her age," Archer said.

Rory turned and mouthed something at Morgan. Morgan was lousy at lipreading, but it seemed a safe bet that it translated to, *I'm going to set him on fire.*

They watched two more witches perform—a very young girl who must only have come into her powers recently, and a boy doing some fairly standard tricks but with appreciable flair. Archer's commentary was predictably irritating, but at least he didn't excessively praise the boy performer for simply existing.

"How come you never participated in the junior exhibitions?" Morgan asked; it dawned on her that she'd never read about it, and surely, given how much press Rory had eventually received, something about it would have been written.

Elemental spellcasting shows could take one of two forms. At exhibitions, anything went, and the judges could score performances on whatever criteria they wished. Like the ones at the festival, they existed just for fun. Competitions were another matter. During a competition, judging followed specific criteria, and witches were scored on their power, control, and artistry. Council-sanctioned competitions started at the local level and ran all the way up to national tournaments.

Competitors were tracked across events, and the biggest ones were by invitation only for the highest-ranked witches.

The man announcing the performers called out a new name, and the witches at the quarters cast a fresh circle. Rory was holding a list of the performers, and it appeared they were about two-thirds of the way through. She folded it and stuck it in her backpack, then pulled out her phone and checked the time.

"Strategy," she answered Morgan. "Lots of serious competitors keep an eye on the junior events to see who the up-and-coming competition might be. My parents and my coach didn't want anyone to gather that intel on me."

The strategy had worked. Rory had taken a lot of people by surprise and garnered a lot of attention during her first competition. She'd ranked in the top ten nationally that year, too, unheard of for an eighteen-year-old.

Competitive spellcasting wasn't an old witches' game—that kind of magic and its subsequent drain took its toll on the body physically. But it wasn't a young person's forte, either. It took years, decades really, to develop enough power and control to rise to the top. Most competitors who were serious about it peaked in their forties. That was one more reason why Rory eventually winning nationals when she was in her mid-twenties had made her a bit of a legend, never mind the setting herself on fire bit.

"That was smart," Morgan said. "You placed third in your performance at the last national's qualifier that year."

"You remember that?" Rory gave her an incredulous look.

Oh shit. She was blushing. "I was a bit of a fan. Before I met you, I mean. Not that I'm not one anymore, but you know. It's different now, obviously."

Rory stopped her babbling by kissing her cheek, and Morgan was torn between grinning like a dumbass or crying like one.

"We need to get going. My dad's helping preside over the group spell circle tonight, so dinner is going to be early. I feel bad about missing Athena's performance," Rory said, referring to the daughter of one of their coven members, "but I'm sure her family is taking video."

As they left the area, a few people called out to Rory, telling her how excited they were to see her perform tomorrow. She waved back with a strained smile that reminded Morgan of a mask. As soon as the crowd had disappeared behind them and the stadium was at their backs, Rory ripped it off.

"This is your fault," she snapped at Archer.

With his sunglasses on, his baby face took on a decidedly douchey appearance, Morgan decided. Very punchable.

"I don't know why you're being so stubborn. I negotiated a prime spot for us in the lineup," Archer said. "Word is spreading, and everyone is excited. Most of the festival is going to show up."

"Fucking wonderful." Rory kicked a pebble down the dirt path. "When I tell everyone that I had nothing to do with the rumor and it was all you getting people's hopes up, I hope you enjoy being hexed."

Archer raised his arms. "I don't understand you. You didn't act like you hated performing at the exhibition today. Why go if you did?"

Morgan darted in front of his path as Rory stormed ahead, and she held up her hand. "You do not know when to drop things, do you?"

For a second, she thought he might he push her out of the way, but she apparently didn't deserve that kind of effort. Archer stepped aside with merely a sigh to retrieve his phone from his pocket, and Morgan charged after Rory.

Rory grabbed her hand and lobbed her a tired smile. "I have to admit I'm in no rush to return to my family. Want to take the scenic route and see which covens are in the lead for the awards?"

Regardless of their score in the scavenger hunt, Harborage's coven was unlikely to be a contender (barring, say, Rory actually performing tomorrow), so Morgan didn't feel particularly invested in who won. That said, as much as she was looking forward to no longer carrying around a full wine bottle and assorted other purchases, she also wasn't looking forward to dinner with the Sandlers. So she readily agreed.

The awards information, along with all sorts of other general festival information, was posted in the registration tent. At this time of day, the people arriving had trickled into nothing, and a couple of bored volunteers sat by the registration tables with their feet up, swapping gossip and spells. They barely glanced at Morgan and Rory as they headed to the back of the tent and the giant bulletin board.

There were coven awards for service and awards for activism, as well as individual awards for each. There were awards for the coven that had the most witches volunteering at the festival, which Morgan considered self-serving but fair. Awards were also given out for the various competitions, such as potion-making, kitchen witchery, and stitching witchery. There was a junior scavenger hunt for the under-eighteens (an easier version of the adult scavenger hunt), scrying competitions for speed and accuracy, and many more games. And, of course, there were awards for those who participated in the exhibitions. Since these were exhibitions and not formal competitions where one witch would be crowned winner, festival judges gave out individual awards for creativity, flair, power, and whatever other categories they chose. Add up all the various awards, and the coven with the most points was declared the overall winner of the Golden Cauldron award.

The awards ceremony was always held at the closing of the last day during the evening bonfires. It was meant to be celebratory, but to Morgan, it always felt bittersweet because it marked the end of the festival. She and her family would have already packed up most of their booth by then, and all that would be left was one more sleep, then they'd load the cars in the morning and start the long drive home to normal life. Sure, she worked while at the festival, but it still took place in a kind of otherworld. When she went home, she would have her friends and her work, but she'd cease being surrounded by her people. Life always felt more magical, for all definitions of that word, at the festival. Maybe that association with its end was one reason why, despite being competitive in general, Morgan didn't care too much about the festival awards.

Although she told herself not to look, her gaze landed on the winners of the potion-making competition, and Morgan sighed as she read what the winning potions were. "Look at that. This is why I don't bother to enter."

Rory understood exactly what she was referring to, and she shifted her attention to where Morgan was looking. This year's runner-up was a potion that could make a person briefly float on air. The winner was one that could show the drinker the face of their true love.

"Scrying in a bottle." Morgan groaned. "I would never even think to try to create something like that."

Rory crossed her arms. "Okay, but what good is a potion that makes you float? Besides that it might have saved me a swim today? It's a silly gimmick. Fun, I guess, and a way for mundanes to experience flying, but just a party trick."

"It's more creative than anything I've tried to do, and it's got to be a lot harder to make than my stuff. And a divination potion is *incredible*."

"Again, I ask—for what purpose? How do you even know if that potion works? All I foresee is a potion that could raise the divorce rate among those who take it."

Morgan snorted. She appreciated that Rory was trying to make her feel better, but all she felt was hopeless. And guilty—she couldn't forget that. How was she supposed to create an anti-love potion when her skills were so clearly subpar?

Rory entwined her arm with Morgan's, and Morgan was too depressed to protest. Nor did she really want to. There was no one else she wanted comfort from more than Rory, however wrong it was.

"Look," Rory said, "you're not creating unique but ultimately pointless potions because you're busy creating ones that are actually useful. That's not a commentary on your skill, but on your professionalism. Maybe you could create a floating potion if you were motivated to do it, or maybe not. But until you're motivated to try something that stretches your talents and skills, you don't know what you're capable of. And for what it's worth, I am completely confident that you are capable of amazing things."

Morgan wanted to believe Rory was right, but she was under a spell. An illicit spell Morgan had made by accident. Because she was capable of making utter disasters, too.

"Thank you."

Rory gave her some major side-eye. "I can see on your face that you're doubting me, but I'm not saying this to make you feel better. I've heard you talk about your work plenty over the last two weeks, and I've bought stuff from your store. Everyone in Harborage has, and we all agree you do excellent work. If you don't trust me, trust Bea's opinion. She wouldn't have complimented you if she didn't mean it."

It was true that she'd talked about potion-making with Rory sometimes, just like Rory had answered her questions about elemental spell work. Morgan had assumed she'd been boring Rory, but what if she hadn't? Some of those conversations had taken place before Morgan had given Rory the love potion. Was it possible, then, that Rory's opinion was untainted by it?

"Although," Rory added as Morgan's mood started to improve, "and I will say this until you get sick of hearing it, you don't need to create anything fancy to be someone special. You don't need a noteworthy potion to be a noteworthy person."

That surely had to be the love potion talking, but the rest . . . Morgan allowed herself some hope. Sure, it was just Rory's opinion, but it was a lot harder to discount *Rory's* opinion than it was her grandmom's. Rory might not be much of a potion-maker, but she wasn't a biased family member, and she was the most powerful witch Morgan knew. Her assessment of Morgan's current skills might be off, but probably not her assessment of Morgan's potential. If Rory believed in her, Morgan would have to trust that she could create that anti-love potion after all.

21

WHEN THEY ARRIVED AT THE SANDLERS' CABIN, THE PLACE WAS IN chaos. With Erika's help, Rory's parents were rushing to get dinner ready so they could prepare for the group spellcasting. Isaac was just getting up from a nap, and his additions to the conversation were groggy and irritable. The baby wanted dinner, too, and was making a fuss.

After Morgan handed over the bottle of wine she'd bought, she and Rory were told their assistance was neither wanted nor needed in the kitchen, and they beat a hasty—and on Morgan's part, grateful—retreat. Lilith was hanging out in their room, and Morgan gave the cat the present she'd been unable to resist buying for her earlier—an enchanted pink bow tie filled with catnip. Since technically the present was for Lilith, Morgan assured herself that she was not screwing up her plan to make Rory fall out of love by buying it. She simply had cat needs; that was all. Until she had one of her own again, she was always adopting the cats around her.

Lilith grudgingly allowed Rory to put the bow tie on her, then seemingly became very confused by what was happening when Rory showed the cat her reflection in the mirror. The magic in the bow tie had given Lilith the appearance of floppy rabbit ears, a cotton ball tail, and eyes more commonly seen on a Snapchat filter.

"I'm not sure if she loves it or hates it," Morgan said as they watched Lilith try to attack the bow tie.

"I'm not sure if she loves or hates *you* right now," Rory said, taking pictures. "I, however, know where I fall. This is going to bring me hours of entertainment. Thank you."

Playtime with Lilith was interrupted by Isaac calling out that dinner was ready, and Rory reluctantly removed the bow tie. Lilith turned her back on Morgan and Rory, and she darted out of the room with all the feline dignity she could muster.

Archer had arrived while they were upstairs, and Morgan was glad she'd contributed to the wine bottles sitting out in the dining room. With the addition of herself and Archer, plus the five Sandlers and Erika, the table was crowded and there was more tension than food. Even Isaac, who was still half-asleep, appeared ready to snap.

Despite that, dinner started off promising. Rory's mother began the meal by complimenting Morgan on the relaxing hand lotion. While Morgan and Rory had been racing for scavenger hunt glory, Rory's parents had stopped by the Bed, Bath, and Broom booth. Wanda had purchased a bottle of the lotion, which she credited with helping her weather the Council's investigation of last night's incident.

Morgan's first thought was that her potion couldn't have done much, given how on edge everyone was. Then she recalled what Rory had told her on the way to dinner, and she forced herself to stop being so negative. Rory kicked Morgan under the table as Morgan tried to graciously accept Wanda's praise, a gesture Morgan took to mean, *See, I told you so.*

Then there was the scavenger hunt to discuss. Rory wasted no time reminding the table that her team had beaten Isaac's.

"No, no, no. Doesn't count. I was exhausted from dealing with the investigation all morning. In no way was that a fair competition." Isaac jerked his thumb in his wife's direction. "She dragged me into it when I should have been napping."

Erika pushed his hand out of her face. "You said, and I quote, *I could do any of the spells involved in my sleep*."

Isaac glared at her. "What? You're on *her* side now? I demand a rematch at the next festival. See you in two years."

"I'm just saying . . ." Erika smirked into her dinner while Isaac glared at the taunting faces Rory made in his direction.

Talk of the investigation took over after that. Isaac confirmed that yes, they believed they'd found the witches responsible. No, they didn't think the intent was malicious, more like a prank that should not have been played. And yes, that was all he could tell them.

Morgan was surprised how little gossip she'd encountered during the day, but then, she hadn't mingled much, and her mind had been elsewhere. People standing next to her could have been talking about the incident, and unless the words "love potion" had escaped their lips, she probably wouldn't have noticed.

Speaking of those two words, Morgan was relieved to see that they didn't seem to mean anything to Isaac—at least he didn't bring anything up, and he was treating her the same way he had since they met. Any oddness Morgan had seen in his behavior earlier had to have been her imagination, which was a relief. There was enough tension present without her being paranoid.

Nothing went awry until dessert, when Erika shared the magical mix-and-match cupcakes she'd bought. They allowed each person to create their own unique combination of flavors from several options, and everyone had a moment of fun teasing Rory's father when he made his a boring vanilla with vanilla frosting. By that point, Morgan had allowed herself to relax a touch. One glass of wine helped, but everyone was on their best behavior. Because of that, Morgan had assumed that she wasn't the only person who'd noticed the tension in the air and was trying to prevent it from creating an explosion, but as it turned out, she was wrong. Some of them had merely been biding their time. Rory's mother lobbed a verbal grenade as Morgan bit into her cupcake (chocolate with raspberry cheesecake frosting).

"I heard you were at the junior spellcasting exhibition," Wanda said to Rory.

Rory's head snapped toward Archer. "Really?"

"Don't look at me," he said, shrugging off her accusation. "You said to drop it, so I dropped it." He sounded too smug for Morgan's taste. He might not have been the one to tell Rory's parents, but he'd certainly been waiting for the subject to arise.

Rory sighed. "Yes, I was at the junior exhibition. The daughter of one of our coven members was performing, and I met another girl at lunch who was also performing. I wanted to offer them encouragement."

"A fan of yours?" Brett asked.

Rory stared at her father, and the remains of her cupcake flattened between her fingers.

Morgan tentatively waded in. "A girl who was nervous about performing. Rory was giving her tips."

Speaking up was a mistake. Instead of disappointing the Sandlers by implying the girl hadn't been a fan, they latched onto Rory's attempt to help her. Even Isaac perked up, as though Rory had taken a positive step toward . . . something.

Shit. As usual, she was opening her mouth when she should be keeping it closed. Morgan once again realized how much she didn't know about why Rory had quit competing, and why it was therefore such a sore subject.

Loud voices overlapped with questions and commentary from everyone but Morgan and Erika, who was quietly feeding bites of her cupcake to a very happy baby. Morgan played with her empty wineglass, trying to think of something to say that would be helpful, although she suspected that her silence was probably the best she could do.

While Archer gave a rundown of what they'd seen at the junior exhibition, Morgan stole glances at Rory, searching for a sign as to what she needed or wanted from her. But Rory kept her head down and her face disturbingly placid.

"I suggested—*again*—to Rory that we could perform together tomorrow," Archer said, "if she'd rather not do it by herself."

Rory had turned her cupcake into crumbs by this point, and Morgan would not have been surprised to see them go flying at Archer. The way Rory covered them with her napkin, calmly, deliberately, with that icy self-control she'd demonstrated time and time again, struck Morgan as somehow scarier. "I don't work well with others."

"You don't work at all these days," her father said.

Rory's eyes flashed. "I have a job."

"And she works very hard at it," Morgan added, relieved to be able to say something helpful at last.

Brett scowled and ignored her. "You threw away a brilliant career, and for what?"

"Another career," Rory said pointedly.

"Dad, let it go." Isaac rubbed his eyes. He sounded more tired than ever, and Morgan could only assume this was not his first failed intervention this week.

The baby chose that moment to spit out a mouthful of frosting, and Isaac and Erika both jumped out of their chairs, fighting over which of them got to go clean him up.

"How do you give up something you spent your entire life working toward?" Rory's mother asked. She sounded genuinely bewildered. "You loved it. It was all you wanted to do since you were in kindergarten."

"Until I didn't, which is the part you're always ignoring." Finally,

Rory had raised her voice. Not a lot, but enough to get her frustration across.

"You could love it again," her mother said. "You took a break. That's fine, but the longer you take to get back in the stadium, the harder it's going to be. The more insurmountable it's going to feel when you get tired of bartending. For now, your fans, the sponsorships—they're waiting for you. But they won't forever, and what happens if the love returns then? And how will you know you won't fall back in love if you don't try?"

If she doesn't want to try, isn't that enough of a clue? The words were on the tip of Morgan's tongue, but she hesitated. An idea, both horrible and brilliant, lit up her brain.

Since last night, she'd been doing small things to annoy Rory, hoping they could break whatever enchantment remained from the love potion. But they hadn't worked. They had, in fact, all backfired. And was it any wonder? She wasn't thinking big enough, bold enough—her perennial fault. She'd been trying to annoy Rory with minor incompatibilities when she should have been trying to royally piss her off. To do that, she needed something momentous, something from which there was no coming back.

"Maybe your mom's right," she said, and the words came out slowly, like each was a lead weight pressing down on her tongue. Her body was fighting her, and her brain was screaming at her to shut up, but there was rarely any stopping her—or her big mouth—when she was on a collision course with a bad idea. "Maybe you should give performing a try tomorrow. Just to see what happens. The other night, you had so much fun."

Rory froze. The entire *world* had frozen for the length of a breath, then an explosion of voices shattered the silence and shook the room.

"Thank you, Morgan!"

"Listen to your girlfriend if you won't listen to us."

Archer said nothing, but the expression of satisfaction on his face, as though his earlier words to her had prompted Morgan's own, felt loudest of all.

Morgan considered crawling under the table. Rory, however, simply stood, pushed in her chair, and walked away.

Morgan thought she might be sick. Did she run after Rory? Did she give her time to cool off? If she were Rory, she wouldn't want Morgan anywhere near her. And besides, Morgan wasn't supposed to try to fix this. She was supposed to be making Rory not like her anymore. But fuck. Now that she might have actually succeeded, her entire body trembled.

Rory's parents were talking to her, or perhaps among themselves. Morgan couldn't tell. Their voices and Archer's were a jumble of noise. She hated them in that moment. Hated everything. Herself included.

"I'm sorry. I need to go." She got up before she knew what she was doing and raced out the front door of the cabin.

Rory was nowhere in sight, but Morgan was positive she'd heard the door close when she left, and Rory couldn't have gotten more than a minute's head start. Despair and guilt washed over her as she leaned against the deck railing and shut her eyes against the slowly setting sun. She didn't even have it in her to text Hazel and ask for consolation. She didn't deserve it, and there was no question that Hazel would tell her so.

Morgan didn't know how long she stayed that way, doing her best to tune out the indecipherable voices drifting through the cabin windows, until something warm brushed her ankle. Lilith had gotten out, and she meowed up at Morgan, then jumped down off the deck.

Was she allowed out? Morgan glanced around, but no answers presented themselves among the trees. "Lilith, come here."

At her name, the cat turned around, meowed again, and kept walking. The way she swayed her head was clear. She wanted Morgan to follow her.

Worried for Lilith, Morgan followed as prompted. Also, the cat had to be the smarter of the two of them, so who was Morgan to argue with her demands?

Lilith was fast, a black blur streaking across the grass. Morgan was not, but the cat was patient. She'd stop and wait for Morgan to catch up, and finally, in that manner, they also caught up to Rory. She was heading toward the stadium.

Lilith raced up to Rory and kept pace beside her in the distance, but if Rory realized Morgan was following, she gave no indication. The stadium had cleared out since the junior exhibition had ended, and Rory walked until she disappeared inside. Morgan found her sitting on the grass in the center of the field where the young witches had performed only hours ago.

Rory didn't look up as Morgan headed over to her. The stadium seemed a lot bigger with no one else around, and the breeze blowing across the field felt especially empty. From this perspective, she could see charred patches of grass and a sparkling film—definitely not dew—that clung to many of the blades. The particular indescribable scent of magic that permeated the grounds was stronger here, heavy in the air.

"I'm sorry." They were inadequate words for an inadequate girlfriend, and tears bit at Morgan's eyes. She wasn't supposed to apologize, but now that she was here, she didn't know how not to.

Rory rested her chin against her knees. Her eyes were unfocused as she stared into space, or maybe as she stared into a memory. "It's not your fault."

That was neither the response Morgan longed to hear nor the one she'd expected. It absolved her too easily and didn't solve their joint problem. "I'm supposed to be helping you, not making you feel worse or siding with your family."

That roused some life into Rory's face. "I thought we were over the idea that this was just about you helping me."

"Are we?" She sat next to Rory since hovering over her seemed worse than sitting with her, and Morgan wondered what to say next. From the ground, the stadium swelled like an enormous cage. Not just imposing, but mind-bendingly so. Morgan had no trouble making a fool of herself in front of a crowd, but imagining those seats filled with people staring down at her—she didn't know how Rory or anyone else did it.

Or maybe she just felt very small in her bad decisions.

Rory, on the other hand, seemed perfectly comfortable, if not at peace. The stadium didn't diminish her in the slightest. Even the sun, dipping below the trees, cast where she sat in a golden glow while Morgan had sat in shadows. The light highlighted her perfect freckles and sharpened the angles of her face. She was half living legend, half mere human. And in Morgan's chest, she remained everything.

That was why she couldn't walk back what she'd said, even if she apologized for it. Even if the pain it caused her was surely as bad as the pain that she was causing Rory.

Rory would heal. Her life would return to normal.

As for herself, Morgan wasn't sure if she'd ever stop hurting.

"The girl from earlier today," Morgan said, grasping for excuses. "Phaedra? She called you an inspiration. That has to mean something. You said so yourself."

That got Rory's attention and she turned toward Morgan. She didn't speak, although her eyebrows said, *Explain*.

So Morgan continued babbling, and what started as an excuse grew in honest conviction. It didn't make up for her not siding with Rory at dinner, but she believed her own words. "It's a gift to be able to make people dream. To inspire them. It's the same as how you said those girls weren't brave enough to approach you until I spoke up. Well, you have that effect on them, too. Who knows what they'll accomplish one day because they've seen what you can do and dare to push themselves? And I get it—if you hate what you're doing, then maybe that gift feels more like a curse—but does it hurt so much to try performing again? If you do and you hate it, at least you'll be able to say to your parents that you gave it a chance. Maybe then they'll drop the issue."

"I don't hate performing." Rory's dark eyes were inscrutable. "I had this whole plan I was going to work on after World's, you know. I want to fly. Not float. Not use a broom or potion or some other gimmick. My goal was to get good enough at manipulating air to actually fly. As you could see from my attempt today, I have a lot of work ahead of me."

"Oh." Well, that was unexpected. Morgan was horribly confused and loath to ask more, considering how much damage she'd already done today.

Lilith rested her head on Rory's feet, and Rory absently stroked her until the cat's eyes closed in contentment. Good for one of them.

Morgan lowered her head, wishing she knew what to say. When she'd been having her post-Nicole crisis, Rory had known exactly how to make her feel better. Just like she had this afternoon. Of course, Rory hadn't been the one to cause her crisis either time. No doubt that helped.

"It's not your fault," Rory said a second time, and the words made Morgan's jaw clench. "I knew going to the exhibition was going to give my family the wrong idea, but I wanted to show my support. It was a risk. Someone was bound to mention it to my parents, even if it wasn't Archer. I knew that and knew how they'd react, but I did it anyway."

"But it is my fault for speaking up about something when I don't understand. Just today, you told me you like the way I'm willing to defend people I care about, and I went and did the opposite." Damn the lump forming in her throat. "You should hate me."

Please don't let Rory hate her. Break up with her, yes. Rory needed to do that, but hate—why did she have to point that out?

Rory almost sounded like she laughed, but it was more of the suggestion of a laugh than any real humor. "Morgan, I don't hate you for speaking your mind. I should have explained myself more before thrusting you into my family drama. It wasn't fair of me, but I'm not used to talking about stuff like this with anyone."

"I offered to help," Morgan said. "Why should you have told me anything? We didn't know each other well, and you never talk about it to anyone. I made my choice."

"We didn't know each other well at first, no. But that changed." The sun kept moving, kept sinking. Rory was half in shadow. "I quit competing because of the pressure. It became too much."

Morgan squinted into the darkness encroaching on Rory's features, searching for clarity. "Like nerves?"

"Not exactly." Lilith looked up at her, as if to ask if Rory was really going to talk about this, and Rory returned to stroking the cat's back. "I liked competing. You know how competitive I am. But the more successful I was, the more pressure I felt from everyone—from fans, from the media, from myself. I told you that all I did was eat, sleep, and practice, and that became eat, sleep, practice, and stress. Everyone wanted to know how I'd top my last trick. Everyone just expected me to win. It began to feel like I owed it to people to do more, to be better, and that started making it all less fun. Not that it was always fun before; it was definitely work. But it only got harder, and the constant worrying that I was letting people down never left me alone."

Rory waved her hand around in an agitated fashion. "I don't mean because of the so-called fans who got nasty if I didn't live up to their personal expectations—fuck those people and their entitlement. If they didn't like a performance, they could try doing it themselves. It's the ones who were kind and excited, the ones who believed in me and were supportive no matter what—they're who lived in my head. They're the ones I cared about and hated disappointing."

Morgan had once been one of those fans, one who always expected more each time. She started to apologize for however insignificant a role she'd played in Rory's stress, but Rory wasn't done.

"For performances like these exhibitions, no one cares much about what you do before you take the field. They're for fun and don't factor into rankings. But for real competitions, the judges ensure that you aren't using any magical enhancements, for obvious reasons. Mundane assistance, though? They don't care about that. I had a prescription for an antianxiety medication. In the days leading up to competitions, I'd take a pill at night so I could sleep. Sometimes I'd take one right before competing, even though that was dangerous because it would mess with my focus. But as long as it wasn't some kind of magical spell or potion, no one cared what I did or why I needed to do it."

The sun seemed to be sinking too quickly, or the earth was spinning out of control like everything else in Morgan's life. Shadows encroached on Rory's face. The more she talked, the younger she looked. The more vulnerable. Morgan recalled the way she'd laughed and insisted she wasn't intimidating, despite having to know how amazed people were by her. Rory couldn't have—wouldn't have—felt such pressure if she hadn't been made constantly aware of how people felt. But was this the reason why she'd scoffed at the word?

Rory closed her eyes. "By the time World's came around, the magical press was predicting I'd place, if not actually win, and all I heard from everyone in my life was that they expected me to blow away the competition. Even with the drugs, I was constantly sick to my stomach, and while I was there, I just . . . snapped. I had this epiphany that I didn't owe it to anyone to win. I didn't even owe it to anyone to compete. And I knew if I continued to medicate before performing, my odds of hurting myself were high. What I'd planned to attempt was too dangerous for that. So, I quit and decided to reassess. I'm not unwilling to return to competing, but I'm not there yet mentally. I need the break still. I need to know that if I do it, I can handle the pressure better."

Fuck, fuck. FUCK. Morgan couldn't believe she'd made Rory feel like she needed to confess all of this, and guilt swallowed her heart. Rory hadn't owed her an explanation. She owed Rory one. She owed Rory a lot. More than she could ever repay for what she'd done.

Morgan longed to hug her and hold her, but she didn't dare. She also longed to kiss away all of Rory's stress, to promise to be the person she could lean on, a safe person who would never again fail to side with her. The temptation was strong, too strong, and she feared if she did the kind, friendly thing, she wouldn't be able to stop herself from doing the things she wasn't allowed to do.

But Rory's words had also shocked Morgan into silence. It hurt to listen to her confession. Hurt to know how much stress Rory had been under. Morgan wished she could have helped her, but of course, this was all in the past. She hadn't known Rory then, and she didn't have a way to help now, either. She'd only made things worse.

Morgan had to say something, though, and when her chest expanded enough to allow her to breathe, what came out was the most pathetic response possible. "I'm so sorry you had to go through that, and I'm sorry I made you feel like you needed to tell me."

Rory reached over and ran her thumb across Morgan's cheek, and Morgan's eyes closed involuntarily. She snapped them open once she realized how easily she'd succumbed to Rory's touch.

Despite the increasing darkness, the confession lightened Rory's face. "Don't be sorry. You had nothing to do with what happened—that was my own head. And you didn't make me feel like I had to do anything. Given the situation I put you in, you should know what's going on. More importantly, I want you to know, and there's no reason for me to hide it from you. I just never told anyone else because it's no one's business."

"Do your parents know?" The question had been weighing on her. Morgan had sided with Rory's parents, and regardless of why she'd done it, she'd hate herself more if they did know and were pressuring Rory regardless.

"No, not really. They know how stressed I was, but they don't know about me taking medication. They think I got performance nerves while at World's, and I just need to be eased back into it. I've thought about telling them the truth, but it's not that easy."

That was something, but Morgan's relief was tainted with confusion. "Why not? They do seem concerned about you."

"I know, and in fairness, they're not entirely wrong about everything." Rory wet her lips and sighed. "We aren't the warmest, fuzziest family, in case you haven't noticed. My parents support us by pushing. Anything they did, they want me and Isaac to do more, to do better. I'm not always fair to them, because I know their hearts are in the right place, but it makes talking to them impossible. Telling them what I just told you—I'd be disappointing them. Weakness is not something a Sandler should show. We push ourselves harder until every soft spot is covered in a callus. We play with fire and pretend the burns we get are no big deal. We're obligated to make them proud—that's our expression of love. I'd hoped showing them I was happy with you in Harborage might be enough to do that. That's the thing parents should be pushing for—right? Wanting their kids to be happy? But they're not going for it."

Morgan swallowed, her thoughts drifting toward the scavenger hunt and Rory's excitement over her flying attempt. Maybe Archer and Rory's parents were right; maybe Rory was too ambitious to be happy giving up competing permanently. Or maybe not. But one thing had been clear—the joy Rory felt at pushing *herself*. She hadn't needed any family to urge her on then.

"Is it because it's not true?" Morgan asked. "You do miss competing."

"Parts of it are true."

"And Archer?" She couldn't stop thinking about his words. "What does he know about it?"

"Only whatever my parents told him. You don't have to feel left out." Morgan blushed, and Rory poked her in the shoulder. "I'm teasing you."

"I know." Morgan hung her head. "Although I did wonder if I was the only one who didn't know what happened. I wish I'd known you then. I wish I could have helped."

Rory pushed strands of Morgan's hair out of her face. "You are helping me. You make me happy—that part is absolutely true. You're funny and fun to be around, and I wasn't lying about admiring your fearlessness. Maybe if I could have channeled a bit more of my inner Morgan Greenwood, I would have been able to laugh off some of that pressure back then."

"Oh, fuck no. Believe me, I would have folded under that pressure like a . . . Shit. I don't know how to make an analogy. Something that folds. Origami?"

Rory laughed. "See? You're hilarious."

Morgan flopped backward onto the grass. "Yeah, that's the nice way of saying I sound like a dumbass."

"Nope. It's me saying you're funny and sweet, and you make every conversation a delight. I'm always happy around you. I could have fun cleaning a bathroom if we did it together."

"I don't know if that's the sweetest thing anyone's ever said to me or the weirdest." She tossed a handful of grass at Rory. "Let's go with weirdest."

Let's go with, sit up, Morgan! Your attempt to infuriate Rory did NOT go as planned (so typical), and you're lying on the grass next to her, and the moon is starting to rise, the stars will be shining soon, it will be a perfectly romantic evening, and you are ACTING LIKE NOTHING IS WRONG WHEN EVERYTHING IS FUCKED-UP.

Morgan shot upright, her heart pounding.

"So, can we talk about your issues now?" Rory asked.

22

"MY ISSUES? WHAT ISSUES?" MORGAN DEMANDED. SHE WAS STILL spinning with the dangerously romantic turn things had taken a moment before.

"How about the way you've been acting strange?" Rory cocked her head to the side. "Look, I know you said this new potion obsession has nothing to do with your ex, but I'm having a hard time believing that, especially now."

Morgan steeled herself, though against what, she wasn't sure. She was bewildered by Rory's accusation. "What do you mean?"

Rory shifted position so she faced Morgan for the first time. "In one breath, you're telling me not to waste my talents. And in the next, you're making deprecating comments about your own. How am I not supposed to wonder if you're pushing me about performing because of your own insecurities? Or because you're feeling like *you're* not living up to your potential?"

"No. Absolutely not." Morgan hugged her knees to her chest.

"Morgan." Rory reached for her arm, and Morgan pulled herself in tighter.

Rory was staring at her in a way that was starting to make Morgan doubt her own words, but that was ridiculous. She was really telling the truth about this. She couldn't give Rory the full explanation, but Rory's assumption was so off base it was ludicrous.

"If you're stressed about your skills or what you're doing with your life," Rory said, "I hope you know you can talk to me about it. Obviously, I'm not a great role model for what to do when stressed, but I think it's a pretty normal thing to question your skills and direction."

"You are a good role model, though. You were smart enough to back away from everything before you hurt yourself. That was a good choice, by the way, and I completely support it, in case you were wondering. Watching you perform was already nerve-racking, and I do not want you doing anything that puts you more at risk."

In fact, if she were actually dating Rory, and Rory was intent on competing, Morgan wasn't sure she'd be able to watch her anymore. She'd have to do it with her hands partially over her eyes or her body half-drunk on a relaxation potion.

"I wasn't wondering, but I'm glad I convinced you." Rory narrowed her eyes. "Now stop changing the subject."

"I wasn't changing the subject. I was responding directly to your comment about not being a good role model. That was also self-deprecation."

Rory started to argue, then shut her mouth and glared. "Fine, I'll allow it. But my point stands."

"What was your point again?" Morgan asked innocently, and she laughed at the expression of disdain Rory shot her.

Yes, Rory had a point. Yes, Morgan was stressed. But Nicole had nothing to do with it. Of that, Morgan was positive. This was all because of her colossal screwup. Because *she* was a colossal screwup. And every time she tried to un-screw-up the situation, she got nowhere. Rory should have been livid with her for what she did at dinner, and instead she was pouring her heart out. It was one more thing that Rory was going to regret later. One more reason she was going to hate Morgan when the truth came out. One more reason she'd feel like a complete fool, and Morgan had no defense for making her feel that way.

If she'd just told Rory the moment that she'd known the truth . . . Fuck. She was back to second-guessing her decision.

Since Rory couldn't possibly know her thoughts, her face must have revealed the extent of the anxieties Morgan was trying to hide. Rory slid closer to Morgan until their arms touched, and Morgan's pulse quickened with the warmth of her body and scent of her skin. "I know you're trying to laugh it all off, but I hope you also know that I'm here for you."

Morgan swallowed. "I do."

She needed to run. She wasn't lying down anymore, but Rory was too close, and it was too dark. They were too alone, and she felt too exposed. Morgan was certain Rory did, as well, and this could not lead to good outcomes. Morgan turned to say something—anything, a bad joke, a bullshit excuse, whatever—but the words stuck in her throat.

Rory's face was mere inches from hers, near enough for Morgan to count her freckles and feel her breath on her lips. Near enough that she once more felt like gravity was pulling their mouths together and her blood was on fire. An aching need was squeezing her around the chest, making Morgan believe she could kiss away Rory's past, touch her cheek and brush away her fears. Hold her so tightly that her own awful mistakes couldn't come between them.

Rory did believe it, or something like it. Morgan could see the conviction in her eyes. They watched her with a tenderness and trust she didn't deserve.

Because it wasn't real.

Was. Not. Real.

Panic sent Morgan flying backward, breaking the spell. How dare her reckless heart leave her alone in the indigo twilight with the woman she loved and couldn't have. Her resolve was strong, but Morgan was too distractable to trust herself.

And now, thanks to her heart, she had a sore ass from scooting away from Rory so quickly.

Not for the first time today, or probably the first time in the last hour, Rory beheld Morgan like she was possessed. "Are you okay? Did I do something wrong?"

"Yes! No! Or, no and no. I don't know." Morgan scrambled to her feet. Adrenaline flooded her veins, quenching the fires that Rory's closeness had ignited. The confusion on Rory's face was going to break her, but she had to stop this. Rory had bewitched her every bit as much as she had accidentally bewitched Rory, and she couldn't trust herself.

"I think we need to . . ." Morgan pressed her hands against her face. What was wrong with her? If she couldn't get this out, she'd been a fool to think she could ever confess the truth about the love potion. "This isn't supposed to be real between us."

Rory said nothing. She bit her lip and simply continued to look at Morgan as though she was the one who'd been bespelled.

"I feel like maybe we're getting confused. We're not sure what's real and what's not, and we're rushing into something that feels real, but it's only because we're here at the festival with all this magic, and we're putting on an act for your family. But once we go home, we'll realize this was a huge mistake. So we should back off temporarily, and if it's not a mistake, then we'll know later. But we shouldn't be so hasty." She gasped for breath, but the intake of oxygen did nothing to ease her dizziness or make her words sound more coherent to her own ears.

Darkness had finished consuming the field. Gone was the romantic twilight of a few minutes ago. Here was night—cold, unfathomable, murky. Sure, there were fireflies twinkling like miniature stars and a rising moon glowing down on them like a crystal orb. But fireflies were only insects, and the moon was waning, which was useful for magic at times, but spoke to crueler powers and secrets and endings.

Morgan felt all three of those associations in her blood, and she didn't like it.

In the dying celestial light, Rory looked more ethereal, too. A shadow of the strong, powerful woman that she was. She, too, climbed to her feet, seemingly guided by the same preternatural calm and grace that had overcome her at dinner.

"You don't mean that," Rory said.

"I do." She didn't. Not exactly, but it was probably the smartest attempt she'd made to handle the situation so far. It wasn't the same as the full truth, but it came close. Perhaps close enough. Once back home, the love potion would have to wear off eventually, and if it took too long, Morgan would create the antidote first.

"I don't believe you. You're acting strange again. You expect me to believe you can't tell the difference between real and fake because we're putting on an act, but the other day you told me you'd had a crush on me long before the festival. How does that make sense?"

It doesn't. Good job there, Morgan.

She'd totally forgotten about saying that, and Morgan struggled to explain herself and came up with nothing. The harder she tried to find the words to justify her sudden suggestion, the flimsier they all sounded.

Her head was spinning, her heart was hurting, and all she wanted to do was collapse to the grass and cry. To scream so loudly that she forced her will on the universe and made it correct itself. But she was not that powerful. Not even Rory was. Witches could only do things like that in movies, and only then to address some great cosmic injustice. Accidental love potions weren't even worthy of miracles in the eyes of Hollywood.

"What about you?" Morgan asked, seizing the first pitiful explanation that came to mind. "You're acting strange, too. All of a sudden, you—Rory Sandler—care about me? Without warning? Does that make sense? Of course, I can't trust that feeling, and you shouldn't, either."

"Without warning?" Rory's stillness broke all at once, and she raised her hands in bewilderment. "What was I supposed to do? Sound an alarm, flash some hazard lights, post signs around town—*Beware, Morgan, flirting ahead*? I thought flirting *was* the warning. Have I been doing this wrong all my life?"

"I don't know! I'm just trying to protect you!"

"Protect me?" Rory's hands dropped to her sides. "Protect me. That's what this is about?"

"Yes." She simply had to explain why, but the words were a jumble of broken consonants and vowels on her tongue. Morgan took a deep breath, then another, hoping to order her thoughts so that when she finally said the truth, it would be . . . well, not perfect. There was no perfect way to say it. But clear and honest, and the least traumatizing as possible.

But while Morgan was forming her plan, Rory had gathered her wits. "This is because of what I told you, isn't it? The medication, the reason I quit competing? Do you think I'm fragile? That I don't know my own mind or emotions?"

The shock of Rory's so very wrong accusation knocked the badly formed confession from Morgan's brain. "What? No."

Rory didn't seem to hear her. "I get it. You are brave and loud, and you don't hesitate to speak your mind and rush to people's defense. So I guess it makes sense that you would think I'm meek and in need of protection from myself."

"No!" Morgan spoke louder this time, cutting Rory off. "That's not what I meant. That's not why."

"Then what is it, Morgan? Because that's the only conclusion I can draw. If you want things to slow down between us, then fine. But that's not what you said. You said you wanted to protect me. But believe me, I am very aware of my feelings and my limitations and my mental health. I have pushed them to the breaking point before, and I don't need to be coddled. If you're worried for yourself, if you don't trust you own feelings, then say so. Be honest."

"I'm trying to be. I just . . ." Need a moment. She just needed a moment so she didn't blurt everything out carelessly like usual. So she didn't utterly wreck Rory with the truth.

Rory sighed. "Fine. When you figure your shit out, let me know." She turned and started walking away. Lilith jumped up and followed.

Morgan didn't, immobilized by her own fucking weakness.

The night swallowed Rory quickly, her black-clad form vanishing into the stadium periphery like she'd never been there in the first place. But her angry words hung in the air, ringing in Morgan's ears, and the memory of how close her face had been stung her skin. Tears flooded Morgan's eyes, and she finally gave in to her emotions and dropped to the grass.

Alone, the air felt so much sharper and the grass so much colder. Even the moon glowed a pitiless light, and the fireflies had disappeared. Morgan rested her head on her knees, and let the tears fall, silently berating herself.

She was careless, sloppy, distractable. She spoke before she thought and acted before she planned. All she'd ever had to go on, magically speaking, was her instincts. They were strong and finely attuned to the energy surrounding her. They'd saved her ass many times when she'd failed to properly follow directions or keep herself on task. But not this time with the relaxation potion. This one time—*one time*—when she'd wanted everything to be better than perfect, she'd let herself become too distracted for her instincts to save her. Her brain had met its match in Rory as surely as her heart had, and neither had stood a chance.

Trying to gain control of herself, Morgan wiped her eyes. She'd tell Rory they would talk more tomorrow. Emotional and physical exhaustion weighed down her mind as well as her limbs. If she attempted anything else tonight, she'd ruin it as badly as, well, what she'd already done. Morgan wasn't sure if Rory would go for that, but the love potion was making her prone to forgiving Morgan's mistakes. For tonight, that was a blessing.

Somehow, she got up. Somehow, she made it back to the Sandlers' cabin. It appeared deserted, and Morgan wasn't about to question small favors. She clomped up the stairs, not bothering with sneaking around. She wanted to give Rory plenty of warning that she was coming.

Just, you know, in case Rory was planning to hex her. Morgan deserved it.

But Rory wasn't in their room, and Morgan didn't see Lilith around, either. She pulled out her phone, but the only messages were in her group chat with Hazel and Andy. Andy had sent a text earlier to let them know she'd arrived, and Morgan had missed a bunch of plans to have fun tonight. Which was fine; Morgan was definitely not up for fun.

She plugged in her phone, brushed her teeth, and spared one longing glance at the bed she'd shared with Rory last night. That had also been a mistake. Morgan retrieved her pillow and spread the extra blankets out on the sofa without unfolding it into a bed. She was too tall for it this way, and it was lumpy, but the lumps were better than the broken mattress springs, so she would deal.

Minutes passed. Hours. Sleep didn't come. She heard Isaac and Erika return and put the baby to bed. Archer made his way upstairs. The cabin filled with hushed voices and creaking floorboards, then fell into silence again. Morgan eventually fell with it into a fitful sleep.

But Rory hadn't returned before she did.

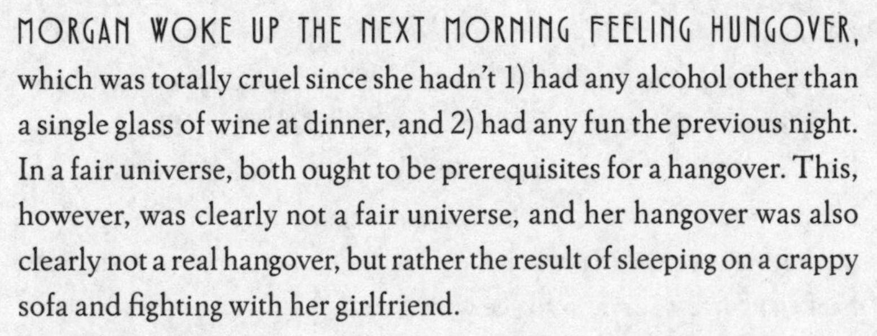

23

MORGAN WOKE UP THE NEXT MORNING FEELING HUNGOVER, which was totally cruel since she hadn't 1) had any alcohol other than a single glass of wine at dinner, and 2) had any fun the previous night. In a fair universe, both ought to be prerequisites for a hangover. This, however, was clearly not a fair universe, and her hangover was also clearly not a real hangover, but rather the result of sleeping on a crappy sofa and fighting with her girlfriend.

Fake girlfriend.

Except, wait. Was that still the case? Had she and her fake girlfriend had a very real breakup?

Morgan closed her eyes against the sunlight peeking through the window covering, but that didn't help the pain in her back and shoulders, and it definitely wasn't going to stop her alarm from going off any minute. Wearily, she climbed off the sofa, took care of the alarm, and looked up to see if she'd woken Rory.

Only Rory wasn't there. The bunk bed hadn't been slept in.

Morgan grabbed the wall, overcome by a wave of anxiety. *Stop it*, she told herself. She would not worry, because there was nothing to worry about. Rory had probably found some friends and crashed elsewhere. No big deal.

Except Rory had wanted so much to avoid her that she hadn't come home last night. That actually seemed like a huge deal.

A huge deal that Morgan had needed to happen. Well, not the staying away part, precisely, but the avoidance part. That had to be a positive sign. Maybe she'd finally broken the love spell.

Morgan tried to take comfort in that, but her chest throbbed along with her unhappy muscles. She got dressed quickly and crept out of the cabin before she accidentally woke up anyone she was in no mood to talk to.

Her outlook didn't improve over the next few hours. Not even the enormous coffee and chocolate muffin she'd bought to console herself helped. Certainly, checking her texts and discovering Rory hadn't sent any didn't. Morgan typed out a quick Are you ok? but as the hours passed without a response, she came to view that as a mistake. Knowing Rory was ignoring her hurt more than assuming she was.

The booth was busy, too, which normally would be enough to keep her mind occupied, but not today. It was the festival's last morning, and people were out purchasing the treats they'd been eyeing but putting off. Hazel, Andy, and other friends stopped by around lunch, but they also hadn't seen Rory.

"She's probably practicing for the exhibition," her mother said, having overheard Morgan's lunch conversation. "I think the entire festival is shutting down to watch. Everyone's excited to see her perform again."

Morgan's stomach rolled at the memory of what Rory had told her last night. This was exactly the sort of pressure that had caused Rory to quit, and she shook her head. "Rory's not performing. Someone signed her up without her permission."

"Are you sure? Why would someone do that?"

"Some people are assholes who thought they could pressure her into it." It was a kinder explanation than the one running through Morgan's head, but her grandmom was in earshot and Morgan had already gotten scolded once for swearing this morning. (For a particularly forceful "what the fuck?" when she saw Grandmom June *and* her mom sporting chartreuse hair today.)

Her mother frowned. "Are you all right? You've been quiet all morning."

"I'm fine. I just think your hair is loud enough for the both of us." When that didn't win her a smile or a sarcastic retort, Morgan let out a whine. "Rory and I had an argument last night."

"Do you want to talk about it?"

Morgan's face clenched with suppressed tears, and she turned away. She was pathetic. She wanted her mom to hold her and lie to her and tell her it would be okay. But it would not be okay, not for her, and she had no idea what was going on with Rory. The love potion's hold on her might have broken or it might not have. Until Rory actually talked to her, Morgan wouldn't know if she was okay, either.

"Not right now," Morgan said, and her voice was thick and ugly.

Her mother hugged her from behind. "I know you stopped coming to me about your crushes a long time ago, but I am full of relationship advice, and I'm here when you need me."

"I know." Morgan hugged her back and returned to packing unsold items and unused ingredients.

Over the next hour, the crowds noticeably thinned, and her mother finally announced that they were shutting down for the last time. "The exhibition is starting soon. We might as well join everyone and head to the stadium."

Morgan wrapped a mortar and pestle in paper and tucked them in the corner of a fresh box. "I told you—Rory's not performing."

"Doesn't matter. No point in staying open if everyone is going," her grandmom said. "We did enough business this week. Let's enjoy the rest of the festival."

Her mother placed an arm around her. "You love watching the spellcasting. Come on, it will cheer you up."

It was unlikely that anything that reminded her of Rory would cheer her up. "I think I'll stay here and keep packing. Less to do tomorrow morning."

Morgan was certain the other two women were exchanging concerned glances behind her back, but they were kind enough not to press the issue.

"I'll text you where we find seats," her mother said. "In case you change your mind."

"Pretty sure your hair will be impossible to miss."

"Smart-ass." Lianne kissed her forehead.

As soon as they left, Morgan pulled out her phone and checked her messages again, but she still had nothing from Rory. *Was* she okay? She hadn't left last night and been attacked, had she? Tripped and fallen somewhere, hit her head and was dying on some secret, hidden trail?

A thousand horrible scenarios flitted through Morgan's brain before she shook them off. Surely Rory's family was on her case about the exhibition. Surely if they hadn't seen or heard from her today, they would have asked Morgan if she knew where Rory was.

Surely.

That eased the tension in her stomach somewhat, but her heart continued to ache.

Morgan finished packing her current box and moved on to sorting through the remaining inventory. They'd sold most of what they'd brought, so it wouldn't take her long to complete this task. And then what? She'd need something to occupy her mind. Not that this was doing a great job, to be fair.

When her phone vibrated, Morgan whipped around for it so quickly she almost knocked if off the counter.

ANDY: Are you coming? You're going to miss Rory.

Here they went again. Morgan took a deep breath.

MORGAN: Rory's not actually performing.

HAZEL: Then why did they just make an announcement that they're changing up the performance order so Rory can go last?

Morgan stared at Hazel's message, trying to understand what the words meant. There had to be a mistake. Hazel must be misinterpreting whatever had happened.

But what if she hadn't? It would make sense for Rory to go last. Who in their right mind would want to follow her?

Morgan dropped the packing tape, grabbed her purse, and ran. She barely remembered to lock up the booth, and by the time she arrived at the exhibition, her side had a massive stitch and her lungs burned like rubbing sandpaper. The stadium was far more crowded than it had been yesterday, but seats remained scattered among the bleachers. Morgan didn't bother heading to where her mother or Hazel had told her they were sitting. She stopped near the steps overlooking the field.

She doubted she'd be able to so easily climb over the fence today. Far more people roamed around below. The performers would be a mix of talents and skill levels, but there would be other pros or former pros, like Rory and Archer, among them. Some of them had coaches, and many had dedicated supporters helping them out. There were also teams of witches casting the protective circle. That made sense when they would expect the spells inside of it to be more powerful and potentially more dangerous. Those witches would take turns, switching off between performers, preventing the circle's power from waning over time.

Morgan's gaze darted among the forms wandering around, searching for Rory. She couldn't shake the fear that this was her fault. That Rory was doing this because Morgan had said she wanted to protect her, and Rory had interpreted that to mean Morgan thought she was weak. She'd said she wasn't ready to perform again, so what else could it be if she wasn't trying to prove Morgan wrong?

Morgan closed her eyes, fighting down panic. For the past year, Rory hadn't performed more than parlor tricks at the Empty Chalice. By her own admission, she hadn't publicly performed without self-medicating for longer. Did she have meds with her? Or had she taken something else? Rory had also told her that at an exhibition like this, no one cared if you used magical assistance. Would Rory try something so bold?

Despite her best attempts to not lose her shit, panic was gaining control over Morgan. She retrieved her phone and sent another desperate message to Rory.

> **MORGAN:** Just tell me you're ok. Please let me know if I can help you.

Please don't do this, is what she wanted to type, but that was only likely to infuriate Rory.

Since she didn't expect a response, she almost dropped her phone as she was putting it away.

> **RORY:** I'm fine. Been busy getting ready. We can talk afterward.

Morgan let out a frustrated scream that caused a cat to bolt out of the arms of the witch standing near her. The woman shot Morgan an annoyed expression before calling out after her furry Princess Piper.

Whatever. Morgan wanted to yell at her that if her cat (or familiar) couldn't handle one brief outburst, how did she think it could handle the action on the field? People needed to take better care of their pets. This wasn't the time for a rant, though, so instead, she rolled her eyes and returned to her phone.

On one hand, finally—she had a response. On the other, it was a bit of a blow-off. Although if Rory was psyching herself up to go out on the field, that might not have anything to do with Morgan.

At a loss and in need of someone to hold her together, Morgan headed toward Hazel and Andy. If nothing else, they knew her relationship with Rory was fake, and Hazel knew about the love potion. They would understand her state of mind better than her family.

People glared at Morgan as she made her way through the bleachers, blocking their view of whoever was on the field. As long as it wasn't Rory, Morgan didn't much care. Hazel squished into Andy to make room for her, and Morgan sat before anyone cursed her height.

"You really didn't know?" Andy asked.

"As of last night, she was adamant that she wasn't going to do it."

Hazel gave Morgan a thoughtful look. "I wonder what changed her mind."

All Morgan could do was shake her head. There'd been no hiding her mood from her friends at lunch, but she hadn't wanted to talk about it. Part of her still didn't. She'd screwed over Rory once with the potion, and if Rory got hurt, Morgan couldn't shake the idea that it would be her fault, as well. It had been her clumsy attempt to make Rory believe they were wrong for each other that had made Rory believe she needed to do this when she wasn't ready.

A figure dressed in a long midnight blue cloak and knee-high boots walked along the sidelines, and it took Morgan a moment to recognize Archer in his performance costume.

In competition, costumes didn't add to a witch's score directly, but there was no question they influenced people's perceptions. Spellcasters adopted styles suitable to their routines—long velvet cloaks, billowing capes, jewel-toned dresses with enormous bell sleeves—all the flowing, gorgeous clothes a witch would never wear without an audience. Morgan would scoff if anyone expected her to dress like that while making a potion, but for competitions and exhibitions, she was as much a sucker for the beauty as anyone else.

Back when she was competing, Rory had her own style. Given the nature of many of her stunts, she opted for more practical but no less eye-catching clothes—tight leather pants, corset-like shirts, and as much bare skin as she could get away with. No doubt the outfits had played a role in Morgan's initial attraction to her, but the jeans and T-shirts Rory preferred at the bar hadn't lessened it.

Morgan swallowed, and she leaned forward for a better view of Archer, hoping to see Rory with him. But Archer was alone.

The performer on the field finished, and people cheered. Morgan realized she hadn't watched a bit of it. She held her phone in her lap, hoping Rory might send another message, but she was too nervous to send one first in case she shattered Rory's concentration.

Another performer took the field, and then another. They had to be getting near the end. Archer came next and did a solo routine with fire and illusions that Morgan had to reluctantly admit was compelling. He was better than the average performer, but he was definitely no Rory. Performing with her would have benefited only him.

At last, another performer took a bow, the audience clapped, the protective circle was dropped to prepare for the next, and Morgan sensed a change in the crowd. A hushed excitement, like an electric charge. It raised the hairs on her neck, so thick it was palpable, or perhaps that was simply her nerves. Next to her, Hazel gave her wrist a light squeeze. Andy flashed her a smile that was equal parts excited and sympathetic, as though she knew Morgan's body was buzzing with barely restrained energy, even if she didn't know precisely why.

"Here we are at the end of the program," came the announcer's amplified voice. She was one of the festival organizers, and she stood near the judging table. Morgan craned her neck, and thought she caught a glimpse of Rory's parents next to her. "It's with great delight that we ask you to welcome our final performer for the afternoon, the current U.S. spellcasting champion—Rory Sandler!"

Current? Right, and no wonder Rory's family was desperate to get her back in the game. Nationals was held only every three years. Morgan had somehow forgotten that no one had had a chance to unseat Rory yet, although it was bound to happen. Even if today marked a permanent change in Rory's choices, she'd been off the competition circuit for almost two years. It was questionable whether there were enough competitions left for her to be able to qualify in time to defend her title.

No one in the crowd cared. Rory was who many of them had come to see, and Morgan found herself standing and clapping along with everyone else. Never mind her heart pounding in her throat or the way her legs twitched with the urge to shove her through the mass of bodies and forcibly pull Rory away.

Rory walked onto the field, and Morgan couldn't help but think about how last night they'd stood in that very same spot. Rory had offered up more of her heart, and Morgan had flung it back at her in one of her disastrous attempts to un-fuck her mistake. She'd gone from being so close to failing Rory by kissing her again to failing Rory by upsetting her instead.

The memories hit Morgan in the head like a jackhammer, and she wondered if they were pounding at Rory as well. One more thing to mess with her focus.

"Breathe," Hazel said, and Morgan tried.

Rory was not dressed to perform. That was no surprise to Morgan since she knew this was a very last-minute decision, but the casualness of her clothes, the seeming lack of care she showed, didn't help Morgan's frayed nerves.

She'd assumed when Rory had said she'd been getting ready, that part of that time had gone into pulling together all aspects of her routine. But the clothes Rory had worn the last couple of days were fancier than what she was currently wearing—jeans and a T-shirt from the Empty

Chalice. Unless she intended this performance to be an advertisement for the bar, Morgan didn't know what to think. Although, she could definitely imagine Rory going through with a performance just for that purpose; it would be like giving her family a magical middle finger.

Rory also didn't appear to have any props or tools with her. That was a bit of a relief. There were no pyres, so presumably she wasn't asking people to try to light her on fire. Whatever she had planned, from this distance, she struck Morgan as utterly calm and in control. She smiled, waved to the crowd, and then bowed in each of the four cardinal directions.

That was the cue for the circle-casting witches. Though Morgan couldn't truly see the barrier they created, their candles flared, and for a brief second, the air around Rory shimmered in the sunlight as a magical field cut her off from the rest of the stadium. All around, people returned to their seats, and excited murmurs swept through the bleachers. Morgan sat with them, her fingers clawing at her shorts to release some of her energy.

On the field, Rory pulled what appeared to be a small white candle from her pocket and set it on a bare patch of grass. So she'd brought something after all. Morgan knew exactly what someone like Rory could do with a single candle, but relatively speaking, it didn't seem too dangerous.

With an imperceptible gesture, Rory lit the candle and began drawing on the flame. It rose to her height above the ground, then kept growing, splitting into four ribbons of fire. Rory stood in the middle of them, in the center of the circle, and spun the flames around the circumference, weaving seemingly random designs in the air. They arced and split, again and again, faster and faster until the dome of the circle itself appeared to burn. Once every inch was lit and Rory was almost impossible to see, she drew her arms in with a swift but fluid gesture. In seconds, the flames were sucked back into the candle, and it extinguished, leaving only a trace of smoke hovering in the air.

The crowd clapped, but Morgan could sense their disappointment. From anyone else, they would have been more appreciative, but Rory brought expectations with her, and Morgan began to understand on a more visceral level what Rory had expressed last night—the very weight of what people wanted from her. It sat in her gut, too.

Rory didn't bow to indicate she was finished, although she remained motionless. She stood with her back straight, but her head bent. Her arms were pulled into her chest.

Morgan leaned forward.

"What is she doing?" the witch behind her whispered into the air.

She wasn't the only one with the question. Confusion was noticeably growing around the stadium. People turned to those sitting near them, and others, like Morgan, strained for a better view. Lots of people held up phones, but their arms wavered like they wondered if it was time to give them a rest.

But Rory *was* moving, so slowly as to be almost imperceptible. Morgan would have missed it, too, were it not for the grass around Rory's feet. It whipped at her ankles, giving her away. She was pulling her entire body in tighter—head lower, arms closer, knees bending—and Morgan held her breath with stress and anticipation.

There were many ways for witches to release the power for a spell. Sometimes, it was nothing more complicated than what Morgan did to ignite the runes on her worktable at Bed, Bath, and Broom. A little spit contained all the power she needed. Sometimes blood sufficed. If a spell required more, sometimes breathing exercises would allow a witch to build and concentrate their power before releasing it with an exhale or the proper hand motion.

Rory was gathering power. A lot of power. Morgan had watched her cast enough protective circles at their coven gatherings to know Rory didn't need this much effort to unleash an impressive amount of magic, so she must be planning something enormous.

Before Morgan could point this out, the stadium exploded.

24

FOR THE LENGTH OF THE BREATH KNOCKED OUT OF HER lungs, Morgan thought Rory had actually blown apart the stadium. Rory had flung her arms wide and her head back, and a wall of power had burst outward from where she stood. It slammed into Morgan, sending her backward in her seat and washing her skin in magic. Every hair on her arms and neck stood on end. Her body tingled and her lungs burned, and on the other side of the stadium, as she blinked the world back into focus, she caught a shimmer of what had once been the protective circle flying away and dissipating. In the distance, the trees shook and dozens of birds took to the sky as the wave of magic rolled into the forest.

People screamed in shock and disbelief. Next to her, Hazel sat as frozen as a statue. Unable to entirely believe what she'd seen, Morgan stood on trembling legs for a better view of Rory.

By all rights, Rory should have collapsed in a heap after that burst of raw power. But then, by all rights, what she'd done should not have been possible. To have overpowered four other witches, and from inside a circle designed to prevent magic from leaking out . . . Morgan's head swam to think of it, but no one was going to leave here today disappointed by the show Rory had given them, that was for damned sure.

Miraculously, Rory remained standing with her arms outstretched and her face passive, seemingly oblivious to the chaos she'd created—the commotion in the stands, the circle-casting witches who had fallen to the grass, the people scrambling around the field, unsure of what to do. Morgan didn't know what to do, either, but her heart and her instincts had aligned to give her body a single directive—move. Get to Rory. Help her.

Morgan maneuvered her way off the bleachers, heading toward the stairs. Most people were too dazed by what had happened to pay her attention. They either parted without word or she had to lightly push by them. Her gaze remained glued to Rory as much as she could allow it, so from the corner of her eye, Morgan noticed the moment Rory moved again, lowering and then reraising her arms over her head. No more than a minute must have passed between her destroying the circle and casting the new spell, and Morgan wondered if this second spell had been her plan all along.

From the clear blue sky above the stadium, a magnificent bolt of purple lightning spiked toward the ground. Morgan couldn't see who or what it hit from her vantage point, but the bolt split in two perhaps ten feet above the grass. The shrieks of surprise and astonishment that had just begun to die away returned in force.

The crowd split in two, as well, with half apparently deciding that Rory had given them more than they'd actually wanted to see. The extra bodies suddenly fleeing toward the exits both helped and hindered Morgan's approach to the field. On the ground, the volunteers and organizers were shaking off their shock, and someone was yelling to clear the stadium.

Rory took her cardinal bows and crumpled to the grass.

There was so much confusion that no one stopped Morgan as she sprinted across the field. Without worrying about the implications or consequences, she fell to her knees next to Rory and wrapped her arms around her. Rory's skin was cold, likely due to the extreme magic depletion, but she was damp with sweat from the exertion. Despite that, her heart beat steadily, and her breaths came easily. In time, she would recover. Rory closed her eyes and leaned into Morgan's embrace. For one precious moment, Morgan allowed herself to not care about anything beyond Rory's well-being.

Was it so terrible to want to help her? To hold her until she knew Rory wasn't going to fall apart? Morgan's conscience warned her to be careful.

"Are you okay?" she asked.

Rory surprised her with a tremulous laugh. "How many times have you asked me that today?"

"So you did read the texts I sent you?"

She nodded, and Morgan sighed. She'd kind of assumed that, and it was hard to blame Rory for being angry at her, all things considered.

"You need food," Morgan said, ignoring these other concerns. "Why isn't anyone here to help you?"

She glanced around. The stadium was emptying rapidly, but scattered people clustered together in the stands excitedly discussing what they'd witnessed. At ground level, most of the important people—judges, council members, festival organizers—had formed huddles filled with agitated conversations. Morgan could no longer see Archer or Rory's parents.

Belatedly, Morgan recalled she had some trail mix in her purse, and she pulled out the bag and handed it to Rory, along with her half-empty water bottle. "Eat."

Rory stuffed a bunch of nuts and dried fruit in her mouth without protest, and some color returned to her cheeks. When she finished chewing, her gaze flitted around the area. "I think the people who were supposed to help me are busy at the moment. There was a lightning strike." She laughed, more strongly this time but also more wild.

Morgan pulled another handful of trail mix from the bag and forced it on her. "How did you blow out that circle? You know what?

Never mind. It's you. But how did you know you *could* do it?" She paused, realization dawning. "That's what you were doing with the fire, wasn't it? You were testing the strength of the circle."

Rory beamed at Morgan, clearly delighted to have been understood. "I didn't know I would be able to take it down, even after that, but it seemed possible, and you only discover your limits by trying to push past them. Overconfident bitch, remember?"

"Sweet stars, you're insane. And the lightning?"

"Oh, that's why I needed to take down the circle."

"Obviously." Since she'd already guessed as much, Morgan rolled her eyes and rested her head against Rory's. "I was so scared you were going to hurt yourself."

"I'm sorry I scared you."

"I'm sorry I made you run away last night. We need to talk about . . . things."

Rory took her hand. "We do."

Morgan's muscles untensed a little. She had no desire to have this talk, but this was progress. Once Rory was back to full strength, she could try to rectify last night's missteps.

To that end, Morgan opened her mouth to ask how else she could help Rory recover and blurted out her biggest misstep yet. "I love you."

FUCK.

You absolute dumbass. Are you sure you weren't actually hit by the lightning? That it didn't kill your last couple of brain cells?

Fact: she could not be sure, but the words had tumbled out of her mouth in a burst of relief.

Also a fact: telling Rory she loved her, regardless of how understandable the reason, was definitely not the best way to undo a love potion's effects.

Also, also a fact: she was clearly a walking disaster.

Rory started to say something in return, and Morgan placed her fingers over her mouth. Under other circumstances, it would have been too intimate a gesture, but if Rory was about to say those same three words back to her, she might lose her shit.

Frankly, there were already far too many people running around the stadium who had lost their shit. Besides, there would be plenty of time for that later when they could talk in private.

That was assuming she couldn't be classified as having lost her shit already, which might be a bad assumption. She had just blurted out *I love you*, after all.

Rory almost started protesting into her hand, but the questions in her eyes flickered away as something else caught her attention. Archer and Isaac were marching in their direction.

While Rory calmly took more of the trail mix, Morgan raised herself to her knees. This way she was only half hovering over Rory. After last night, she didn't want to insult Rory by throwing herself between Rory and the men, but damn it, she'd intended to be a shield during the festival, and the furious expressions on the men's faces roused her protective instincts.

"What the hell did you think you were doing?" Isaac didn't bother to keep his voice down. "You could have killed Mom and Dad."

Mom and Dad?

Morgan's jaw dropped. She hadn't thought to ask Rory if the lightning had been aimed at anyone, and she hadn't been able to see where it touched the ground. In retrospect, perhaps she should have assumed who the targets were. Or that there were targets at all.

Rory washed down the trail mix with a sip of water. "I was in complete control the entire time. No one was hurt."

Isaac's face was scarlet with pure rage. "That's not the point. If you had fucked up, you could have killed people."

Morgan suspected she was seeing the Inquisitor side of Isaac for the first time. He'd trained to protect others from their own kind's power, and Rory had just provided the most dramatic example of why in years. No wonder he was furious.

"Isn't that the point?" Rory asked with a shrug. "Really. I could kill any of us at any time, and the reason I don't is because I *choose* not to. My choice. I would like all my choices as respected as this one."

Isaac breathed deeply into his hands. "That's what this was about?"

"If you'd like it to be. It's also about how I was signed up for this party against my wishes, so I decided to have fun with it." She smiled up at Morgan. "You convinced me to see if I could just have fun."

She what? Morgan wasn't sure how to respond to that. Good for Rory? She hoped Rory did have fun, but holy shit. Her plan had backfired *again*?

Luckily, Morgan didn't have to say anything. Archer jumped in first. "That was your idea of fun? You'll be lucky if the Council doesn't take your powers for this. You could have killed a Council member with your recklessness. I take everything I've said back. We could not possibly work together. Don't contact me if you want to return to competing."

He spun around and stormed off like he couldn't get away fast enough to save his own reputation.

Rory burst into giggles. "Do you think I scared him?"

Morgan combed her fingers through Rory's hair, which was sticking straight up in places. Rory might scoff, but Archer's words worried her. "Is he right about what they could do?" Morgan asked Isaac.

Groaning, Isaac lowered his hands. "No. Taking away someone's powers is a last resort measure, and she didn't actually hurt anyone. But I wouldn't be surprised if some sort of formal warning or other punishment is given."

"Please." Rory pulled Morgan's hand away, then ran her fingers through her hair herself, making it stick up again. "I'm just a bartender from a small town in Maine. Ask Mom. I'm harmless. A nobody."

"You are a pain in the ass," Isaac said, and he stalked off in the same direction as Archer had.

Rory grinned in the most adorable way, and Morgan inched away from her before temptation could dig its hooks into her skin.

"Do you want to leave?" Morgan asked.

"Yes." Rory wobbled, and she plopped back down. "Give me another second."

"She's one of my coven members!" Verbena's voice cut through the confusion around the stadium perimeter. "I want to make sure she's all right!"

A few unfamiliar witches were trying to cut off access to the performance field, Verbena's included, and Morgan noticed for the first time that several dozen people hung around the edges of the field, gawking openly or snapping photos while pretending to help. Nicole was among them, and Morgan turned away before Nicole caught her looking. She must have gotten down here right before they started holding people back.

"I can go talk to Verbena," Morgan said, searching for a reason to not be the focus of Nicole's attention.

Rory grabbed her arm, though, and she waved to Verbena with her free hand. "Stay," she told Morgan. "I need support."

"Oh, so *now* you want to be around me." Morgan hoped that came out as an attempt at humor, but she suspected pain undercut her tone.

"For the moment." Rory resealed the trail mix bag and handed it back. "It's hard to stay angry when you're taking care of me."

"Good. That was my devious plot."

Rory tossed a peanut at her. "I am sorry I worried you. I went for a long walk last night with Lilith, which turned out to be a mistake, because Lilith decided after a short time that she didn't want to walk anymore, and I had to hold her. Anyway, I had to think on some things." Rory grimaced. "While schlepping around an eight-pound cat. Do not recommend."

Apparently, Morgan had been carrying more tension around inside than she realized, because Rory's explanation had her sighing with relief. "I panicked when I saw you hadn't come to bed last night. Where did you sleep?"

"In the cabin, but on the sofa downstairs. I didn't want to wake you by climbing into bed."

Of course. So they'd both been uncomfortable for nothing.

"I also slept on the sofa," Morgan said. "In the room."

"Figures. Oh, look. We're getting more company. Time to try leaving again."

Sure enough, four more people were heading their way, Rory's parents counting for two of them. However close the lightning had come to hitting them, they appeared fully recovered from the shock and no worse for the experience. The other two witches were dressed in festival organizer shirts with enamel pins that marked them as members of the Council. Rory gave the same cocky wave to her parents as she'd given to Verbena.

"Ms. Sandler." The older of the two council members stepped forward, then seemed to reconsider such a bold move. "You'll be getting a formal notice, but as a courtesy to you and your mother, we want you to know now that the Council has voted to give you a three-year suspension from participating in any Council-sanctioned competitions or exhibitions."

"That's it?" Rory asked, and Morgan couldn't decide if she sounded disappointed.

"It's ridiculous." Wanda Sandler crossed her arms as the two other witches strode away. "They wanted to give you a five-year suspension, but I talked them down from that."

"What would I do without you?" Rory muttered, and Morgan had no problem detecting the sarcasm that time.

Had that been Rory's plan all along? Get herself banned? She'd wanted a break and her parents off her back about it. Now there was nothing her family could do to prevent her from taking one.

"Congratulations on formally ruining your career," Brett said. He opened his mouth to add more, then seemed to think better of it. Instead, he stuck his hands in his pockets, pulled out a piece of smoky quartz, and began turning it over in his palm, casting some sort of spell on himself.

At least Morgan hoped it was on himself. Smoky quartz was usually used in protective or shielding magic, so the odds were good.

"Thank you, but it's hardly ruined. If anything, I just made a bigger name for myself." Rory wavered on her feet, and Morgan held out a steadying hand. "You should be proud."

Rory had a point. Morgan was positive that if she went online, dozens of videos of Rory blasting that circle apart would already be posted all over the Internet. That alone would have been enough to dominate any other magical news. Add in that Rory had enough power left to conjure lightning afterward, and it was all anyone was going to talk about for weeks. The suspension was just icing on the publicity cake. If Rory returned to competing after it ended, the anticipation would likely generate enough magical energy to blow out a hundred protective circles.

What that meant for Rory and how she'd felt crushed by the weight of such pressure, Morgan wasn't sure. Would she be able to handle it in three years' time? She seemed okay for the moment, but Morgan didn't know how she'd reached her decision to perform or if she'd taken any potions to help her through it.

Wanda's face lit up and she nodded slowly, apparently sharing Morgan's publicity-related thoughts. "This will eventually be a positive moment in her career. She's right." She turned from her husband to her daughter. "But was the suspension worth it? If you were that adamant about taking a few years off, why didn't you say so?"

Why hadn't Rory said so? Was she *serious*?

Anger roared in Morgan's blood, fighting to escape. She snapped her attention between Rory and her parents, waiting for Rory to let out her own fury.

"Of course, we want to support you," Brett added.

Rory only stared at her parents in disbelief.

Morgan tried counting to ten to give Rory the chance to respond, but Rory seemed lost for words. As usual, Morgan was not, and she made it to five before they exploded out of her as fierce and furious as the spell that broke the protective circle. "Are you kidding me? You're going to act like she hasn't been telling you for days—months, years, for all I know—that she wanted to take a break? How many times did she say it yesterday alone? Don't you dare act like this is new information. Don't you dare gaslight her like that. She's your *daughter.* You don't do that to the people you love!"

Morgan caught her breath, dimly aware that her voice had been raised loud enough to draw the attention of multiple people in the vicinity. She would probably regret that later. She would probably regret all of this, because if the Sandlers didn't attempt to hex her tongue off, they were better people than she was giving them credit for.

And she . . . she was not as good as she was pretending. Her words rattled around in her brain and settled in her gut with a sickening feeling.

Oh, sweet fucking stars, didn't all her lying and pretending mean she'd essentially been doing the exact same thing to Rory these past two days?

25

IN THE UNCOMFORTABLE PAUSE THAT HAD FOLLOWED MORGAN'S outburst, Rory found the energy to stumble away from her parents, half dragging Morgan with her.

Amid her other concerns, Morgan worried that Rory was overexerting herself in her haste to separate Morgan from her family. But Rory's strength appeared to be returning quickly, although she told Morgan she didn't want to stop and talk to any of the gathering witches who were waiting for her outside the stadium until she'd sorted out what to say publicly, particularly about the suspension. No formal announcement had been made yet, but naturally the rumor had already spread beyond the stadium walls as if by magic. Which was likely the actual cause. Morgan had always theorized that witches who were good at scrying were the reason why the magical community's gossip spread faster than the speed of texting.

Rory feigned being more tired than she was, leaning on Morgan as she smiled and waved to the people who cheered her on and yelled about the unfairness of the ban.

"Where do you want to go?" Morgan asked, assuming the answer would not be her family's cabin.

"Away," Rory said.

Away ended up being one of the open-air buildings that had been hosting workshops during the last few days. The workshops had all ended and the area was cleared out, but the wooden tables and benches were part of the festival grounds and so remained. Rory was walking normally by the time they reached the closest building, but she seemed grateful to sit again.

"Can I get you more food?" Morgan asked. The vendor area was nearby, through a path in the trees, and while the majority of the shops had closed down, most of the food proprietors would remain open through dinnertime.

"I'm fine. What I need is a good night's sleep, that's all." Rory made a wry face. "I didn't exactly get one last night."

"Yeah, me neither." Nor did Morgan foresee a good one anytime soon.

She fell silent, wondering where to start the conversation she and Rory needed to have and discarding her options one by one. Like a coward. She knew that's what she was being. Maybe it was what she'd been all along.

Rory also seemed content to delay, however, so it wasn't only her. She pressed her fingertips together, staring off into the trees. Every few seconds, her phone went off, as it had been doing since she'd turned it back on after leaving the stadium.

Rory scowled at the most recent intrusion and shut the phone off again. "I have not missed everything about performing, that's for sure. It was fun, though."

"Really?" All she wanted was for Rory to be happy. It wouldn't assuage Morgan's guilt for any role she might have played in Rory's decision, but as long as Rory had enjoyed herself, Morgan could focus on her other—more pressing—reason for feeling guilty. "I'm glad, and I'm so sorry if I made you feel like you needed to do it. To prove me wrong, or something. I don't think you're weak. Far from it."

Rory took her hand, and Morgan was too surprised to pull away. "Like I said, I was angry with you, but I know your heart is in the right place. I might have overreacted and been feeling defensive. You kind of blindsided me with some of what you said last night, and we need to talk about that, but I promise I didn't go out there today to prove you wrong. If anything, I did it to prove you were right."

"I was right?" A squirrel snapped a tree branch nearby, jostling Morgan's already jumbled thoughts. "You must be wrong. I'm never right."

"About that, you are very incorrect. But I'm not wrong."

Morgan rubbed her overtired and overstressed head. "Are you trying to confuse me? What are we talking about again?"

Rory grinned, and Morgan's heart swelled. She'd started taking it for granted that she could make Rory laugh, and she knew it wouldn't—couldn't—happen much longer. She had to savor what she could, and while the love potion might be overriding Rory's true feelings for her, Morgan hoped the moments of happiness Rory had would still mean something once she knew the truth.

"You were right," Rory said, letting go of her hand, "about it being good to put myself out there, and to remind me that I wouldn't know what I could handle until I tried. Like breaking the circle, it's all theory until you test yourself. I was able to shake off the pressure enough to quit two years ago. How would I know if I could shake off the pressure and have fun unless I gave it a shot?"

"I don't quite remember saying that."

"You didn't exactly, but it's how I interpreted what you said. In a way, it's what you've been doing all along. Like how you pushed me to go dancing the other night. I always stayed away from the concerts because it's too loud and overwhelming. But I went for you, and I had fun. And when you spoke up for me yesterday at lunch, something good happened then, too." Rory tilted her head back, looking up into the building's wood ceiling. "So when I stopped being defensive and thought about the reasons you gave for me performing, it seemed like it wasn't a bad idea to listen to you."

Morgan shook her head. As much as she wanted to be a fount of wisdom, that was so far from the truth it was laughable. "But I wouldn't have said any of what I did if I'd known why you quit. I'm always talking when I'm better off keeping my mouth shut."

"Or maybe the world is not always better off when you keep your mouth shut. If you kept your mouth shut at the bar two weeks ago, we wouldn't be here, would we?" Rory raised an eyebrow.

No, they wouldn't, but Morgan couldn't bring herself to acknowledge that, seeing as her plan to help Rory had all gone to shit. Besides, those other things Rory mentioned—she didn't know that Morgan had done them to annoy her. To make her believe they were incompatible. Worse—if she liked Morgan for doing them, wasn't that proof that they were *actually* incompatible?

"You can't be happy about what I did. I shouldn't have forced you to go dancing when you said you didn't want to! It was rude."

"What was rude was me outright refusing originally," Rory said to Morgan's ever-increasing confusion. "I was making up rules because our relationship was supposed to be fake. But I'd never simply refuse to do something my real girlfriend wanted that badly. I can't know I'd enjoy everything, but I'd want to give it a try for her sake. And that's what happened. You would do it for me. I know you would because look at what you've already done for me, and I'm not just talking about how you tried one of my lime-flavored rugelach despite hating citrus."

Morgan hadn't even remembered the cookie incident until now. Absurd, in retrospect, that she'd made such a big fuss in her own head about offending Rory. Like, *that* was drama? Her two-week-younger self had been piteously naive.

"What else have I done?" Morgan asked.

Rory's expression was incredulous. "You offered to do *this*—be my fake girlfriend—because I was stressed about my family. You agreed to my unfair demands to make me happy. And you did it without even the possibility of enjoying it."

"It's not like my motives were entirely selfless. I did hope there was some chance that if we spent time together, things wouldn't always stay fake."

"So? It doesn't change my point. You cared enough to try, and we know it's not so fake anymore."

No, Morgan didn't suppose it changed anything, but that only made her feel worse. She needed to end this lie. It just fucking hurt, so she kept delaying and searching for excuses.

Morgan lowered her head to her knees and attempted to control her breathing, seeking the power in herself like she would to work magic. Intent. Will. Purpose. Those same intangible concepts had gotten her into this mess, and she needed them to get her out of it.

"Our relationship *is* fake," Morgan said, hating how her voice trembled. "You just don't see it."

Rory made a noise somewhere between a sigh and a groan. "I did say we had to have this talk, didn't I? Come on, Morgan. You really expect me to believe that we can't tell the difference between what's real and what's not?"

"But it's true."

"Yes, when you ran onto the field this afternoon to help me, that felt very fake." The sarcasm dripped from Rory's words. "Why are you so adamant about pretending? You said yourself that you're a lousy liar, and you absolutely are. That's why I know you're lying now, and not when you told me you loved me."

Tears burned behind Morgan's eyes. She hadn't cried so many times in such short duration since high school. Even when Nicole had dumped her, she'd had one good cry and one get-completely-drunk-with-friends night, and then one spell to help her banish her feelings. She hadn't shed a tear since. But lately, she was weeping like an oozing wound, and perhaps that made sense. Her heart was breaking. Not just for her own crushed hopes this time, but because she was going to hurt Rory as well.

"That's because I wasn't lying about that," Morgan said into her knees. "But you are lying in a way, and you don't know it."

Rory pulled Morgan's hair back with a gentle hand. "I swear to the gods, I'm going to kill your ex for putting it in your head that—"

"I gave you a love potion." Morgan snapped her head up. Rory's touch had been more than she could take. She had to get this out. No more hesitating. No more delaying by searching for perfect words that didn't exist.

Silence filled the air, as heavy as that moment after a strenuous spell was cast. As though time and space were suspended.

"What?" Rory asked quietly, and the silence popped, flooding Morgan's senses with the horrible weight of what she'd finally admitted.

Morgan sniffed, and she wanted to gag on the smell of the building's old, weathered wood and the traces of countless pungent herbs that had been absorbed into its fibers.

"I gave you a love potion," she repeated, her voice barely louder than a whisper. For something that had been so easy to do that she hadn't realized she was doing it, admitting that she'd done it felt like someone was dragging dull razor blades through her insides. Every word drew another jagged slice.

She couldn't leave it at that simple sentence, though. She couldn't justify her actions, but the need to explain kept the word vomit going, and once Morgan started, she couldn't stop herself. She had to make Rory believe she'd never willingly hurt her.

"It was an accident, and I am so, so sorry. I never meant to do it. I'd mislabeled some ingredients, and I was distracted and didn't double-check anything . . . That potion I'm obsessed with making—I'm trying to create an antidote. I mean, the love potion should wear off anyway, and I don't know why it hasn't yet. But I will fix it. I will fix you. I just didn't want to tell you at first because I thought that if I could convince you that we were all wrong for each other, that might be a less traumatic way to break the enchantment. But it's so hard because I do love you, and I realized I have to stop hiding the truth, even if it hurts. I've been lying to you like your parents have, and you deserve better. And I'm sorry."

She'd barely paused for a breath, and the speech left Morgan winded. Gasping, she waited. Waited for Rory to yell at her, to curse her, to fling every bit of shit at her that she deserved.

But Rory didn't say anything. She gaped at Morgan with that tiny V between her eyebrows, looking so completely lost that Morgan crumbled. Every word she'd spoken had shredded her a bit more, and she was collapsing in on herself. Unable to breathe. Unable to keep her head up. She'd wanted to be the world's best fake girlfriend, then the best real girlfriend, but she was, in fact, the world's worst friend.

Clouds rolled in with the evening sky, the air hummed with birdsong, and Morgan was slowly dying of shame and guilt and her own selfish pain until she couldn't take it any longer.

"I'm sorry," Morgan whispered again, and then she turned and fled before she was too broken to move.

Tears blurred her vision. It was amazing that the lumpy ground didn't trip her feet. If Rory had called out after her, she would have fallen for sure, but Rory was silent, at least until Morgan had disappeared down the path that would take her to the Sandlers' cabin. If Rory screamed then, if she cursed Morgan or hexed her into the wind, Morgan didn't hear it. Her ears were filled with the sound of her labored breathing. Sniffling and running were a bad combination—who'd have thought? But she had to get to the cabin and grab her things before Rory returned. She couldn't face her again tonight, or honestly, ever.

That also meant that whatever happened next between Rory and her family, Morgan couldn't help her. She felt awful about that, but her outburst at Rory's parents probably ensured her presence would only make things worse anyway. She had multiple reasons to flee.

Morgan flung open the cabin door and charged immediately up to the bedroom, ignoring the voices coming from the kitchen. Someone—it sounded like Isaac—called out for Rory, and since she wasn't Rory, Morgan didn't respond. She had to be fast. It was a toss-up as to which of the Sandlers was last on her list of people she wanted to run into, but after her confession, Isaac was a strong contender.

Lilith was in the bedroom, lazing on the sofa, and Morgan swallowed past the lump in her throat, finally pausing to catch her breath and pet Rory's cat one last time. "It was nice meeting you," Morgan told her.

She suspected Lilith would pick up on Rory's mood soon enough, like a good familiar (despite Rory saying she was a bad one), and that was another reason to hurry. Morgan didn't need to be clawed so that her outsides looked like what her insides felt like.

At the moment, though, Lilith blinked at Morgan, her green eyes eerily human in their confusion.

Morgan began shoving her belongings into her pack when her hand hit a paper box, and she pulled out the chocolates Rory had given her. A fresh spasm of regret almost knocked her over. That had been a good day. An almost perfect day in spite of running into Nicole.

And it was all a lie.

Sweet stars, she ought to be thankful it hadn't seemed like a better day at the time and that they'd never tested those chocolates. Morgan closed her eyes and shuddered, then dropped the chocolates on the desk. Rory would likely toss them—she would in her place—but that should be her decision. Morgan had stolen enough choices from her already.

On that thought, Morgan ran her fingers over the snowflake obsidian bracelet. Ironic that she could use protection from negative energy more than ever, but this, too, should belong to Rory. She yanked it off, surprised to not be immediately blasted by all the rage Rory must be directing her way.

Then again, Rory was more methodical than she was. Maybe she was channeling her anger and pain to cast a hex in Morgan's direction later. Morgan couldn't blame her, and she didn't see the point in trying to ward herself. She deserved whatever Rory did to her, and besides, it wasn't like she was a match for her magically. As Rory had proven only an hour or so ago, she could kill anyone anytime she wanted to with a decisive lightning strike. Morgan might be feeling more confident in her potion-making skills lately, but there was no potion to ward against death by sky incineration.

Of course, she didn't really think Rory would want to kill her. Hex her a little, maybe. That wouldn't even go against Council rules, since witches were allowed to defend themselves from other witches, and Morgan had clearly been the instigator in this situation.

Behind her, Lilith let out a questioning meow, and Morgan shook her head. "They're hers."

In response, Lilith knocked both items to the floor, and Morgan jumped. With a sigh, because she had neither the time nor the emotional fortitude to explain herself to a cat, she picked up the box and the bracelet and set them back on the desk. "Rory will tell you why later."

Morgan assumed. When she got her own cat, she expected she'd torture it with long, drawn-out weepy tales of how she'd lost the love of her life. (Hopefully, any cat she adopted would just be a cat, and therefore not get too angry about her constant moping.)

Her explanation seemed to satisfy Lilith, since she didn't knock the objects over a second time, and Morgan stuffed her sleep shirt into her pack, wadding it up in a ball. It was a terrible packing job, even for her, but it would do until she got to her mother's tent. That, she'd decided, was where she would go. Hazel and Andy would want to talk—Andy didn't know about the love potion—and Morgan couldn't do it. Eventually, yes. Tonight, no. But her mother and grandmom would let her be quietly morose, and they'd discuss the shop and make plans for leaving tomorrow, which meant, if she was really lucky, Morgan would find a few minutes here and there where she could think about anything other than Rory.

26

Stir clockwise nine times in rhythm with your pulse.

Morgan reread the sentence. How in the name of Aphrodite did she feel her pulse strongly enough to stir in time with it? Who came up with this damned potion recipe anyway?

Right, her grandmom. Morgan had never asked her if it worked, since it was an illicit potion that she shouldn't be messing with in the first place.

Here went nothing. She closed her eyes and focused her power inward. For the past five days since she'd returned from the festival, her pulse had seemed to be running at full speed, as though her heart could power her beyond the consequences of her actions if she only kept moving. But here, in Bed, Bath, and Broom's back room with the worktable powered up, her pulse was slow and steady. Magical headspace existed in a realm beyond reality, as magic did.

Morgan stirred the potion once, twice, three times. Each full rotation of her pestle turned it a darker pink and the liquid grew thicker. Then, on the ninth turn, the pink completely vanished, leaving her with a colorless potion the viscosity of warm maple syrup. It even smelled ever so slightly sweet.

According to Grandmom June's notes, the potion was best made during a full moon, but Morgan didn't have time to wait for that. Besides, best did not mean it was necessary. It was merely a suggestion, like the best-by date on the yogurt she'd found in her fridge and had eaten for lunch that day, because she couldn't bring herself to set foot in a grocery store and hadn't anticipated how much more expensive grocery delivery was. She hadn't gotten sick yet, so all was probably fine. Or it would be until she ran out of old yogurt, raisin bread, and coffee.

It was the coffee that would do her in. She'd have to suck it up and pay the grocery delivery markup because she couldn't do without, especially since she wasn't sleeping.

Unless . . . Morgan tapped the table's glowing rune for protection. She could try using magic to disguise herself. It was a thought, but she would need supplies, which meant a trip to the store, and that meant she was back to square one. Maybe Hazel could be bribed.

Morgan dug her nails into her palm to snap herself out of this thought loop and back to business. The love potion should be finished, and she was simply going to have to trust that she'd made it correctly for experimentation purposes.

It looked so innocuous. So innocent. So not the same color or viscosity as the potion she'd given Rory, but then the spells hadn't been identical, only similar enough for concern. Morgan had already tried remaking the potion she thought she'd given to Rory, and none of her three attempts had come out looking like she recalled the original had. But it didn't matter. She needed potions she could experiment with, so here she was.

Creating a brand-new potion was always a challenge. Although Morgan had never done it before, she was quite familiar with the anxiety of trying a new-to-her potion for the first time and guessing whether she'd made it correctly. There were methods for testing efficacy, of course, though none were as guaranteed to work as the most obvious—using herself as a guinea pig. That, she couldn't afford to do, however. Not to mention it was generally considered a terrible idea for obvious reasons. So she had to rely on less efficacious and slower but safer methods.

Morgan rubbed her hand over the worktable, deactivating the runes, and yawned. Her tiredness was part magic depletion and part simple exhaustion. For the past several days, she'd only slept one night out of every three because even her restless brain couldn't fight the need for sleep that long. She was due for another crash anytime, and it couldn't come soon enough.

As if on cue, her elbow resting against the worktable slipped, and she lost her balance. Morgan's arm shot out, and she smacked her brazier as she attempted to steady herself. Hot incense went flying. Embers of burning herbs scattered across the table and winked harmlessly out, but the back of her hand screeched in pain from where some landed on her skin.

Morgan screamed silently, cursing her overtired body. That could have been worse, though. She could have knocked over one of the candles.

On that thought, she hauled herself back to her feet and snuffed out the flames.

With her head aching and the room shifting in and out of focus, Morgan grabbed her cheese crackers from the counter and sank to the floor with the box. Once she got her brain back in check—or as in check as it ever was—she'd examine the purported love potion.

A light tap on the door preceded Morgan's mom sticking her head into the room. "I was told you were still here."

"I'm here." Morgan licked bright orange crumbs from her fingers. "As I suppose you can see. Don't mind me."

Lianne stepped inside and shut the door behind her. "Liv just closed the shop. You should go home. As happy as I am to see you spreading your wings on this new secret project, I'm worried you're overworking yourself as a way to cope. I'm not saying having a few too many drinks and blasting 'I Will Survive' while dancing around with a hairbrush is as productive as what you're doing, but I'm not sure this strategy is healthy, either."

A few too many drinks and singing along to Gloria Gaynor sounded like a time-wasting luxury Morgan couldn't afford. "I can't stop. I've never screwed anything up so badly before."

Let her mom just think she was trying to keep her mind off the pain. She wouldn't be entirely wrong.

Lianne frowned, and once again, Morgan was struck by how similar they looked, especially now that her mother's hair was back to blond. "Whatever you think you screwed up, if Rory can't see beyond a mistake and accept your apology, that's on her. You deserve better."

Morgan snorted. "You're supposed to say that. You're my mother. No one puts up with my shit who doesn't have to. Even Dad dumped me when I didn't go to college."

In fairness, he'd dumped both of them, but her parents had divorced twenty years ago, and her mother seemed well over it by this point.

"Oh, sweetie. That's not true." Lianne kissed her head. "Your father simply doesn't handle magic well, like a lot of mundanes. I'm pretty sure he'd hoped you would grow up to be more like him, but your power weirded him out. You didn't disappoint him or screw anything up. He disappointed us."

"Magic didn't weird him out enough to not marry you."

Her mother conceded the point with a grimace, sliding to the floor next to Morgan. "Not at first. I'm sure he thought he'd be fine with it. But even then, part of me knew he wouldn't be, and your grandmom warned me, too. Hell, every coven member with a tarot deck or a scrying crystal warned me, not that it took any divination talent to see it.

But I wanted to believe we could make it work, and I still believe marrying him was the right decision—he gave me you."

"Oh." All these years, she'd assumed her father had grown more distant because he was disappointed that she hadn't wanted to go to school where he taught. He'd never hidden the fact that he'd wanted her to be driven academically like he was, but Morgan had already decided by high school that she wanted to work at Bed, Bath, and Broom. Could her father have felt like she was growing distant from him instead of the other way around?

Lianne wrapped her arms around Morgan, and Morgan leaned into her. She remembered what Rory had said, about how in her family you pushed on and didn't expose vulnerability. As glad as Morgan was that she didn't feel that pressure, there were limits to how willing she was to pour her heart out. Though part of her longed to confess the truth, and maybe beg her mother for assistance with the potion, it wasn't smart. She'd created the problem, so it was hers to fix. Telling her mom the truth would put her in an awkward and potentially fraught position with the Witch Council.

But, while she wouldn't confide in her mother or stop working, maybe a small amount of comfort could keep her going longer.

"I need to get home and feed the cats," her mother said at last. "I don't suppose you want to come over for dinner?"

The thought of food made Morgan reel. The cheese crackers were her limit. Besides, she had the potion she'd just completed to test. "I want to finish up here."

Lianne didn't seem surprised. "Can I get you something before I go?"

Yes, an entirely new life would be helpful. One where she wasn't a magical disaster.

Morgan rubbed the burning patch of skin on the back of her hand. She should run that under cold water, but that would take energy and coordination. Then maybe she should put some burn salve on it, but she could get that herself. “I’m good. I’m going to leave as soon as I finish cleaning up the mess on the worktable.”

“Okay.” Her mother did not sound like she believed her, which was fair. Morgan had no intention of leaving soon. “Have a good night then, sweetie. Try to get some rest.”

Her mom kissed her head once more before heading out, and the crackers turned to salty dust in Morgan’s mouth as she listened to the main door being locked.

Her phone buzzed with a text as Morgan closed the cracker box. Conveniently, it was on the floor with her, so Morgan braced herself and checked it.

HAZEL: We will see you at the Empty Chalice in twenty minutes.

Sweet stars, Hazel was getting bossy.

Before she could think better of it and pretend she hadn’t seen the message, Morgan wrote back.

MORGAN: No.

Seriously, had Hazel lost her mind? Wound her Princess Leia buns too tightly? Inhaled too much incense smoke? Morgan couldn’t bring herself to go to Hannaford for groceries. Like she was going to barge into the Empty Chalice, the very last place in Harborage where she’d be welcome? She wouldn’t be surprised if Rory had put wards up around the doorway to stop her from entering. But if she had, Morgan would never know, because she could never, ever show her face in there again.

HAZEL: I have it on good authority that Rory isn’t working a shift tonight, and you need to take a break. Whatever happened to your

theory that inspiration only comes when
you're doing something else?

Smoke inhalation or not, Hazel was with-it enough to toss Morgan's own words back at her. Annoying. Also, irrelevant. Morgan did not have time to wait around for inspiration, which was why she was scouring every potion book she could find for assistance.

MORGAN: According to Verbena, genius is 1% inspiration and 99% perspiration.

HAZEL: I'm 99% sure that's actually according to Thomas Edison.

MORGAN: Even better. When has Verbena ever invented a light bulb?

HAZEL: Morgan, I'm worried about you. How about I come over, and we make our own margaritas?

Damn it. First her mother, now Hazel. It was hard having people who cared about you when you didn't feel like you deserved them. Morgan swallowed down her latest round of weeping with a drink of cold water.

MORGAN: Worry about Rory. I'm fine.

HAZEL: My heart is big enough for you both.

HAZEL: That's it. I'm coming over with a bottle of that hideously pink premade margarita stuff.

MORGAN: You can't. I'm working. Go hang out with people who don't suck.

Shit. Was that too much? Hazel was going to freak out, so Morgan quickly tried to scale back the extent of her self-loathing.

MORGAN: I mean, I had an idea this morning, and I'm busy. I think I'm onto something.

Morgan watched Hazel's ". . ." appear and disappear on her screen as she ate some more crackers.

Her idea wasn't specifically for how to create an anti-love potion, but for what seemed like a logical first step in creating one. That is, she needed to understand the basis of what all potions that could override a person's mood or general mental state had in common. It stood to reason that there was *something*.

Magic often looked random and chaotic to those who couldn't do it, and sometimes to those who could, but there was a rule or reason for every seemingly inconsequential step. A reason why you stirred one potion clockwise sometimes and counterclockwise other times. A reason why some spells had to be performed during certain moon phases, while for others, it made less of a difference. A reason for colors or smells or why one plant or crystal or word was chosen over another. Once Morgan figured out what the underlying rules were to mood- and mind-altering potions, that would become the blueprint for how she broke that kind of spell.

Previously, she'd been trying to formulate a potion that would counter each individual ingredient she'd used in the love potion, but that was only scratching the surface. She needed to understand each ingredient's role in the spell's efficacy to choose the proper counter-ingredient and add it in the proper way. Otherwise, she was looking at possible endless configurations since most ingredients had many potential uses.

All of this bordered on magical theory, which Morgan detested. If she couldn't intuit an ingredient or instruction, she tended to struggle. When she was making a new potion for the first time, like the love potion she'd just completed, she understood enough of what was going on, and why, to be fairly confident of her results. But intuition alone was not going to cut it here. She would rely on it to help her see the greater pattern, but she had to put in the work and do the research for that to happen.

It was painfully ironic that the only reason she was convinced she could do this was because of Rory. Even before the love potion, Rory had believed in Morgan's skills and power. And Morgan believed in Rory. So it was time for her to do what Rory (and Grandmom June) had suggested—stretch her talent and skills and see what she could really do. Would she be successful? Only time would tell, but Morgan was determined. If Rory could eat, sleep, and practice her way to greatness, she could do the same, though likely without the sleep.

To that end, Morgan had been gathering what knowledge she could about potions that overrode free will. Love potions, charming potions, truth potions, and even lesser mood-altering potions—ones like the relaxation potion that she made regularly—were all variations of that same spell. Morgan already knew how to tweak the relaxation potion's theme for different outcomes. Once she'd made several of each other type of potion, she therefore had reason to hope that the larger pattern would present itself.

For the moment, the hardest part was finding potion recipes that were known to work. Since most of these potions were illicit except under specific circumstances, witches could be kind of cagey as to whether they'd ever tested their handiwork. They were also classics, though, so everyone had a formula they claimed had been handed down in the family for generations, most since before the Witch Council had officially banned their use.

Hazel wrote back at last.

> **HAZEL:** Fine, but I'm stopping by tomorrow, and I'm going to make sure you're eating and sleeping.

Perfect.

> **MORGAN:** About that . . . I could use some groceries.

Hazel was as likely to throw eggs at her as she was to buy them for her, but if the universe hadn't wanted her to take the opening, it shouldn't have provided one. That was logic.

Five minutes and a third of a box of crackers later, Morgan climbed to her feet and washed orange dust off her hands in the sink. She was back at the point where she could distinguish between overtiredness and the effects of magic depletion. Progress. She even gave herself a pep talk, promising to go home after no more than a cursory examination of the love potion.

Her phone chimed again, and she groaned. No doubt it was Andy this time, also attempting to lure her out of her self-imposed cage. How was she supposed to fix her mistake with all these interruptions?

> **RORY:** Morgan, for fuck's sake, will you respond to my messages?

Morgan banged her non-injured hand against the love potion's bowl, and a few drops splashed over the side. Shit. With her heart back to pounding at full speed, Morgan wiped her hand off on her shirt and swiped away the text. Then, to keep temptation at bay, she turned off her phone.

Rory was finally sounding pissed off at her. That had to be a positive sign. In fact, Rory wasn't actually being rational in her anger. If she were, she'd recall that Morgan *had* responded to her. Granted, it had only been once, but she'd reiterated that she was working on an antidote, and she'd explained that in the meantime, the best way to counteract the potion was for them to stay away from each other.

Morgan wasn't entirely certain about the veracity of that advice, but intuition told her it was true. Convenient, but true. She still was too ashamed to be anywhere near Rory, never mind speak to her, but she would apologize a thousand more times over text if that's what Rory wanted. Except Rory *didn't* seem to want that, and that was unfortunate since Morgan couldn't do anything else.

Barely holding herself together, Morgan poured the remains of the potion into a bottle, labeled it, and tucked it safely away where no one else would stumble upon it until . . . well, tomorrow. Given how late it was and how she would be the first person here in the morning, there was no real risk of anyone else finding it. But Morgan had learned her lesson about sloppiness. She would be careless with her labeling and storage no more.

27

"EXPLAIN YOURSELF." A FEW DAYS LATER, HAZEL SHOVED ASIDE an empty Chinese food takeout container, a pile of junk mail, and the broken phone charger on Morgan's counter. On the square of space she created, she set down a shopping bag.

On some level, Morgan knew she was embarrassed by the disaster that had overtaken her apartment since returning from the NEWT Festival, but she was too distracted by life to care at the moment. One day, that would change. Or so she hoped.

Morgan held out her phone. "I'm adopting a cat."

"That's not what I meant."

"I thought you'd be proud of me. I took a break from work. I went to the shelter, met a bunch of kitties, and filled out the paperwork." She pressed her phone in Hazel's face. "Look at her! Isn't she precious?"

Hazel took the phone, and her face softened as she saw the sweet, gray-haired cat that had spent the morning nuzzling Morgan's ankles. "What happened to her poor ear?"

"Right?" Morgan took the phone back and poked at the picture. "She's had a rough life so far, but I'm going to spoil her and make her the happiest cat ever."

Hazel leaned against the counter, winding her long braid around her hand. "Are you sure you're not adopting a cat because you're feeling sad and looking for something to love you?"

Morgan scowled and set her phone down amid the clutter. "No, but this was my plan since before the festival, so I'm sure it's fine. We bonded. It's fate. Her name is Luna."

"Then explain to me," Hazel said. "Why could you take the time to go to the shelter, but not the time to stop by the Broom Closet and pick up your own spell supplies?"

Morgan cleared her throat. "The shelter is outside of town, and it didn't seem likely that I'd run into Rory there."

"Morgan."

"Whereas the Broom Closet is downtown and across the street from the Empty Chalice. Odds of a Rory sighting are exponentially higher." Morgan wrapped her arms around herself, imagining a chill more so than feeling one. The late August afternoon heat was only starting to dissipate, but most of her apartment's windows faced east, so there was a light ocean breeze wafting in.

"Yeah, speaking of Rory." Hazel continued over Morgan's low whine. "Would you please stop being a coward and talk to her? She's miserable. She asked me to tell you that, by the way. Not the miserable part, but the coward part. I'm sorry to say it, but she's not wrong."

Unable to argue the point, Morgan turned her back on Hazel under the guise of loading several days' worth of dirty dishes into her dishwasher. "I don't know what else she wants me to say! I'm doing my best to make it up to her the only way I can—by staying away and trying to break the spell. If she has something else she wants from me, I wish she would tell me what so I could do it."

Hazel crossed her arms. "What she wants is for you to talk to her."

"How am I supposed to face her after what I did?"

"I don't know, but don't you owe it to her to do that?"

"Why would she want to see me?"

"You could try asking her!"

With a scream, Morgan gave up on the dishes and flopped on her sofa. Hugging a pillow to her chest, she curled up in a ball. "Maybe she just wants to hex me in person."

From the sound of Hazel's sigh, she was rolling her eyes, but Morgan had her face buried in blue microsuede. "Has she hexed you?"

"Not that I'm aware of, but my phone charger died, I burned myself with incense, sloshed a potion, and the dental floss has broken in my mouth four days in a row. So, on the other hand, possibly."

"Has she reported you to the Council?"

"Also, not that I'm aware of." Morgan hadn't given that possibility much consideration. That was unwise on her part, but she'd been too caught up in her work on the anti-love potion to think about much else.

Well, she'd thought about a cat, but that was because she could do something about a cat. She could do nothing about Rory reporting her if Rory chose to, which Rory would be well within her rights to do. Even if she didn't want to go through official channels, it would be easy enough to call her brother and tell him everything.

"She should have reported me," Morgan said into the pillow.

"Why? It was an accident."

"Because it means she's being nice to me still." Morgan sat and tossed the pillow aside. "She's not angry enough, and that tells me she hasn't broken free of the potion. It's been a week since I told her the truth. How can it not have worn off, especially when she should be furious at me?"

Hazel reached into the bag she'd brought and began unloading the contents. "Good grief, is that what these are for? It looks like you're planning on doing a banishing spell."

"I am." Morgan rubbed her eyes. "I've made progress on my potion, but it's not right yet. I'm positive my feelings for Rory are interfering, just like they interfered when I was trying to make her the relaxation potion. I don't think I can make her an anti-love potion while I'm in love with her."

Morgan sorted through the rest of the banishing spell supplies—the ones Hazel hadn't obtained for her—which were sitting on her living room table. She'd brought home all of the dried herbs she needed from the store, and she already had a cheap mirror and the small knife she used for magical bloodletting. Getting the energy to cast the spell—that would be its own problem given her sleep issues.

Despite that potential setback, over the past few days, she'd prepared a variety of new-to-her potions, including the love potion, and the pattern she'd been searching for among them . . . Morgan thought she understood it.

It turned out, however, that understanding it and using it to the right effect were not quite the same thing. Which, duh. But her frustration was doubling every day. She was doing something right, that much was certain. The latest potion she'd created reacted strongly with all of the free will–altering potions, turning each of them some shade of green. It was an interesting development and it might suggest it had potential uses if Morgan had the energy to care, but she didn't. Because it wasn't useful to *her.* It was too generic. She needed it to counteract a love potion—specifically, the love potion she'd accidentally created and given to Rory—which meant she needed to hone that botched potion until it didn't interact with any other type.

Hence the banishing spell. If her feelings for Rory had messed up her intentions once, it stood to reason they could mess up her intentions again. A banishing spell wasn't a perfect solution—banishing emotions was difficult—but it was worth a shot. After all, one had helped Morgan get over Nicole.

Or maybe finally seeing Nicole for the kind of person she was had done it, and the spell was merely a formality.

Sweet stars, Morgan hoped not. She'd rather believe that it had worked once so it would work again.

Oblivious to Morgan's spiraling, Hazel tossed the black pillar candle around in her hands. "How is it fair for you to do this? Why do you deserve to banish your feelings for Rory while she's stuck with hers for you?"

"None of this is fair, or I wouldn't have hurt her." Morgan snatched the candle away. "Do you think it would work if she did her own banishing spell? I don't think so, because she'd just be trying to banish a spell while under a spell, and not her true feelings, but if it might work, you could suggest she try it. I can't do it for her. It would definitely backfire, and anyway, I've messed with her emotions enough without her permission."

"Slow down." Hazel held up her hands. "You're probably right. But also, who's to say she hasn't tried?"

"She probably has. But still." Morgan gave Hazel a hopeful look. "You could suggest it."

"You can talk to her and do it yourself."

So they were back to that.

"Tell me about your progress," Hazel said after a moment. "I can help you brainstorm."

Although Morgan got the sense that Hazel simply wanted to hang out and ensure she wasn't going to work herself to death, Morgan knew she needed the break. But she wouldn't give in that easily. "Okay, but first you need to fill me in on what's going on with you and Rory's friend from the festival."

"There's not much to tell," Hazel said, a touch too quickly. "We're just seeing how things go."

"Liar. Don't hold back. I need uplifting news."

Hearing about an improvement in her friend's love life didn't seem like the best way to deal with her own misery, but for Hazel she'd make an exception. If someone around here was going to be happy, Morgan couldn't think of anyone more deserving.

"What happens," Hazel asked an hour later as she watched to make sure Morgan was eating her sub, "when you test this new potion of yours with the actual potion you gave Rory? You said it reacts with all of the others, but there's nothing even slightly different about that one?"

"I don't have the actual potion I gave Rory," Morgan said, picking apart the sandwich in search of more pickle chips. "Only the replicas I made."

"You never took it back?"

The bite of dinner landed heavily in Morgan's stomach. "She didn't have it with her at the festival, or I would have. I assumed she tossed it when she got home, so I haven't asked."

Hadn't she? Wouldn't she?

Doubt crept over Morgan's brain. She had told Rory what the potion was. She must have. And yet Morgan had no memory of doing so. That entire conversation after the exhibition was hazy in her mind, but she must have.

Must. Have.

Unless she hadn't.

Unless that was why the potion hadn't worn off. Because Rory had re-dosed, perhaps more than once, since they returned home?

Fuck.

FUCK.

"Morgan?"

Hazel's voice snapped Morgan back to the present, but a shiver ran down her spine. "What if I didn't tell Rory to stop taking the potion? What if she doesn't know what it is?"

"Why wouldn't you tell her?"

"I don't know! I think I did, but what if I didn't? That could explain why she's still miserable. It's not that I created a super effective potion; it's because she took more." Morgan dragged her hands through her hair, but they didn't get very far thanks to her inability to care about it lately. Brushing? What was that? She'd only showered earlier because of her trip to the shelter, and her hair had dried in a tangled mess.

Since that was the least of her problems, Morgan yanked her fingers free, ripping strands out as she did. Her mouth had gone dry, and her heart was racing. The smell of her sub turned her stomach, and she pushed it away.

"Okay, calm down." Hazel climbed on the sofa behind her, trying to fix the bird's nest attached to Morgan's head. The sensation of Hazel's competent hands, though gentle and caring, was nothing like when Rory had touched her hair, and the memory brought a fresh wave of pain and shame with it. "Call her, find out if she has the potion, and get it back if she does."

"Can you?" Morgan loathed herself for asking, but she couldn't stop her mouth.

"No, but I will be right here for moral support, fixing your hair because it's been physically paining me to look at it this entire time."

"What if she strikes me with lightning the moment she sees me?" Morgan whimpered, and Hazel tugged on her head in a way that had to have been intentionally painful.

"If she was going to do that, I think it would already be done. It's Rory. Do you think she needs to see you to hit you?"

Point to Hazel. No, Rory fucking Sandler did not need to see her to strike her down. The love of Morgan's life was the scariest witch she'd ever met, but never once this entire time had Morgan ever felt frightened of Rory's wrath. It was only partly, she had to acknowledge, because she deserved it. But it was also because Rory was too kind, too good. Too perfect.

Morgan's heart hurt, and ugh, she was going to cry again.

"Quit stalling," Hazel said. "This is important. What if you're right and you forgot?"

Right, right. With her eyes half-closed, Morgan typed.

MORGAN: I need back the potion I gave you.

"That's what you're going with?" Hazel asked, peering over her shoulder.

"Presumptuous of you to assume I have the will to hit send."

"Morgan."

"Fine." She closed her eyes the rest of the way, hit the button, and instantly regretted not starting off with another apology.

Rory wrote back almost immediately.

RORY: You want the relaxation potion?

Shit. There was her confirmation that she hadn't told Rory what it was.

MORGAN: It's not a relaxation potion. That's what I screwed up.

RORY: You know where I live.

"Can you—"

"No," Hazel said.

RORY: Don't even think of asking Hazel to get it for you.

"Too late," Morgan muttered.

RORY: It's been a whole fucking week. You OWE ME.

"She's not wrong," Hazel said, finishing with Morgan's hair. "And at least you look fit for going out in public now."

"What questions can she have?" Morgan said, staring at her phone. "I don't have any answers for how to fix this yet."

Hazel sighed and packed up the remains of her sandwich. "Instead of freaking out immediately, why don't you wait and see?"

28

MORGAN OPTED TO WALK RATHER THAN DRIVE, WHICH WOULD have been the sensible option as the wind was picking up and thunder rumbled in the distance. This allowed her to delay longer while ostensibly making progress, and it spared her the possibility of a distraught car crash on the way home. Although it might not spare her a good soaking if rain accompanied the thunder. Still, it was one of those rare evenings when the air thrummed with power. The breeze was warm, the pressure was dropping, and the world felt more alive. It would have been a perfect night to do the banishing spell she'd been planning on. Even the moon was in the ideal phase.

But the rush of all that chaotic energy barely touched Morgan. She was aware of it, she noted it, but it didn't sink into her bones or lift her spirits. All she could think about was how she'd been caught in a thunderstorm that day she'd kissed Rory.

Morgan squeezed her eyes tight against the lingering memory, and she stumbled on a patch of uneven sidewalk. Her ankle cried out, and she cursed silently. Her distracted clumsiness seemed like an omen, far more than the weather did, and she was tempted to use her injury as an excuse to turn around and go home. Except her ankle wasn't too damaged to walk on, and she was currently closer to Rory's than she was to her own place.

Rory must have seen her approach, because she opened her door as Morgan limped up the walkway. "Are you okay?"

"Why are you asking me that?"

"You're limping."

Her lower lip trembled. "Why do you care?"

"Ugh. Fine. Would you please move your ass inside?" Rory cast furtive glances down her street, then backed up into the condo.

Unsure what to make of that exchange, Morgan sped up her hobbling.

Since the last time she'd been here, Rory had hung a wooden pentacle on the back of her door, and it glowed faintly with power. Like many witches, Morgan maintained a similar ward. They were usually cast to keep out evil, be it living or dead. But Rory hadn't bothered with one previously, which raised the question of what had changed. Morgan's initial assumption, that it was her whom Rory wanted to keep out, had to be dismissed as quickly as it had popped to mind since she passed through the doorway without issue.

Morgan tore her gaze from the intricately carved design as Rory locked the door. That complete, Rory stepped over to the sofa and sat on the arm directly across from Morgan. The lights were dim, augmented by a few flickering candles that gave off the soothing scents of vanilla and lavender.

Rory looked like she could use soothing. Hazel had said she was miserable, and somehow Morgan hadn't quite let that description penetrate her thick skull, but there was no missing it in person. The circles under Rory's eyes matched her own, and her freckles stood out starker against her pallid skin. She wore none of her usual jewelry or makeup, and her leggings and loose shirt were a reflection of the attire Morgan had been living in.

It was hard to believe she was the same woman who'd confidently stood in a crowded stadium one week ago and demonstrated a power that continued to dominate the witch community's discourse. In this moment, she was spun glass—breathtakingly beautiful but fragile, and quite capable of leaving you bloody if you damaged her.

She was everything that made Morgan's heart pound harder in her chest.

"Was there a blue SUV outside?" Rory asked.

The question cut through Morgan's mental fog, and she realized she'd been staring at Rory. "Um, I don't know?"

"What about a white car with Massachusetts plates or a black SUV with New York ones?"

Morgan scratched her neck and glanced over her shoulder as though she could see through the closed door. "I wasn't really looking. It's kind of why I tripped on my way over. I was distracted. Sorry."

"Don't worry about it. I didn't see them when I let you in, but I wasn't sure if they were lurking down the street."

"Who's they?"

Rory grimaced. "Gossip reporters. They're coming from all over the area. When I'm at work, they're hanging around the Chalice, not drinking enough to earn their stools, but not giving me a reason to kick them out aside from the never-ending questions about my career."

"Witches?"

"Mostly." She snorted. "If they were mundanes, they'd be easier to scare off."

Come to think of it, Morgan had heard from Hazel that the Empty Chalice was extra busy the other night. After the show Rory had given, she wasn't surprised. "I'm sorry."

"Would you stop saying that? It's getting annoying."

"I'm sor—"

Rory cut her off with a glare.

"Right." Morgan wet her lips and hung her head. "Is that why you have the ward?"

Rory nodded. "I got tired of them knocking on my door. Now I don't hear it unless it's someone I want to hear. Which is basically no one."

Lilith plodded down the stairs and curled up on a chair by the windows. Her green eyes fixed on Morgan, and she cleaned a paw, apparently waiting for the show to start.

Rory tapped her fingers against the sofa arm. The time for pleasantries, such as they'd been, was over, and her dark eyes grew sharper. Morgan recognized the same deliberate calmness about Rory that she'd seen when Rory was furious at her family. Her exhaustion had masked it at first, but she was waking up.

"I have questions," Rory said. "I was stunned after what you told me, and by the time I'd processed it, you'd run off. And then you wouldn't respond to my texts, and honestly, I didn't want to have this conversation over the phone anyway."

"I'm—" Morgan cut herself off this time. Her throat was getting thick.

"Yeah, I know." Rory stared up at her ceiling as though searching for goddess-given strength. "When did you realize you gave me a love potion?"

Morgan grabbed the kitchen counter to hold herself up, unable to meet Rory's gaze. "Thursday. Morning or noon, I can't remember."

"It took you two days to tell me."

"Yes."

"And that's why you were trying to avoid me so much during that time?"

Morgan nodded, unsure she could form more words.

"Why? Why the fuck did you wait two days?" Rory didn't exactly raise her voice, but her frustration was a palpable punch to the chest.

The tears Morgan had been holding back finally burst out, and she slid to the floor. She'd known this was going to happen. Not the questions Rory would ask, or how she'd express her anger. But her response to it all. She was pathetic, and Rory must despise her, but she couldn't help herself.

"I was so embarrassed," Morgan whispered, staring at her knees. "And ashamed, and I felt so awful. I thought if I could undo it—break the enchantment, create an antidote—then I could spare you the pain of knowing what happened. I almost told you Friday morning, but at breakfast you were talking about how horrible it must be to have been given a charming potion, and I wanted to prevent you from knowing your free will had been overridden that way. And then I almost told you again that night, but I hesitated, and you ran off before I could bring myself to do it. I swear, I wasn't just trying to protect myself. I thought I was being kinder to you. But I finally realized that was just me taking away another choice from you. You deserved the truth and to decide what to do with it."

Since she couldn't bear to look at Rory, Morgan had no idea what was passing over her face, but she guessed. Anger. Disgust. Contempt. Everything she was feeling directed at herself.

Through her tears, she saw Rory's bare feet touch the ground and wander out of view. Morgan attempted to pull herself together. She was a bubbling mess of wet, snotty failure, but she'd managed to avoid more apologies as requested. It didn't feel like much of a win.

"You're right," Rory said. "I deserved the truth as soon as you knew it."

"I know that now."

"I believe you, and I believe you didn't do it on purpose."

Morgan raised her head ever so slightly. Her eyes burned like hot ashes had been dumped in them, but she took relief in those words. Rory might hate her, but she didn't think Morgan was that terrible a person. It might be the best she could hope for.

"Next question," Rory said. Morgan steeled herself, then blinked in surprise a moment later when Rory sat by her on the floor. "How do you accidentally make a love potion?"

It was harder to avoid Rory's face when she was down on the cold tile with her, but Morgan gave it her best effort. "I'd mislabeled some ingredients and wasn't paying attention. It was the day after we first kissed. The practice kiss, I mean. I kept thinking about it and was distracted. Between the wrong herbs and my misplaced intentions, it made sense."

"So you don't actually know what you gave me was a love potion. You assumed?"

"I mean, I don't know for sure, no. A relaxation potion works on mood, and a love potion works on emotions. It's not the same, but there are similarities among all potions that work on the mind that way. So when I discovered I must have used yarrow in the potion, and I remembered I'd been distracted—like I said, it made sense."

Rory rested her head in her hands. "Because there are similarities in the potions, and the day before I'd told you about my feelings for you."

"Yes." She understood that Rory was simply trying to get her facts straight, and she owed Rory as much of an explanation as she wanted. But sweet stars, did Rory not understand how much this was hurting her to admit? Or did she not care?

"Did it ever occur to you, even once, that my feelings might be real?"

The question surprised Morgan, but she thought back. Maybe, for a moment, she had considered it, but the possibility had been as insubstantial as a dandelion puff and dismissed as easily on the wind. Dreams were ephemeral, and that was all being with Rory had ever amounted to.

Rory must have seen this on her face, and she sighed. "It never once occurred to you that 'hey, I'm a beautiful, talented, funny, caring person, and Rory's feelings for me might have nothing to do with this random potion I created that's similar to, but not exactly like, a love potion'?"

Morgan shook her head. "But that's not what happened."

Rory held up a finger. "This is because of your ex, isn't it? She made you believe that you aren't worthy of being loved, so I couldn't possibly have real feelings for you."

"And she was right!" Frustrated, miserable energy coursed through Morgan's veins, propelling her to her feet. "Look at what a screwup I am. Look at what I did."

Rory stood, too. "She's not right. Your fault is not that you are untalented or a small thinker or any of the other bullshit she said to you. If you were to have a serious flaw, it's your propensity to believe the worst about yourself. And that's what led you to jump to the worst possible conclusion."

Morgan had no rebuttal to that since it was also true.

Rory stalked by her, retrieved a bottle from one of her cabinets, and tossed it at Morgan. The relaxation potion. Morgan's relief at getting it back quickly turned to dismay. The bottle was empty. Maybe there were traces left she could use for the antidote, but it wouldn't be much. The only upside was that Rory couldn't take any more of it. But then, she'd taken a lot. Who knew how long the effects would linger in her blood?

"This was the love potion?" Rory asked. When Morgan nodded, Rory leaned against the counter, shaking as she cried. Or was she laughing? Morgan couldn't tell which; Rory's hands covered her face. "I can't believe you dragged us through this for a week. An entire, shitty week! No, over a week—ten days!"

"I'm sorry."

"You really should be." Rory took a deep breath and wiped away her tears. "You really, truly should be, because I never used a drop of it."

29

THUNDER SHOOK THE SKY. LILITH BOUNDED OFF HER CHAIR and streaked up the stairs. Morgan stared at the spot the cat had vacated, trying to make sense of what had happened. What she'd just heard.

But it didn't make sense.

If Rory hadn't taken any of the potion, then . . .

Morgan thought she might faint. She must have heard wrong, but when she tried asking Rory to repeat herself, her words failed. Her words never failed. Yet all she managed was a barely audible, "What?"

"I really was going to take some the night you gave it to me," Rory said. She crossed back into the living room and shot a confused glance to where Lilith had disappeared. "Lilith was acting weird that night. There might have been a mouse. Anyway, I was watching her and not paying attention, and my hand smacked the bottle. I'd already removed the stopper, and the potion went everywhere. Unlike with the ice cream at the festival, I wasn't prepared, so I didn't have a chance of saving it. I didn't tell you because I felt bad. You'd taken the time to make it special for me, and I'd completely wasted it."

Morgan clasped a hand over her mouth and whimpered. She still couldn't speak. Her mind was reeling, struggling to understand what was going on. Was this how Rory had felt when Morgan had told her that she'd given her a love potion? If so, no wonder Rory had gaped at her. Some things were too much to absorb all at once.

She didn't know what or how to feel. Happy and relieved and furious at herself, yes. But that didn't seem to quite capture the storm raging inside of her. There were a million more feelings flying through her veins, and her heart couldn't settle down long enough for her to understand any of them. This had to be what shock was like.

Rory didn't seem to be faring much better. She really was both laughing and crying at once. Morgan would do that, too, if only she could do anything, including hold herself up. She slid to the floor again on shaky knees.

"If you had just talked to me at the time," Rory said, running her hands through her hair. "If you'd just explained about the potion, I would have told you all of this then. Ten days, Morgan."

Rory saying her name broke Morgan out of her stupor. She was crying. What the fuck? How did she have any water left inside of her at this point? "I'm sorry."

Rory laughed through her tears, not sounding entirely stable herself. "I know. We've been over this. You should be. I'm so pissed off at you. I want to scream."

That was fair. Just because Rory hadn't been bespelled didn't mean she shouldn't be furious. Morgan's elation warred with her guilt. Hope with her fear. Had she messed everything up too much for Rory to ever forgive her?

She curled into a ball on the chilly floor, and suddenly Rory's arms wrapped around her, and her lips pressed into the back of Morgan's head. The lavender scent of Rory's shampoo filled her senses. Morgan grasped at her arms, turning, daring to look Rory in the face at last.

Rory rested her forehead against Morgan's. "You are the sweetest, funniest, most wonderful person I've ever met, and by far, the most infuriating. But I love you. No potions or spells or other interferences required. You are all that I need. You've always been enough."

"Really?" She should have said something smarter than that, but hearing Rory say "I love you," and finally believing that Rory meant it, was too much. Morgan's entire being had latched onto those words too strongly for her to move, so anything more profound or coherent was a lost cause.

"Really."

Morgan took a deep breath, aiming—if not for something more profound—then for something more meaningful. "I love you, too."

Rory's lips twitched as though she was on the verge of laughing again. "I know, and I understand why you jumped to the conclusions you did. Considering I recently threatened my own parents with lightning, I'm not sure how fair it is of me to judge anyone for overreacting."

"That's not the same thing."

"Not exactly, but look—I'm admitting that I haven't always made the best choices lately when it comes to my own issues. Don't protest too much. And besides, as much as I want to storm off and not speak to you ever again, that would be punishing me. Since I have a feeling you've punished yourself plenty this past week, I'm just going to hope you learned some sort of lesson about communication?"

Morgan sniffed and wiped away her tears. It had been a long ten days. Ten days of feeling sick to her stomach and mourning the best thing to ever happen to her. Ten days of believing she'd hurt someone she loved. If Rory wasn't kicking Morgan out of her life, she might have to learn to live with Morgan oversharing from now on.

She brushed her thumb down Rory's arm, still not entirely convinced this was real. Needing proof that Rory was solid, was here, wasn't going away. "Yes, I think it's fair to say I have. About communication *and* organization."

Rory nodded, her lips achingly close to Morgan's and stirring her blood, tossing a heady amount of need into the potent cocktail of emotions wracking Morgan's body. "I hope you've also learned that anyone who wishes you were something else doesn't deserve you for who you are, and they aren't worth a single additional thought."

Morgan took a deep breath. "Can I promise to try? That's going to take more time. But I will work on it if you'll help me."

Helping her wouldn't take much effort. Knowing Rory loved her and wanted to be with her, in spite of everything, was going a long way to repairing Morgan's crushed self-confidence.

Rory snorted. "Already negotiating with me? I guess that's a step in the right direction."

"Maybe I just want to hear you say nice things about me again. I'm still worried you're going to strike *me* with lightning next."

"Well, you owe me." Rory smiled mischievously, and Morgan's pulse quickened. Damn it. She wanted to kiss her so badly, but she wasn't entirely sure how Rory would feel about that. "We'll see how you pay up before I decide."

"What else do you want to know?"

"You should assume I want to know everything, to be safe. But . . ." Rory entwined her calloused and scarred fingers with Morgan's. "I meant you owe me all of the kisses that I was denied over the last week due to your misplaced freak-out. I'm collecting, with interest. I expect you to be very good about making it up to me."

"Oh." Her heart skipped. "I can do that."

Can do that. Like it wasn't *all* that she wanted to do.

If Morgan hadn't already dissolved into a puddle of teary goo, she would have now, but her heart could only swell so much.

With her free hand, Morgan reached up and skimmed the softness of Rory's cheek. Disbelief, guilt, hope—everything inside her was coalescing around one dominant emotion. Joy. She'd come here expecting more pain, but the pain was all floating away. No, she was floating, leaving it behind. Leaving everything behind but the sensation of

Rory's skin and the feel of her breath, the flutter of her eyelashes as Morgan traced her finger around Rory's mouth.

She leaned over and touched her lips to Rory's nose, each freckle calling for her attention. She wanted to love them all. Rory had no idea what she'd asked of her.

By the time Morgan kissed a third one, Rory's silent laughter made it hard to go on. "Seriously?"

Morgan's cheeks burned. "I'm not apologizing for loving your freckles."

"Good. Please don't apologize for anything else tonight."

But that was exactly what Morgan intended to do, although maybe not with words, and it was going to be the best apology of her life.

Resisting the freckles' lure, Morgan took Rory's lips in her own. And, oh, sweet stars. Kissing Rory's face hadn't prepared Morgan for the sheer need that bloomed inside of her. Rory's mouth was soft and sweet, and as hungry as Morgan's own. She tugged on Rory's lower lip, trying to be gentle, to taste her and not devour her. But there was Rory's tongue, and Rory's fingers twisting through her hair, and the pleasure spiking through Morgan's body was going to make her lose control.

Never mind that the tile floor was cold and unwelcoming. Rory's body was warm and melting into hers. Morgan's hand slipped up Rory's leg, searching the curve of her thigh and the rise of her hip for more skin. She was so close but awkward inches away, and Morgan needed more.

Ten days of abject misery compounded an entire year of yearning. But when Morgan used to daydream about kissing Rory, it was never like this. Now she knew who Rory really was—generous and unnervingly organized, and not nearly as quiet as she seemed. Funny, although she didn't think of herself that way. As competitive as Morgan was, but also so ambitious she believed if she tried hard enough, it was possible to create a spell that would allow her to fly with the birds. She called herself an overconfident bitch, but she was tender on the inside, and she hid her fears behind a carefully crafted mask, also like Morgan. She wasn't unattainable and unapproachable because she was perfect, but she *was* perfect for Morgan.

Morgan didn't realize she'd lost another tear until Rory's finger gently brushed it away.

"Another question," Rory said, pulling back and sitting up straighter. Her hair was mussed, her lips were red, and the last thing Morgan wanted was to stop kissing her, but she'd answer as many questions as Rory had. "The antidote you said you were working on—how is it going? An anti-love potion would be a pretty big deal. It could be that important potion you wanted to make."

"It could be, but I haven't finished it, if that's what you're asking."

"These things take time."

Morgan rested her head against Rory's, fighting a smile. "You're trying to encourage me to keep working on this, but you don't need to. I knew it would take time, but I haven't felt like I *had* time because of what was at stake. But what I did have was a plan."

"Why the past tense? You could keep at it. Tell me."

Morgan raised her head. "Now?" Just because she would answer Rory's questions didn't mean she wanted to delay the kissing that much longer.

Rory slid an arm around Morgan's neck. "You said the word 'plan.' You, Morgan Greenwood, intuitive witch and creature of chaos, have a plan. This is turning me on."

Morgan laughed into her shoulder. "Fine, but only because I've always dreamed of meeting your Virgo approval."

So, for the second time this evening (and after nestling herself against the crook of Rory's neck), Morgan explained how she'd been creating different types of mind- and mood-altering potions and studying them until she could understand their basis, and how her work had resulted in a potion that was close but not quite right. "I thought it might help if I had the potion I gave you, but since there's none left, then I need—"

Rory cleared her throat.

"Since there's none left, *and* we can't say whether it actually was a love potion or not . . ." She paused while Rory confirmed this was an acceptable revision. "Then, if I do decide to keep working on it, I need to figure out how to proceed next. It's going to take a lot of effort to get from a potion that interacts with all mind-altering potions to a distilled anti-love potion, and since we're in the clear on any love potions, I'm not sure it's worth the effort."

Morgan waited for Rory to say something, probably that she should keep working on the potion for its own sake, but Rory was chewing her lip. Her expression did not scream turned-on, as promised. Rather, it said, *I'm about to get nerdy.*

"*All* potions of that type?" Rory asked.

"Of the ones I've tried making. Which may or may not be any good, since I'm making illicit potions that therefore can't have any verifiable record of success. Why?"

Rory ran her fingers down Morgan's arm and entwined their hands. "I'm thinking as a bartender here. Have you heard of those strips you can use to test your drink for mundane drugs?"

Morgan wracked her brain. They sounded vaguely familiar, like something she'd read about once or a friend had mentioned. She'd never seen them or used them, although she could imagine them being helpful if you were at a party or surrounded by people you didn't know.

Or at a festival with so-called friends wanting to play a nasty prank?

Morgan sucked in a breath as she realized what Rory was suggesting. She'd thought her new potion might have a use for something, given how it interacted with the mind-altering ones, but she'd been too focused on her specific task to recognize the possibilities. "I would need to do so much more work to make sure this potion really does what I think it does, but the potential . . . The whole charming-potion ordeal could have been avoided."

"It doesn't help if you trust the person giving you the drink," Rory said, "but yeah. Lots of potential there." She kissed Morgan's forehead. "And in there, too. I told you so."

Although it was a chaste kiss, Morgan shivered as she grinned. "You're brilliant."

Rory pretended to smack her. "It's your work. I'm just pushing you to see beyond your self-imposed limits like a good coach does."

"Fine. We're both brilliant." She went to kiss Rory back, and in her exuberance, she knocked them both to the cold floor. "But now my question for you—are you truly turned on by my ability to create and follow a plan? Because, as you've pointed out, it's been ten days since we last kissed."

"Technically, it hasn't even been ten minutes since we last kissed. But does this mean you're not itching to race off to your workshop and get back to work now that you've seen the project's potential?" Rory slid out from under Morgan and tugged them both to their feet.

"Are you kicking me out?" She reached over to kiss Rory again, but Rory pulled away with a smirk.

She led Morgan past the stairs to the loft and into another room. Her bedroom, from the looks of it. Rory flicked her wrist, and a couple of candles ignited, sending shadows dancing over the walls.

"I'd never kick you out, but I couldn't stand the tile any longer when there are much better places to kiss you," Rory said.

Morgan's hands dipped to Rory's hips and the hem of her shirt. "No objections, but I will kiss you anywhere."

"Yes, you can." She pressed her body against Morgan's, all sweet curves and warm heat, and she wrapped her arms around Morgan's neck. "My prior offer stands."

Oh. *You can kiss me anywhere you want,* Morgan remembered her saying from the cabin. She didn't know whether Rory had misinterpreted her comment, or if she was simply taking advantage of the opening. She didn't much care, either. The invitation had been made, and Morgan accepted.

She pulled lightly on the shirt, and Rory stepped back and yanked it off. She was wearing a sports bra underneath, hardly revealing, but the sight of all that skin made Morgan dizzy. Standing was proving difficult in the face of so much temptation. She took a step closer, and Rory took another back. Then Rory pulled off her sports bra.

Oh fuck. Morgan pushed her against the bed, her knees shaking. Their mouths collided again as Rory scrambled backward, and Morgan pressed her against the blanket so she could look at her better. It wasn't enough, though. She needed to touch her. To taste her.

"Take your shirt off," Rory said, and Morgan tossed it on the floor.

The moment apart gave her the chance to breathe, and she stared at Rory. She was so beautiful and staring back at Morgan in a way that made Morgan feel the same. Her body was painfully on edge, and her nipples puckered further beneath the tight fabric of her bra. She glided her hand up Rory's stomach, ready to jump out of her skin as Rory sucked in a breath. With her thumbs, she circled the swells of Rory's breasts, caressed all that delicious skin until Rory was squirming, and so was she.

"Morgan." Rory reached up and grabbed at her legs.

So she bent down and kissed Rory again—her mouth, her chin, down her throat—savoring her moans and relishing every twist and wiggle of Rory's body. Her breasts next, sucking and nipping at each one, her skin like silk against Morgan's tongue. Then her stomach, her hips. She slid off Rory's pants and pressed her mouth down her thighs.

Tearstained and tired as she might be, Morgan poured her heart into every kiss. Each one a promise. Each one a bit of magic. Each one driving her closer to oblivion.

Rory stuffed her wrist in her mouth to muffle her cries. She sat up and watched Morgan through half-closed eyes until Morgan spread her legs and kissed the sweet spot between them. Then she flopped back against the bed with a moan that Morgan was positive she'd take into her dreams tonight.

When Rory buckled and shattered beneath her tongue, Morgan was reluctant to stop tasting her. Her body was ready to burst. The scent of Rory's skin had permeated hers, and she craved more. Morgan kissed her way back down Rory's legs, then up her torso, lingering over her breasts, until Rory's breathing slowed to normal.

Nestling her head against Rory's, she draped an arm over her stomach. "Please tell me I have a lot more debt to work off."

Rory's laugh exploded out of her, and she turned languidly on her side and brushed back Morgan's hair off her cheek. "I love you. You are adorable."

Morgan closed her eyes and willed herself not to start weeping again. "I love you, too. And I've loved you longer. I had a crush on you since we met."

"Are we making a competition out of this, too?" Rory ran her fingers down Morgan's shoulder and under the lace of her bra.

Morgan's breath hitched. Rory was striking her with lightning after all. Her finger sent jolts of arousal shooting through Morgan's body, pulsing between her legs. "I'm up for the challenge."

"Are you? Good. Because I've heard I can be intimidating." Rory slipped the bra strap off Morgan's shoulder and peeled the lace back to grant further access to Morgan's skin.

Morgan shivered. "You are. Were. But you make up for it by being one of the kindest, most generous people I know. I'd say smartest and most talented, too, but honestly, that's part of the reason why you're intimidating, so it doesn't count."

Rory made a noise of disbelief and took Morgan's nipple in her mouth, which led to a lot more noises from Morgan. She gripped the blanket, struggling to breathe.

"And despite this," Rory said, raising her head right before Morgan began to plead with her, "you avoided talking to me in more than monosyllables for a year. It sucked because you were so funny and everyone loves you, and I wanted to be your friend." She reached under Morgan's partially arched back to unhook her bra. "More than your friend, honestly. You weren't the only one with a crush."

What? Morgan started upright in shock, but Rory hovered over her, and she stopped herself right before their heads collided. Rory hadn't told her that back at the festival, and she laughed at the expression on Morgan's face. If Rory had told her *that* during the festival, it could have changed everything. She might never have jumped to conclusions about the potion.

"You what?" Morgan managed to squeak out. "It never occurred to me that you would ever look at me twice."

"Why not? Because of everything I've already told you about how wonderful and gorgeous you are? Definitely reasons to be indifferent to someone."

Rory dipped her head and lavished attention on Morgan's other breast, and it was becoming very difficult to talk. "But . . ."

"Morgan." Rory pulled on the elastic of Morgan's leggings, and Morgan helped her tug them off. She wanted to contemplate this new information, but she had no ability. She also wanted to stare at Rory, who was lying next to her, gloriously naked, but her eyes were closing of their own accord as Rory kissed the spot between her breasts.

"Do you really think I'd have agreed to practice kiss you if I didn't want to really kiss you?" Rory asked.

"Oh." Her eyes flew open. Such a possibility had been too ludicrous to consider at the time.

"I love you, but we need to work on your logic skills so you stop jumping to silly conclusions."

Oh. She couldn't protest, not that there was anything to protest, because Rory's fingers had slipped beneath her underwear.

She was all nerves, all need. No chill. She pushed her underwear off to give Rory better access, and when Rory tipped her head, her tongue circling and flicking and tormenting Morgan's nipples, she begged for more. She came soon after Rory slipped a second finger inside her, her thumb on Morgan's clit coaxing her over the edge.

Morgan sank into the bed as the spasms stopped, wondering if her heart would ever slow down. Especially as Rory ran her wet fingers up Morgan's body. She painted Morgan's areolas and licked up the mess she'd made, and Morgan almost came a second time.

She grabbed Rory's hand. "I thought I was supposed to be owing *you*."

Rory grinned and kissed her shoulder, settling in next to her. "You are, and we have plenty of time. You don't intend to walk home in the storm, do you?"

Morgan shifted closer, and realized Rory was right. It had started to rain at some point, and she could hear the light patter on the windows. It would be the perfect sound to drift off to while surrounded by Rory's bedding. Not to mention Rory's body. "If you're not kicking me out."

"I would be most upset if you tried to leave."

"Oh, thank the stars." She closed her eyes. Contentment was making her lack of sleep catch up to her, but Morgan didn't want to sleep. "You'll have to force me to leave."

"Sounds unfortunate. I'll do my best to avoid it."

They fell into silence for a moment, Rory's fingers idly tracing patterns across Morgan's stomach. Then they stopped abruptly, and Rory raised her head.

"Actually, I do have another question for you," she said.

Morgan swallowed. "Okay?"

"At the festival, you said you'd tried to convince me that we were wrong for each other as a way to break your nonexistent love potion." She propped her head up on her arm and frowned at Morgan. "What did you do? I don't remember that."

"Oh, but the dancing, and the way I was so obnoxious to that guy who negged you at lunch." Morgan paused at the confusion on Rory's face. "Acting recklessly during the scavenger hunt? Suggesting you should listen to your family and perform? All things you hated. Only you never got upset with me about them. They all backfired. I couldn't even do that right."

Rory bit her lip, laughing silently. "Of course they backfired. They are all very *you* things. How could you believe being yourself would make me not like you?"

Morgan opened her mouth to protest the characterization, but . . . Well, Rory wasn't wrong, was she? Everything she'd done with the intention of making Rory dislike her had simply involved Morgan being her loud and pushy self. And Rory liked it. Liked her. Called her vibrant.

Sweet stars, she'd started this fake relationship willing to contort herself into whatever shape she needed to win over Rory, when the truth was, her real self had been enough all along—just like Rory had said.

Morgan let out a squeal and rolled over, pulling Rory against her once again. "What happened with your family? I kind of blew it at the end there, and I know you don't want me apologizing anymore, so I won't say it, but . . ."

"Ah, yeah. Family." Rory tensed and peeled herself free of Morgan's excitable limbs. "Let's just say it was not a great day at the cabin after our conversation. But things will be fine. My father isn't thrilled, but my mother apologized. I finally told them about the meds. As I suspected, they thought I had a confidence problem, and that performing in a low-key environment like the festival would help me overcome it. We talked for a while, and it went better than I feared. They're being supportive and actually feel guilty for making me feel like I couldn't talk to them, so I'm feeling guilty for making them feel guilty, and . . . Well, that's family. Will either of them listen better in the future? Who knows. But in the end, you did exactly what I'd wanted. They are convinced that I'm happy with my life, so there's no need to feel bad about that. And for what it's worth, they thought you ran off because of your outburst at the stadium, and I didn't correct them. Oh, that reminds me."

To Morgan's dismay, Rory jumped off the bed and disappeared. While she was gone, Morgan climbed under the sheets. Although they'd rumpled them, of course Rory had made her bed this morning. Morgan would expect nothing less.

She rested her head on Rory's pillow. Pulled Rory's blanket up to her shoulders. Sniffed the fabric to breathe in Rory's scent. Morgan hadn't realized it was possible to feel this happy. She'd thought she'd felt it that day Rory had taken her up on her offer to be her fake girlfriend, and again when she'd kissed Rory at the cabin, but this was an altogether different kind of happiness. That happiness had been an ecstatic, jump-around-for-joy happiness. A wild, drunken kind. This was the sort of hard-won happiness that seeped into your bones and filled in your cracks. It pieced together the bits that other people had broken and softened the jagged edges they left behind. It was the kind that made her feel whole. Not merely needed, but actually wanted.

"You left some stuff behind," Rory said. She paused in the doorway, taking in the way Morgan had made herself at home in the bed. "Go ahead and get comfortable."

"I did." Morgan lifted her head from the pillow and hugged it to her chest. Her eyes opened wider, seeing what Rory was holding.

She climbed into bed next to Morgan and fastened the snowflake obsidian bracelet to her wrist. "That was for you, and so are these."

Morgan took the box of chocolate orgasms. "I can't believe you didn't trash them."

"Are you kidding? Do you know how much money magic like this costs? I figured if I didn't get to give them back to you, I'd eventually be in the mood to eat them myself one day." Rory opened the box with a grin. "I'm going to enjoy sharing them much more."

30

"THIS IS AMAZING. HAVE I TOLD YOU THAT BEFORE?" SHE HAD definitely told Rory that before, but it didn't hurt to say it again.

Morgan let out a soft moan as she swallowed another sip of the autumn cocktail. It would be leaving the Empty Chalice's menu at the end of the month, and she was going to miss it. Rory had somehow made a drink that was as if everything pumpkin spice collided with a warm apple pie while fiery trees rained down leaves and bonfires scented a frost-tinged breeze. And it all went down smooth with a sweet, smoky finish that made her think of mulled cider. Pure magic in a glass, not even counting the sugared apple slices that maintained their freshly cut appearance on the rim. "You are a genius. Forget blowing out protective circles—this is your calling."

"High praise coming from someone whose favorite season is summer." Rory garnished two glasses of the Empty Chalice's signature sangria with more apple slices and passed them over to the waiting server.

As the temperatures had grown cooler and the days shorter over the last three months, Morgan had mourned the loss of shorts weather while Rory had rejoiced in pulling out flannels and sweaters. Since they made for cozy cuddling, Morgan didn't mind nearly as much as she pretended to. In fact, now that the fun parts of fall were over—pumpkin season, leaf-peeping, and of course, Halloween—Morgan was looking forward to snow. She envisioned many winter nights curled up together, whether it was in front of Rory's woodstove or by her apartment's ancient radiators. Naturally, they would have to trade off so that Lilith and Luna could each join in.

"I did try explaining your real talent to some of those reporters," Morgan said, "but all they wanted to talk about was Rory Sandler's triumphant return to elemental spellcasting. Like you're good at it or something."

Videos of Rory at the NEWT Festival, speculation about her motives, and calls to lift her suspension were everywhere online, and it had taken weeks before the trail of witches—reporters and fans from as far as the West Coast—had stopped hogging all the seats at the Empty Chalice for a chance to talk to her. For the bar, it had been a financial windfall. For the locals, it had been worse than dealing with regular summer weekends. And for Rory, it had been exhausting. But Morgan had carefully watched how she was handling the pressure, ready to be her shield, but only if Rory asked for it.

She'd also, with a little hesitancy, offered to make Rory another relaxation potion, and Rory had declined. Not, she'd assured Morgan, because she didn't trust her, but because she didn't want to risk developing a habit of relying on any substances to relax. So instead, Morgan had done all she could to be there however Rory needed her, be it listening to her vent, making jokes, or her favorite—kissing Rory into oblivion. She'd only once jumped between Rory and a particularly pushy photographer, which Morgan thought showed great restraint on her part.

As it turned out, Rory had handled the situation better than she herself had expected. Although knowing she had two years before she needed to seriously consider whether to return to competing, and three before she actually could, had probably helped. In the meantime, Rory had decided she would start working on flying. That way she'd be ready, regardless of her choice.

Still, although witchy gossip sites and social media remained rife with discussion, everyone in the Harborage coven was relieved when life around town finally returned to normal. Morgan had been busy, too, over the last few months, and after the news she'd received today, she was going to be busier.

That was why she was at the Empty Chalice tonight. It was a chance to have a small celebration before the word got out. Morgan had wanted to wait until tomorrow, when Rory had the night off, but Rory had insisted she share her news with Hazel and Andy right away. Tomorrow, Rory had promised, they could celebrate alone, and Morgan had not been about to argue with that plan.

On cue, Hazel and Andy entered the bar and made their way over. There was no live music tonight, and the windows had been fitted back into their frames, but the lights overhead twinkled like always, the candle flames danced, and Morgan could almost smell the ocean if she thought about it hard enough. Although Rory was stuck behind the bar, Morgan couldn't think of a better place to celebrate. In a way, everything had begun here.

She twirled the bracelet Rory had given her around her wrist impatiently, although she wasn't in need of any protection.

"I was told there was a celebration?" Andy slipped onto the stool to Morgan's left, and she narrowed her eyes in Hazel's direction. Given that Andy had been the last of the group to find out everything that had happened between Morgan and Rory, she was suspicious of being left out.

Hazel shrugged.

The only person who knew what Morgan had been working on

was Rory. Well, and also Rory's mother, since she was on the Witch Council.

Rory placed drink napkins in front of the new arrivals. "We're celebrating Morgan's success. Bask in her presence. She's going to be famous."

"What did you do?" Hazel asked. "And why didn't we know about it?"

"And is this place going to be overrun again?" Andy asked. "Because that sucked."

"Doubtful, and you're learning about it now. Hush." Morgan sipped her drink with a smile. "I made a potion."

Hazel and Andy stared at her, waiting for the details, but Morgan was magically wandering through a pumpkin patch.

"She made a completely brand-new, never-been-made-before-that-anyone's-aware-of potion," Rory clarified for her. "And it's going to be the most important potion developed in a long time."

Once Morgan's goal changed from developing an anti-love potion to a potion-detecting potion, it had taken another month of her time to perfect it, and a letter to Rory's mother, as an official representative of the Council, to be allowed sanctioned access to the sorts of forbidden potions she needed to truly test it. To Morgan's surprise, Wanda Sandler had been intrigued and not petty enough to hold a grudge. If anything, Rory seemed to think her mother was enamored with Morgan—not only had Morgan proven herself highly skilled, she'd stood up for Wanda's daughter.

Even more surprisingly, Morgan was less excited about a powerful witch praising her talent than she was simply relieved that Rory's mother didn't hate her.

It was funny. Her potion was about to be endorsed by the Witch Council—a feat that was going to make her famous among magical circles—and that wasn't going to be the highlight of her year. It wasn't even going to be the highlight of her month. That had been last week when she and Rory had introduced Lilith and Luna. After some initial hesitancy on Luna's part, Lilith had won her over, and Rory had commented that it was a good thing they got along in case they ended up seeing a lot more of each other. Morgan had tried—and utterly failed—not to read more into that, and Hazel had finally taken away her tarot cards after she'd obsessively attempted to divine their meaning.

Whatever, though. She had priorities, damn it. She'd spent so much of the last few years believing the only way she would ever be happy was if she could prove her magical worth. And now that she'd created a potion that could do just that, she didn't feel the need for it after all.

That wasn't to say she wasn't proud of the work she'd put in or the potion's potential for good, but maybe she believed what Rory had been telling her all along—she was already enough. It wasn't so hard, really, when she was surrounded by supportive family and friends, and a dark-eyed witch with adorable nose freckles who was only intimidating to people who didn't know her, and who smiled at Morgan like she was the most amazing sight in the world.

Morgan found herself beaming at Rory's praise as she explained what she'd created, what the next steps were to make more, and how the Council wanted to contract her recipe so there would be plenty of potion available at the national convention next year.

When she finished, Rory set two of the autumn cocktails down in front of Hazel and Andy so they could toast. Then she came out from behind the bar and kissed Morgan's cheek. "See? I told you that you were brilliant, and I'm always right."

"So overconfident."

Rory cackled, and her expression wrinkled those freckles. "You should try it more. When you so confidently explained your work to the Council, it looked good on you."

"I've always been confident in my ability to make a mess."

Rory wrapped her arms around her and lowered her voice. "And yet making a mess of things is only your second biggest talent after making potions. No, wait, third, and I won't say what the second is in public."

Morgan melted a little, and she pulled Rory closer by her shirt for a better kiss. "No wonder I love you so much."

ACKNOWLEDGMENTS

Every book is special because every book contains pieces of the writer, no matter how small or fleeting those pieces are. *This Spells Disaster*, however, will always hold a unique place in my heart for one significant reason—it's the first book I've published (though not written) with a central f/f relationship.

Like many people I know, I didn't realize I was queer until my thirties. This, in spite of me spending my teens and early twenties insisting that one day I'd fall in love with a person, not a gender. Perhaps unsurprisingly for a writer, it was books that made me realize a truth that now seems so obvious—both the books I read, and just as importantly, the ones I kept being drawn to write without understanding why, until the epiphany poked me in the brain and I *finally* went, "Huh, well I guess things make sense now." (What I'm saying is, earning a degree in psychology emphatically does *not* make you any better at introspection.)

Anyway, since then, I've been seeking out more queer romances, and more books of all genres with f/f relationships in them, and I'm extremely happy to be able to contribute one of my books to the growing number of queer romances available. Maybe twenty-year-old me would have figured things out sooner if she'd had access to the number and variety of books that I do today.

Romance and fantasy are my two favorite genres, and after having written both separately, I'm thrilled that I've finally been able to combine them into one personally meaningful book. I'm grateful to my agent, Rebecca Strauss, for being the first person to suggest I try my hand at a witch romance. She probably doesn't remember it, but on our first call, when she offered me representation for a contemporary romance, I asked her about writing paranormal or fantasy romance, too, and her response was something along the lines of, "Maybe one day that would be a good idea, but let's put a pin in it for now." That was many books and many more years ago, and I've been thankful for her honest career guidance and excellent editorial notes (that only occasionally make me curl into the fetal position) ever since.

I'm also super thankful for my editor, Sarah Blumenstock, who, coincidentally, suggested I write a witch romance around the same time as Rebecca did. I might have screamed with happiness, but that's between me and my email.

My editorial team of Sarah and Liz Sellers worked their magic on *This Spells Disaster* to make this book far better than I could ever do alone. (I cannot write anything about Sarah without throwing in at least one pun, so there it is.) Huge thanks as well to my marketer, Elisha Katz, my publicist, Kristin Cipolla, and my copy editor, Marianne Aguiar—all heroes in their own domains. Did you check out this book because of the absolutely stunning cover? Credit goes to Wendy Stephens for the amazing illustration and Katie Anderson for the cover design.

I can't express enough gratitude to all my fellow writers who took the time to read and say such nice things about Morgan's and Rory's story: Ali Hazelwood, Alicia Thompson, Sarah Hawley, and Courtney Kae. Knowing people are reading your book is scary. Knowing people whose books you've loved are reading it is unspeakably terrifying, no matter how kind they are.

Aside from the fabulous people already mentioned by name above, I need to acknowledge a few more people for all the advice, support, and occasional great ideas they provided while I was working on this book: Nekesa Afia, Olivia Blacke, Eliza Jane Brazier, Lyn Liao Butler, India Holton, Sarah Zachrich Jeng, Amy Lea, Mia P. Manansala, and Lynn Painter. There are too many people in my various groups and chats to name individually, plus the ever-present fear that I'll accidentally leave someone out, but the Berkletes and Y-Nots have been the best support systems a writer could ask for, and I'm so glad to know you all.

As always, I'm grateful for my wonderful family (I miss you, Dad, although I'm not sure I'd want you to read this one) and for my delightfully not-quite-chaotic-neutral husband. I know this isn't the sci-fi epic you continue to wait for, dear, but it's a step in that direction.

Photo provided by the author

TORI ANNE MARTIN lives in New England, where she collects pen names, tattoos, and hoodies in shades of gray and black. Previously, she collected degrees, including a doctorate in psychology, where she studied interpersonal power, consent, and sexual assault. She much prefers writing romance. If you can't find her online, it's because she's lost in the woods.

CONNECT ONLINE

ToriAnneMartin.com

TAMartinAuthor

TA_Martin